Gopal sensed its presence. Turning slowly, he glanced over his left shoulder. The naga hovered about ten feet in the air, rhythmically flapping its black, leathery wings. Like a feather, it floated down, perching on the altar. Pearl claws wrapped around the edge of the cold stone, scratching the hard surface, the sound grating on Gopal's nerves. Coiling its black serpent body, the naga held its hooded head high. Its forked tongue slithered from its cavernous mouth and twitched, sniffing Gopal. A slow hiss seeped past glistening fangs. The dead stare of its black, polished eyes reflected its prey. All noise died. The jungle submitted to its lord.

Petrified, his palms sweating against his bow, Gopal could only watch. Black wings swung wide, extending to their full length, blotting out the sun. Hypnotized by the naga's heavy-lidded stare, he was powerless.

In his mind, he heard his grandfather's warning: "Don't look into its eyes. . . ."

Other TSR® Books

THE NINE GATES

Phillip Brugalette

THE NINE GATES

First printing: August 1992
Printed in the United States of America
Library of Congress Catalog Card Number:91-66496

9 8 7 6 5 4 3 2 1

ISBN: 1-56076-399-X

TSR, Inc.
P.O. Box 756
Lake Geneva, WI 53147
U.S.A.

TSR Ltd.
120 Church End, Cherry Hinton
Cambridge CB1 3LB
United Kingdom

Sincere thanks to Howard Hendrix, for getting me started; to Bruce McAllister, for getting me finished; and to Srila Prabhupada, for showing me The Whorl.

"Never was there a time . . ."

Map: LANDS OF BHU

- Mt. Kuru
- City of Hiranya
- City of Toshana
- Sarps River
- Talavana Forest
- Durga Temple
- Kingdom of Goloka
- Forest of Driti
- Forest of Angas
- Goverdhan Valley
- Toshana River
- Plains of Vrindaban
- Rudra Temple
- Kindom of Radhakunde

PROLOGUE

NEVER WAS THERE A TIME during his third life as a mystic that Vyasa had missed the Brahma-murta, that brief moment before sunrise: the most sacred time of day.

Today he woke late and didn't understand why. Why this morning, after three lifetimes? The sleep mantra had never failed him before. Rising quickly from his mat, he rushed to the uncovered window and looked to the east and the dark before dawn. He couldn't see down to the lake, but he knew the way. He'd been following it for two decades.

Quickly the mystic prostrated himself on the cold floor before his icon of the deva Paramatma—the maintainer of whorls. Its large, dark pupils stared, all-knowing, from its even larger white eyes. Vyasa chanted his obeisance. *"Jai Om."*

Still hurrying, he gently placed the icon in the cloth pouch that hung on the bare wall, which felt cold this early morning. Swiftly he moved about the room gathering his incense, the charcoal, the sacred clay, his meditation beads, and a brass bowl. Then he grabbed his crescent-tipped staff and hurried, alone and silent, through the still passages of the temple. The catacombs were dark, but he needed no light; the path was well worn, like the lines in his face that had been darkened by years of meditating in the warm sun of the planet Bhu. The way was in his flesh, etched in his mind.

He barely felt the tattered woolen chotta that kept his chest and shoulders warm; or heard his footsteps echoing through the empty marble shrine; or noticed the tap his staff's wooden tip made each time it struck the hard, cold surface. He rushed on, knowing the entrance to the hermitage was just ahead. In his mind, he already saw the cool waters of the bathing ghat and smelled the fragrant malati flowers that bloomed along the familiar muddy shore of the lake. He stepped out to meet the brisk air, high above the morning mist, and continued down the steps. He found himself stopping suddenly at the twisted kadamba tree that stood by the stone stairway.

The sages say this tree is sacred, Vyasa mused. To be born as a kadamba tree meant your next birth would be on a planet of Sveta-dvipa—the First Whorl—among the planets of the devas. The devas, through performance of prescribed rituals and the required number of births, were incarnated to their posts as controllers of the forces of nature and guardians of Bhu—the Second Whorl—the whorl of men. Although not eternal, the devas were not considered mortal, since their lifetimes were calculated in the thousands of thousands of years and they could be killed with special weapons and mantras.

After living the life of a deva, a particular being might petition the manus—the creators and lawgivers of the Bhu-mandala universe—to serve another lifetime. But the devas could still commit offenses against the manus and be forced to be reincarnated in the Second Whorl and take lives as men.

It was a boon to find a kadamba tree, since such a birth was rare, and its leaves, when used with the proper mantras, could secure for the finder a place in Sveta-dvipa. This was Vyasa's goal, having reached the level of treta, his third incarnation as a mystic.

Vyasa spoke to the tree. "How are you this morning? I offer my humble obeisance to one as special as you."

The tree didn't answer. It always had before, in a voice that didn't need the words of men. It would whisper when the wind touched its branches or vibrate its leaves into a song that only the treta-mystic could hear. It had always answered, "Yes, old friend, and a higher birth awaits us after these bodies are discarded."

Today there was no sound, no motion, no vibration, nothing that could be a voice. "Is something wrong?" Vyasa asked, still paused on the step. "Have I offended you?"

Vyasa saw it then. A single branch was twisted as if the tree knew pain. Had it always been there—such a small thing—and he simply hadn't noticed? No, he would have noticed. He and the tree had come to know each other well since the pilgrims had stopped coming.

There were, he saw now, other differences as well. The leaves on the lower branches were dead. How could this be? He had seen them green just yesterday. Reaching with his left hand, he gently bent a small branch from the upper reaches down toward him. The buds had withered. In a single night? The cold enclosed him. All this in a single night? He was afraid.

Probably just a sudden change in the weather. He had to go on. His rituals had to continue, in spite of his fear, if he was to reach his goal. He longed for the serenity of meditation, to be free from the material entrapments of this whorl. He had come so far, was so close to reaching the prize of the treta-mystic—rebirth as a deva. He didn't want anything to stand in his way, not now, not after three lifetimes.

The dawn called again. He gathered the few usable leaves and hurried on. At the bottom of the steep stairway he had to look back one last time at the tree, that ancient sentry, and wonder.

Finally reaching the ruin that jutted into the lake like a pier, Vyasa shivered. The air gusts were even colder near the water, as if a giant door somewhere in the universe had been left open.

He tossed the chotta over his left shoulder. He needed to make his mind do what it had always done before so readily and easily—to withdraw from this whorl.

The morning stillness and his thoughts were interrupted by the clamor of unexpected visitors. Turning, he smiled. A troop of monkeys scampered from the brush to drink from the cool reservoir. The sight lightened the mystic's heart.

Five large males, scouting the terrain, led the pack. The largest of the group signaled an all-clear, and the females scurried to the water's edge. Some carried suckling infants cradled beneath, while others had adolescents riding atop their strong backs. Holding firmly to the shoreline, they dipped their faces into the cool waters. The adolescents played while the adult males stood watch. Their chattering echoed through the abandoned, hollow halls of the temple, filling it with life.

Vyasa looked back at the ancient temple, its reliefs now cracked and covered with sand. He remembered when it had been visited by more than monkeys, when priests ignited sacrificial fires, when the altars were covered with offerings of fruit and flowers for the devas, when the chanting of worshipers rose on incense clouds until it reached the halls at Sveta-dvipa.

Sometimes he thought he heard the chants of the priests offering their sacrifices to the deva Vayu—controller of the winds—and Indra—ruler of Sveta-dvipa and controller of rain—hoping their petitions would convince these celestial beings to release the precious waters.

Suddenly, the monkeys stopped drinking. The males stood at attention, guarded, their heads upright, their back hairs stiff from fear. The largest of the males screamed an alarm, and the families scurried back to the protection of the forest.

The monkey's shrill cries made the hairs on the back of Vyasa's neck stand on end. Why be startled? he thought. A water snake probably scared them off. There are plenty of snakes at this time of day.

Dismissing his unease, he chased the strange cold from his bones and crouched on the cool surface of the ruin, placing his chotta upon the hard stone as a sitting place. He removed his sandals and took hold of his ankles, folding his legs into the lotus sitting position. The morning stiffness creaked from his joints. It felt good.

Opening the pouch, he removed the icon. He never tired of admiring the workmanship of its maker. He cherished the flat-nubbed hands, one holding a painted conch shell, the other, a lotus flower. A peacock-feathered crown, majestically carved, topped the head.

He counted the individual rows of red, yellow, and green flowers that formed a painted garland across the wooden figure's chest. When the devas wished it, Vyasa could actually smell the flowers, but today there was no scent. The bright paint covering the figure had faded. Curious, Vyasa turned it over. Color was missing from its arms and feet. Why hadn't he noticed before? The image of the branch on the kadamba tree flashed across his mind. He sat, looking first at the wooden figure, then back up the steps to the lone tree.

I am a third-incarnation mystic, he assured himself, but even three lifetimes still left him a man. He needed to cross over, to reach the next step. He brushed the sand from the ground. His offering had to be prepared, and quickly! He needed to focus his thoughts, to get on with the ritual.

Vyasa took a piece of coal from his pouch and placed it before his object of meditation. "Agni," he chanted, invoking the deva of fire to ignite the fuel. "Obeisance to Agni, mouth of the devas. Through you all the devas feed." He held his breath and stared at the coal. Would it light? Would this day return to him? The coal sparked, burning red.

A puff of warm breath escaped from between his lips. He reached into the pouch to remove a small packet containing grains of incense. He chanted, "Nayana pathagami, bavatume." Sprinkling the grains and the kadamba leaves on the hot coal sent a white cloud of heavily perfumed smoke billowing into the morning air just as the first of the sun's rays highlighted the cracks on the temple ruin. Dawn!

Quickly but carefully, for the slightest mistake would spoil the rite, Vyasa unwrapped the sacred clay, chipping off a small fragment. Not to lose or waste even the smallest bit, he covered the remaining piece and returned it to his pouch. He placed the chip in his left palm and added drops of water from his bowl, turning the clay to paste. With his finger as a brush, he marked his forehead with three vertical lines that converged to form a **V** between his eyes—the symbol of the treta-mystic—all the time glancing nervously at the sun.

He placed the first meditation bead between his thumb and index finger, but his fingers were too numb to grip the rounded wood, and his hand trembled uncontrollably. Nervous perspiration filled his palm—not the palm of a treta-mystic. He looked into the eyes of the icon to engage his sense of sight. He inhaled the sweet fragrance of the incense to engage his sense of smell. He sounded the sacred mantra, "*Jai Om*," to engage his sense of hearing. He had to withdraw into a trance.

Instead, the left side of his body, his arm, and eye quivered. His heart palpitated. A she-jackal howled and leaped to the top of a temple column. The animal vomited fire and disappeared. Vyasa fingered his beads and stopped chanting, his mind unwillingly diverted to something stirring . . . something inside the temple.

From within the shadows of his sanctuary, a milk-white cow emerged and walked down the stone steps. The apparition walked into the dark water of the lake, slowly submerging, disappearing from sight. Ripples in the water spread from where the animal vanished. Bubbles, rising from beneath, ceased. The small waves that had disturbed the calm of the lake settled, again becoming one with the surface. Vyasa sat motionless, staring into the cold water, mourning his fate.

A loud screeching, unhampered by the muffling liquid, came from deep within the still water, startling Vyasa from his thoughts. He leaned over the edge and peered at the black glass surface, his beads held firmly. Something splashed beneath, but the dark water kept him from seeing anything but his own reflection. Afraid to take his eyes from the liquid mirror, he stared, listening to the strange cries. When a snow-white owl sprang from the water, splashing him, Vyasa jumped back, moving his hands to protect his face and causing his beads to swing wildly.

"The messenger of Yama, Lord of the Dead," he stuttered to the emptiness of his hermitage. Cold drops of water rolled from his face and hands. "*Jai Om*," he chanted for protection. His fingers instinctively reached for the string of beads, only to find that they were gone.

He searched his lap and the surface of the ruin, but the beads swung above his head, clutched in the creature's talons. The owl's red eyes glowed on a circular facial disk of radiating feathers. Vyasa was afraid. Like an arrow, this symbol of foreboding shot straight up to impossible heights until it was a mere speck in the sky, disappearing just as a black cloud materialized in an otherwise cloudless sky. Growing in size, the dark mist moved against the wind, hovered above the temple and the lake, and blotted out the sun that had just begun to reveal itself.

Again Vyasa chanted, "*Jai Om!*" and the mantra broke the enchantment of the vapor as the cloud descended. Like a shroud, it fell into the water around him. Assuming the shape of two dark hands, it churned the still water to foam. A strange, intruding wind swept up from between the parted waves, climbing the sides of the ruin. The icy gale crept along the smooth surface, extinguishing his incense offering and sweeping the coal into the cold water where the hot ember sizzled out.

Vyasa turned back to the surface of the ruin. His pouch, the brass bowl, the sacred clay, even his sandals, had vanished! Desperately he grabbed his staff and clutched it to his chest. "You weren't quick enough to take this from me!" He cried tearfully.

Suddenly the icon stirred. Life airs filled the little wooden figure. Its celestial eyes blinked. Holding its ground against the dark tempest, the icon spoke.

"The mountains are throbbing. I hear cloudless thunder. I see bolts from a darkened sky. The rays of sun decline, and the stars fight among themselves. A dark wind blows from the Third Whorl, blasting dust everywhere, turning light to darkness. The clouds will rain blood."

Vyasa kneeled and moaned. "What am I to do?"

"The Asura, Kali, has broken the seal of Bila-svarga, unleashing from that whorl the demon races and worshipers of the black art of the Pisaca. The balance of the Bhu-mandala universe has been breached."

Had Vyasa heard correctly? "How could this have come to be?"

"With help from the enchantress Maya, Kali has discovered the lost dvars—the portals between the three whorls. The hordes of Bila-svarga will use these doorways to enter Bhu, where they will assume human form and—"

As dark suddenly overtook dawn, Vyasa grabbed for the icon, but the figure was swept into the black water by the inky vapor. Alone, the mystic stood on the windswept ruin, his left hand still outstretched. His right hand gripped the saffron cloth wrapping of his tridunda—the crescent-tipped staff standing as straight and tall as its master.

Dark waves crashed against the walls of the ancient ruin, spraying Vyasa's stoic face, splashing and chilling his bare feet. Icy winds pierced his flesh, blowing his chotta around his neck. The tattered ends of the wrap flapped wildly against his back. His long silver hair whipped his face, brushing his blazing eyes—eyes that had been witness to three lifetimes.

Vyasa looked at his empty hand. He knew that before he could gain the prize he sought, before he could attain the whorl of the devas, there were further tests to pass, tests greater than any he had known in his previous lives. He had been called to restore the balance.

He . . . and another.

ONE

GOPAL ALWAYS ENJOYED THE MARKET. It was where his dreams took the form of the exotic visitors that passed through his small village with their caravans. Although the kingdom of Goloka was only a watering hole for them, their presence was a dream come true for him. Today there would be two, maybe even three, caravans setting up in the square.

With his closest friend, Nimai, trailing behind, he hurried through the narrow streets, now cramped with farmers' carts, merchants, peddlers, and herders.

"Mother of Daksa! Watch where you're going!" he heard. The warning was too late and Gopal, in his rush, found himself in the midst of a small herd of goats. The animals scattered, fleeing into the open doorways of the small dung- and mud-brick homes. The screams of surprise that came from within the buildings combined with the goats' frightened cries and Gopal's light-hearted laughter. The animals were swept back into the street by women clutching small wicker brooms, which they waved wildly above their heads. Their complaints mixed with the angry cries of the people in the street as they searched for the instigator of this foolish prank, but Gopal had quickly moved on. Nimai had trouble keeping up.

Gopal's black topknot darted between the turbans of businessmen and the long, unkempt hair of ascetics who had come from the mountains. An ox cart, stuck in traffic, blocked his path, so he took a shortcut, running through a passage between the buildings that was too narrow for carts or herds. He came out on the other end and paused, gazing at the wonder of the market.

Still trying to keep up, and unable to see through the wall of shoppers, Nimai crashed into Gopal, who fell face-first onto a cart piled high with mangos, bananas, and white figs.

"By the gods! What do you think you're doing?" the vendor screamed, watching his crops spill and roll along the ground between the feet of strolling patrons. The fruit was squashed as people slid on the man's livelihood.

Sitting among the fruit, Gopal laughed at the sight he and his friend had caused.

"I'm sorry," he heard from a cracked, frightened voice. It was Nimai, apologizing and bending to pick up any unblemished fruit. "It was my . . . I mean . . . I didn't mean to . . . I'll help get it." Nimai gathered the spilled crops and soon was joined by the beggars that usually followed the caravans. Their pushing turned to frenzy as they shoved each other to retrieve what they thought was free fruit.

From within the melee of a hundred hands, Gopal grabbed Nimai by the back of the shirt and pulled his god-brother from the dust and confusion.

"Well done," he said with a laugh as he took Nimai from the street. His eyes met those of the angry fruit vendor. "I think we'd better get away from here!"

He dragged Nimai by the arm through the swelling crowd to the other end of the plaza, where the market swarmed with activity. Makeshift shops stood wherever there was space. Heavy cotton pandals, with woven designs of multicolored geometric shapes, lined the streets. These

awnings were supported by long, thick bamboo poles from
the rain forests in the east and shaded the market from the
Golokan sun.

Carts of all sizes, each brimming with produce or crafts,
filled the plaza's center. Shoppers scrambled, haggling
over prices. Shouts mixed with clouds of smoke that rose
from the many stoves, and the smell of lentils from the
urad dal soups drifted on the warm air, blending with the
scented displays of turmeric, cayenne, asafetida, black
cumin, and cinnamon from the spice carts. Wheat-flour
pooris sizzled and ballooned in the hot ghee that simmered
in large copper kettles.

Jewelers rang silver bells, drawing attention to their
chains of gold bracelets, earrings, and rings. Pottery of all
shapes and sizes hung from wooden poles while potters furiously pumped their wheels, their crusted hands molding
shapeless lumps of clay into objects of use. Large brass vessels lined the street, and the pounding of busy hammers
echoed from deep within warm shops. Exotic young wom-
en, huddled in circles, meticulously strung piles of flower
petals into white, yellow, and pink garlands that, when
displayed, swayed in the wind, their delicate fragrances
dancing upon Gopal's senses. A tailor prepared a woven
carpet of colorful hand-blocked designs for delivery to a
rich customer while two young boys, hired to carry the pur-
chase, waited anxiously nearby, mentally spending the
small wage they would receive for their labor.

Caravan merchants waved silk cloth above the heads of
strolling husbands. Occasionally a merchant would whisper
less-than-respectful remarks to the wives trailing behind,
embarrassing some of the women whose jingling necklaces,
rows of gold bracelets, and silver ankle bells played a pecu-
liar tune to their hurried pace. Clay jugs filled with wine
and bronze vases filled with lotus-scented water glided past
atop the heads of young female bearers. Above Gopal's
head, cotton garments of green, yellow, orange, and purple waved in the wind as they were hung out for their dyes

to dry, the sun glistening on the occasional golden thread.

A shenai's haunting music captured Gopal's ear. Snakes, hypnotized by their charmers' swaying instruments, danced in straw baskets. The high, clear song of flutes combined with the swirling dust and the cries of animals being struck by their herders' sticks.

Gopal turned to the cries. "Sweets! Sweets from the south! Milk-sweets, to light up the palate!" He inhaled the sweet scent of fresh sandesh cheese fudge and rasgula cheese balls in orange flower syrup.

Turning, he saw the most beautiful woman in all the three whorls. Her rounded hips swayed slowly to the fingered beat of a drum as her slender arms lifted and her palms met, forming a triangle above her head. Gopal's breathing quickened when her long, thin fingers, tipped with red, pointed fingernails, clanged small brass cymbals. His ears tingled with each delicate clash. Her body glistened behind golden veils while Gopal's imagination followed droplets of sweat down into her soft garments. Still swaying, she pushed her hips forward, forcing the thin silk to brush aside, revealing the smooth upper portion of her thighs.

"As soft as a broad sand bank," Gopal said with a sigh.

Oblivious to all but this entrancing beauty, Gopal stepped forward to get closer, right into the path of a train of brightly painted elephants. Nimai grabbed him by the shoulders with two hands, pulling him back.

"Move away, young fools!" Gopal heard the master cry from atop the first beast. When the animals swayed past, each heavy step caused sand to explode from the road as the bells decorating the animals' feet beat a dirge. With Nimai still holding his shoulders, Gopal shifted from side to side, straining to see the dancer through this forest of legs as the elephant caravan passed.

Gopal eventually was drawn to a magician standing on a waist-high platform on the far side of the crowd. With his friend in tow, Gopal meandered over to the conjurer of wonders and watched in awe when the illusionist removed

a large gem from the mouth of a passing stranger. The
crowd applauded this magical feat. Then the magician
held the green, prune-size gem above his turban, catching
the sun's rays, illuminating the stone. The jewel turned into a beacon and the magician directed the magnified light
into the faces of the audience, which already glowed in
wonder. Gopal blinked when the sweeping beam swung
across his eyes.

"They're probably working together," he heard Nimai
whisper. Gopal waited for the black spots that dotted his
world to fade. "The magician and that man from the
crowd. It's a trick," Nimai insisted.

Gopal wouldn't believe that! He believed in magic. Before he could respond to his friend's disbelief, another hypnotic voice found him. He turned to his left and saw the
crescent-tipped staff of a mystic. From the markings on the
man's forehead, Gopal knew he was a treta-mystic. Here in
Goloka? he wondered. This was a treat! Mystics of such
birth were rare and usually lived as hermits in the northern
mountains.

This one dressed in tattered saffron robes. A cotton chotta adorned his shoulders as the man sat, cross-legged and
barefoot in the sandy street. Long silver hair touched the
ground at the mystic's back. Unknown to Gopal, Vyasa
had come in search of "the other" that the devas had chosen to help him complete his task.

"Strange and wondrous places have I seen," Gopal heard
the mystic sing.

"Tell us," begged a woman dressed in merchant's finery.
Her hair was decorated with elaborate combs of silver and
gold, and a silk veil, held by jewel-studded pins, covered
her face. Tossing a coin into the small wooden bowl the
storyteller kept before him, she implored, "Tell us more."

Vyasa had no interest in money, but it was customary to
offer some form of alms to ascetics. He let the coin lie
where it landed, for something of greater importance had
caught the mystic's eye—Gopal and Nimai had joined the

audience. The two boys were oddly matched, as one wore the clean white silk of the ruling Varna class, and the other, the dull, homespun cotton of the lowly Sudra. But there were bonds that even a treta-mystic could not see, and Gopal's royal birth meant little to the boy.

"In my previous lives I traveled among the Three Whorls of the Bhu-mandala," Vyasa said charmingly.

That was all Gopal needed to hear. "We've got to get up front." He forced his way through the crowd with Nimai reluctantly following.

"I remember one journey to the edge of the whorl." When Vyasa pointed, the entire crowd turned, as if with one head, to look toward the clouds. "I visited the gardens of Soma, attended by creatures of angelic beauty."

"The gardens of Ushana-sukra," Gopal heard whispered among the amused onlookers. Even more quickly now, he pushed his way under elbows and arms, through the sweet perfumes of ladies and the foul scents of men. He knew of the gardens.

"Yes! Such places exist!" continued the teller of the tale. "It is in such a place, they say, that there is a tree of blessings, a magical tree that can grant any wish."

"Well, old man," said a merchant, tossing another coin into the mystic's bowl, "tell us! What did you wish?" Everyone broke into laughter at the thought of what a man's wish might be.

Vyasa paused, looking at the two boys emerging from his audience. He knew his search had ended. He needed to disperse the crowd and learn more about this boy he had been sent to find. "I would tell you, but I am afraid there are ears too young for the rest of my tale."

The crowd turned to Gopal and Nimai. "Off with you!" blurted a drunken gentleman standing beside them. The man wiped at wine that dripped from the sides of his mouth; his other hand loosely gripped his silver cup. With force that matched an elephant's, the man pushed Gopal and Nimai back, spilling the drink across his belly and splashing the boys. "A curse on these two," he slurred at his reflection, staring back from inside the empty cup.

"Get them away!" yelled another. "I want to hear the rest." The audience grumbled, annoyed at the delay.

Awkwardly pushed from hand to hand, Gopal and Nimai soon found themselves outside the mocking group. "We will be seventeen this harvest," Gopal shouted, bending to pick up a stone from the ground at his feet. Vyasa liked the boy's spirit. He was like a wild horse that needed to be tamed.

"It's just the imagination of a hungry old man," said Nimai, grabbing Gopal's arm and stopping the stone. "There are no such places!"

Gopal wouldn't hear it. "There are such places!" There had to be! But it was a voice from behind that made him lower his arm.

"There they are!" It was the fruit vendor, brandishing a long stick. He stood with a soldier, brought with the caravans for protection and armed with a spear. "Those are the ones," cried the merchant, pointing his stick. "Arrest those two!" Gopal dropped the stone and ran into the mass of shoppers. Nimai, without thinking, followed him through the path Gopal had forced in his haste. "Come back here, you thieves!" yelled the vendor. "Curse your miserable lives!"

Fortunately, the crowd, like water, quickly closed behind the boys, making escape easy. The vendor could be seen beating the crowd with his stick, still trying to follow, while the soldier stood by, annoyed at the time he had wasted.

Gopal and Nimai found themselves on a narrow street and in even more trouble. Just ahead, beyond the shoppers' heads and shops' awnings, was Cittahari.

"My sister!" Gopal cried, not knowing if Nimai had seen her.

"Citty? Here?" said Nimai.

Gopal frantically looked for a place to hide. "Quick, follow me!" he shouted, as if the Lord of the Dead were coming for his due. Grabbing Nimai by the arm, he led him up a wooden staircase. "We can hide . . . on the roof."

"Gopal?" Citty waved her hand above the heads of the crowd, her other hand trying to keep her veil from falling from her head. It was against the law for an unmarried girl to have an uncovered head in public, but everyone knew how much Gopal's sister hated following those laws.

Maybe she hadn't seen where they went, Gopal hoped, swinging up to the rooftop and crouching low in a corner. He heard her call again; her voice floated up from the street below like a reed that wouldn't stay underwater.

She persisted. "You'd better come out, and I mean now!" He heard his younger sister's cries, and he frowned. He didn't want to go, not now! "Father is getting ready for the fire sacrifice. He wants you there!"

Gopal peered carefully over the roof's edge. Citty was looking up and down the street, squinting, then looking up to the ledges of the roofs, checking each of them. She was nothing if not thorough, he reminded himself. Even their father said that. "I know you can hear me, Gopal!" She yelled again, cupping her hands around her mouth, allowing her shouts to rise above the banter of the people on the street.

Beside him on the roof, their elbows rubbing, Nimai whispered, "Are you going to answer?"

"No!" Gopal replied. "I know what she wants. It's time for the yagna! I don't want to go!" Gopal was tired of the rituals, as his friend knew. Being the son of a simha was nothing to crow about, though everyone thought it was. He didn't want to be bothered with any more royal duties. He wanted to visit the places the mystic in the market had talked about. He wished to travel the Bhu-mandala, to find the Garbhodaka Ocean at the very bottom of the Whorl of Bhu, and to see for himself the giant timangala fish. He had even heard of the vast Ocean of Milk, churned by the devas in their battle with the Asuras during the Bhu-mandala Wars, when Bila-svarga, the Third Whorl, was sealed . . . forever!

Most of all, Gopal dared to imagine himself entering the place where no mortal had ever traveled—Sveta-dvipa, the whorl of the devas. That's what Gopal wanted, not some ceremony for farmers to placate their deities.

Citty called again and Gopal and Nimai peered down. "Now she's talking to Prema's two sons," Gopal said. Nimai looked into the crowded street below, but couldn't see Cittahari. "There." Gopal pointed. "In front of their father's shop." Nimai saw her then, holding a new sword in her hand. One of the brothers snatched it back. "That place is probably the only thing that could divert her," said Gopal. "I know how badly she must want that sword."

"Such a wish is forbidden by the Laws of the Manus," snapped Nimai, shocked at the thought.

Gopal ignored his friend's outburst. Many a night they had spent arguing about the laws. "She must be asking if they've seen us." Gopal knew the brothers wouldn't tell, even if they did know. They were his friends. He turned from the street, perspiring and thirsty, and looked around the dusty roof. He'd always thought that the karma of being of the First Order of the Varna—born to a royal family—should have gotten him more than this. To him, his royalty was nothing more than words and useless duty.

His sister called his name again. She sounded close now, right below. He couldn't hide up here forever, but he didn't want to go. Performing rituals so cows would give more milk? That was the duty of a herdsman, not the son of a simha! No one, not even Nimai, really understood how he felt. Even his father had laughed when he had said it, but it was true.

"It's your duty," he heard Nimai remind him.

Paying his friend no mind, he stood and leaned over the ledge to see if his sister had left. He didn't see her. She was probably hiding, waiting for him to stick his head out too far.

"As son of the simha of Goloka—" Nimai started to say, as he stood to join his friend.

"Get back," Gopal warned, pushing Nimai from the ledge. "She may see you!" Gopal sat again as well. "I know about my duty. The traditions are important to my father, not to me."

"Don't let anyone else hear you mock the Laws of the Manus," his friend warned.

Turning away, Gopal leaned over the wall that ran around the roof. Again he looked for his sister. There she was! He ducked back when her eyes scanned the surrounding rooftops.

"I don't know why you feel like that," said Nimai. "I like it here. Just look around you. Out there, away from the village, farms spread out as far as we can see. And there," he said, pointing to the hills that sloped to meet the mountain, "cows graze in the pastures. We have our own market, where everything is brought to us. We are safe here. We have everything we could want. We never have to leave."

Gopal saw it all differently, though he and Nimai looked at the same things. The mountains were something to go beyond, not something to close him in and keep him safe. "You stay!" he replied. "When the time comes, I'm leaving."

Gopal wondered if his friend would ever understand. Nimai was from the Sudra class, and just being with the simha's son must seem like a blessing to him. But why should class matter? He liked Nimai; they were god-brothers. He wanted Nimai to go with him . . . someday. "Aren't you curious to see what's over that mountain, beyond those clouds?" Gopal urged, wiping the sweat from his forehead. How long had they been up here?

"You know no member of the simha's family can leave the kingdom," Nimai sternly reminded his friend. "It is forbidden by the Laws of—"

"I know the law! I've been taught all the vidhis."

But Nimai went on. "We shouldn't meddle with karma. This is where fate has cast us," his friend calmly reasoned. "Haven't you heard the lesson of the wedge-pulling monkey?"

Frustrated by his futile attempts to get Nimai to understand, Gopal turned from the mountain in the distance. Sliding his back down the wall, he rested on the roof's hot surface. He preferred listening to the street, to the music and excitement radiating from the market. Maybe no one would ever understand how he felt.

Trying to be consoling, Nimai moved close. "Did you ever hear the story?" his friend asked again.

"No," Gopal responded, hugging his knees to his chest. Looking up, he shielded his eyes from the bright sun with his hand. Black clouds, heavy with rain, drifted toward the mountain, passing his village.

"Then listen," Nimai urged, placing a hand on Gopal's shoulder, still intent on telling him the story.

Nimai seemed excited at the prospect of knowing something that he didn't. Can I stop you? thought Gopal. Looking down at the scorched surface, he picked up a small stick that lay between his feet. In the sand and dust, he scratched a drawing of clouds.

Nimai tried to start the story. "There was a city—"

"What region?" Gopal questioned, smiling at the agitation he tried to stir.

"That isn't important . . . any region. Let me finish."

Gopal half-listened, scratching his dreams on the surface of the roof while Nimai told how, one day, a troop of monkeys came upon a half-built temple, where there lay a tremendous anjana log. A worker had begun to split the log with a wedge of acacia wood that he'd left stuck in the crack. While the monkeys played on the woodpile, one of them thoughtlessly straddled the log, finding it curious that someone had stuck a wedge in such a place. Gopal hid his smile when Nimai imitated the talking monkey, but nothing would keep Nimai from continuing.

"The careless monkey seized the wedge with both hands and worked it loose. What happened when the log closed on his private parts, you know without being told. So you see," Nimai concluded, "meddling with karma should be avoided. Leave things as they are. Your questions will lead only to pain." Nimai turned to find Gopal standing again, leaning against the wall.

Gopal rubbed away the drawing of the cloud with his sandaled foot. Nimai stood with him.

"Where did you hear that story?" Gopal asked, annoyed at the reasoning to which his friend had so easily fallen prey.

"From my grandfather," said Nimai.

Gopal preferred the stories of his own grandfather. He turned again to look for his sister. Leaning over the ledge as far as he could, and looking up the street to its end, he thought his sister had gone.

"There you are!" He heard from behind, and turned to that familiar voice. "Well! I knew I'd find you near the market. Father is on his way to the north field to prepare for the sacrifice. He expects you there!" She stopped suddenly. Stepping closer, she looked curiously at her brother's dust-covered, fruit-smeared shirt. She sniffed. Her nostrils flared.

"Do I smell wine?" she asked, the way a sister does when she thinks she's caught her brother doing something he shouldn't. Before Gopal could explain, she smiled and said, "I'll go and tell them you're on your way. . . . That's all I'll tell, so hurry." She turned, pulled her veil over her head again, and ran down the steps as quietly as she had come up.

Gopal looked at Nimai. "Come on, we'd better go." He smiled a sly smile. "I'll race you to my house . . . through the market!"

*　*　*　*　*

At the field, the farmers and herdsmen gathered, waiting for their king's command. The simha, dressed in his ceremonial white robe, his chest draped with a garland of lotus flowers, peered over the heads of his subjects, looking for his son.

When Gopal and Nimai finally arrived, they quickly moved to stand beside Gopal's father. Padma gave a stern look and, with two fingers, drew his black mustache away from his mouth as he usually did before he chastised his son. Today, though, he was more anxious to get on with the ceremony than to lecture on lateness.

"I want to get closer!" Gopal heard. Turning, he saw his sister fidgeting. His mother was pulling on the back of his sister's sari, trying to keep the veil on the girl's head with one hand and keep her in place with the other. "And why do I have to wear this," he heard her complain. "Why can't I wear a warrior's vest?"

"It is not for you!" Lila reminded, adjusting her own silk-embroidered sari.

"My hand held a blade today," Citty bragged, forcing herself free and making her way to the front, next to her brother.

"It is not your place, or the place of any Golokan woman," their mother called, embarrassed by her daughter's display. She begged the other women to excuse her daughter's behavior, but they merely stared respectfully. Quickly she followed the girl. "The law! Besides at your age—" Lila realized she was drawing too much attention.

Citty was out of their mother's reach. "I don't care," she muttered. "Gopal is right. The old ways no longer make sense. I can hold my own with any other fifteen-year-old girl . . . or boy," she challenged, and turned to measure herself against Nimai. The top of her head reached his eyes. "And one even older." She laughed, her twinkling brown eyes looking up, meeting Gopal's gaze.

"Sssh," he advised with a smile. His sister was probably right. "The yagna is beginning."

All work stopped for the yagna, a ceremony held every spring to protect the village and farms. Simha Padma, Gopal, and Goloka's other leading men were to lead the procession of priests who carried offerings of rice, wheat, bananas, and other fruits, while the villagers—along with a specially selected cow, bull, elephant, and water buffalo—marched three times around a chosen field. Padma's duty was to recite prayers to Indra, controller of fire. Gopal was to assist with the fire sacrifice.

When all was ready, his father began the prayer:

> "Lord Indra, I pray and beseech you,
> That you may be gracious and favorable to us.
> For this cause I have ordained
> That an offering be carried 'round this land;
> That you may ward off all diseases,
> Visible and invisible,
> And all barrenness from our fields and our women.
> Cast away all misfortune that we may suffer."

The completion of the invocation was a signal for the drummers to start. The beat of the clay mrdungas was joined by the clash of small brass cymbals and the banging of gongs. Children rang bells, and the chanting of "Glories to Indra!" filled the hot, dry afternoon air as the Golokans danced along the designated path, their hands reaching for the heavens, as they hoped their prayers would. When the procession came full circle, they reached the priests who had been busily preparing a pit for the sacrifice.

The villagers quieted their drums and singing. Then, to Gopal's surprise, the mystic from the market sat with the village priests. It wasn't often that a village had the honor of hosting a treta-mystic, and Padma, being a religious man and a strict follower of tradition, apparently had taken the mystic's presence as an auspicious sign and invited the ascetic to lead the sacrifice.

After Vyasa had taken the special seat in the sacred circle of priests, he took up a small silver spoon that had been laid before him and dipped it into a bowl of clarified butter. While uttering "Sva-ha," the sacred syllables for sacrifice, he poured the ghee onto a small flame, fueling the sacrificial fire.

"Sva-ha," repeated the priests as the ghee ignited into a fountain of fire and black smoke. The scent of burning butter rose with their chants. Other priests took their cue and tossed their articles of sacrifice into the growing flames. Grains sizzled and cracked. Vyasa chanted again. The echo of the priests was followed by fruit, which they tossed into the fire. After each offering, Vyasa made the sacred sound.

Gopal, sitting across from the mystic, poured a small cup of cow's milk onto the flame as an offering to the deva Bhumi, Mother of Bhu. Next he presented a lighted oil lamp, waving the small flame before a copper pot containing mango leaves and coconut, symbols of regeneration and cosmic fertility. Seeing the mangos reminded Gopal of the scene he and Nimai had caused at the market. He couldn't hide the smile on his face, much to his father's disapproval.

With the final offerings made, the musicians picked up their drums to play again, this time with more reverence. The cymbals joined, followed by the single clang of the gong, and the priests, in unison, uttered the most sacred syllable, "Om."

Everyone fell into a meditative trance. With closed eyes, unconsciously swaying, the people listened to the priests' soothing chants. The entire group became as one—everyone except Gopal, who had become diverted. Something was different about the tone of their guest's voice, but why should that be? There was nothing different about today's sacrifice. The mystic probably had performed yagnas like this a hundred times. While everyone else closed their eyes, Gopal kept his open, watching the mystic.

He had heard other visiting mystics interpret the astrological signs of the jyoti, and he had laughed when these strange visitors from the mountains had frightened the other boys with tales of Asuras and Rakshasas. Gopal had even heard that treta-mystics could leave their bodies and, in another form, travel to other planets.

The mystic opened his eyes. Priests never did that during a sacrifice! Gopal knew this, for he had attended many. The mystic looked up. A tremendous black thundercloud had rolled in from the west. The mystic stared at the darkening sky. Gopal looked at the strange cloud, then back at Vyasa, watching both for the duration of the yagna. Nothing happened, at least nothing that Gopal could see. When the sun had set, their guest signaled the end of the ceremony.

The priests quickly gathered ash from the fire into large silver bowls. Rising to their feet, these holy men walked to where the animals had been tied and spread small amounts of the ash on the beasts' heads. The priests then turned to the royal family. As with the animals, small amounts of ash were to be rubbed into their hair. Gopal's father received the first blessing, and Gopal was next. Out of respect for his father, he acted the part, bowing humbly, as was his duty, and allowed a priest to rub the ashes on his head. When the holy man moved on to the rest of his family, Gopal rose from his place and faced the mystic.

Vyasa was still staring, only this time at him! What Gopal saw wasn't an angry stare, or a happy one, for that matter. It wasn't the look he received from his father when he mispronounced his mantras, or when he daydreamed during his warrior-arts lessons. This look was strange. The mystic's face had become like stone, lifeless, as if its features had been carved by some unknown hand. Gopal was scared. For the first time in his life, the stare from a mystic terrified him.

TWO

WITH MORNING CAME THE DUTY Gopal dreaded most. According to the Laws of the Manus, it was called an istagosti, a meeting called by a simha to hear the complaints of the men of his kingdom. Even a kingdom as small as Goloka had to follow these laws.

While putting on the purple ceremonial robe worn at such a meeting, Gopal scoffed at the law. Why should he have to listen to the squabbling of old men and farmers?

"Because it is your duty as heir to the throne!" his father would say. "And control that tongue of yours, or you will offend the manus," he would warn. As usual, his father's reasoning won. After all, he was the simha. Just once, Gopal wanted to win. Just once, he wanted his father to listen to what he had to say.

However reluctant, Gopal was on his way to the istagosti. The uneasiness the mystic had left with him hadn't gone away with last night's dreams. Even Nimai, dressed in his finest gray cotton tunic, noticed his friend's restlessness. It was obvious that something was bothering Gopal when they met outside the meeting hall. Gopal didn't want to discuss it.

As they stood outside the building, constructed for such meetings many years before by his grandfather, Gopal noticed how the fronds on the old pitched roof needed replacing. The building was nothing more than another dung-and-mud structure, but it had withstood the test of heat and monsoon. It was the same with most of the buildings in Goloka. Everything suddenly seemed in need of repair, as if the spark that gives life to everything, even inanimate objects, had been extinguished.

It wasn't only that; other things had changed since yesterday. Familiar things seemed foreign. It was like seeing his village for the first time. Had it been the strange cloud he had seen last night? Did it still hang over the village . . . over him? He looked up, but the sky was clear.

The priests had talked to his father about an evil wind called krura-lochana, or something like that. Maybe he should have been more attentive. It was supposed to be a dark wind from Bila-svarga, believed to carry drought and famine, to change weather, to contaminate all who breathed it, even animals. The old men called it a cosmic disease, an infection that traveled the Bhu-mandala. Once contacted, a kingdom could only be cleansed by the performance of vidhis—rituals prescribed by the Laws of the Manus. But Bila-svarga had been sealed after the war with the devas.

What was he thinking anyway? These things weren't his concern. He wanted to leave this tiny place his father called a kingdom. He hadn't asked to be born into the family of a simha. Karma had cast his fate. He wondered . . .

As he entered the building, the sudden burst of warmth from within comforted him, making him realize how cold it really was outside . . . even if it was still spring. The hall was vacant, except for the priests. The light from outside shone through spaces in the old frond roof. The timbers stood, warped and splintered, like an old man's staff, barely able to carry the weight. At the other end of the room, before the village altar, priests busily prepared the morning offerings of rice, dates, and warm milk with bananas. On the altar were the statuettes of the major devas: Lord Indra, Agni, and Vayu; Varuna, guardian of the seas and oceans; Vivaswan, keeper of light; and Chandra, ruler of the moons of Bhu. In their center stood the deva worshiped by the simhas of Goloka, the four-armed Paramatma. And, barely visible if you didn't know where to look, a six-inch figure of Bhumi, Gopal's favorite, nestled among the rest. Bhumi was his namesake, for Bhumi often took the form of a cow and "Gopal" meant "protector of the cow-mother."

The decorated altar always stirred Gopal's fascination with the whori. If the size of a universe is related to the number of heads of its creators, then how large must the universe of the thousand-headed creators be? The thought bewildered him, but still he thirsted for more knowledge. His questions knew no bounds; only his life in Goloka did.

The scent from a thick cloud of resin incense rose from the altar. The fuel had ignited. Its glow reflected off the misty incense haze, spilling light from the windows and illuminating the meetinghouse like a beacon in the middle of the village.

The village men entered. Some came alone, others in small groups. The ones with wives separated from the women at the door. While the husbands entered, mingling with the other male villagers, the wives took seats outside. Prohibited by law from taking part in an istagosti, the women, some cradling infants, brought cloth to mend or brass to polish. They huddled in small groups by the windows while their children played nearby.

As the men took their seats on the dirt floor, Gopal took his place on a platform, on a cushion to the left of where his father would sit. Nimai took a moment to see to the wishes of his own father, who was being helped to a place toward the back of the hall. Nimai's father, Sahadeva, had never been the same after his wife was killed by a bakasura beast. The poor man had been mauled while trying to save her, and the loss of a hand and a leg, for a farmer, was worse than death. Now, unable to work, he had been forced to live as a Sudra, on the simha's welfare.

"It is a simha's responsibility to care for his people," Gopal remembered his father saying. But Sahadeva saw it as a curse and blamed the simha for not protecting the village.

Watching Nimai help the man made Gopal happy. He and Nimai could still be friends in spite of their fathers' ill feelings. He was very fond of Nimai: his wide-eyed innocence, his fear of anything different, his loyalty as a friend—even if they were from different social classes and even if Nimai didn't understand him. Finally getting permission from his own father, Nimai took a seat in front to act as a diversion for Gopal.

A priest who had been standing near the entrance announced, "Obeisance to Padma, Simha of Goloka."

The men obediently bowed. "Jai Padma," they chanted in voices of cold sincerity while Gopal's father marched down the center aisle. Padma circled the fire pit with his entourage of priests and took his royal seat on a sana of silk cushions. The respect his father commanded engendered a curious admiration in the boy. Would men bow for him when he became simha? he wondered.

While his father received honors, Gopal's mother was forced by law to stay outside. According to tradition, she was treated to a special seat at the window closest to her husband.

Also forced outside, Citty protested, convinced she could solve the problems better than most men. Gopal knew Citty enjoyed the meetings more than he did. Who didn't? Law or not, he would have loved to let her enter . . . just once, just to see the faces of the old men and priests. The thought alone made him smile. What would Padma say? Gopal laughed to himself, then looked around, fearing his father's stern stare, but Padma was talking to the mystic, Vyasa, and hadn't noticed.

When all looked ready, Gopal struck a small brass gong,
bringing everyone to attention. Slowly the assembly came
to order, voices lowered, and the last of the villagers took
their seats.

"Pradhumna, of the family of Matilla," his father announced, "has petitioned the council, that he may speak
first."

Pradhumna represented the second class of Goloka—the
farmers, craftsmen, and herdsmen. His family had always
been respected and, but for his birth in the order of Vaisha,
Pradhumna could have made a good simha. Pradhumna
rose from the assembly, supporting himself with the herding staff of his family, and approached the council. Since it
was forbidden for Vaishas to wear turbans, a hood from his
green-and white-striped robe—the colors of his family—
protected his head from the cold. Reaching the front of the
assembly, he uncovered his head, as was the custom, and
addressed the council.

"My farm is not producing, in spite of our continuing
sacrifices to Indra." He turned from the council to the audience. "We are getting frost in late spring that is ruining our
crops." He pointed to the fire pit. "See how we need a fire
this morning. This behavior for the seasons is unheard of."

"Lord Indra has forsaken us!" screamed a voice. Gopal
quickly searched the audience for the cause of the rude interruption. No one was to speak without the simha's permission. The villagers obviously were restless this morning.

"My animals can barely give enough milk for my family
to live on," came another angry comment, diverting
Gopal's attention. Gopal realized this behavior was unheard of at an istagosti. What had come over these people?
Everyone in the hall began to stir, mumbling like rolling
thunder, complaining among themselves.

"Shanti. Shanti," his father commanded in a soft, calm
voice. Raising his two hands, his father motioned for everyone to be still. "Everyone will be heard, but we must have
peace. You will speak in turn." Still respectful of their

simha, the men slowly quieted. The serenity his father displayed relaxed even Gopal.

"And the marketplace," continued Pradhumna. "Every day there are more caravans than our wells can serve. Three more wells have dried up this month alone." Weren't the caravans a good thing? They were for Gopal. "There is no room," the farmer continued, "and still they set up their tents."

Gopal glanced at his father. The simha sat calmly on his sana.

"Yes, Sunanda," said Padma, recognizing a villager who had his hand raised. "You also may speak to this assembly." Gopal knew it was wise of his father to call on another to maintain order, but he didn't know how much longer order would last. Sunanda, also of the Vaisha class, rose to his feet but stood at his place, resting on his staff. Was this a subtle display of disrespect? wondered Gopal.

"The market has been overrun by outsiders," said Sunanda, "while farmers and herdsmen, who have lived their lives in the hills of Goloka, starve!" He turned to the assembly. "We can't compete with these foreigners." Heads nodded. The mumbling resumed.

"It is not the foreigners," said Vyasa. As the simha's guest, he was the only one who could speak without asking permission. "Too many temple altars stand empty. The offerings to the devas have decreased." The assembly quieted.

"The manus are offended!" shouted a priest. "I saw another shooting star last night." Gopal worried. His grandfather had said that demons enter the whorl on falling stars.

"We are being punished!" screamed another. "The devas have forsaken us!"

Vyasa stood at his place. "It is *krura-lochana*."

There was that word. The air suddenly was cold and still, frozen in space. The incense cloud stopped rising and clung to the ceiling. No one spoke. No one breathed. The door flew open, and a cold gust rushed in, carrying bits of the parched land. It blew the robes of the gathered men, who covered their eyes. Sand, like a thousand darts, pricked their faces. A second gust fanned the fire. Shadows flared to the height of the ceiling's wooden rafters, as if dancing with the flames. The fire leaped ten . . . fifteen . . . twenty feet into the air. Nimai, startled by the sudden burst of heat and flame, fell over. Citty stood to her feet, stretching to see through the window. Gopal sat in awe.

Where the flames had reached, a giant appeared, engulfed in fire and smoke. Gopal counted six, seven—no, eight arms extending from a bare human chest. It had human hands, each finger tipped with a black claw that curled into a hook. More smoke cleared, revealing the head of a magnificent, golden-maned lion. The creature's head nearly touched the building's roof.

Gopal touched his dagger. What should he do? He wiped the sweat from his face. Padma sat in place, one hand on his own dagger. Gopal followed his father's lead and waited.

Looking to the sky, the creature released a thunderous roar, shaking the ground and tearing bamboo fronds from the roof. Outside, frightened branches shook loose their leaves, showering the children and the women who cowered from the roar. The ground turned to a collage of foliage.

Within, Gopal crouched low, frozen by the vision, his ears still ringing. When the echo of the beast's cry faded from the hall, the figure of flesh, smoke, and flame spoke to the assembly.

"Eternal time has been changed!" it growled, twisting its head in mute agony. "There are disruptions in the seasons. Greed, anger, deceit, foul means of livelihood, cheating, and fighting among friends usher in the reign of the Asura king Kali Yuga—the Age of Kali. The seal of Bilasvarga has been broken!" Each of the vision's eight limbs reached for the sky in torment.

The Age of Kali? Is that what it said? An Asura? Here on Bhu? In human form?

A whirlwind of hot air and dust circled outside the assembly hall, tossing the saris of the women, who hugged their children close. After wrapping itself around the building, the whirlwind burst through the door. Sweeping a path through the dirt and cowering villagers, it rushed to the fire, tousling the men's hair and clothing. The wind whirled into the fire pit to engulf the creature and, scooping it up through the already tattered roof, disappeared. With the fire extinguished, the spell broke. The men were convinced that their doom was near, and the assembly's grumbling grew into panic.

Padma rose to his feet. "Please, we must maintain order!" Nothing happened. Everyone on the platform stood. "This will be dealt with," Gopal's father assured, again motioning with his hands. The simha tried to get everyone to return to their seats, but this time the complaints grew louder than his royal command.

Vyasa whispered into Padma's ear. Gopal heard a word—"dvar." With Padma and Vyasa leading the way, the council members left, followed by the troubled and frightened assembly.

* * * * *

That night, within the comfort of their home, Gopal noticed how distraught his father was during their evening meal. His mother also noticed.

"Is it the istagosti that has upset you, my husband?" she asked, placing a serving of chapati before the simha. Being within the privacy of their home, the women were able to uncover their heads. Lila's long brown hair fell in front of her as she placed food before the men, and she had to sweep it out of the way. The Laws of the Manus prohibited women from cutting their hair.

Gopal's father placed a handful of rice on one of the flatbreads, rolled it up, and took a bite. "Not just that," Padma replied. He lifted his empty cup to drink and fingered his black beard, as he often did when something bothered him. "Citty, my daughter, bring me some cold water."

"Yes, Father," Citty replied. She took the bucket from the shelf and filled a clay pitcher. At least at home she didn't need to wear her veil, and she happily let her hair, as black as her brother's, hang loose. Many times she had tried to convince Gopal to cut it short for her. Tempted as he was, he respected his father enough to refrain.

Padma continued as Citty filled her father's cup. "I was willing to overlook the other omens that krura-lochana has befallen us. Now, with the appearance of that creature . . ." Padma lowered his cup, grasping it tightly with both hands. He looked up at his son.

Gopal felt obligated to say something. "Maybe the treta-mystic can use his powers to rid us of our trouble. A mystic can provide the answers you seek."

"Perhaps Gopal is right," offered Lila, also attempting to calm her husband. "Here, have some more rice. Gopal, you, too. Take some more rice with your soup. Citty, get more rice, and more pepper for your father." Citty brought the pepper and a large bowl of rice from the fire. Resting the rice on the table, she spooned another serving for the men.

"He already has," Padma replied.

Gopal, having been distracted by his mother's diversion, looked at his father. "What?"

"Vyasa has given me the answer," Padma calmly explained, taking another sip from his cup. Slowly he put the cup down. "Gopal, it is up to you."

Gopal nearly gagged on the rice he had just put to his mouth. Quickly he reached for a cup of water and sipped. The water wet his dry throat, allowing the lump to go down.

"Wha—what?" he stuttered. What was up to him? He listened intently.

"After the istagosti, I asked the mystic to consult the jyoti. He found the stars in favor of your performing the vidhi of purification."

Gopal turned to the bang of a metal plate his mother had dropped. "Forgive my clumsiness," she begged, fear lighting her eyes as she bent to pick up the plate.

Padma ignored her and continued. "You must bring back the claw of the naga. As the manus dictate, only the slaying of the Black Serpent and the taking of its claw will free our village from the krura-lochana." Gopal knew the laws. He had read them many times. "Our people need something to show that the manus have not forsaken us. This vidhi could be the sign they seek."

Gopal didn't believe what he was hearing. Now the traditions were getting dangerous. He wanted to say something, but what?

"You may leave tomorrow before Brahma-murta. That would be auspicious! And you must not forget to fast the whole day . . . from the moment you wake. Make an offering to Paramatma, to beg his protection."

Gopal's eyes widened, his throat dry again. Nervously he rubbed the drops of moisture that had gathered on the sides of his metal cup. The shining metal reflected his troubled face. He was too surprised by all of this to drink.

Gopal panicked. "Isn't it true that the serpent nests in the Temple of Durga?" His father nodded. His mother looked down at the floor. "The old men say the temple is haunted!" he blurted. Citty stopped cleaning the table, forgetting about taking her turn to eat. She took the seat across from her brother.

"You must have been too young to remember the story," his father explained, seeing Citty's sudden curiosity, "and the demon sent—"

"I think she was only five," added Lila, trying to appear calm and also taking a seat at the table.

Had time passed that quickly? Gopal sighed. I'm suddenly old enough to perform a vidhi? But am I? He thought about the law as his sister spoke.

"Father? Please tell me about the temple and the demon," she pleaded, smirking at her brother.

Stepping away from the table, Gopal went to the altar. There lay the law book. He took up the ancient text and touched it to his forehead. Returning to his place at the table, he sat. Gopal stared at the cover . . . then opened it.

"Yes, tell her," Gopal chided, looking up. "I wouldn't want to go . . . and not remember everything."

His mother, hearing the hesitation in Gopal's voice, tried to console him. "It's just a story."

"Well, tell us, Father," his sister again implored, setting the plates to the side and resting her arms on the wooden table, her hands clasped together.

Gopal searched through the book for a way out of the vidhi while his father told how some worshipers of Durga—the only female deva allowed to take part in battle—had been unceremoniously smoking ganja. In their intoxicated state, they abducted a devotee of Rudra—deva of annihilation—to sacrifice to their deity. Before Durga could stop them, they defiled her altar with the blood of their poor captive.

Gopal knew the story well. He'd heard it before, from his grandfather. Where was the Law of the vidhi? Frantic, he searched the ancient manuscript. The perspiration on his hands made it difficult to turn the pages. The rustling of the stiff paper grew under his worried fingers.

His sister, fidgeting on her cushion, pulled herself closer to the table. "What about the demon?"

She would ask that! Gopal thought, looking at her excited expression. Why couldn't she have been born a boy?

Padma explained that when Durga knew she had lost control of her followers, she called for the Destroyer himself, to make atonement for the loss of the innocent life. When Rudra appeared, he saw the slaughtered remains of his own faithful disciple and cried.

The rattle of a wooden spoon grew loud against a metal

bowl as Gopal's mother, trying not to listen, noisily emptied the half-full bowls of rice.

Her husband continued. "Rudra's sorrow turned to anger. His blue skin burned red. His eyes blazed like lightning. Laughing like a madman, he tore a fistful of hair
from his head, dashing the strands to the ground. The devotees of Durga stood petrified." His father, pretending to
grab his own hair, rose from his seat, sliding the sitting
cushion back. Then Padma threw the imaginary strands to
the ground.

Gopal stopped turning pages. His father droned on, telling how, from the strands, Rudra's anger rose, personified
as the black demon Virabhadra, who stood as high as the
sky. Padma reached with both hands, as high as he could,
until standing on his toes. Citty looked up, wide-eyed,
grabbing the edge of the table to keep from falling back.
Gopal leaned forward to rest his forehead in the palms of
his hands, again searching the pages. He heard Padma rant
on, telling how a garland of human heads swayed around
the demon's neck.

"The heads still lived," said Padma, "screaming in their
misery. As bright as three suns, the creature's hair burned
like fire. With a thousand arms, each sporting a different
weapon, Rudra's creation waved its hands above the heads
of the multitude of miscreants."

Padma told how Virabhadra slaughtered all who had attended the bogus sacrifice. Their severed limbs were strewn
about the temple altar as the demon chopped and cut his
victims. The offenders had tried to flee, but, like weeds,
were plucked up by the demon's inescapable reach. So pro-
fuse was the carnage that a river of blood was supposed to
have flowed from the demon's hands as he beheaded and
gutted his foul prey. The blood ran down the temple's
stone steps, into the forest below. At last the words his father spoke distracted him, and Gopal had to stop reading
and listen.

"The goddess wept at the sight of the horror she had

called upon her own followers. Finally she begged Rudra to withdraw his creation, but, by then, there were no survivors. The temple, abandoned by Durga, stands empty to this day."

Citty sat up straight on her pillowed seat. "And Gopal has to go there tomorrow?" She grinned, turning to meet his sneer. He looked back to the book, his fingers searching for a way out.

His father laughed, probably trying to defuse the fears in his son's mind. "Like your mother said, it is just a story!" Padma turned to Gopal and said, in that familiar, calm voice, "Your task is of a much more serious nature. The well-being of Goloka will depend on your bringing back the claw of the naga."

There it was, the page he was looking for! "Father? I'm not yet seven and ten years in this life. And it says it right here—Sloka 25:3. The age set down by the Laws of the Manus for performance of this vidhi is eight and ten."

"Karma has chosen you," his father calmly reasoned. "And, like you have said so often, times have changed, and change calls for new ways."

For the first time in Gopal's life, his father had listened to something he had said. He must be cursed! It was the only explanation.

Before Gopal could utter another word in his defense, his father moved away from the table. Taking a knife from the shelf by the door, Padma walked outside, into the dark.

"I will make you a new bow," he called back. "It will be ready for you in the morning."

What could Gopal do? He couldn't disobey. That would bring shame and disgrace to his family and his ancestors. He was expected to perform the vidhi. It was dictated by the Laws of the Manus! The entire kingdom of Goloka would be cursed if he didn't. Why had he even been born? He pushed the law book to the center of the table and rested his elbows on the hard surface. Holding his chin in his hands, sitting quietly, he stared at the book, the cause of his misery.

From the corner of his eye, he noticed his mother run to the door, watching his father disappear into the darkness. Then she turned her head, looking worriedly over her shoulder at him but saying nothing.

His sister also looked at him. Then she smiled—a strange smile—and started stacking the metal plates. She avoided his eyes and dipped her fingers into the half-filled cups, lifting them from the table, pretending to be concerned with cleaning up. Without speaking, his mother and sister finished cleaning the plates. Neither of them bothered to eat that night.

THREE

IN HIS ROOM, GOPAL RESTED on his mat, listening to dogs scrounging through the family's trash pit. The echoes of their snarling mixed with the grunts of hogs as the scavengers squabbled over choice scraps in the ravine near his home. His teeth vibrated to the claws of monkeys scratching the tiles as they scampered across the roof above him. In his mind, he saw the lion-headed creature whisked into the sky, and the thousand-armed demon rampaging through the temple. How could he sleep? He was torn; torn between the responsibilities of his birthright, his duty to the law, and the responsibility he believed he owed to himself. Were the manus playing a cruel joke on him? Was that what this was all about? He had wanted to leave Goloka and now the manus were letting him go—to perform the vidhi. It wasn't funny! Had he actually offended the manus? Nimai and his father had warned him. Lying in bed with his thoughts was torture, so he was thankful when the pre-dawn came.

Still barefoot, and wearing only a modest sleeping cloth around his waist, he quietly slipped outside. A chill shook his body. It was still so cold. He folded his arms across his bare chest. Anything was better than being back in his room.

He knew his first duty, to go to the well. After pulling up the clay jug and taking the three sips of water for purification, he washed his feet, hands, and mouth, and rushed back indoors. In the outer room he found the white cotton tunic, pants, and leather belt his mother had laid out the night before. As he dressed, he could still see her face, her worried eyes that had looked right through him. Looking around the chilled room, he pictured his sister helping to clean up, she too, looking worried. But his father wasn't worried, for this was a vidhi for the son of the simha, and the bow his father had carved was leaning against the family altar. Kneeling before the four-armed, brass figure of Paramatma, its white, conch-shell eyes staring, he offered incense.

Rising to his feet, he took the bow, and his own leather case of arrows. The seven shafts reminded him of his last lesson with his father. They had been in the north field practicing the art of the bow: he, his father, and the other boys in their ashram-school, when Padma had said, "Behold the snakebird in that tree."

He and the other boys answered. "Yes, Prabhu, we see it."

Then to Gopal, as he was the son of the simha, his father said, "What do you see? Do you see the beast, the tree, me, or the other students?"

"I see the tree, and you, the other boys, and the beast," he confidently replied.

"Then stand aside," his father ordered, to Gopal's bewilderment.

The simha asked the same question of all the students, one after another. The answer was always the same: "I see the tree, and you, the other boys, and the beast."

One by one they were told to stand aside. Then, Padma took his own bow, aimed . . . and upon release of the arrow, the snakebird fell dead. "That is all for today!" he abruptly announced and sent them home without an explanation.

What more were they supposed to see? Gopal never did get an answer, and the question still annoyed him. Angrily, he picked up his sandals and dagger, and, with his father's words still gnawing at him, he stormed into the cool, dim pre-dawn, leaving his father, mother, and sister sleeping. He saw no need to wake them. Everyone knew what he had to do.

The morning air made him yawn. The little sleep he had managed to capture still dulled his senses. He stretched his arms, the bow and sandals in one hand, the arrows and dagger in the other. Breathing deeply, he inhaled the scent of dung, burned and fresh, that permeated his village. Sandalwood and camphor burned on the altars of the Go-lokan homes and mixed with the dung air, forming a sweet haze that drifted on the breezes. The shrill screams of pea-cocks and their hens, their senses waking them to the ap-proaching dawn, startled him. Their high-pitched cries from their perches high in the surrounding acacia trees broke the stillness of the sleeping village.

Gopal looked at the home of his birth. To the side, Anu, his black ox, stood unusually quiet in its pen. "Are you waiting for your bath?" Gopal asked. He remembered rac-ing the animal to the shore against the other boys. Anu always won. He had to touch his pet. Seeing his master ap-proaching, Anu raised his coal-black head. "No, my friend," Gopal whispered. "We're not going for your bath today. You'll have to wait. When I return, I'll race with you to the river." He patted the animal on the head and rubbed between its eyes. "You like that, don't you?" He smiled, but the animal's hide felt cold to the touch, sending a shiv-er through Gopal's fingers. It was time—time to get to the task at hand. It would get too hot when the sun came up. Heavily burdened rain clouds drifted overhead, still with-holding their precious cargo from his village. If only his arrow could reach that high and pierce a cloud. Slinging the bow and arrows over his shoulder, tucking the dagger into his belt, and slipping the sandals on his cold feet, he hesitantly set out. Along the edge of the outer village lay the narrow footpath that would take him to the temple and the naga.

His grandfather had told him of the mythical creature. Had time passed that quickly? He could still hear Dristaketu, Padma's father, explaining how special black cobras were chosen by the manus to live to the age of one hundred years and begin another life as the winged serpent of legend.

The gentle old man Gopal had loved so dearly would sit at the table, surrounded by family, and tell his stories. With green eyes sparkling like jewels, amused at his own tales of wonder, the man would speak in a soft, hoarse voice. "The black serpent grows to over twenty-six feet in length, with a wingspan of at least twelve feet. Each giant wing is tipped with pearl-colored, daggered claws, strong enough to tear from their roots the giant bamboo forests of Angar."

Laughing to himself as he walked beneath the moonlight, Gopal recalled how he used to scare his sister, who must have been about seven at the time, by pretending to become the serpent. He would chase her through the fields . . . until his grandfather made him stop. Gopal straightened his smile. That was a game. . . . This is a vidhi, and no longer a story to frighten his sister.

"Remember not to meet its stare," he could still hear his grandfather warn. "For the naga casts a hypnotic trance to freeze its prey. Once bitten, you have less than a minute to chant your death mantra."

Coming upon a giant arjuna tree lying stricken across his path, Gopal paused to rest. He was thirsty. How foolish of him, forgetting to bring water. Maybe he would find a stream along the way. Water doesn't break a fast, does it? he wondered

The forest was thickening into jungle. The dawn air was

cool and very still. He took his bow in both hands and removed an arrow from its case. Pressing the reed to the string gave him the sense of reassurance he sought. There was noise above: a bird—a snow-white owl. His arrow's tip became his eye as he traced the course the bird flew. Taking careful aim, imagining the arrow soaring to catch the bird in flight, he thought of that day with his father.

There was the owl, sliding on the icy air, its white wings opened wide, slicing space. There were the trees, standing tall, like guards along the walls of a fort. There, in his hand, was the bow, freshly trimmed by his father's blade. He saw his own hand, his young, tense fingers wrapped, sweating, about the former tree limb, now a weapon. What more was he supposed to see? The owl disappeared into the thick cover of branches suspended above the path. Frustrated, Gopal lowered the arrow.

The woods chattered. A monkey hopped among the branches. Small animals squeaked, hummed, clicked, and stirred under the leaves and brush, giving life to a forest carpet. Something scurried within the bamboo that grew along the path. The thick stalks gave him an idea. The vidhi would have to wait. Taking hold of a reed, he used his dagger to cut a piece the length of his forearm. Some music to accompany him on his journey, now that's a good idea. So, using a skill also taught him by his father, Gopal fashioned a reed flute. This would show his father! At least there was something he remembered from his lessons.

With the bow and arrows again secured to his back, and the flute in hand, he continued through the thickening jungle, neglecting to notice his dagger, lying where he had left it on a tree trunk.

In this new heedless mood, and with the seeming pleasantness around him, Gopal remembered a rhyme his mother had sung to him and his sister whenever they were afraid. He played the tune and sang the words to himself, still walking, as carefree as a cow going to pasture.

Always in the lands of Bhu,
Through Golokan clouds and rain,
The devas smile with celestial eyes,
Forever and a day.

The fanciful melody flowed from his flute. The notes
filled the mountainside and his heart. The morning sun
burned through the low-hanging clouds, through the treetops, bathing Gopal's back with warm, comforting rays
and illuminating the side of sky-high cliffs. Through dense
growth stood the massive stone walls and fallen columns of
an ancient temple carved from rock that seemed to climb to
the halls of Sveta-dvipa.

Gopal's flute playing stopped. The last note lingered
with his final exhaled breath, then disappeared, consumed
by the scene before him. He couldn't remember breathing
in. The fresh reed still pressed against his parted lips.

Above towered the image of a woman—no, a deva—
carved into dark rock. She sat atop a giant bakasura beast;
its two grimalkin heads turned, twisting, looking back
from four gemstone eyes that radiated fear at their undis-
puted sovereign.

He counted the arms of this warrior. There were eight,
each carrying a different weapon. The forest growth made
the weapons hard to see, but he could distinguish the
shapes of a trident and an arrow; what looked like a flower,
maybe a lotus; a shield; part of a discus; an axe—was that
fire? There was a sword, its deadly tip broken where the
cliff had given way to the roots of a giant banyan tree that
sat atop it, its upper branches vanishing in clouds that
passed like ships in the ocean sky.

The giant relief was cracked and stained, aged by Vayu's
wind and Indra's rain. It hung over the temple ruins,
watching, peering down on all who entered, peering down
on him, a boy, standing with a child's flute pressed to the
lips of a gaping mouth.

Realizing the foolishness of his whim, Gopal slowly

tucked the instrument into his belt, looking to see what creatures might have been within earshot of his song. He turned ever so slowly, slipping the bow from his shoulder, blindly feeling for an arrow, careful not to damage the feathered guide to the shaft. He removed an arrow and listened. Without the flute's song, an uneasy quiet fell upon the jungle. No birds or animals usually found in such a lush place disturbed the air that had grown solid around him. Had he frightened them off? Had something else frightened them off?

His arrow led his turn. The jungle had wasted no time in reclaiming its domain. Towering trees and webbed vines now covered most of this once splendid place. Although the temple was in ruins, Gopal could appreciate its majesty.

A high-pitched cry came from behind one of the sturdy columns. The bow slipped from Gopal's hand. He was afraid to look. Was it a peacock . . . or the tortured souls of Durga's devotees crying for their offenses? A chill slithered up his back. Shaking it from his shoulders, he carefully bent to retrieve his weapon. He was afraid to take his eyes from the surrounding jungle. He blindly felt the ground at his feet, his fingers begging for the touch of his weapon, finally touching the bow. Mercy, the arrow was there too. He joined the arrow with the string as his mind raced. Could the demon Virabhadra, his taste for blood unappeased, have returned?

Gopal realized his mortality. He looked back at the path that had brought him this far. He could leave. He could join a caravan . . . or . . . he could act, not react. Stay in control, that's what Padma would say.

Slowly, he climbed the massive stone steps that led to the unholy altar, stretching his legs to keep an even pace. Each step became a struggle, each struggle a conquest. He breathed deeply. The climb was tiring. The stairs were too big for a mortal's stride. Only the legs of a giant could span these steps. He struggled to keep his balance against the awkwardness of the ascent, all the time keeping a watchful eye on his surroundings.

The steep stairs were bordered by massive stone walls and covered with reaching limbs and staring brush. He couldn't see over the top of the wall. Anything could be hiding there.

He must be mad to be here. Breaking the Laws of the Manus had never bothered him before. But now, he had no choice! Isn't that how it always was? He wanted adventure, but not like this! This wasn't of his choosing. It didn't matter, though; nothing mattered anymore but to perform the vidhi and get back home. If he was ever to see the market again, he had to focus his mind. Marbled Agasura lizards scampered between the wide cracks of the stone wall, examining him with their bulging eyes. They had no doubts of his madness. In his uneasiness, Gopal counted the steps. At one hundred and eight he reached the top and stopped, bending at the waist to catch his breath. He rested his bow across his knees.

The altar of Durga was circled by twelve twenty-foot granite columns that stood like soldiers asleep at their posts from a mystic's charm. Some, in their enchanted slumber, had become overgrown with vines, while others had given way to the expanding jungle that now enclosed the ruins and lay crumbled on the ground like flesh-stripped bones. Tall, thick, spiked bamboo shoots had forced their way through the cracks of these fallen granite soldiers. The ceiling of the temple lay scattered about on the ground, having shattered the marble floor, which now rose or sank to different levels under the crushing weight of the collapsed roof. Wild grasses grew from the recesses.

Cautiously, he walked around the larger blocks, his readied arrow again leading the way. Gopal tried to balance himself on the slanting surface by holding onto a rock with one hand, but slipped. This was it, he thought. He was dead for sure. Sliding down, he clawed at the hard surface, scraping his fingertips. In his pain he let go of his weapon and landed in a muddy clump of kusha grasses. Insects, like none he had ever seen in Goloka, fluttered, crawled, and slithered from the disturbance he had brought to their nests. Quickly, he grabbed his bow and climbed out of the shallow crevice onto a flat surface. He stared upward, into a cloudless sky—the same sky that watched over Goloka— expecting the giant naga to appear at any moment. It was too quiet.

Slowly, very cautiously now, Gopal approached the altar, walking up the smaller steps that led to the marble surface. Imagining the temple before it was in ruins, he thought he heard the ghosts of Durga's devotees dancing and chanting the praises of the deva. He thought he saw the frightened captive, struggling as they dragged him to the altar, and heard the screams as he was finally sacrificed. It was terrible. Gopal shuddered, then closed his mind.

Standing on his tiptoes, he looked at the unholy surface. He wiped gray soot from the top of the altar with his finger, sniffing the powdery substance. He didn't recognize the scent and wiped away the layer of ash, revealing something underneath. Frightened by his discovery, he quickly backed away, wiping his sticky fingers on his shirt and stumbling over a fallen column. Fear forced him to check his weapon. The touch of the shaft to the string renewed his strength. He took a needed breath. The scent of wild tulsi in the air reminded him of the basil his mother used in her cooking.

Carefully, Gopal rose to his feet. In slow motion, he walked to the rear of the altar, all the time keeping his back to the stone. His arrow still pointed the way. Something darted from its hiding place beneath the altar and crossed his path. His arrow met its mark and a large, mud-brown jungle rat lay quivering while its death screech rattled the walls. "That's remaining calm," he muttered, his self-ridicule carried away on a sudden breeze. He had to get hold of himself or this wouldn't end as planned. But it was too late for plans! If the sound of his flute had not announced his arrival, the cries of the rat did.

Wild Vanecara monkeys scrambled through the branches, chattering at the contest about to take place, their eyes glowing like windows to the sky. Even the lizards scampered up the cracks to higher levels in the walls, as if hoping to get a better view.

Gopal sensed its presence. Turning slowly, he glanced over his left shoulder. The naga hovered about ten feet in the air, rhythmically flapping its black, leathery wings. Like a feather, it floated down, perching on the altar. Pearl claws wrapped around the edge of the cold stone, scratching the hard surface, the sound grating on Gopal's nerves. Coiling its black serpent body, the naga held its hooded head high. Its forked tongue slithered from its cavernous mouth and twitched, sniffing Gopal. A slow hiss seeped past glistening fangs. The dead stare of its black, polished eyes reflected its prey. All noise died. The jungle submitted to its lord.

Petrified, his palms sweating against his bow, Gopal could only watch. Black wings swung wide, extending to their full length, blotting out the sun. Hypnotized by the naga's heavy-lidded stare, he was powerless. Its wings creaked forward like giant teak doors on rusted hinges, permitting the sun to flood through its gate, blinding him.

His mind called out, *Jai Om*, the mantra shaking him free. He quickly rubbed his eyes with his left hand, but the salted sweat stung them. Grabbing a handful of shirt, Gopal rubbed his eyes. Slowly, his vision cleared, and he heard his grandfather's warning: "Don't look into its eyes!" But Gopal's heart now beat to the slow hypnotic flap of the serpent's wings. All he could hear was the beat. He fought to keep control of his mind and reached for another arrow. The giant naga lifted itself over him, breaking the spell. He chanted, "*Jai Om*." The serpent swiped at the arrow case, knocking the arrows across the temple and scattering them out of reach. The naga was playing, earning its due, he reasoned crazily. It was returning the karma he had earned for scaring his sister. The giant's shadow skimmed along the ground, brushing his sandaled feet. The shadow's icy touch forced him to look up. The naga circled.

The snakes in the market! Slowly, Gopal reached for his flute. Leaning the bow against his side, he pressed the instrument to his lips. His fingers found the holes. His mouth was dry and parched. He tried to swallow, but couldn't. Then he heard it, the tune, coming from the flute, as if someone else were playing. The sweet song filled the air. The words filled his head: Always in the lands of Bhu . . .

Should he believe his eyes? Was it possible? The giant serpent returned to its perch. Its wings, like a cape, folded around its coiled body. Its hiss sounded less aggressive. Remembering the trick of the snake charmers, he slowly swayed the reed from side to side, drawing the naga's attention. It was working. The serpent's head swayed to the movement of his flute.

As one part of him played, another part of him planned. His eyes darted to the lifeless form of the rat. The arrow! The force of the shot had taken it almost straight through the rodent. It might be possible . . . if he could pull the arrow the rest of the way through. Maybe . . . ? Without hesitation, he dropped the flute, grabbed his bow, and dashed for the dead rodent. The lifeless animal dangled from the feathered shaft. Gopal grabbed for it and lost his footing.

He landed in a ditch. The dirt walls were too steep and high to climb out. Gopal looked in both directions, but it was no use, he couldn't see to the ends. He pulled the arrow through the rat's carcass. The animal's quills pricked his chafed and scratched hands. Ignoring the gelled blood clumping on his hands, he tossed the dead rodent aside and looked for his bow. He panicked, searching the ground at his feet. The bow was leaning against the earthen wall. He grabbed it and pushed himself against the wall of the trench.

Loose dirt sprinkled Gopal's head and shoulders as he readied his bow. The arrow was wet, his hands slippery. It was hard to line the reed with the string. The stench of the blood that caked his hands and arms filled the sun-baked ditch. He couldn't hear any sounds from the jungle. . . . Even the wind had stopped. Beads of sweat formed on his forehead and rolled down his smooth young skin. The air grew solid again. It was hard to breathe.

Suddenly, the naga's shadow crawled down the opposite wall, slinking across the floor of the ditch to Gopal's feet. He turned cold when the shade climbed his legs, felt crushing pressure when the shadow's weight moved across his chest to his neck. It covered his face. It was suffocating him. Then, just as quickly, it moved on. Like a drowning man breaking surface, Gopal breathed life back into his lungs. Color returned to his cheeks as the naga rose above the temple, well above the cliffs, and continued to climb straight up, up to the abode of the devas, it seemed.

Gopal squinted up into the sun's glare, his hand shielding his eyes. He was barely able to see, but what he saw was enough. The naga turned, beginning its decent. It fell straight at him like a spear, its wings tucked close. Sweat dripped from Gopal's face. His palms were wet again and he was afraid the bow would slip. He quickly wiped his hands on his shirt.

The winged serpent's fangs glistened, as if already tasting blood.

Gopal pulled back on the feathered shaft.

The beast opened its claws.

Gopal held his breath.

The naga's eyes blazed.

Gopal pulled back on the bow string.

The serpent's wings opened wide.

A little more, a little more. Not yet! Wait . . . Wait!

The naga released a screaming cry.

Once again Gopal heard his father's questions: "What do you see? Do you see the beast? Do you see the tree? Or me? Or the other students?" Was that question to haunt him to the World of the Dead? No. . . . He understood!

"I see *only* the beast! Not the tree, not you, not any-one."

The naga readied to strike.

"I see only the serpent. I see only its head. I see only the spot between its eyes. Now!" The arrow released, finding its mark between the snake's coal-black eyes.

But still the creature came with blinding speed, and Gopal leaped to his right as the naga crashed into the wall, breaking the arrow that stung its head. Dust, dirt, and rocks exploded. Blinded, the naga reached for Gopal, grabbing the boy's bow instead.

Gopal backed away, just out of reach, the tip of his arrow still embedded in the serpent's skull, still leeching the crea-ture's life airs. The naga, whirling in its death frenzy, broke the bow. Thrashing in the soil, throwing its hooded, ser-pent head straight up, it extended its body to full length. With wings stretched, its claws searched for the thief who had stolen its life. Its black eyes glowed, radiating anger, as it reached out. Gopal stood, motionless, afraid of giving away his position.

Then the naga, as if chanting its own death mantra, gave one last, blood-choked scream, a scream that made the temple columns quake and the trench rattle. Like a wave, the death scream rolled both ways along the ditch, filling the trench, spilling over the walls, flooding the temple are-na, and finally fading into a jungle that stood gaping at what it had witnessed.

Gopal crouched low, protecting his ears from the cry as the naga's last breath seeped from between its fangs. Its lifeless black tongue hung limp, and a cloud of white smoke billowed from the black snake's mouth. Gopal was still afraid, because the cloud took shape—human shape. In seconds, the mistlike specter solidified, becoming dis-tinguishable.

"Vyasa?"

"You have nothing to fear, my young friend. I have come for you."

Maybe those words were meant to be comforting, but for Gopal, they brought terror. His only thought was to flee. He searched for a way out of the ditch, but he was still trapped.

"The Spirit of Foreboding made itself known to me," the mystic explained, "first at my hermitage and again at the yagna. The appearance at the assembly was for your benefit."

"How could it have been for my benefit?" Gopal asked. "I was only at the meeting because—"

"You heard it describe the coming of Kali. I thought we had more time," the mystic sadly admitted. "My calculations of the jyoti must have been misguided. It was Kali's magic—he has the help of a powerful sorceress."

Vyasa went on to tell how the ancient scriptures warned of the coming of Kali the Asura, a demon with great powers gained through sacrifice and the blood of innocents, who had spent many aeons trying to break the bonds of Bila-svarga. Now Kali's plans were to conquer the Whorls of the Bhu-mandala, to overthrow the devas and destroy the manus.

"It appears Kali has succeeded with part of his plan," Vyasa explained. "He and his consort, Maya, used their mystic powers to transform into rain which, disguised as a shower, fell on the grain fields of the King of Klesa. When the king ate the grain grown in the field, Kali and Maya entered his body. Then the king impregnated his wife, allowing the two to enter her womb. The queen gave birth to twins—a brother and sister—unknowingly giving Kali and Maya human form. Kali's escape to Bhu has contaminated the entire universe.

"That has nothing to do with me!" Gopal blurted.

"The twins have already sacrificed their parents," Vyasa warned. "Now, citing their royal births, they have claimed all of Bhu as their domain." Vyasa rose to his feet.

Gopal feared the seriousness of the mystic's eyes. Vyasa's face looked like it had that day at the yagna. Worst of all,

Gopal feared his own involvement. "Well? What are you going to do?" he asked. "You're a treta-mystic. You have the power. . . . Don't you?"

Vyasa once again sat on the ground beside the boy. "I must go along and help you if I am to reach my goal." The mystic's words were final.

"Go along? Help me?"

"It is you who have been chosen to complete this vidhi."

"Me?" Gopal was no longer a passive listener. He pleaded, "I'm—I'm just a boy! I know nothing about demons. My family is waiting in Goloka for me to assume my place as the next simha. The village needs me. It's where I belong. My karma is to reign after my father." Gopal sat, tired, scared, bewildered. "What about the krura-lochana?"

"Kali *is* krura-lochana!" Vyasa tried to calm the boy. "You passed the first test by killing the naga." The mystic smiled. "I have faith in your ability."

"Why me?" Gopal asked.

"I have more to tell you, but not here." Standing again, Vyasa motioned for Gopal to follow and quickly found a place where they could climb out of the ditch. Reaching the surface, Vyasa looked to the thick cover of trees at the other end of the temple and waved his hands, motioning for someone to join them. "Come out!" he yelled. "It is safe now. Come here!" Vyasa turned to Gopal. "I was able to save these two. They will join you. Go to Radhakunde and I will tell you more."

Gopal brushed the dirt from his clothes. Wiping the blood that had dried on his hands, he looked across the clearing, not really understanding the mystic. What did he mean, he was able to save these two? What two? Gopal was about to turn and ask the mystic to explain when two figures approached from across the temple grounds.

"Nimai! Citty! Am I glad to see you!" Running, he met his sister and best friend near the altar. "You won't believe what I've been through!" he exclaimed, relieved to be with the two people dearest to him.

"We know," his sister confessed, obviously worried.

"Yes," added Nimai. "We followed you this morning, when you left Goloka. We saw everything. When you fell over the edge of the ditch, and didn't . . . well . . . we thought—"

"What took you so long?" demanded his sister. She grabbed his forearm, annoyed. "You scared us!"

"After I killed the naga, the mystic appeared. He told me this incredible tale of an Asura king."

Citty, releasing him from her grip, looked puzzled. She glanced over at Nimai.

"Wait," Gopal urged, seeing their looks of disbelief. "Have him tell you himself." He turned back to where Vyasa had been standing. "He's gone!" Gopal ran back to the edge of the ditch.

"Wait!" Citty yelled. "Where are you going?" She ran after her brother, catching him as he was about to leap into the trench. "Nimai! Help me hold him."

Nimai caught up to them and grabbed Gopal by the waist, pulling him away from the edge. Hesitantly, Nimai peered into the ditch. "It's the naga!"

"But I saw him," Gopal insisted, breaking free and running farther along the edge. Nimai and Citty ran to catch up. Gopal spun around, looking at the stone columns that seemed to lean toward him, into the jungle that moved closer, and up into the treetops that reached down for him. He looked at Citty and Nimai, whose faces came and went as he spun. He looked everywhere, searching for the mystic, until his sister grabbed him by the shoulders, stopping his dizzy rotations. The surrounding jungle spun for a few moments more.

"He waved and called you over to me!" Gopal persisted.

Nimai looked confused. "You waved to us! You called us over!"

Gopal didn't know what to think anymore. He wasn't feeling very well. Seeing his face turn white, his sister's expression turned to concern. She handed him a flask and motioned for him to sit. "Have some water," she offered. "You need to rest."

Gopal gulped the water quickly, allowing its refreshing coolness to splash on his flushed skin. Wiping the drops from his chin, he noticed for the first time the dried blood on his hands and arms. He brushed his sweat-dampened hair back from his face, revealing a gash on his forehead. Citty poured water on the end of her sari and gently cleansed the wound. Gopal jerked away, startled by the sting.

"It's all right," she consoled. "It doesn't look serious." She tore a piece of fabric from her hem and made a bandage to wrap around the wound. "Hold still," she ordered, tying the cloth. "There! That should stop the bleeding. When you feel up to it," she suggested, wiping her hands on her dress, "we should start back for Goloka."

"The claw!" Rising quickly, still holding his head with both hands, Gopal fell back to his seat.

"You are weak from the wound. Let me do it?" His sister begged. "Let me get the claw! . . . I'm part of the family."

"The law!" Warned Nimai.

Gopal nodded to his sister. "Get it."

Citty smiled. "Nimai, give me the dagger."

Nimai hesitated, but after Gopal gave him a scathing look, reluctantly surrendered the weapon.

Citty took the dagger, showing it to her brother. "Remember this?" She smiled again. "You left it on the path."

Gopal thought he recognized the blade as his, but the world was spinning right now and all he wanted was for it to stop.

With Gopal's dagger in hand, Citty climbed into the ditch, ready to claim the prize. She walked along the bottom of the trench toward the place where Nimai had seen the naga. The serpent lay crumpled before her. Brave and proud, Citty grabbed the stiffened wing and held the claw. Then she paused. "Someday I will be the one to complete a vidhi," she thought. Cutting away the hard leathery flesh, and freeing the prize, she triumphantly raised the severed claw aloft. When held up to the sunlight, the monster's claw shriveled as if withered by a thousand years. It had turned to bone under stretched and hardened leather. Quickly climbing out of the trench, Citty found Nimai helping Gopal to his feet. "Here's your knife," she said, offering her brother the blood-stained blade.

Gopal was feeling a little better now; the spinning in his head had stopped. "Why don't you carry it back?" he suggested, refusing the knife. "You earned the right." Nimai looked at his friend, shaking his head in disagreement.

Citty only noticed the condition of the dagger and, gathering up a handful of cloth, wiped the bloodied blade on the silk. Smiling at the thought of finally carrying a weapon, she tucked it into a fold in her garment. "Here, this is yours!" she said, proudly relinquishing the claw. "You must carry this back to our father. This, *you* earned!"

Gopal remained silent, staring at the naga's severed claw.

"Your wound has stopped bleeding," Citty noticed. "Are you ready to leave?"

"I'm ready!" answered Nimai.

Gopal didn't say anything.

"Gopal?" Citty looked at him, worried. "I said, are you ready to go?"

Gopal stared at the talon, thinking about the vidhi, about Kali. Had he dreamed it? Touching the wound, feeling the swelling above his eye, he looked at his blood-stained hand. Had it all been the result of a blow to his head? Again he looked at the shriveled claw. The naga was real. "Yes," he finally answered, tucking the claw into his belt. "I want to go home!"

FOUR

THE JOURNEY DOWN THE MOUNTAIN was uneventful. Gopal didn't mention Vyasa. How could he talk about what he didn't understand? He wasn't sure it had even happened. No one seemed concerned about it. Nimai looked happy to be away from the temple and heading back to Goloka. And Citty? Citty had a grin the size of a crescent moon. Her face could have lit the way, had it been nightfall. All she could think about was the dagger tucked in her clothes.

What was he bringing back? he asked himself. The naga's claw? Did he even have the right to carry it? His sister was the one who had cut it from the beast. Vyasa was, in some way, responsible for the creature's death, even if he wasn't sure exactly how. And the vidhi . . . ?

At last they rounded the final turn in the steep path that would return Gopal to the shelter of his village, and maybe a hero's welcome, deserved or not. Through the trees appeared clouds of dense, black smoke. There were no ceremonies planned that Gopal could think of to account for such a dark display.

Without a word, his pace quickened. The stamp of his sandals grew louder on the hardening path. The echoes of four more feet joined his in a song of hurried footsteps, as did the familiar shrills of peacocks, the frantic chattering of monkeys, and the howl of a lone bakasura beast. The hurried concert grew louder, the beat faster, the song more frantic, while his feet, no longer under his control, carried him down the mountainside.

Leaving the trail, Gopal stopped. He searched for a place, anyplace on the ridge that would give him a better view. He found one and, still without a word, rushed to the ledge. As Gopal looked from the bluff, his face paled. He tore the bandage from his head and twisted the bloody cloth around his hand. His sister fell to her knees. Nimai's eyes widened, his mouth hanging open at the sight before them. Goloka—the village of their childhood—was in flames!

Villagers, friends, and neighbors fled in all directions. Hordes of soldiers, like none Gopal had ever seen before, slashed and sliced at everything that moved. Through the curtain of smoke and clouds, abruptly parted by the wind, he could see some village men taking a stand in the marketplace—or what used to be the marketplace. Carts stood crushed and abandoned. Torn pandals waved flames and smoke.

The tongues of merchants and shoppers no longer argued over prices, for their bodies now lay scattered about the streets and shops. The wheels of the potters had been stilled. The hammers of the smiths now were wielded as weapons in the center of an assemblage where Padma stood, commanding the few who remained of his loyal subjects. From his vantage point on the ridge, Gopal watched, stunned and helpless. Mounted warriors, like flood waters rushing from a broken levy, converged on the small band of men attempting to defend the village. The market—that place of wonder and escape—became a scene of unspeakable horror.

"They have no chance!" screamed his sister. Rising to her feet, bewildered, she lunged forward, toward the edge of the cliff. Gopal grabbed her.

"What can we do?" Nimai wept, looking at Gopal, at City clutching her brother in terror, then to the village below.

Seeing Nimai's tears, Gopal also wanted to cry. He unconsciously touched the claw hanging from his belt, igniting a spark somewhere in his mind. He forced the tears back. "Nothing, if we stand here," he responded. "Let's go!" Thoughts of the dead naga and Vyasa flashed through Gopal's mind as he tore through the brush. What was happening? Why were these things happening to his family and his village? Gopal knew what he had to do—reach his father—there was nothing else to think about, not now! He didn't have to turn to see if City and Nimai were keeping up; he could hear their hurried footsteps.

All other noise faded until they neared the village, when the pain-filled screams of women and children once again rent the air. Gopal's eyes filled with tears as he drew closer. Why hadn't any people come running toward them? The screams fell silent. The three reached the edge of the village, standing in the road that had, that same morning, carried them away . . . a road now strewn with the headless bodies of their neighbors. The dead lay scattered in small heaps. Mothers lay upon the bodies of their children. The bodies of the men lay where they had fallen. The only movement came when the wind lifted the fine, top layer of sand to cover the dead. None had been spared . . . all had been beheaded.

Why had this terrible atrocity been committed against Goloka? What offenses could an entire village have committed to raise the wrath of the manus with such a vengeance? Gopal's questions were muted by the ghastly scene.

The backs of the dark assailants, like thundering storm clouds, rode into Goloka's depths with the heads of some of their victims held high on the tips of swords, tridents, and spears. Their bronze armor reflected the fires they left in their wake. Glowing with a ghostly haze, the flames highlighted the fruits of this dark harvest. The faces of the severed heads revealed the innocence of the victims. Cries of victory, more like the howls of beasts after the kill, swirled and stung Gopal's heart. "Is this my fault?" he cried aloud. Was this the karma he had incurred? Was everyone in Goloka to pay the price for his thoughts? He had never felt so alone, standing in the middle of the road among the innocent dead.

Citty leaned over the body of a child that lay at her feet. It had been trampled by the horses, its head, crushed like a clay doll, an unworthy trophy. She stared down at the mangled, toylike body while Gopal, in his fear, backed away, moving against the cold of a wall where Nimai already stood, as if the hard brick would bring comfort. Citty, her eyes red from tears, was lifting a tiny, lifeless hand. Her own sun-darkened skin contrasted sharply with the whitened, blood-drained flesh of the limp, little fingers.

Unseen by the girl, a soldier appeared in the doorway behind Citty. He stepped out from the building, unaware of Gopal and Nimai, who were not within his angle of vision.

The soldier was a giant figure of a man—if he was a man. His face was covered with thick red fur, as was his head. What little skin showed looked like leather and was copper in color. Golden earrings dangled from pointed ears. Yet, all other features said this was a man. The soldier carried a bronze helmet in one fur-covered hand and a bottle in the other, as if he had just finished drinking. His red tongue curled over his black upper lip to catch the drops of wine that spilled out. Black, pointed fingernails gleamed when he brushed the wet hairs from around his mouth.

Could this be one of the creatures Gopal had learned of in ashram? One of the races of Rakshasa? He had read how one of these races could assume the forms of horses, buffalo, and tigers at will. Some had even been known to have a hundred heads. But the Rakshasa races had been imprisoned on Rahu after the war with the devas. Hadn't they?

A dented brass armor plate covering a leather vest hung over the warrior's chest and back. A carving that adorned the front intrigued Gopal, who stood frozen, half in fright, half in wonder, forgetting his sister was in danger. Reflected in the fires, engraved on the armor, was a trident. Its three black, lightening bolt blades were encircled by a many-pointed star. Gopal had never seen such a symbol before, not even in any of the numerous caravans that had passed through Goloka.

Seeing only the girl, the soldier prepared to claim another prize. He grinned, a spike-toothed grin that stretched from ear to ear. Two tusks that protruded from his widening smile rose like ivory gates, releasing eight fangs. Quietly placing the empty bottle on the ground beside him, the ogre wiped the wine from his dark, wet lips. His tongue slithered forth to catch what his hand had missed. Then he silently removed his sword and stepped into the street. The dust of the road exploded under his booted foot like a splash in the ocean. The giant blade glowed in the light of the flames that burned in a nearby building.

"Citty, look out!" Without a thought for his own safety, Gopal lunged, throwing himself on the soldier's bronze, shell-covered back where he clung like a cat to the cold metal. The man-beast turned in alarm as Gopal wrapped one arm tightly around the soldier's neck. He searched in vain for his dagger, the one he had given to Citty. Still, he had the advantage of surprise because his frenzied kicking and thrashing knocked the creature off balance. They fell like a giant tree, shaking the ground. The sword fell from the surprised warrior's grasp as Gopal, pounding furiously on the warrior's back with his fists, attempted to pin the creature to the ground. "His sword!" Gopal panted. "Get the sword!" he called to Nimai.

Nimai stood, embedded to the wall. His face said he 'dn't hear his friend's frantic cry.

The Rakshasa reached behind him, but Gopal beat back the large hand. Letting go of his helmet, the soldier again reached back, this time with both hands, trying to swat the boy off his back. Gopal needed help.

Nimai remained stiff, unable to move, still looking at the bodies. "We have entered a nightmare," he moaned, over and over again.

Citty came to her senses and quickly crawled toward the sword, her sari, dragging on the ground, hindering her. She had to reach the sword! By the time her fingers finally touched the handle of the huge weapon, the soldier had managed to grab hold of Gopal with one of his hands, ripping the boy from his back and hurling him onto the ground. Trying to stand, Citty struggled to lift the heavy weapon above her head, a task that seemed impossible. The soldier went after Gopal, who lay stunned and helpless. Citty, using both hands, mustered all the strength she could to raise the huge blade.

The creature straddled Gopal's waist and slapped him, amused at the boy's foolish bravery. "You are brave for a flea!" he snarled. "But your tiny head will still be worth the time it takes to slice it off." The Rakshasa, holding one hand firmly around Gopal's throat, reached for his dagger.

Gopal stared into the last face he thought he would ever see—such an ugly one—as the fur on the creature's hand pricked his neck. Thinking it was the end, Gopal chanted to himself, *Jai Om*.

Out of view, his sister stood with the sword resting on one shoulder, which quickly grew numb under the great weight of the blade. The sharp edges pierced her soft skin, turning the silk under the heavy metal red. The man-beast raised his dagger, preparing to do his evil deed. Citty put all the force of her bloodied shoulder and upper body into lifting the weapon as high as it would go.

The Rakshasa's dagger was raised.

The blade in Citty's hands glowed.

Both weapons came down.

The sword blade fell across the back of the soldier's neck, stopping the movement of his hand. The soldier's arm stiffened, his palm opened, and the smaller blade dropped free. With his other hand, the bewildered soldier reached behind him, trying to find the source of the sharp pain that filled his neck and spine as the weight of the razor-edged sword, barely guided by Citty, sliced, like a blade through soft cheese, into his neck.

The look of surprise on the man-beast's face etched itself forever in Gopal's mind. Foul blood dripped from the wound. The tear widened, and the head fell forward. Mixed with the blood came a flash of blue light, blinding Gopal, who blinked frantically. When his vision returned, with it came the expression on the creature's face. It brought a bad taste to Gopal's mouth, not the taste of revenge, but of sickness.

The blade in Citty's hands was still making its downward swing. His sister's face was red and her eyes were shut tight. Her teeth were grinding within a mouth twisted with anxiety, grimacing with pain. She couldn't hold back the blow!

Gopal knew the heavy blade wasn't stopping, that it was coming for him next! He tried to move but couldn't. The weight of the headless soldier pinned him to the ground.

Citty pulled with all her might on the sword's handle, forcing her entire body back until she lost her balance and fell backward to the ground.

By luck, or the will of the manus, Gopal managed to force his head to the side. His neck strained from the tension. The blade hit the dirt, slicing into the road, the very tip scratching the taut skin of Gopal's neck, splashing dust onto his red, sweat-covered cheeks.

Breathing freely once again, Gopal spit the dirt from his mouth. The sword was so close he could see and smell the wet blood that smeared its edge. One of his eyes stared back at him, reflected in the polished metal. His other eye saw the dead soldier's head, lying where it had rolled, wobbling, in the road. A cold, bewildered stare was frozen on its horrible, now pale, almost human face.

Gopal also saw the bottoms of two sandaled feet. Sprawled in the road beside him was his sister, the sword's handle resting in her lap. The bloodied tip of the blade stuck in the dirt, inches from his face. Panting, Citty stared down the length of the blade. Horror glazed her eyes.

"Help! Get it off me!" Gopal cried.

Citty dropped the weapon. "You're alive!" She turned to Nimai, who still leaned against the wall. "Nimai!" It took a few seconds for her voice to penetrate their friend, who was petrified with fear. "Nimai!" At last Nimai turned. A tense, pale expression masked his face. He looked like he wanted to throw up. "Nimai! Please . . . come help me!" The third call hit a nerve. Nimai peeled himself from the wall and ran to his friends.

Gopal breathed heavily from the weight of the stiffening body. Nimai and Citty pushed . . . again . . . again. Finally the body rolled off and Gopal sat up, still panting, staring at the corpse. He looked at his sister. "I've never seen a man so big," he puffed.

"If he is a man," said Citty.

"Is he a giant?" asked Nimai, seeming to return to himself.

"I think he's a Rakshasa." Gopal guessed.

"He must be about eight feet tall," Citty remarked, collapsing to her knees beside her brother. She couldn't hold back any longer. She hugged him, half from relief, half from fear.

He smiled, trying to defuse the fright he himself was feeling. "Now he's only seven feet!" Gopal whispered, turning to meet his sister's reddened eyes. He dared to smile. She dared to join him. He glanced at the severed head of the Rakshasa, then turned to study the soldier's armor. Remembering the strange carving, he warily approached the body.

"Help me roll him over," he said. "Quickly, before any more come." Citty and Nimai rushed to Gopal's side and rolled the body onto its back. It was easier this time, with three of them. "There!" said Gopal, pointing, then crouching next to the breast-plate. Nimai stood and moved away. He looked lost in other thoughts.

Citty joined her brother, holding her nose. "He stinks!"

"I know. Here, look at this. Have you ever seen this symbol before?"

Citty looked. "A trident . . . inside a star!"

"But what does it mean?" Gopal was frustrated by the strange ornamentation.

Citty was counting. "Twenty-eight!"

"What?" His sister's comment confused him.

"I said, twenty-eight."

Gopal looked at her, still confused by the strange remark.

"There are twenty-eight points on the star."

Oh, he thought, finally understanding. "But what does it mean? I've never seen it before." He turned to ask Nimai, who was standing in the middle of the road. "Nimai, come look at this."

Nimai was again staring at the headless corpses, then at Gopal and Citty. A strange look returned to his face. Rising to their feet, Gopal and his sister went to their friend. "Their heads!" gasped Nimai. "They're doomed! The Laws of the Manus say that severing the head prevents the atma from transmigrating to another body at death."

"It's all right," Gopal assured Nimai, taking him by the shoulders, not knowing what else to say. Gopal knew it wasn't all right.

Nimai wasn't fooled. "No, it's not! Their life forces will wander between the whorls for eternity. . . . My father! We must find him." Nimai pushed away, about to run. "Where? Which way?"

Gopal remembered the scene they had witnessed from the cliff. "The market! We need to get to the marketplace."

"We'd all better find something to use to defend ourselves first," said Citty. She knew the soldier's heavy sword would be useless and reached for the dagger Gopal had given her. "Here, you'd better keep this," she suggested, handing it to Nimai who stared at the body at his feet.

"There!" Gopal pointed across the road to a dead villager, unrecognizable to the three since his head was missing. "He has a dagger in his belt. Stay against this wall, I'll get it." He quickly scurried to the corpse, retrieving the weapon.

"And there's another," whispered Citty, pointing. "Near the body of the soldier."

"Get it, quickly," Gopal ordered, "and be careful."

Citty grabbed the dagger from the dirt—the dagger that had almost claimed her brother's head. Picking it up, she realized it too was not of ordinary size. "It's more like a short sword," she said, running back.

Gopal smiled. "I'm sure you can handle it." Looking at Nimai, he was unsure of his friend's state of mind. Nimai was staring blankly at the dagger he had been given.

They moved quickly along walls, ducking behind abandoned carts, staying close to the few buildings not yet engulfed in flames as bands of mounted soldiers roamed the streets, driving captives before them. Gopal and his companions hid among the structures smoldering in the aftermath of the attack. Gopal had often walked these very streets on his way to his favorite place in all the three whorls, but all that had changed—forever!

The sound of more hooves, muffled by the dirt streets, grew louder. They ducked into the doorway of a small shop, its insides gutted, the body of the proprietor lying among the ruins, headless. "Down," Gopal whispered. Citty and Nimai crouched beside him, their panting the only sound within the room. The sound of charging horses grew, until six black steeds rushed past.

Remembering what he knew about the Rakshasa's ability to change form, Gopal couldn't help wonder which would take the shape of the horses and which would be the riders?

The riders' screams, like servants of the Lord of the Dead, filled their hideaway, shaking the charred rafters and driving the strange thought from his head.

The churned-up dust and dirt from the street formed a cloud that rushed into the open doorway of their hiding place. Afraid of being discovered, they tried to muffle their coughs. When it seemed clear, Gopal cautiously peeked out, then stepped into the road, looking in all directions. "Come on!" Citty and Nimai followed without question.

Reaching the end of the street, Gopal urged Citty and Nimai to take shelter behind a cart. He couldn't help noticing how similar the cart was to the fruit cart they had spilled just a few days earlier. On his own now, he continued along the wall to the market, following the cold stillness of the stone, as the cries of battle echoed ahead. The clash of metal against metal, metal against wood, and metal against bone grew louder. He cautiously neared the end of the street—a street that only days before had led to wonder and excitement.

Then, around the corner of a building, in the square, he found what nightmares were made from. Rakshasas were hacking at what remained of the small band of villagers. Without mercy they cut down their victims while the cries of the helpless men filled the square. Their screams echoed like the death screams of the naga. Gopal held his hands over his ears but couldn't stop the shrill cries of the victims or the howls of the attackers from penetrating. He watched, helpless.

One villager tried to stop a sword with bare hands, which his attacker hacked off in a fit of rage and laughter. The defenseless man bent over his bleeding stumps, the pain and horror draining from his eyes. The giant severed the man's head and grabbed the prize by the hair as the convulsing body slumped over on its side. A bit of blue light flashed from the villager's body and rose to join the growing shimmer hanging in the air—the atmas of the lost.

Gopal placed his hand over his mouth, gagging. The

heads of the fallen were raised high on the ends of their tormentors' weapons. Gopal's teeth unconsciously clenched around his longest finger, drawing blood.

The few remaining villagers fought on with sticks, hammers, and hoes. They were men he knew: Bashkara, the cowherd; Nalini Kanta, a potter; Advaita, the tailor; men he had known all his life, men who had visited his family, eaten at their table. Today, they were butchered. One by one, the villagers fell, beheaded, each ejecting the same flash of light as their life force escaped.

Another villager was fighting from where he lay on the ground. It was Sahadeva, Nimai's father. Armed with a spear, Sahadeva jabbed at the horseman who stood laughing above him. Unable to stand, the crippled man tried in vain to defend himself as the horse reared, bringing its front legs down without mercy. Sahadeva's body twitched beneath the stomping hooves of the beast. Finally, the mounted soldier took the spear from Sahadeva's own hand and turned it on the villager.

The soldier dismounted, severing Sahadeva's screaming head. Laughing with the voice of a beast, the warrior impaled the head onto the spear. With his trophy held high for all to see, the Rakshasa howled and snorted, joined by his animal comrade and his unholy brothers. The shouts of victory drowned out the desperate cries of the last villagers.

Then, to his horror, Gopal recognized the whitened, blood-drained head of his own father, held high on swordpoint. His cries of rage and grief were swallowed by the howls of the invaders and the crackling of fires. Gopal's beloved marketplace was in flames, his father dead, his village in ruins. The last sounds of Goloka faded . . . finally ending.

The taste of his own blood was on Gopal's lips. Pulling his hand from his mouth, he turned away. He could no longer look at the destruction of the people and things that had held a special place in his heart . . . in his life. His face was red, and his eyes were swollen with tears. He wiped the drops from his cheeks and the blood from his finger. He was still alive. Why? he sobbed. Why hadn't he been with his father? He should take his dagger and go charging into the square. He could kill at least one before they killed him. He should die with his father, he reasoned, but then Gopal remembered his sister and Nimai, hiding behind the cart. He couldn't leave them, not now, not like this. The sounds of killing had stopped; the soldiers were finishing in the square. Fearing for his sister and his friend, he quickly returned to them.

"What's going on?" asked Nimai, seeing Gopal come running.

Gopal's pale expression turned Citty's concern to dread. "Is there anything we can do?" she asked, already knowing the answer.

"It's too late to help them." His eyes looked down at the claw, then up to meet his sister's stare. "It's time we took care of ourselves."

"My father! What about my father?" Nimai cried. "We have to find him. He'll worry."

"He was there, in the market, alongside his simha. I saw him. He died bravely. They all did!"

"His head," pleaded Nimai.

"It was severed . . . as was my father's . . . and all the rest."

Nimai didn't try to hold back his tears. "What do we do now?"

Gopal looked back down the road to the market. "Those demons will soon be finishing their black deeds, and there are probably other soldiers in the rest of the village. We need to hide until it's safe to leave."

Citty tried to pinpoint their location among the ruins. "There! Isn't that the shop of Kuvera?" Nimai and Gopal looked in the direction she indicated.

Nimai answered first. "Yes! I recognize it. Gopal and I hid on the roof—"

"Let's try it," Gopal said, rushing across the road and

into the shop, pushing past a broken door that still hung from one of its hinges. The shop, like the others, had been ransacked, robbed of everything valuable. Broken remains of furniture, like dismembered skeletons, lay scattered. There were no bodies.

"Get down," whispered Citty urgently.

Rakshasa soldiers, holding three young girls on rope leashes, marched past the window. One stopped to peer in through the broken pane. "Mother of Maya!" they heard him complain, while sniffing through the broken window with large black nostrils. "They've already been here too! Let's try down that way," he grumbled and with a growl motioned for the others to follow, giving his prisoner a shove forward, forcing her down the street.

Did he say Maya? Gopal wondered. Wasn't that one of the names Vyasa had mentioned? He turned to Citty and Nimai. "They're gone," he told them. "Maybe we are safe now."

"At least for a while," his sister added. Citty started walking around the room, poking through the refuse. Suddenly she noticed something under a broken table. "Come here! Look, I've found a trapdoor."

Gopal and Nimai moved the remains of the table and carefully opened the wooden door. As they peered into the dark hole, the smell of musty dirt and dampness leaped out. The fires outside grew, lighting the inside of their hideaway. Anyone who looked in could see them.

"We have no choice," claimed Gopal and jumped down, followed by Citty and, finally, Nimai. The floor of the cellar was strewn with open wooden crates and chests. Large footprints disturbed the surface of the sand. "It's obvious they've already been down here, too!" said Gopal, turning over a box to sit on. "Let's hope the manus have mercy on us and don't let the fire get this far. It looks like we'll have to stay here for a while."

"Maybe Vayu will blow the fire away from us," Citty joked.

"What are those creatures?" asked Nimai, his face still white with fear. "You called them Rockshers?"

"Rakshasa," Gopal calmly corrected, understanding his friend's confusion. Although all boys learned the Laws of the Manus, the children of Sudras were not permitted to attend ashram schools and knew little about the Whorls of the Bhu-mandala. "From what I learned from my father," Gopal offered, "I think they are of the races of Rakshasa."

"Races?" asked Citty curiously. She also, being a girl, had not been permitted in the ashram.

"Some are celestial, while others are more goblin, imp, or ogre. They haunt cemeteries, animate dead bodies, disturb sacrifices, and ensnare and devour mortal beings." Gopal suddenly found use for his education and felt pride in his knowledge. "The third race is more monstrous. They are relentless, powerful enemies of the devas! I think they are what we faced today. They have many powers and can take the form of certain animals or," he continued, holding out his hand, "they may appear as small as thumbs."

Nimai looked around the floor. "The thought of tiny creatures crawling up my legs gives me chills." He stomped the area around him, bringing momentary smiles to Citty and Gopal.

As young people will, the three soon became more concerned with their present circumstances than with the events of the past hours or the things yet to come. "I say we rest," yawned Nimai. "I'm tired. I need sleep. There's still the chance this might be a dream."

"What else can we do?" Citty agreed. "Why don't you both rest, and I'll keep watch. I'll wake one of you when I feel sleepy." When no one objected, she took her sword and walked to a place below the trapdoor to stand guard.

Gopal sat alone in a darkened corner. The flickering of the fires showed through the cracks in the floor at the far end of the room, casting shadows that danced on the wall and on the empty crates that lay around the floor. In his mind the shadows turned into the men in the market, some becoming Rakshasas, and others, villagers. Again Nimai's father died alongside his own as the eerie scene played again and again in the dancing, flickering reflections.

Gopal also saw his sister in a new light. She was no longer a child to frighten with stories. She was living the part of the warrior she had always dreamed of being. Her apparent fearlessness worried Gopal though, not because she was braver than he was, but because she was his sister, and all he had left. He was happy to have her with him. . . . It was the thought of losing her that scared him.

Nimai also had crawled into a corner and closed his eyes. Gopal's dagger lay beside him. Citty leaned against a cracked wooden chest, staring at the floor above her.

A thought suddenly occurred to Gopal. Sahadeva and his father had rarely spoken to each other, but they had willingly fought and died together. Would he and Nimai be willing to do the same? Would he have made a stand as his father did, had he been simha?

Suddenly Gopal realized with dismay, I *am* the simha. He closed his eyes, hoping that when he opened them, the shadows would be gone. It was no use, for the shadows were still there, though they had changed, and now his mother's face appeared on the wall. How could he have forgotten about her? Where was she?

The shades of fire transformed again, this time taking the form of the temple of Durga. The mystic! Vyasa said he had saved Citty and Nimai. Why hadn't he warned Padma? Gopal was tiring. The questions went on, but made less and less sense. His eyes closed. He forced them open, looking around the darkening cellar. His sister was still sitting under the closed trapdoor, still looking up, her sword held tight in her small hand.

Again the questions clogged his brain. How could Rakshasas have escaped from Rahu? What were they doing on Bhu? What could they want with an out-of-the-way place like Goloka? Did this have anything to do with what the

mystic had told him? He had heard the soldier say "Maya."
And the symbol of the trident in the star? Did the twenty-eight points mean something? Why twenty-eight?

His eyelids were so heavy. He fought to keep them open.
Radhakunde. Vyasa said to go there. Gopal could keep his
eyes open no longer. He told himself he could close them
. . . but not go to sleep . . . just rest for a minute. He
listened to his own advice. He wanted to cry. Was a simha
allowed to cry? What did the Laws of the Manus say? The
pain was too much for a boy. Gopal wept quietly, trying to
conceal what he thought to be weakness. Finally, he closed
his eyes and slept.

FIVE

GOPAL OPENED HIS EYES slowly. Above him, all was quiet. No horses stomped, no shouts filtered down to the dark cellar. There were no peacocks wooing their hens, no dogs chasing monkeys, no hogs snorting their way through the piles of trash, and no herders driving their animals through the village streets. There were no children, no farmers, no merchants, no caravans. There was no market. Goloka was lifeless. It hadn't been a dream.

Sunlight filtered through the cracks of the wooden floor, illuminating the shadowy surroundings. The fire hadn't reached them. They hadn't been discovered. They were alive. He, Nimai—Gopal looked for Nimai and found him, still sleeping quietly in the same place. Citty? Gopal's eyes scanned the small cellar. He sat up quickly, looking around the room. "Citty?" Citty was gone.

Gopal jumped to his feet and rushed to Nimai, violently shaking his sleeping friend. "Nimai! Nimai!" He tried to whisper, not knowing if they were safe from discovery and fearing the worst.

Nimai's eyes unstuck and opened. "What? Where?" he

stammered, sitting up and shading his face from the broken rays of light. "Gopal?" Nimai rubbed his eyes. Thoughts quickly organized in his head, chasing the remnants of a dream. "What? What is it?"

"Where's Citty?"

Nimai rubbed his eyes again, looking past his kneeling friend. He focused on objects not so near, on things around the room that revived memories. "Isn't she here?"

"No, she's not here! What happened to her?" Again Gopal shook his half-sleeping friend, as if Nimai should know the answer. "Come on. We have to find her." He turned toward the open trapdoor.

"Here," Gopal heard from behind. "Here." Nimai was holding Gopal's dagger. "This is yours. I feel funny using it. It wasn't meant to be used by a Sudra. Let's trade."

Having his own dagger back didn't mean that much to Gopal, whose primary concern was for his sister. A blade was a blade, but Nimai seemed intent on making the switch, and Gopal figured it couldn't hurt, especially if it made Nimai feel better. At least he was acting like himself again. "If you really feel it's important," said Gopal, exchanging knives with his friend. He looked at the dagger Padma had given him when he was twelve. It was the one he had left on the path to the temple, the one that Citty had used to cut the claw from the naga . . . and now Citty was gone. The morning sun bathed his face. He took a deep breath. "Let's go," he ordered, and tipped one of the larger crates on end.

They climbed up through the opening into the partially burned shop. They had to cover their eyes from the light that glared through the collapsed ceiling. As their eyes slowly adjusted, they cautiously stepped into the street of what had been their village.

"They've destroyed everything!" said Nimai, surveying the scattered rubble. Goloka was a burned-out ruin. Smoldering buildings lined the silent, death-haunted streets. "I had hoped that what I remembered about yesterday would have been a dream. It wasn't." Nimai gasped as he stubbed his toe on something sharp . . . Citty's sword.

Gopal grabbed the weapon, which was covered with dried blood. His eyes swelled with tears. It couldn't be his sister's blood. It couldn't! He had to believe that she was alive, that she had been taken captive, not killed.

Why had he fallen asleep? It was all his fault, not just Citty disappearing, but everything. Why would the mystic have saved her, just to allow her to be captured by the Rakshasas? There had to be a reason. Gopal had to hold on to that hope, if he was to go on. "We have to go to Radhakunde," he said, to Nimai's surprise. "There's nothing for us here." Nimai nodded. There were no words for what he felt.

They walked . . . through the ruins, past shops that had brought life to them and the village. Rats searched for food in streets the boys had played in as children. Was that so long ago? The brick aqueduct that ran down the side of the street was dry, strewn with the bodies of villagers and maybe a Rakshasa or two—a feast for the crows and jackals. Death was everywhere. Instead of the shouts of businessmen, greetings between friends, or the sounds of children playing at their mothers' feet, the street was filled with silence and the dead bodies of their neighbors lying in the sun.

Debris blocked the path. Frustrated, Gopal tossed a plank of charred wood at a crow. "Get away!" he screamed, his voice the only sound. The black bird flew to the safety of a collapsed rooftop, hardly phased by the sudden outburst, ready to return after Gopal had passed. Those were the only words Gopal spoke. All that remained were unanswered questions.

The familiar scents of sandalwood and camphor had been replaced by the smell of burned wood, bloodied corpses, and Rakshasa feces that dotted the streets—the final offense committed on his village. Unsure of their safety, Gopal and Nimai stayed within the shadows and alleyways. After what felt like forever, they reached the outskirts of the village.

Gopal stopped and looked back at what had been his home. He tried not to cry, but the tears came regardless. Nimai also wept as Gopal put his arm around his friend's shoulders.

"You see what's happened here?" Gopal asked. "The Rakshasas were thorough. They are experts in their art. If, by the will of the manus, anyone managed to escape, they surely have run off into the hills. The thing to do now is to find the mystic. He will know what happened to Citty . . . and what has happened to our whorl. Do you understand?" Gopal asked. "We have no other choice."

Nimai looked at Gopal solemnly and nodded. "You are my friend and simha. . . . I trust you with my life."

SIX

BEFORE THEM STOOD THE FOREST and beyond was the Goverdhan Valley. Once barriers imposed by the Laws of the Manus, they were now Gopal's gateway. However, just as Gopal was about to embark on his journey into the forest, the brush crackled under some huge weight.

"Rakshasas!" feared Nimai, tears swelling his eyes.

Gopal listened, but said nothing. Slowly, he slid his dagger from its case, pointing it toward the sound of the snapping reeds. "Would Rakshasas be so noisy?" Gopal whispered, pausing.

"I don't know," said Nimai, frozen behind his simha.

Loud snorting came from within the stand of slowly moving bamboo. The tops of the tall grasses bent. The parting reeds moved toward them. "Do you see anything?" Nimai whispered.

Gopal made no reply, but bravely stood his ground. "Who's there?" he finally challenged.

"You were never very patient," said Nimai.

The sound of thunder parted the tall brush and bamboo and a black, snorting form emerged from the edge of the surrounding forest. "Anu?" remarked Gopal, relieved at the sight of his ox stepping into the small clearing.

Nimai wasn't ready to relax. "Are you sure it's not some Rakshasa trick?"

"I don't think Rakshasas can take the form of oxen. Anu?" Holding his left hand out to his pet, and tucking his dagger back into his belt with his right, Gopal walked to meet the animal. "It is you!" He smiled with delight. Quickly, he rubbed his four-legged friend between its two huge eyes.

"At least something got away." Nimai joined Gopal in petting the beast. "How did it find its way here? Is it a gift from the manus?" Gopal just shook his head. "At least we won't have to walk," said Nimai. "Where was it you said you . . . we were supposed to go?"

"Radhakunde," Gopal answered, "is where we are supposed to go." He smiled at Nimai and grasped his friend's hand. "Radhakunde," he whispered, looking to the east. His voice faded into the distance as he thought of foreign lands and the adventure for which he had always longed . . . but at what price?

"Where is Radhakunde?"

"I remember seeing merchants from Radhakunde," Gopal recalled, "with a caravan." The caravans seemed like a thousand years ago, he thought, but continued, "I think there was a vendor of brass from Radhakunde with them once." He remembered the cape his mother had bought at the market for Citty. The thought of his mother and sister stung his heart.

"Well?" asked Nimai.

Gopal cocked his head, puzzled. "Well what?"

"Where is Radhakunde?"

Gopal laughed, torn from his somber thoughts by his friend's persistence. "On the other side of the hills that rise in the east, beyond the valley," he replied. "There should be a river a half day's journey from there. If I'm right, we follow it downstream."

"What are we waiting for?" Nimai asked, seeing his friend again donning a mask of contemplation.

"Right!" Gopal shook himself free of the self-induced trance. "Jindu," he commanded to the ox, but got no response. "Jindu," he said, more sternly this time. Following the familiar command of his master, the ox bent his front legs, then his hind legs, lowering himself to the ground for boarding. "Jump on." Gopal smiled as Nimai climbed awkwardly atop the ox. Breaking a thin branch from a nearby pipal tree to drive his pet, Gopal jumped on behind his friend. Slowly, but steadily, they rode off together. The huge, swaggering, black beast looked like a great boulder that had worked itself loose from the side of a mountain. They followed a path, away from the smoldering ruins of their abandoned village, through the forest to the pastures.

"Rudh," commanded Gopal, who sat farther back from the beast's huge, crescent-horned head. The ox stopped abruptly.

Nimai unexpectedly bolted forward, grabbing onto the horns to keep from tumbling over the animal's face. The ox twisted his huge head, looked back, and snorted hot, wet air. "Tell me when you're going to stop," Nimai yelled in embarrassment. Gopal laughed. Nimai regained his balance and straightened the dagger that hung from his side.

Gopal had stopped to gaze out over the rolling pastures that bordered Goloka. Because of the Laws of the Manus, he had never been allowed to come this far before. Golden grasses waved like an ocean, smooth and soft like peacock feathers.

Gopal's feelings were mixed. He was excited about the adventure he had spent his life waiting for, but ahead lay the unknown. His parents were dead. His village was destroyed. He could only hope to find his sister still alive.

Gopal smacked Anu on the rump. "Vrtpra!" he commanded, and the ox continued its slow, heavy walk. Like a ship, it parted the sea of grass that brushed against four dangling feet, the tall blades sliding between their open-toed sandals, until they reached the bottom of a hill.

Nimai was getting restless and bored. Even though Anu was the fastest ox in the boys' races back home, riding atop the plodding animal got monotonous. "Race you to the top," he shouted, quickly sliding from the beast and darting off.

"Wait!" Gopal hesitated, not sure if charging over the hill was the safest thing to be doing. After all, he was simha now, and his friend was his subject—even if the only one. But youth won over caution and Gopal gave in to his friend's whim and his own innocence. "I'll beat you," he yelled, and swung his leg over the ox's back, jumped to the ground among the high grasses, and joined the race. Anyone watching would have seen only two moving gaps in the rolling pastures, since neither of the boys was taller than the reeds they pushed aside in their race. Anu appeared like a desolate, black island in an ocean of gold.

Nimai was first to reach the top of the hill. Anu trailed along behind Gopal, the ox knowing well enough to follow his master. "I was right!" said Gopal, catching his breath and looking at the rushing waters in the distance. "The River Toshana." Nimai knelt on one knee, breathing heavily. "It should only be another half day's journey," Gopal announced, proud of the success of his newly tested leadership. Without waiting to be told, Nimai hoisted himself back atop the crouching beast. Gopal once again climbed on behind, and the journey continued.

As figured, in a half day's time they stood at the shore of the river. "If we follow the bank, in another day we could be in Radhakunde."

"Maybe sooner," Nimai said, "if my eyes aren't playing tricks on me. Look!" He pointed up the river. "Are those boats?"

"Yes," Gopal answered, but not with the same enthusiasm. He still vividly remembered the destruction of Goloka and wasn't sure they should be out in the open. "Maybe we should—" he began, but it was too late. Nimai was waving. They had been seen.

Three small boats, each guided by a single boatman, came within shouting distance of the shore. Two of the boatmen were yelling at the third, warning him to stay with them. The third boatman ignored the cries of his companions and guided the vessel toward shore. "Shanti. Shanti," he greeted. The man looked ordinary enough. He had a trim, gray beard and hair to match, which seemed radiant against his black skin. His clothing seemed well kept and his arms looked strong for a man of his apparent age. "I am in need of some company," he called, guiding the narrow wooden craft toward the sand. "I'm called Stoka." The boat brushed the mud shore, splitting the reeds that grew along the river's edge. Gopal felt for his dagger, but saw no weapons on the boatman or in the vessel, at least none in plain view. "It's been some time since I've seen anyone along these shores." The boatman eyed the two boys. "Where might you be traveling?"

"We're going to Radhakunde," Gopal cautiously answered, looking into the vessel for signs of other passengers or anything not to his liking.

"If you can use the company," blurted Nimai, "we can use the ride."

"You have a deal," replied Stoka, "for the cost of your labor when we reach the end of our journey." Four bales of cloth were lashed to the center of the small boat. "But I don't think I can take that fine beast you lead."

Gopal looked into the eyes of the ox, then back to the top of the hill, then both ways along the river. "What do you think?" he whispered. Nimai came closer, sensing his hesitation.

"He seems safe enough," Nimai said, looking at the boatman. "At least he's not eight feet tall." He smiled.

"And who might you two be?" called the stranger.

"I'm Nimai," Gopal heard, before he could think whether to reply with the truth. His friend was already attempting to steady the boat with his foot. It appeared the decision was made.

"Well, let me give you a hand," Stoka replied, letting go of the rudder and gracefully walked the length of the vessel. "Watch your step," he sang as the boat bobbed.

Nimai grabbed hold of Stoka's hand, and before Gopal knew it, took a seat on one of the bales of cotton cloth.

"Ah, this feels good! Wake me when we reach Radha-kunde."

The boatman reached out to help Gopal. Gopal felt for his dagger, then paused and turned to Anu. "I can't take you any farther," he apologized, "but there are cool waters, and plenty of grass for you to eat around here." The animal stared. "Maybe we will be able to come back for you."

The ox lowered its head. Gopal moved close to the animal's face. To Gopal, leaving Anu was like losing another piece of his past. He hesitated at the thought.

"Come on," yelled Nimai. "It's getting dark, and I'm getting hungry."

"Yes, and we don't want to be on the river at night," called the boatman. "Not these days," he advised. "Surya will soon lower his disc behind the horizon."

Gopal gave his pet one last whack, sending the animal running some yards up the slope. He tossed the herding stick aside to accept the boatman's callused hand and took a seat. "We have been through much these last few days and are in need of rest and direction."

"And food," Nimai said, his eyes already closing.

"Well . . . rest you have, there is food ahead, and perhaps I can give you direction."

Gopal sat at the bow of the narrow boat. Stoka handed him a bamboo pole. "Use this to push us from the shore while I take my place at the rudder." Gopal looked at the pole, unfamiliar with such things. "With both hands," the boatman instructed. "You will have to let go of the dagger."

Stoka had a curious smile. Maybe I can trust this stranger, Gopal thought. He decided to take the chance. Taking the pole with both hands, Gopal stood, pushing the end of the bamboo reed into the mud and the craft back into the current of the Toshana.

Nimai was already sleeping on the bale of cotton. Their ferryman smiled, looking as contented as the denizens of Soma after a winefest. "You are fortunate that I came along when I did," said Stoka. "Since the war broke out, not many people chance traveling."

"Is that why your friends yelled at you?" asked Gopal.

"I've never listened to them before." He smiled, his eyes scanning the river ahead. "Hasn't the news reached you?" Stoka carefully examined the hem of Nimai's shirt. "I can see why you haven't heard. This weave—" He rubbed the cloth between his fingers. "You come from a small village. I am a weaver by trade . . . not a boatman." He let go of the shirt, leaving Nimai unaware of his touch. "That is a weave from the valleys to the west, beyond the Plains of Goverdhan, and the forests of Driti. "I would guess—" He touched Nimai's shirt again. "—Goloka." He let go of the cloth. "Village homespun." Gopal was impressed. "I know my craft, but your clothing . . . " He looked at the boy. "It is not like that of your sleeping friend here."

Gopal thought to himself, Don't answer.

"Do you know the simha Padma?" The weaver noticed the claw hanging from Gopal's belt. "Maybe you know more than you appear to. Isn't that the claw of a naga? . . . You look too young to have such a prize."

Gopal glanced down at the talon, unsure of what to say. "What war were you talking about?" he prodded, wanting to learn more before he revealed anything about himself.

Realizing Gopal wasn't about to talk, Stoka answered, "The self-proclaimed simha of all Bhu, the new King of Klesa, has sent emissaries from beyond the mountains in the west. He is asking all the simhas of Bhu to give tribute to him and his consort. Ha!" laughed the boatman, one hand wiping his mouth, his other guiding the craft. "What he really wants is to rule it all. The tribute is an excuse for conquest. He knows they won't pay!"

"Those soldiers that attacked our village . . ." Gopal blurted.

"Then you do know about it?"

"You are right about where we are from. Goloka has been destroyed." Gopal realized his openness, but too late. "Everyone was killed." He remembered what happened to his sister. "Or captured." He still refused to believe the worst.

"But the claw you carry. You . . . are a simha?"

"I became simha after my father died defending his village," Gopal confessed. "We barely escaped."

"If you are the son of Padma, you have nothing to fear from me," said Stoka, to Gopal's relief. "But guard your head. High prices are being paid for such a prize these days."

Gopal decided to take the risk and tell all. "I have come looking for the mystic, Vyasa. Have you heard of him? I was told he would be at Radhakunde."

"Vyasa?" mused Stoka, scratching his short, straggly beard. "Vyasa, hmmm. I only go to Radhakunde when I have cloth to sell. It's not where I live, you know. I live farther up the river, where—"

"Do you know him?" Gopal repeated.

"No, I am afraid I don't. But I can take you someplace where someone might, a place called The Bala Inn. If he is to be found, alive or dead, that would be the place to find out." Suddenly, Stoka sat up tall, like a cat hearing things people can't. Without explaining, he let the boat glide to shore, where it slid to a halt in the wet sand.

"What is it?" asked Gopal, also sitting up, trying to look downriver. An unnatural fog bank rolled toward them along the water's surface.

"Quiet!" Stoka commanded. "Don't you hear it?"

Suddenly, Gopal did. A drum. No, many drums, all beating at exactly the same moment, like one great drum, in perfect time with each other. "What is—" Gopal was about to ask when a wall of long, sleek shadows appeared, following the curtain of moving fog. The drum beats grew louder and the high-pitched bows of a hundred teak battle canoes—no, more than a hundred, more than he could count—glided past, down the middle of the river. Atop the front of each canoe was a flag. Gopal tried to make out the first, but it went past too quickly. They must be soldiers. Gopal knew from Stoka's expression that it wasn't the time to ask questions, so he sat quietly, within the cover of the reeds, while the regatta passed, its wake tossing their boat. Gopal held on tightly with both hands. Nimai slept soundly, undisturbed by the rocking.

Each canoe held at least a hundred warriors, each man, on each boat, rowing in perfect time with every other man on every other boat. It was as if their arms connected to one brain that pulsed directions with the beat of each drummer on board each vessel. It was amazing, the precision displayed as each oar sprang up from the river to the combined beat of over a hundred drums. Then, every oar jerked forward, splashed down, and rowed, pulling against the current. Springing up again, each oar jerked forward, and again splashed down in perfect harmony. Like a school of hundred-armed sea creatures from the Ocean of Garbhodaka, each armlike oar reached out from between the colored shields that lined each vessel as the army slipped past in the coming night.

As suddenly as they had appeared, the war canoes faded. The waters returned to their normal ebb. The wake along the shore relaxed, returning to the slow, easy, rocking motion that had preceded the canoes' passage. Before Gopal could form the question, Stoka answered. "The army of Drona, Simha of Radhakunde. His mystic uses the fog to hide their canoes. Drona's mystic is good—old for this life, but good. They go to meet the armies of Kali. May the manus have mercy on them," he said gravely.

The way Stoka said, "mercy on them" Gopal wasn't sure if he meant Kali . . . or the army of Drona.

"We will stay here until first light. It isn't safe on the

river in the dark."

Gopal was no longer tired. He was too anxious to sleep. There seemed little else to say, so he looked to the banks of the river. Water fowl hunted among the reeds for fish, a quick splash signaling when they found their prey. The waves now caressed the reeds standing guard at the bank and rocked the boat like a cradle. Between the sounds of the birds and the rolling waves, Nimai's snoring kept an unusual beat. For Gopal, the sounds of the night finally gave way to sleep.

* * * * *

"Radhakunde!" Gopal woke to Stoka's shouts. Without waking his guest, Stoka had set his boat back on the river as promised. "Radhakunde!" he shouted again, pointing to a brush-strewn shoreline ahead. Except for two similiar boats, overturned on the beach, the riverbank was deserted. The weaver guided his craft toward a small wooden pier. "My friends have made it safely," Stoka noticed.

"Where's the inn?" wondered Gopal, for the beach, and the riverbank as far back as he could see, lay deserted.

"Radhakunde is farther up that way, over the bank." Stoka pointed to a well-trodden path leading over the rise, hidden if you didn't know where to look. "You can't see the city from here. Help unload first and I'll take you part of the way." Stoka guided the boat to the mooring and, grabbing a rope from the bottom of the craft, stood, balancing himself on the bales. Carefully, the old man stepped over Nimai, who was still asleep, and leaped from the vessel when it came alongside the dock. Stoka quickly wrapped the end of the rope around a post, bringing the craft to an abrupt halt, jarring Nimai and rolling him off his soft bed of cotton onto the narrow deck.

"Ouch," he shouted, sitting up, sleep still swelling his eyes. "Where am I?" he mumbled. Recognizing his companion, and seeing the boatman standing on the pier, he remembered. "How long . . . have I been asleep?" His stomach rumbled louder than his head. "When can we eat?"

"Soon enough." Gopal laughed. Nimai made things seem normal. "Help with the bales."

With the cargo on the beach, secured and covered from the elements, they followed Stoka along the path. The sun rose high above desolate fields and the outline of the roofs of a walled city in the distance. The city wasn't as big as Gopal had expected. It was only slightly larger than Goloka. But here there was still movement beyond the wide open teak and iron gates. People, animals, and merchants' carts brought back fond memories as they passed under the gateway and the cautious eyes of two well armed guards atop the archway. Stoka's wave turned the guards' attention to other matters.

In the plaza, three streets led away from a brick well, which was busy with women and children drawing the day's water supply. The children hurried to their mothers' skirts at the sight of the two strangers. Some of the women gathered close together, obviously watching the newcomers.

Gopal looked first at himself and then at Nimai. "What do they find so amusing?"

"They don't get many strangers here anymore," said Stoka.

The familiar and comforting noises that came from within the shops on either side caused all concern for their strange and ragged appearance to fade. Men drove small herds of goats past them. Shop shutters flew open to greet the new business day. The scent of morning teas floated on the smoke from outdoor stoves. Gopal stared into the dull eyes of the few oxen that passed. He looked, worried, at the horses, remembering the form some of the Rakshasas had taken in Goloka, but said nothing to their host.

"Well, this is where we part ways," announced their guide, reaching into a pouch hanging from his belt.

"Here, take this." He handed Gopal five small coins. "For helping with the cargo." Gopal hesitated. "The first treasure for a new simha's coffers." Stoka grinned from between sparse teeth.

Knowing they had no money, Gopal humbly accepted. "Thanks, we—"

"My business is down that way," Stoka continued, ignoring the boy, "and yours is just up that road and on your left. You can't miss it. Ask for Canura, the owner of the place. He might know about this Vyasa you are seeking. If he can't help, he probably will know who can."

"Thanks again," said Gopal.

Stoka walked off, greeting two men who had been coming down the street, and went in through the door of a tailor's shop.

"So this is Radhakunde," said Nimai, suddenly pleased at being in a foreign city, even a relatively small one.

Gopal wasn't at all pleased. "Is this what I waited my whole life to see?" he wondered aloud. Nimai didn't answer, but was more wide-eyed then Gopal would have believed. They followed Stoka's directions down a street which reminded Gopal of Goloka, although business appeared slow in comparison. Shopkeepers swapped stories of the previous day's events, each bragging how they made better deals than the other and arguing over who had cheated and who had been cheated. Like Golokans, they shared their food, drinks, and tales freely.

"There doesn't seem to be a war on," Nimai said. "Maybe Stoka exaggerated."

Was that possible? Gopal thought. What about the canoes that had passed them last night?

At the top of the street's slight incline, Nimai was first to notice the sign: Bala Inn. It was written in the script of the manus, the universal script of Bhu. The weather-stained, chipped placard hung on rusted chains above a door as stained and chipped as the sign. Above the sign's lettering were the carved figures of two men, leaning on each other, arms around each other's shoulder, each holding herding staffs in their other hands.

"I suppose it's meant to be inviting," said Gopal, standing below the sign as it swayed and creaked. A cool breeze had moved in from the river, reminding Gopal and Nimai of their scant clothing and making the inside of the inn seem more inviting. Without hesitating, Nimai pushed the heavy door open, stepping into a poorly lit room. The gust followed him in, traveling from table to table, blowing out the candles closest to the entrance. Amid angry moans, Gopal quickly closed the door behind him.

More candles glowed faintly from the centers of some tables toward the back. Around the low tables, in the glow of the dim lights, several patrons sat on cushions. The air was thick with incense, camphor, and cooked lentils, which together covered an underlying foul smell, as if the windows had never, or rarely, been opened. No one in the room paid attention to Gopal and Nimai, or seemed to, once they had entered.

Ahead of them was a counter, behind which sat a heavy man. The owner, Gopal supposed. The man wiped the area in front of Nimai, who had wasted no time in taking the last clean cushion. Most of the people, at knee-high tables, sat on the chipped and cracked tile floor. I'm also hungry, Gopal thought, but the dinginess of the place enhanced the foul-smelling air, and he wondered if eating here was such a good idea.

"What can I do for you two men?" snickered the innkeeper, smiling at the sight of the two ragged strangers.

"Is that dahl I smell?" asked Nimai. "And do you have something good to drink?"

The innkeeper looked again, this time, to get a better look at Gopal. "You boys look a little young to be traveling. Can you pay?"

Gopal fingered the coins Stoka had given him. He tossed them on the counter. Two coins spun around, getting the attention of the innkeeper and at least one patron, hidden by the dark.

"We can pay," Gopal answered. "Is the food worth it?"

The innkeeper turned to a pot steaming over the fire. "I guess that depends on how hungry you are." Taking a ladle that hung near the fire, he wiped it on his stained shirt. Then he filled two mugs that he took from a wooden shelf. "Water or—" He leaned on the counter, close to Nimai. "—how about some honey wine?" Placing the soup-filled mugs in front of his customers, he spilled some of the thick broth.

"Water," replied Gopal.

"I'll try the wine," said Nimai enthusiastically, eyeing the soup as if a feast had been placed before him.

"Here, have some chapatis. You can have the bread for free. It'll just go stale. We don't get much business lately." He took three soup-covered coins from the counter, wiped them on his already stained sleeve and held them, one at a time, up to the faint light of an oil lamp that swayed from the ceiling.

Gopal placed the two remaining coins in his pouch as the innkeeper returned with a cup of wine and a pitcher of water. "You look a bit young for wine," he said, placing the drink before Nimai, who already had a mouth full of soup and bread.

"Age is measured in more ways than years," answered Gopal.

"In these times . . . I suppose it is," the innkeeper replied. His always curious stare noticed the claw on the boy's belt.

Gopal quickly covered it with the tattered end of his shirt. "We were told to ask for Canura," he said, pouring water for himself and trying to divert the man's attention. "A weaver who brought us downriver said this Canura might be able to help us."

"A weaver you say? What might this weaver be called?" The innkeeper folded his arms across his chest, appearing to know more than his demeanor would suggest.

"Stoka," Gopal replied. "He's elderly, with a beard and—"

The wrinkles on the landlord's forehead relaxed. "That fool!" He laughed. "Is he still bringing his bales down-river? Get himself killed, he will! I'm surprised he wasn't drowned by Drona's war canoes." The innkeeper relaxed his stance. "I'm Canura. How can I help you?"

"We're looking for the mystic called Vyasa."

"And he is looking for you," came a voice from a dark-ened table off to the corner behind them.

Canura turned from his customers, knowing when he was no longer needed . . . and when things were no longer his business.

SEVEN

OUTSIDE THE CITY OF RADHAKUNDE, on the Plains of Vrindaban, Drona was leading his army to meet the armies of Kali: a Rakshasa army numbering over a hundred thousand strong.

Drona sounded his conch-shell horn, and the alarm was echoed by the horns of his generals. With full strength they showered arrows, iron bludgeons, swords, tridents, lances, pikes, spears, and bhusundi weapons upon the army of the Asura.

Kali's army released a shower of arrows, guided by the hidden hand of Maya. The enchanted Rakshasa weapons shattered the weapons of Drona like the blasting wind scatters the clouds, and the arrows of the Rakshasas easily pierced the shields and bodies of their enemies.

Amidst the carnage, Drona heard a tremendous sound like the roar of the ocean. From the sky a great dust storm approached from all directions until the whole sky was overcast. Thunder clapped, lightning flashed, and before the simha and his army, atop a hill, Kali and Maya appeared, held high on golden palanquins.

Atop the backs of twenty Rakshasas, the King of Klesa was held high on an elaborate platform. Kali, covered in silver armor, held a golden shield in one hand and a jewel-studded spear in the other as he sat on his throne. His eyes sparkled like silver pearls in a black pool at the sight before him. Long hair, black as pitch, curled over his shoulders from under a golden helmet that shone like a thousand suns over the Rakshasas. Seeing the glow from their lord, the Rakshasas cheered and howled.

Next to Kali was his consort, Maya. She was as beautiful as Kali was handsome, with black polished skin which had been bathed in perfumed oils, and dressed in purple silk robes. Atop her head, beneath hair as black as her brother's, she wore a crown made from the skull of her human mother. Her own blue eyes radiated, enchanting all who beheld her beauty. The sorceress held a silver staff, as tall and sleek as its mistress, that she raised above her head. From her own throne, also held high on the backs of Rakshasa servants, Maya rose and chanted her battle charm.

> "May Kali churn this enemy.
> Slay these armies of Drona a thousandfold
> And tear asunder these enemies."

With the chanting of Maya's mantra, Drona thought the time of the dissolution had come. The sound of a fierce sea with great foaming waves and a loud roaring came between the two armies. A great black cloud was visible in the sky, and from all directions hailstones fell on Drona's soldiers, along with lances, clubs, swords, and great pieces of stone. Maya continued:

> "Great is the net of thee, Kali,
> Prepared to slay these armies."

With the signal from his sister, Kali raised his spear, and the Rakshasas charged, their courage heightened by the charms of Maya. While the army of Drona was being showered with serpents, Maya chanted:

> "To death do I hand them over.
> With fetters they have been bound.
> To Kali do I lead them captive.
> Let more than thousands be slain."

The armies clashed and thousands of soldiers swarmed over each other. "The devas shall run from our might. Ghandharvas and Apsarasas, mystics and simhas, none shall escape," Maya vowed as the soldiers of Drona, overcome by the magic charms of the sorceress, fell to the Asura. Maya turned to her consort and, holding a chalice high, offered a salute to her brother. "This sacrificial drink of gharma has been heated by the fire of revenge. To drink is to slay." With that toast, the twins drank to victory as the few survivors of Drona's force were pursued and killed. Maya and Kali watched from their exalted places, and Maya chanted to their future.

> "Conquered, do you flee,
> Repelled by my charm, do you run.
> Repulsed by my power, not one shall be saved.
> All of Bhu shall shriek.
> Let Sveta-dvipa tremble with fright.
> The armies of the devas shall we conquer!

* * * * *

Still within the darkness of the Bala Inn, two boys turned to the voice that had greeted them. A candle stub, centered on the table, suddenly burst into light, and the flash revealed the deep wrinkles of a stoic face framed by long silver hair. It was the mystic, Vyasa.

Gopal rushed to the figure seated in the corner. There were a million things to say, a million questions to ask. Nimai followed close behind.

"Be seated," invited their host.

Gopal, being first, sat closest to the mystic. Nimai moved his meal to the table and continued to sip his soup, content to be warm and fed. Gopal was about to speak when Vyasa raised his hand, stopping him. "I know what has occurred; we share the same path." The mystic paused. A man moved from a table to the door, opening it. The wind rushed in, carrying with it sand from the road. The door quickly closed. Vyasa waited a moment and lowered his voice to a whisper. "It seems our karma in this life has crossed."

"Then you know about Goloka?"

"Yes," Vyasa replied. "I saw Kali's army in the sacrificial fire. I was powerless to stop them."

"And you let me go after the naga . . . when you knew my family and village were in danger?"

"That was the one thing I could do. I convinced your father to let you perform the vidhi."

"But why?" Gopal's voice was an anxious mixture of tears and anger. The thought of his father . . .

"You had to be spared. You are of the First Root-Race of Chayya. Do you know what that means?"

"I know it means I am in the line of the simhas of—"

"No! It is more, much more," Vyasa insisted. "You, and your kind, are the descendants of the devas of Sveta-dvipa. You, and all the rightful simha families, are descended from the First Root-Race, the first beings planted by the first devas, at the time of Bhu's creation. You are the great-great-great-grandchildren of the devas."

Maybe, at another time, in another place, this news would have brought Gopal excitement beyond his greatest dreams, but not now, not after what had happened to his family and his sister. Now, it only meant trouble.

Vyasa explained how in the time of creation each of the devas agreed to have one hundred children, to be planted among the planets of the Second Whorl of Bhu. These children became the first simhas. Gopal's family was descended from the deva, Paramatma. Vyasa continued, "Kali has made his first goal the destruction of the Race of Chayya. It is his first act of revenge against the devas for imprisoning the Asuras in Bila-svarga. Goloka is just one of the kingdoms already destroyed. Kali released the Rakshasas from Rahu to join him as his army. These man-beasts have been unleashed throughout Bhu."

Vyasa looked deep into Gopal's eyes, making the boy uncomfortable. "Being of the blood of the devas, it is your duty, and the duty of all the Chayya, to stop Kali. He must be driven back to the hellish whorl he came from, and the portal must be sealed again . . . or he must be killed. It is your karma, your rasa as simha . . . as Chayya." Vyasa saw the look on Gopal's face, part terror, part confusion. "It is my karma to help you," the mystic explained, "or I will not be allowed to take a higher birth when this body dies."

Gopal felt naked before the mystic. "I have no knowledge of these things. I've spent my entire life in ritual and tradition. I can't—"

"Everything you need to defeat the demon is within the City of Nine Gates," said the mystic.

"Where? What is this place?"

"That, you must discover by yourself."

Gopal's heart was heavy, but before he could think of himself, or the whorl, he had to find Citty. "Kali will have to wait," he said. "If karma is to rule my life, than let my karma take me to Citty! I want only to find my sister. Perhaps we can join up with Drona. We saw his war canoes yesterday; he can help us."

Being a treta-mystic, Vyasa already knew of Drona's defeat. He had to calm the boy, to teach him Bhakti—the art of the treta-mystic, if he . . . they . . . were to survive. "Intelligence is our real strength," he advised. "Do you know the story of the rabbit and the lion?"

Gopal stared at the candle in the center of the table. He didn't want to hear more stories! He wanted to do something—to find his sister, but Nimai was ready to listen. "I've never heard it," he mumbled between sips of the soup.

So the mystic told the story of a fierce lion, drunk with pride, who slaughtered the weaker animals without mercy, until one day all the animals of the forest came together before this evil king and promised that if the lion would remain at home, each day they would send him one animal of the forest.

When a rabbit's turn came, it being rabbit-day, the chosen rabbit reflected on how it might be possible to kill the lion, who was much more powerful than he. So the rabbit went very slowly, arriving late in the day before the lion, with his plan. The rabbit lied and explained how all the animals recognized that the rabbits' turn had come, and because he was quite small, they had dispatched five other rabbits with him. In mid-journey, he claimed, a great beast had jumped out of the ground and eaten his four companions, leaving only him, a meager meal.

The lion, disliking the competition, asked the rabbit to show him this thief. So the rabbit brought the evil king to a well he had passed, and the lion, seeing his own reflection in the water and thinking it to be the beast, gave a great roar. From within the well issued an echoed roar twice as loud. This the lion heard, and thinking it a challenge, hurled himself down . . . to meet his death.

"So, my young friend, that is why I say, intelligence is power," Vyasa concluded.

"So we find a well and get Kali to jump in?" Nimai, feeling relaxed from the wine he had drunk, smiled.

Vyasa smiled. "Let Drona do what he must. We will take another course."

Gopal thought about the words of the mystic. He still preferred to be fighting with Drona. With the help of a great simha, he could find his sister. Gopal grew angry at the decision being made for him.

Seeing the disgruntled look on Gopal's face, Vyasa explained further. "To stop a serpent, we need to cut off the head," he whispered, again looking around the dark, dank room. "Kali never controls his armies in battle. His sister is the real threat. It is from Maya that he draws his power, and from blood she draws hers." Vyasa took hold of Gopal's hand. "To stop Kali, we need to cut off the source of his strength. Kill the consort, and Kali's real form will be revealed for all to see. Only then will he be vulnerable. That is our task."

"To find my sister," Gopal responded angrily, pulling his hand away, "*that* is my task." There was a pause as the mystic and the boy stared at each other. The momentary silence broke when the door flew open, and with more wind came a tall figure through the door. The intruder headed straight for the visitors from Goloka. Gopal grabbed for his dagger. Nimai put down his wine.

"Put your weapon away," Vyasa urged. "He is with me."

The newcomer was Sudama, a student of Vyasa's. He was taller than either Gopal or Nimai and wore the saffron robes of a celibate student of the mystic arts. As was the custom for a brahmacari, his head was clean-shaven, except for the long strands of hair left at the back of his head that flowed down to his waist. The young man, who was about twenty-one years of age, approached and crouched next to the mystic. "Prabhu," he addressed his master, "Kali's armies have advanced. Drona is dead, beheaded, and his army destroyed. Radhakunde is without defense."

These words reached the ears of the others in the room. The few sober patrons scurried off, knocking cups to the floor in their rush to the front door. Canura threw a pail of water onto the fire, where it sizzled like a hundred snakes and billowed a cloud of thick smoke into the already stuffy room. Quickly, he walked around gathering cups, pouring their contents on the heads of those either sleeping or too drunk to heed the warning. "We're closing," he announced, pulling men to their feet. "Get out! Get out! Best you find someplace to take shelter. Anywhere but here! Everyone out!" he shouted, continuing to pour water and wine on the still slumbering men.

Vyasa rose to his feet. The saffron wrapped tridunda, with its crescent-moon tip, was grasped in one long-fingered hand. "This way." The mystic tilted his staff, pointing toward the wall at the back of the darkened room. "Dvar," he chanted, and a door appeared that no one had noticed when they had entered.

Gopal also stood. Nimai tried to stand and fell over. The honey-wine had taken its toll. Gopal grabbed Nimai's arm and dragged him along, following Vyasa through the opening that had, by the mystic's command, come into being. There was a small clearing behind the inn, surrounded by a forest of acacia trees on two sides. Steep cliffs rose like a giant wall, disappearing into the clouds, hampering any chance of escape.

The mystic pointed the tridunda, this time at the side of the rocky cliffs, and chanted, "Parvatah-pathah." Before disbelieving eyes, a path appeared that wound its way up the high, rocky wall. "We will go to my ashram," Vyasa instructed. "Sudama, you go ahead to lead the way." Vyasa tilted his head, indicating that they should follow Sudama.

Nimai still clutched the cup, half filled with the thick wine; only Gopal kept him from falling. With Vyasa hurrying them along, Gopal found himself alongside the one the mystic had called Sudama. "How does he make paths and doors appear and disappear?" Gopal asked, catching Sudama off-guard.

"You mean Vyasa?"

"Yes."

Sudama seemed unchallenged by the question. "They were always there, just covered from your sight, like the sun on a cloudy day. Vyasa can bring or take away the clouds."

"Oh," Gopal answered, not understanding and almost sorry he had asked. He hurried to keep ahead of the spry mystic, who prodded Nimai with his staff to keep the boy from slowing until they had climbed the mountain path and reached a large ledge.

Vyasa moved to the edge, where he stood tall against the red sky. The setting sun shed a pale light on the mystic, who stood overlooking a canyon road that wound its way through the valley to the gates of Radhakunde. "There they are," said Vyasa, pointing to the glow of moving torches.

Nimai, who was almost able to stand on his own now, but still a bit wobbly, rushed to the edge of the cliff. Gopal followed, fearing his friend wouldn't be able to stop, but Nimai did stop. Looking down at Radhakunde, the two friends felt a strange uneasiness, as if events were repeating themselves. The hollow sea-sound of military conch-shell horns echoed from below, leading the way to the defenseless city. "Is that what's left of the army of Drona?" asked Nimai.

"I'm afraid not," Vyasa replied. "That, my children, is the army of Kali."

The force of thousands, aglow with torches and armed with spears, tridents, axes, clubs, and swords, was like a horde of insects, covering the canyon floor, making the road look alive. The glow from the Rakshasa's armor made them appear even larger as they rode atop elephant mounts. Each beast's long, white tusks were painted with the same symbols Gopal had seen in Goloka. Decorations of gold rings clashed with the glow of their horse-drawn, armor-covered chariots. These mounted soldiers led rows of spear-carrying foot soldiers that, from above, looked like a giant serpent, slithering along the valley floor.

Suddenly, something captured Sudama's attention. "Coming this way," he warned. "Everyone down." These words held emotion—fear!

They fell to the ground as one unit, all except Nimai. "Where? I don't see anything. What is he talking—"

Gopal grabbed Nimai by the belt, pulling him down on top of him, finally getting him to let loose of the cup. The clay cup rolled along the rock-strewn path, finally coming to rest against a clump of wild grass. Then there was silence.

A warrior was climbing up the path on the sloping valley wall, heading right toward them. He was big, probably another Rakshasa. Gopal looked to Vyasa for direction.

Vyasa thought that the boy's training should begin. "What do you think?" asked the mystic, before Gopal could speak, startling the boy.

"He could be a scout for Kali. Someone should move down and stop him," Gopal blurted, without much thought or planning.

Vyasa nodded. "You go. Take Nimai with you."

Nimai suddenly sobered.

Gopal's mind went blank. Everything he had learned from his father was forgotten. Taking a deep breath, he calmed himself. He'd played games like this in the hills with his friends. This wasn't much different, except that if he failed, this time he wouldn't get up and go home. The intruder was getting closer. If he didn't do something, Vyasa would never help him find his sister. Or so he thought.

"Nimai, you climb down to the left," Gopal ordered. "I'll move to the right. The rest of you wait here and take him from the front while we close in from the sides." That was how they did it in the game, so Gopal took a place within the thicket on the other side of Nimai, where the path widened.

The soldier drew nearer. Nimai's outline showed on the opposite side. Gopal wondered if he was putting too much trust in the mystic. He looked down at his dagger. He finally removed it from its sheath. Twigs broke under a heavy foot. The sound left little room for changing plans.

The soldier drew close enough for Gopal to see his face. He was almost within reach. It was a Rakshasa, as big and ugly as the one from Goloka. They could have been twins. In one of his massive hands the Rakshasa held a tree branch that had been trimmed of its leaves and branches. He was using it to help him climb the rugged mountain path. The handle of the huge sword that stuck out from behind his left shoulder gave Gopal a shudder.

The soldier was about to cross his path. Gopal changed the dagger from his right to his left hand, and then back again, worrying that the sweat on his palms might cause the blade to slip. He wiped his hand on his shirt sleeve and grasped the dagger in anticipation. What should he do?

In Gopal's moment of hesitation, Nimai, brave with wine, leaped from behind a large rock onto the soldier. Gopal's jaw dropped. Nimai had been catapulted through the air, onto a thorn bush where each tortured movement he made got him more ensnared. If Gopal didn't act he could lose the chance—and his friend. He leaped with newly found strength onto the warrior and just as quickly found himself heaved into the air, landing on his back in the path before his assailant. "May the manus have mercy on me," he stammered.

Nimai had pulled himself together and was making another charge from the side. Gopal, thinking it would take both of them, jumped to his feet, turned, and again lunged toward the warrior. When the two reached the spot where the soldier stood, the fighter stepped aside, laughing. Gopal and Nimai crashed into each other, falling flat to the ground. The soldier tossed away the branch and unsheathed his sword.

"Paramatma protect me!" Gopal pleaded. The gleam of the metal blade shone above his and Nimai's heads when a sound vibration, like rolling thunder, rippled down the valley path, shaking the very ground that Gopal clutched in fear. Two words, "Maha shakti," were all he heard as the mantra engulfed, then passed him. Like a wave, the sound vibration wrinkled the air, rolled over Gopal, and hit the warrior. The soldier tumbled backward, down the path, dead. Gopal, still frightened, cautiously lifted his head. Vyasa stood with Sudama about ten yards up the path. Had the mystic been the source of the unusual weapon?

"I think we have had enough amusement for one night," said the mystic. "Sudama, go help Nimai. I will help our other neophyte warrior over there,"—he pointed to Gopal, who was cowering on the ground—"before they injure each other."

Sudama carried out his master's wish, helping Nimai to his feet and brushing the thorns from the boy's back. "Did you see what the mystic did?" Nimai asked excitedly. "He pointed his tridunda at the warrior and chanted, 'Maha shakti.' The air moved . . . like a wall of water, it hit the soldier. Imagine having such power!" Sudama ignored the boy's rantings.

"What's going on?" asked Gopal, still brushing sand from his sleeves. "Were you trying to get us killed? Letting us attack a Rakshasa, when the whole time you had the power to stop him."

"It was your plan," the mystic reminded. Vyasa looked down the path from which the Rakshasa had come. "Let us get back to the cave before we are really discovered. I will explain."

Led by Sudama, they reached a place about twenty yards from the ledge where, behind the dried brush that hung from the side of the mountain wall, there was a cleft in the rock. They had to slip through sideways to enter the narrow opening.

What? No mantras? thought Gopal, still annoyed at his own foolish display. With daylight fading behind them, and only darkness ahead, Gopal heard the mystic whisper, "Jyotis." The word echoed down the passage, carrying light with the moving vibration. The path that lay before them was suddenly bright. With the mystic in the lead, they traveled through the underground passage, which seemed to lead to the very heart of the mountain. No one spoke. No one questioned. They quietly followed to their journey's end, where the passageway emptied onto a ledge that hung over a well-lit cavern chamber. There were no torches or lamps anywhere. The light revealed a winding rock staircase that had been carved from the walls of the ancient cavern. Strangely, the chamber was warm, not cold or damp like caves usually were. Even the air didn't smell musty, but instead was sweet, herbal, enlivening. Below was a firepit, but it was much too small to be used for warmth.

At the bottom, to one side of the fire, a small wooden platform stood. A sana? Gopal thought, being reminded of the sitting place of his father. On top of the platform was a cushion, a plain clay cup, a wooden bowl, and a book. Around the platform, scattered on the sandy floor, were several straw sitting mats. In front of the platform was a large brass bowl from which emanated a continuous stream of incense smoke, the source of the sweet scent.

Along the rock and dirt walls of the cave were wooden shelves with different sized clay and glass bowls. The colored glass reflected Gopal's image in each container, making a hundred Gopals, each as amused and confused as the next. The glass vessels revealed contents of different hues, some liquid, and some of a sandy consistency. On other shelves were various leather and cloth bags, also filled to different degrees, with what Gopal couldn't tell. Finally, Gopal broke the silence. "Is it the rocks that are giving off the light?"

"Mystic trickery," retorted Nimai. "Maybe the secret is in those bags and jars." Nimai had quickly sobered, enamored of the powers displayed by the mystic, though he had always disbelieved the existence of such things in the past.

Reaching the center of the cavern, Vyasa took his seat on the platform, laying the tridunda beside him. His student took a seat on the mat at the foot of the platform and, taking some tiny colored pebbles from a straw container, tossed them into the brass bowl. The grains ignited, sending a burst of herbal scented smoke into the air. "Sudama," the mystic ordered, "prepare some sandalwood paste and ash of cotton. Our young simha has a wound."

Gopal was surprised; he wasn't aware of having been wounded. Blood seeped through his shirt and he grabbed his waist. Sudama quickly returned and, after removing Gopal's shirt, started dressing the boy's wound. Vyasa offered food to the guests.

"Take it away!" yelled Gopal, refusing the hospitality of his host and startling Nimai. "I want some questions answered!" Sudama also was startled by the abrasiveness of the boy; he did not act like a student should. "Why are we hiding in this hole?" Gopal demanded. "We should be out there, looking for my sister! Not sitting around some mystic burrow."

"Let me take care of your outer wound first," Vyasa replied. "Sword wounds are usually easier to heal than those of the heart." Taking the book from the platform, the mystic gently flipped through the yellow-tinted pages. "Yes, here it is." Then, handing the book to Sudama, he said, "Recite that verse."

Sudama looked down at the page and read:

"For the weak who challenge mighty foes
A battle to abide
Like elephants with broken tusks
Return with drooping pride."

The point made, Vyasa turned to Sudama. "Prepare a mixture of nutmeg powder in rain water to help our guests sleep." Sudama hurried to complete the orders of his master while the others sat silently, watching the unquestioned service of the student to his teacher. Gopal was unable to calm his temper and his face showed it. "That is why the devas have sent you to me," Vyasa said, as if reading Gopal's mind. "To learn! With the seal of Bila-svarga broken, there are vibrations in the air that can have a strange effect on the mind and body of the untrained. Take your outburst, for example."

Gopal thought he understood. "Do you mean krura-lochana?"

Vyasa smiled. "Yes. The krura-lochana has been released

by Kali, or should I say his sorceress-sister, Maya. Their goal is to contaminate the whorl."

"Then Maya's powers must be very strong," said Gopal, feeling he was making progress in understanding his new teacher.

"Or maybe you are weak," answered the mystic. "We shall see in due course. We shall see. Now we should eat and get some rest. There will be plenty for all to do. Tomorrow, we must find your sister."

Gopal didn't speak anymore and, after quietly nourishing himself on the cooked grains Sudama had provided, lay down on a straw mat. Calmed by the nutmeg potion, and protected by the mystic powers of their host, they all prepared for sleep. As Nimai slept off his first encounter with an intoxicant, Gopal stared at the cave ceiling, at the walls that sparkled with magic charms, reflecting on the words he had heard this day. He knew he would have to trust Vyasa and Sudama if he was to find Citty, but when he thought no one would know what he was thinking, he cursed the devas for bringing him into this.

EIGHT

THE NEXT MORNING, THE FIRE WAS OUT, but the scent of sweet mints and sandalwood still filled the cavern, comforting Gopal as he lay on the ground, though he could not truly relax knowing Citty was out there. He had to know if she was alive.

A dark green, cotton chotta covered his legs and a new, saffron-colored cotton shirt, neatly folded, was at his side. Dressing, he noticed that some cloth bags were missing from the shelf on the wall—and that was not all that was missing. He was alone in the cave. Putting on his sandals, and wrapping the soft, warm chotta around his shoulders, he ran up the lighted staircase and into the passageway.

At the cave's narrow entrance, darkness greeted him. It should have been morning by now, but there were no stars, only a black backdrop that should be the sky. He squeezed through the crevice and saw the others, standing before a wall of cloud-black smoke. Faint rays of golden sunlight slipped through the gaps in a near-solid cloud mass.

"What's causing it?"

Nimai jumped, startled by the voice from behind. "You

finally got up. I was about to go and get you."

"What's happened?" Gopal tightened the chotta around him, more from fear than from the morning chill.

"There, at the end of the valley," Sudama answered, "is—or was—Radhakunde." At the end of the canyon was the source of the dark smoke curtain, an ember glow coming from the burning city. "Another city has fallen to the Asura," said Sudama, throwing a small rock to the ground. He turned and angrily walked back toward the cave.

"He doesn't act much like a brahmacari," Nimai said, straightening the new, gray chotta that he wore.

"I can understand how he feels," said Gopal. "I wish we were doing something instead of just waiting around." He suddenly realized someone else was missing. "Vyasa! Where is Vyasa?"

"Sudama said he went to check something on the Rakshasa's armor, something he had noticed yesterday. Then he was going to Radhakunde." Nimai looked back to the cave. "I'm going to see if there's anything to eat."

Gopal was alone again. The clouds of smoke finally began to give way to the wind and sun. The valley, like a ghostly river, glowed in a haze of grays, blacks, whites, and reds that swirled in smoky whirlpools, rushing with gusts that swept through the canyon. This was the second city he had seen destroyed. Maybe if he hadn't come to Radhakunde . . .

Sunlight peeked from between the clouds that had begun to disperse like ghost ships sailing for separate ports. Someone was approaching. Gopal turned to face the sound. It could be anyone, or anything, maybe even another Rakshasa scout. He hid behind the fallen tree and waited, his dagger held firmly, the chotta over his head for cover.

"Namas te," greeted the mystic. "You finally tired of sleeping I see."

Gopal peered out from behind the log. How could the mystic have seen him?

Vyasa looked past him. "Where are the others?"

"Sudama and Nimai are in the cave."

"We must join them . . . I found something."

When they entered, Sudama was spooning hot grains onto banana leaf plates, where it lumped together. Vyasa accepted a plate of grains, and some fruit, but placed it by his side uneaten. "Food is the least of our concerns now," he said. "I found more than destruction in Radhakunde."

Gopal held a warm leaf heavy with cooked cereal in his palms. He was too hungry to refuse. Nimai had already finished his first portion and was on his second.

The mystic's voice revealed the horror in his heart. "I found evidence of the Pisaca," said Vyasa. Sudama at once stopped serving; he understood the importance of his master's words. Vyasa continued slowly. "Besides the severing of heads, I saw the symbols of Bhutanatha. . . . We have more than Kali to deal with." The mystic's expression turned grave.

Gopal put the food down. "Who?"

"He calls himself Bhutanatha," repeated the mystic. "It means 'Conquerer of Bhu.' He is the high priest of the Pisaca—a cult of the black art. Their symbol is a black trident, surrounded by twenty-eight stars," the mystic explained, not entirely to Gopal's surprise. "I noticed it on the armor of the Rakshasa we killed yesterday. I went to Radhakunde to find more evidence to support my suspicions."

"What does he want with us?" Gopal was worried. Things were getting too complicated.

Sudama offered an explanation. "The three blades of the trident symbolize the Three Whorls. The twenty-eight stars are the number of kingdoms in Bila-svarga. Bhutanatha had always vowed that someday the Pisaca would encircle the Three Whorls of the Bhu-mandala."

"I saw that symbol," Gopal said excitedly. "In Goloka, we killed a Rakshasa who had the same symbol emblazoned on his armor." Gopal remembered how his sister had saved his life.

"It is worse than I feared," Vyasa admitted. "Kali has

already liberated the Rakshasas from the planet Rahu to
serve in his army. They alone would make formidable foes.
If Kali has also entered an alliance with the Lord of Narakatala and is bringing the kingdoms of the Third Whorl to
join him . . . " Vyasa rested his tridunda against his left
shoulder and folded his arms across his chest. "We are up
against an extremely dangerous opponent, my students!
No one on Bhu is safe now."

"Citty!" stammered Gopal. "We must find my sister."

Vyasa stood to his feet. "That is our first business." With
his tridunda in hand again, he commanded, "Bring your
weapons!" As the mystic rushed up the stone stairwell to the
passageway, Sudama stopped performing his menial tasks.
Taking his single reed staff—the dunda of the brahmacari—
and a dagger, he prepared to follow his master.

"What are we getting involved in?" Nimai asked. Gopal
couldn't answer.

"Nothing more than is your destiny," Sudama answered.
The student looked down at the claw of the naga dangling
from Gopal's belt. "You carry the talon of a simha and, for
someone who appears not to have reached the age of vidhi,
that is quite a deed." Without waiting, Sudama ran up the
passageway with Nimai following.

Gopal took the claw in his hand and listened to the echo
of Nimai and Sudama's footsteps fade. Had he the right to
carry the talon? he asked himself. Hadn't Vyasa arranged
the vidhi? He wasn't an actor in this play, thought the boy,
he was a puppet. First his father pulled his strings, and now
Vyasa was his master, and if not the mystic, then the devas
. . . or the manus. He looked at the claw, then tucked it
under his new shirt. Straightening his dagger, he shouted
to the empty cavern for the devas and manus to hear, "I'll
play my role, but only to protect my sister. When she is
safe, I will cut all the strings and go my own way!" The
echo of his words rang from the cavern walls, as if his challenge might bring some reply, but it didn't, and the sound
faded away. Grabbing his chotta, he ran up the stairs, into

the passageway, and after the others.

Nimai feared for their lives. "If only I had the mystic's power," he mumbled as Gopal caught up with him. Gopal didn't know what to say.

Vyasa and his student had disappeared down the mountain path. Gopal and Nimai hurried to catch up, struggling to keep pace. Neither spoke. They had finally caught up when Vyasa suddenly stopped and placed a finger against his lips. "Sudama has gone ahead. He motioned for us to wait here. There he is," the mystic said, pointing, "by the clearing, where that stream bends. See him?"

Sudama was looking through the white ganda bushes that grew wild in the region, into a clearing. "He's waving," Gopal said. "He wants us to come." With Gopal going first, they joined Sudama, who crouched over a body. Gopal's heart quickened; he rushed to get a better view. Sudama was wiping blood from the person's face. Gopal moved to the other side of the student. "Is he going to be all right?"

"I don't know."

They had found a man about forty years old. Vyasa joined them, recognizing the stranger. "He is Nakula, a merchant from Radhakunde." Seeing the man's desperate condition, Vyasa took over. "Sudama, find some tagara leaves or jatamamsi—quickly!"

Sudama looked over at his master. "I already applied a poultice of comfrey and yarrow," he said, going off to do his master's bidding.

"Good," said the mystic. "The herbs may revive him."

"*May* revive him?" Gopal looked down at the wounded man. "Aren't you a treta-mystic?"

"Don't worry," Vyasa assured.

Gopal did worry—about his sister and everything else. Around the clearing, scarlet java, yellow champa, and blue aparajita surrounded them. A crystal stream crossed their path. How could a scene as beautiful as this hold such terror?

The man turned white and Vyasa grabbed one of his

hands. "He's cold. . . . He's going to die." Sudama finally returned, carrying something which he emptied from his hands into Vyasa's. The mystic quickly ground the leaves between his palms, turning his skin red. Sudama ran back to the stream, returning with water in his cupped hands. Vyasa sat Nakula up and held his cupped hands, filled with the crushed herbs, over the wounded man's mouth as Sudama slowly poured the water from his hands into the mystic's, who directed the herbal mixture to the dying man's purple lips. The red brew of Ayur Healing dripped across Nakula's lips and cheeks as Vyasa chanted:

> "Let death flee hence,
> Exorcised by Agni and Soma,
> With the herb of sacrifice,
> I overcome the Pisaca,
> And rob them of their property.
> All evil, do I slay.
> Let all harmful things scatter!"

Nakula opened his eyes. He mumbled something, his hands wildly searching, grabbing only air. Vyasa grabbed one of the man's hands and held tight. "They took her!" Nakula cried, grabbing for the mystic, but missing, his free hand falling lifeless to his side. Gopal thought the stranger was talking about his sister, Citty. The mystic took both of the man's hands in his. "It happened so fast," Nakula went on, pausing first for a breath. ". . . My daughter! We escaped from the city. I couldn't find my wife, and we had to leave! They were everywhere!" Vyasa rubbed the man's cheek and forehead, trying to calm him. "I was standing in the clearing. I thought we were safe. I heard splashing." The man's voice was gargled; his skin turned pale.

"When I turned, I saw two, maybe three, of these white, withered things leaping from the stream. I swear I could see their skeletons through their skin. They grabbed my daughter and were pulling her down into the stream. I took out my dagger and ran after her, but she disappeared . . . into the water."The wound was taking its toll. Nakula whispered, "I waded in to find her, and more of those things leaped out to grab me. I started slashing and chanting for the devas to protect me, then I felt something hit me on the head." Nakula's eyelids fell shut. His head slumped forward.

"He's dead," said Vyasa.

"What happened?" said Gopal. "What is going on?"

Vyasa stood and, deep in thought, walked to the edge of the stream, ignoring Gopal's question for questions of his own. But Gopal followed, expecting to be answered. "That man was touched by Pisaca poison," Vyasa explained. "To die at the hand of the Pisaca is to be condemned to slavery in Bila-svarga as a trishna." Gopal's expression showed he had no knowledge of such things. "It is a tormented existence as a slave to the followers of Bhutanatha." Gopal's eyes showed the fear he felt for his sister as Vyasa looked at his student. "Sudama has learned the Healing Art of Ayur well. He will make a fine healer some day. The mixture we gave Nakula and the mantra I chanted sometimes counteract the black arts."

"*Sometimes?*" gasped Gopal, realizing he was depending on these people to help him find Citty.

"Nothing in this whorl is guaranteed," replied the mystic. "If the godhead wants to save you, nothing can kill you. If the godhead wants to kill you, nothing can save you. We mystics are here in case the godhead wants to save you." He smiled a humble smile. "I fear the man's daughter has been taken to Bila-svarga, and I fear the same has happened to your sister."

Now Gopal turned pale. "Taken to Bila-Svarga? What do you mean?" He remembered the girls being led through Goloka.

Vyasa crouched by the sparkling current. Taking a handful of the clear water, he let it drip through his fingers. He wiped his hand on the tattered chotta he still wore over his shoulders. "Considering Nakula's condition when we found him, it is obvious that he encountered the devotees of Bhutanatha—the Pisaca."

Gopal glanced back at the body of the stranger, at Nimai standing and staring. He crouched beside the mystic. "Is Citty dead?"

"No, I don't think so." Vyasa continued peering into the rushing water. "She is alive." Again he paused, still staring into the waters. "At least for a while." He slapped the water, splashing and disturbing its flow. "If I am right . . . " The mystic's words and thoughts went inward. Gopal watched the face of the mystic, waiting for more. "Sometimes . . . they take Second Whorl women for their sacrifices," Vyasa said.

"What?" Gopal couldn't believe what he was hearing. "We have to do something!" he clamored, quickly rising and stepping with one foot into the cold stream. "Why are we just standing—"

"Calm down," said Sudama, joining them and answering for the mystic. Nimai was behind him. Gopal's sandal rested beneath the bubbling water. Stepping back, he shook his foot like some wet animal, splashing cold drops on Sudama and the mystic. "If there is anything Vyasa can do," Sudama explained, "he will."

"Here, take this." Vyasa, to keep the boy's mind occupied, handed Gopal some green, pungent powder from his pouch. "Sprinkle this in a circle around the clearing." Gopal took the powder, bringing it up to his nose. "Garlic and ash have been known to repel the Pisaca." Gopal turned his nose from the mixture and grudgingly followed the mystic's instruction. Hesitantly, he walked to the edge of the clearing, sprinkling the powder as he went and mumbling to himself. "Puppet," Vyasa thought he heard.

"I'll keep my dagger where I can find it," Gopal called back, "just in case your bag of tricks doesn't work."

"There must be something more happening, something that I am not aware of. . . . " Vyasa's voice faded to silence, as if he were continuing the discussion with someone else, somewhere else. The mystic entered a trance. Then the words started coming from Vyasa's mouth again; he had returned.

" . . . I don't think they realized Nakula was there at first when they grabbed his daughter. They weren't sure he was alone even then, otherwise they would have surely killed and mutilated him. They left quickly . . . perhaps afraid there might be others."

"Then there were only a few of them," said Sudama as Gopal rejoined them.

"That is my guess."

"So we follow the stream?" asked Gopal, ready to go. Vyasa nodded, and together they walked along the water. Gopal, thinking about what might be happening to his sister, wished they would move faster, but this time he kept his thoughts to himself. The woods were unusually quiet for the late morning, without the sound of birds. Even the chatter of monkeys, usually found in this part of the forest, was absent. Although he wasn't in Goloka, Gopal knew that the animals shouldn't be any different here, but it wasn't the animals that gave real concern. Cautiously, he looked beyond each tree and shrub, expecting someone or something to jump out from behind them or fall upon them from the branches.

When the stream widened, absorbing the path, they all had to balance themselves on the slippery stones. Sudama slipped and was drenched to the waist, but, as a true brahmacari, he didn't allow his discomfort to hamper his task. Gopal had to admire Sudama. The student had direction. He knew what he wanted and was following the course to achieve it. He seemed loyal to Vyasa, and was reaping the fruits of his loyalty. A Healer of the Art of Ayur? Is that what Vyasa had said was Sudama's goal? The brahmacari's dedication was evident. Maybe he could learn something from these people after all.

The strange quiet, complete except for their own muffled steps on the moss-covered ground and occasional splashing, soon made everyone uneasy. Vyasa, who was just ahead of Gopal, came to an abrupt halt, and Gopal, lost in thought, walked into the back of the mystic, jarring himself back to the present. "What is it?" he asked, looking at Vyasa and trying to draw attention from his clumsiness. Nimai rested on the ground, taking advantage of the break.

"Sudama has found something."

Sudama was ahead about fifty yards now, where the forest appeared to end with a row of tamarind trees. He stood at a place where the path spilled into a clearing, holding his hand up, gesturing for them to stop. He called back, "Come up here!" and stepped past the trees.

Coming out from the forest, they joined the student at the entrance of a small temple. The white marble structure was stained with leaves and covered with vines that crawled out of the forest. Like fingers, the vines wrapped around two columns that guarded a dark entrance. Carved into the marble archway, held by the columns, a relief depicted the Dance of Annihilation, and circling the four-armed, dancing deva were the Flames of Destruction—the all-devouring fires of the manus. "A temple to Rudra . . . actually, a crematorium," said the mystic. "I think we have our answer."

Gopal cautiously walked to the bottom step of the temple, trying to see into the darkened hall. "What do you mean?"

"It is possible to use the ashes of the dead," Vyasa answered, "as a catalyst for travel to other planets." Gopal turned to face the mystic. Even Sudama and Nimai moved closer. "If I am correct," Vyasa continued, "they have returned to Narakatala—the planet of Bhutanatha, in the Third Whorl of Bila-svarga—through there. It is on Narakatala that we will find your sister."

Gopal turned and climbed the first three steps, then stopped and looked back. "Let's go!" he said, dagger in hand, his foot pressed to the edge of another marble step.

"What are you waiting for?"

"Not so fast, my daring young friend," warned Sudama, grabbing Gopal by the arm. "Learn well the wisdom of the treta-mystic." Sudama chanted:

> "A warrior failing to prepare for battle,
> And rushing in mad desire,
> Plunges like a brahma moth,
> Headlong into fire."

"First, we must prepare ourselves," said Vyasa. "Listen to Sudama."

"Prepare? For what?" Gopal challenged. "If they went through, then let's go in after them. I'm not afraid! Is that what you're thinking? That's what it is, isn't it?"

"Let him go," ordered Vyasa and Sudama did.

Gopal ran up the rest of the stairs, his dagger before him, and rushed headlong into the temple. Within seconds he emerged. "There's nothing in there but a marble altar and some big clay vases!"

Vyasa motioned for him to come down. "Hand me that stick," he instructed, pointing to the ground. Annoyed, Gopal did as the mystic requested. Vyasa, holding the twig out, called upon the deva of fire. A small flame appeared on the tip of the branch. "Touch the flame!" he ordered.

Gopal hesitated, looking at Sudama, who nodded. He held out his hand. Nimai howled with laughter as Gopal burned himself. "It's not funny!" shouted Gopal, shaking his aching fingers. "It hurts!"

Vyasa smiled. "I am sure it does. You were not prepared!" Gopal's face reddened like the tips of his fingers. The tingling sensation in his hand grew more intense. "Asking you to touch the flame," the mystic said, "is like asking you to enter fire. In your present state, you burned."

"I know that!" snapped the unwilling student.

"Listen," said Sudama.

"To enter fire," admonished the mystic, "you must

become fire! To travel to other whorls, we must take bodies suitable for such a journey. We must shed the bodies of this whorl, for the coverings of another." Gopal wasn't sure he liked that idea, or even understood what the mystic had in mind, but for his sister was he willing to try anything. "Sudama, see to Gopal's burn." The mystic removed another small packet from his pouch and sprinkled the contents into the air, causing the dried leaves to scatter across the temple steps. Gopal looked to Sudama, who was standing beside him, for some explanation. Nimai sniffed the air before him, and the scattered herb snowed down on the steps of the temple.

"It will form a field of protection," said Sudama, "so no one can use the temple to come behind us."

"Gopal," Vyasa continued, "go back to the stream and get some wet clay. Meet us inside." The boy went to the water, neglecting to take anything to carry the clay, while Nimai and the mystics entered the crematorium. The inside was dark and cold. It looked as if it hadn't been used in a long time, at least not by anything from this whorl. Twigs and dried grass lay piled in the corners of the room. Leaves, blown in through the entry, covered the floor with a carpet of orange, brown, and yellow that cracked and crumbled under the feet of the visitors. Gopal entered with his cupped hands, waiting for someone to tell him what to do with the clay dripping through his fingers. Against the wall stood a marble altar with teakwood panels covering the front, from the floor to the altar's surface. Carved into the wood was a figure of the Rudra—the Destroyer. A garland of snakes hung around his neck, and a fountain that emanated from the deva's head became a river that ran through the carving, along the bottom of the ornate trim, to the opposite side of the altar where the magical waters transformed into a mountain. Atop that stood a lone tree.

On the floor, between the entrance and the altar, a brass firepit for the cremations was sunk into the marble. It was filled with dried leaves, twigs, and other forest debris that had gathered over time. Above, the roof rose to form a large, round opening that allowed smoke to escape. Carved into the ceiling were scenes that Gopal could not recognize, scenes that defied description. There were scenes of planets within the Three Whorls; of many-headed, many-armed beings; of creatures of all shapes, some recognizable as snakes, or birds, and some like nothing Gopal had ever heard described by either his father or grandfather. He did recognize a naga.

"The opening above is to allow the atma of the deceased to travel to its next body." Gopal tilted his head down. His gaze met Vyasa's, who glanced at the mud in the boy's hands. Gopal didn't know what to say. He stood there, with the wet clay, dripping. "Put it there," directed the mystic, pointing to a place on the altar. "Nimai, gather some twigs and put them on the altar, and some straw too. Sudama, I will need some strands of spider web."

"Yes, Prabhu," Sudama replied, searching the corners of the crematorium. "Here, will this be enough?"

"Yes, place them there, on the kindling. We will need to mark ourselves with the names of the devas which will grant us the bodies necessary to travel outside this whorl. As you apply the clay, chant each name."

Nimai whispered to Gopal. "I don't like the idea of wiping wet clay on myself, or even think of leaving this whorl. It was hard enough to leave Goloka." Then he spoke to the mystic directly. "Are you sure this will work?"

"Sometimes." Vyasa smiled. Gopal didn't appreciate the mystic's humor; he was worried about his sister.

"I don't think I know the names," Nimai confessed, hoping he might not be able to go along.

"Then I will help." The mystic took a small amount of the clay and placed it in his left palm. After dipping his right middle finger in the clay, he marked his head. "First the forehead, Om Kesaveya," he chanted, marking himself with two lines that converged between his eyebrows.

Each of them, standing in a circle around the mystic,

took a small dab of clay on their fingers and repeated the words chanted by the mystic. Vyasa continued the rite, chanting the appropriate name for each part of the body. Gopal, finding he had used all the clay in his palm, took more from the altar and continued to follow the mystic's lead.

"Now, take seats against the front wall of the altar, and face the pit," said Vyasa, "and listen carefully." The wet clay hardened on Gopal's body, cracking as he twisted.

Soon, the room glowed from the fire Vyasa created on the marble altar. The radiating warmth chased the chill that clung to the marble walls and their skin. Vyasa took a twig from the floor and touched it to the fire. The end of the stick caught the flame, which he transferred to the cold pit. The twig ignited the dry grass and kindling within the hole. "I am going to add moss to the flames. It will cause a sweet mist to fill the temple. Breathe softly, and again chant after me." Gopal took a deep breath. Who would believe this was happening? Only a few days ago . . .

Vyasa added the bits of moss, and, as predicted, the small hall filled with the sweet haze that floated with the ashes to the ceiling and out through the opened dome. "Yanti deva-vrata-devan," the mystic chanted, his voice rising with the haze, out through the opening.

"Yanti deva-vrata-devan," they responded. The marble hall echoed their verse and their chants spilled from the high, narrow, openings in the east wall, usually reserved for the morning sun to light the way for the dead. Their chants rushed like a wind, down the steps and into the forest.

"Yanti deva-vrata-devan," sang the treta-mystic.

"Yanti deva-vrata-devan." Their chorus rose to the skies above the crematorium.

Gopal leaned back against the hard, dusty wall of the altar as dizziness rushed to his head and his scalp felt like a thousand insects had nested in his hair. The tingle worked its way from his head down into his arms. His chest numbed. His breathing became taxed. He was afraid, but he trusted Vyasa. He had to.

He relaxed. His breathing was slow but painless. The tingle moved to his legs, to his feet, to his toes. The room tilted, or appeared to. He couldn't tell. He tried to focus on the large clay urns lined up near the walls. They doubled in number. He tried to stand, falling against the wall behind him, catching himself with his hand. The tingle left his legs. The numbness was gone from his chest. His vision was beginning to clear.

Looking down, startled, he jumped back. There he was, still sitting against the wall, asleep. Him! His body—or someone that looked exactly like him, a mirror image. He looked at himself, still sitting in place.

"We have separated from ourselves," Vyasa answered to all the questions in Gopal's mind.

Nimai also stood, and, coming to the same realization as Gopal, walked closer to the mystic. Nimai wasn't amused. "What tricks have you performed on me?" Annoyed at himself for having taken part in the mystic's game, Nimai worriedly felt his chest and face. "This must be an offense to the manus."

"Calm yourself," said the mystic.

"Which self should I calm?" Nimai snapped, still obviously afraid.

"You are fine. Just see!" Vyasa pointed to the mirror image of Nimai, which was also sleeping, propped against the wall. "Your body is getting a much needed rest. You will appreciate it when we return," Vyasa explained. "I have separated our subtle selves—our minds, intelligence, and atma—from our bodies. We are in our astral forms. You will still feel like flesh and blood, but only this subtle self can travel through the covering that surrounds our whorl." This explanation was still not to Nimai's satisfaction. The boy walked over to his double, touching it on the arm. "Come Nimai," Vyasa called, "you will be fine. We are not finished." It wasn't until Gopal nodded his head in approval, that Nimai finally agreed.

Gathering the ashes of the dead from an urn, Vyasa sprinkled them into the fire that still burned on the altar. A cloud of white smoke, instead of rising as is the nature of smoke, spilled over the marble, like liquid, to the floor below. Like a great flat snake, the smoke turned and climbed the air to the ceiling where it sparkled as if sprinkled with thousands of studded jewels. It was almost too bright to look at. "It looks like a curtain," said Gopal, at the marvel before him.

"Yes, it does," replied the mystic. Then, after motioning with his hand, Vyasa stepped through the smoky-white veil. "This way—follow me!" he called, and vanished.

Gopal took a final glance at himself sitting by the wall. Thinking of his sister, he went next, followed by Sudama, and finally Nimai.

NINE

AFTER HE STEPPED THROUGH THE VEIL of smoke,
Gopal's foot disappeared into a pale blue, swirling mist
that floated along the ground. The ground-level cloud
moved in disoriented currents around him and the others.
The mist wet his skin like a kitten licking his legs, tickling
his open toes and bare ankles. The ground under his feet
was also soft.

As he emerged from the temple with the others, Gopal
knew he had left Bhu far behind. The smell in the air reminded him of something he had smelled in the pastures
of Goloka when an animal from one of the herds would
become lost and fall into a ravine where it starved and
died—the smell of rotting meat. That was how he usually
found the missing animal, by following the smell of the
dead and rotting carcass.

That was the smell of Narakatala.

They were in a forest. The trees were short, no more than
five or six feet in height, twisted and hunched over, with
contorted, leafless branches that extended almost straight
up, as if reaching for something. The wind that vibrated

through this forest made a sound like the wailing of a thousand tortured children.

"The atmas of those unworthy of even a moving form," whispered Vyasa. "Here they stand, rooted in place, crying for mercy, the transmigrated souls of the cursed."

Gopal adjusted his chotta, wrapping it more tightly around his bare neck.

"We must be careful," said Vyasa. "The Hounds of Sarama will know we are not of this whorl. They can sniff out the bodies we left behind the portal."

"What would become of us?" asked Gopal.

"We probably would be making a deal with Bhutanatha ourselves," said Nimai. "Suppose we take care of the business we came for and get out of here."

Vyasa agreed. "We are wasting time. I suggest we separate. Sudama and Nimai, make your way around to our right. Gopal and I will go that way, along that road."

Sudama touched the end of his dunda, and at the sound "dipika," the end of his staff glowed faintly, like a dim lantern. The brahmacari, with Nimai following close behind, pushed his way through the dimly lit brush, deeper into the forest. Before long, the light faded into the darkness.

Vyasa did the same as Sudama and ignited his tridunda. "Come. We will try going this way." He walked quickly, on what felt like a road. The same pale blue mist covered most of the surface, except in places where there were slopes or large boulders, or where the tortured trees grew. Everything was dark. The glow of the mystic's light couldn't penetrate the darkness very far. It allowed them to see about twenty-five feet away.

"I don't understand," Gopal confessed.

"What is it that you don't understand?"

"The temple we came out of is the same temple we went into on Bhu. How can the same place exist on two whorls?"

"I suspected the possibility when we first found the temple near the stream," Vyasa explained. "Our being here confirms my suspicions."

Vyasa explained how, ages ago, the devas had constructed special temples called dvars. With the proper mantras, a traveler could pass through a dvar into the whorl and planet of their choice. This was during a time before the Wars, before Bila-svarga was sealed. After Bila-svarga was closed off, it was believed that the devas destroyed all of the dvar temples, but they obviously hadn't.

Off in the distance, Vyasa saw two dim yellow lights dancing above the ever-present mist. "Nagaratna."

"What?" Gopal wasn't sure if Vyasa was talking about the same thing he was watching.

"Jeweled serpents. The lights you see. Many life forms that have evolved here have their own light. The lights you see are the jewels on the hoods of serpents."

"Real jewels?"

"As real as the venom of the snake that carries it."

Continuing to glance back at the jewels that danced, Gopal didn't immediately see what Vyasa noticed next. Two coal-black bulls were hitched to a coach. Their beacon eyes scanned the ground through the haze, catching the attention of the mystic. A fire from within the mist cast its glow on the animals, who stamped at the ground with cloven hooves. White smoke gushed from their nostrils. Two horns, over three feet in length, extended straight up from each of their heads. To these, a rope, or something that was supposed to be a rein, was attached.

One animal, smelling the strangers, turned. Its eye-shine crossed their path. Gopal rubbed the glare from his face and stopped. The faces of the bulls weren't the faces of animals, but of men, and looked like large pink masks stretched to fit the bodies of the creatures they had become.

Gopal said nothing, but stood, open-mouthed and sick. Was this how his wishes to see the whorl were to be fulfilled? If he had known, he never would have left Goloka.

The mystic, without fear, shined his own light on the beasts. "Trishna," Vyasa whispered as light swept across the two animals, then to the coach, and then to the glow around the fire that burned within the mist.

The shadows of four figures danced on the side of the coach. The flames flickered and threw sparks to the sound of a shenai that one of the hooded figures was playing.

"Remember," advised the mystic, "they will not know we are not from this whorl. Most Asuras are not very bright. Follow my directions. Do not eat or drink anything. It will reveal your real form." Vyasa dimmed the light of his staff until it was no more.

Outside the reach of the fire's glow, they heard the clashing of goblets and the specter's song. They still weren't close enough to see the faces of the merrymakers.

> "To one who has climbed the mighty steeps,
> Thus blazing a trail for many to follow,
> The gatherer of souls, and heads to take,
> Bhutanatha, we worship with offerings.
> Off with you, spirits! Rampage in hell!
> For him the gods have prepared this place.
> Grant us a realm where we might live,
> Where days and nights still rotate.
> For Bhutanatha, press the Soma,
> To Bhutanatha, offer sacrifice."

They sang, swaying to the music, spilling their drinks, only stopping long enough to refill their cups.

"It seems they know about the war on Bhu," whispered Vyasa, still out of sight of the toasters of the Lord of the Narakatala. "They mentioned the taking of heads. What has me worried is that they are singing of the rotating of day and night. There is no daylight here . . . but there is on Bhu."

"What—"

"Wait," urged Vyasa.

The shadows sang again.

"Present to Bhutanatha an offering rich in grume;
Come forward and take your place.
May he conduct us to the light,
So that in its midst we may live forever!
The offering steeped most richly in blood
Present now to the Royal of Royals.
We offer ourselves to the seer of old,
To the Master who will show us the way.
FForFor Bhutanatha, press the Soma,
To Bhutanatha, offer sacrifice."

The toasters screamed this time, crashing their cups together, spilling the Soma on themselves and the ground as they broke into what could only be described as ghoulish laughter.

Gopal, standing to get a better look, leaned forward, holding a thin branch he thought would support his weight. The dead branch snapped, and he tumbled into the edge of the firelight.

The revellers turned to the disruption, reaching for their weapons, each squinting through the glow into the shadows around them.

Vyasa stepped into the light, helping Gopal out of the wet mist. "Greetings!" called the mystic.

The hooded figures raised their weapons.

"Do not be alarmed! We were enchanted by your song and saw best not to disturb your toast. There is no reason to fear us."

He's telling them not to be alarmed? thought Gopal. They don't need to fear us?

One creature, trying to steady himself, stepped forward to get a better look. Yellow lights glowed at the places that should be eyes. The glow of the sockets highlighted a pale-gray, peeled, blistered, and rotted face.

"It's just an old one and a little one," the reveller laughed, turning and falling back to his place by the fire.

"Welcome strangers," yelled another from the mist.

Emerging from the blue haze, he tossed the hood from his head. His face was as pale and raw as the first, like something once buried. The others removed their hoods, each revealing the same hideous features in different proportions.

"Join us," the one closest invited. "A toast to our master!" he rasped, joining cups with another. The two hands crashed together. One finger broke off and fell into the other's cup.

"Look what you did to my drink." The creature removed the finger from the cup and tossed it into the fire. It wiggled for a second, sizzled, toasted black, and popped into flame, consumed by the larger fire. The one who had lost the digit laughed uncontrollably at the sight. The rest joined in with wild howling.

"They look dead," whispered Gopal, hesitating to accept the gracious offer to join them.

"As we understand death, they are," said Vyasa, taking him by the arm and moving closer. "We enjoyed your song," the mystic praised, taking a seat near the fire. He tugged on Gopal to sit; the boy was gawking at their hosts.

"He will free us from Bila-svarga," creaked one, to the approval of the others, who crashed cups.

Another turned from his drink to the mystic. "Bhutanatha has promised to take all who will follow to the upper planets."

"Out of this hole," laughed another. "Into the light!"

"To take new, young bodies of clean, warm flesh."

"To touch young bodies of clean, warm flesh," another howled. His red tongue wiped across his pale upper lip. His crusted gray hand, its flesh peeling from the fingers like dried paper, probed under a torn and crusted garment, feeling the equally raw flesh of one of the others.

"To taste young bodies of clean, warm flesh," yelled another. Two of them rolled in the mist, laughing and giggling like children. Joining goblets, they drank another toast.

One moved closer to Gopal. "I am called Mustika," he

slurred. The skin on his face was torn and dangling. When he shook his head from side to side, it looked as if his head was loosely fastened to his neck. He took another sip from his goblet. The liquid spilled from the sides of his lips and down over his neck and chest.

The sight was too much for Gopal.

"What are you staring at?" Mustika growled. Then, looking into his cup, he saw the thing that had gained Gopal's attention. Floating in the Soma brew was his nose, a green, blistered, fleshy chunk of Mustika's face. "Hum-mmm," mouthed the creature at the sight. Mustika scooped his flesh from within the cup and held it out to the others, laughing.

Gopal stared at the gaping hole in the middle of Musti-ka's face.

"Better watch it," yelled another, called Mura, from across the fire. "Next time you'll blow your whole head off!"

The creatures thought it was the funniest thing they had ever seen. Mustika threw the nose across the fire, hitting the one who had made the joke.

Laughing, Mura grabbed the nose and placed the flesh over his own nose, sending all except Gopal and Vyasa into hysterical laughter. Mura tossed the nose into the fire. It too twitched, sizzled, toasted black and exploded, and, being larger than a finger, tossed sparks on everyone. This time applause joined the laughter.

Gopal wasn't laughing.

"I know what you need," Mustika offered, falling on his side. "Have some of our Soma." Mustika handed the same saliva-covered cup in which the nose had floated to Gopal, who pushed it to the side, spilling it on Mustika's lap and on the ground. "Now look what you've done!" Mustika wept, sniffing, or trying to, since he had no nose. He was like a child that had broken his favorite toy. "Kubja," he whined to the short, fat member of the party. "Get the barrel and bring more for our clumsy guest.

Rolling to his side for balance, Kubja grabbed the wheel of the coach for support. Like an elephant from a mud bath, he pulled himself up and out of the mist. The coach rocked from side to side from the weight. The bulls snorted in confusion and scanned the dark sky with their eyes.

"We would be happy to join you in your toast," said Vyasa, "on another occasion. We are fasting from food and drink."

Mustika ignored the mystic. Kubja handed his friend another cup which was passed to Gopal. "This is Baka," Mustika said, gesturing to his right. "And that one," he said, pointing across the circle, "is Mura, the funny one."

Mura pretended to remove his own nose. Gopal thought the thing was smiling, but it was hard to tell since Mura's upper lip flopped over his mouth.

"And I am Vyasa," the mystic added, hoping to divert Mustika's attention from the boy. Gopal had placed the drink on the ground.

"Are you on your way to the Mahayagna?" asked Mura, casually peeling a strip of gray, raw flesh from his arm and tossing it into the fire, just to hear the sizzle.

"The great sacrifice?" Vyasa responded, recognizing the word and ignoring the repulsive display. "Yes! That is why we are fasting, in preparation for the Mahayagna."

Gopal couldn't help stare at the creatures sitting around the fire. This had to be dream—a bad dream. Was this what he had waited a lifetime to see? What he wouldn't give to be back in Goloka, in a time before the naga. Then he remembered . . . his sister was somewhere in this horrible place. He felt sick.

Mustika reached over, and, taking the cup from the ground, he handed it to Gopal. "I don't think Soma breaks a fast. Do you, Kubja?"

Kubja, swaying like a bull elephant, slowly walked behind the boy.

Gopal looked at Vyasa, hoping to get some help. He could feel Kubja behind him.

"I think you are right!" Kubja huffed. Gopal looked over his left shoulder at the mass of rotting flesh called Kubja.

"Drink up!" Kubja slurped through dripping lips that twisted and hung from his face. "You don't want to insult us. Do you?" He spit, and one of his lips fell to the ground, disappearing into the mist in front of Gopal.

"Throw it into the fire," said Mustika.

"Yes, throw it in," yelled Mura. "Make it sizzle."

Gopal looked at Vyasa.

Vyasa nodded.

Gopal cringed at the thought of touching the foul flap of skin, but he searched and found it. Quickly, without looking, he tossed it into the flames, where it sizzled to everyone's delight, popped, and disappeared.

Mustika, not diverted by the game, grabbed another goblet, and, taking the boy by the hair, pulled his head back. Kubja, still standing behind, placed a knife to Gopal's throat.

"Now drink this!" Mustika demanded, attempting to pour the drink through Gopal's tightly sealed lips. "Or I will have Kubja cut off your pretty little head, and we will pour it down your hollowed neck," he threatened through gritted, black teeth.

Vyasa pointed his tridunda at Kubja and chanted. "Maha shakti!"

Gopal recognized the sound as the vibration rippled through the air to Kubja, severing the thing's head.

Before Mustika could react, Kubja's head tumbled into the mist. The massive, headless body wobbled this way and that. Gopal thought he would be crushed, but it fell backward, shaking the ground.

Vyasa, wielding his staff, next stuck the drunken Mustika, right in the face, above the hole where his nose had been. Mustika's face split wide from the force of the mystic's blow. The creature howled, and the pitch of his shriek made Gopal's teeth hurt. A foul liquid oozed from Mustika's mouth, replacing the scream. The gash widened on the front of his head, and he fell over and vanished into the blue haze.

Gopal, finding himself covered in the obnoxious substance, hesitated. "Fight!" called Vyasa. Gopal grabbed his dagger and leaped across the fire onto the unsuspecting Mura, throwing him over backward.

Unable to see past his elbow, Gopal knew he had the creature by the neck. Without hesitation, he plunged the dagger into the blue haze, finding Mura's throat. When he removed the blade, the same liquid erupted from the wound, out of the mist, onto Gopal's hands. Repulsed, he dropped the now sticky dagger and fell back.

From out of the ground cloud came Mura, clutching the wound in his neck with one hand. He stood to his feet and stumbled toward Gopal.

Frantic at having dropped his dagger, Gopal searched the wet, soft surface under the haze, desperately trying to recover his weapon. He couldn't find it and stood, defenseless, in front of the fire.

Mura's other skinless hand, with bony fingers outstretched, reached for him. Gopal rolled out of the way, and Mura fell into the flames. The creature sizzled, twitched, toasted black, and screamed an ear-piercing scream before exploding into flying gray flesh.

Meanwhile the mystic was busy repelling the blows of Baka's axe. Vyasa, still using the tridunda, knocked the axe from Baka's hands. After a blow to the belly and another to the back of the head, Baka tumbled forward and fell lifeless to the ground.

"Are you all right?" Vyasa asked, standing over the body.

"I am!" Gopal answered, looking with distaste at the substance still covering him.

Vyasa looked over his staff. He looked over Gopal. "You will need to clean yourself quickly. That is likely to be poison."

Gopal held out his hands, his fingers spread wide. He felt even worse now.

"See if there is anything in the wagon you can change into. Wait!" Vyasa bent to pick up something from the mist. It was Gopal's dagger. "Here," said the mystic. "You don't want to lose this."

Gopal found robes similar to the ones worn by their now dead hosts and some scented oils, used in certain rituals. After wiping himself clean with his chotta and covering his body with some oil, he put on a long, gray robe. He tossed the soiled chotta into the fire.

"By the manus!" yelled Vyasa, waving his hand through the air in front of his face. "What did you put on?"

Gopal raised his arm to his nose. "It isn't so bad. It was all I could find."

Vyasa was done teasing. "We are not too late to save your sister. If they were going to the sacrifice, then she is still alive! We will use this wagon to continue our journey."

"But where do we go from here?"

"To Alakapuri, the city of Bhutanatha. It is there we will find your sister."

"You've been here before?"

Vyasa gave no answer.

"What about Sudama and Nimai?"

"They will find us," Vyasa replied. "Sudama knows of Alakapuri. Put the Soma back in the carriage; it is highly prized here. I will check the trishnas."

The carriage bumped and creaked as they moved slowly down the road. Dark woods lined their path. Vyasa recited the word for lamp, and again his tridunda lit the way.

"The sun never shines here?"

"Never," replied the mystic. "Surya would never permit his rays to light the Whorl of the Asuras. Narakatala is the darkest of the lower planets."

Gopal thought of Citty. How frightened she must be in this place! "I will kill all of them if they harmed my sister." His upper lip rose and stiffened.

"I can understand how you feel," Vyasa consoled, "but if we are to complete the vidhi, you must control your temper. It is to Maya's advantage to make you feel anger." Vyasa, while keeping control of the reins, turned to the boy. "You will become a creature without will, a spiritless shell." He pulled on the reins to keep the animals straight. "Like these poor beasts, every action controlled by a master."

Gopal understood the example. "How can I control my anger?" he asked.

"By controlling your mind," the mystic answered, pulling back on the reins and stopping. "Take the reins." Gopal followed his direction and soon had the wagon moving again. "We are like this coach," the mystic continued, "pulled by our senses instead of beasts. These reins are like the mind. The mind is for controlling the senses, and the mind should be controlled by your intelligence." He smiled, shaking the reins in Gopal's hands and causing the trishnas to quicken their pace. A rut in the road bounced the right side of the wagon, throwing Gopal into the air and causing him to lose his hold on the reins. Vyasa laughed and once more took control of the coach.

The forest grew even more dense on both sides. The trees were taller and arched over the road, turning it even darker. Vyasa held his tridunda higher, chanting "Jyotis." The tip of the staff began to glow brighter than before, and the beam of light continued projecting onto the road ahead.

Where the light hit the road, they could see the ever present mist, hugging the ground. So thick was the slithering fog that the path the wagon wheels cut quickly sealed, leaving no trace of their presence on the dark highway.

Suddenly, before them stood a barricade. As the sound of the wagon came within range, the lanky, almost fleshless figure of a man stepped onto the road. He couldn't have been more than four feet high. Dented, tarnished armor covered the pale-white skin that draped over a small skeletal frame. Long, silky white hair dangled, lifeless, from under a dull and dented helmet. A small human skull swung on a chain from the tip of his spear.

Vyasa dimmed the light. The soldier approached.

Piercing red eyes, embedded in a milk-white, bare-boned face, threw narrow beams of light. The soldier's eyeshine was warm on Gopal's skin.

"Be calm," Vyasa reminded. "Remember, they do not know who we are. Follow my lead."

The soldier moved to the center of the road to block their passage, the spear held across his body.

Vyasa pulled back on the reins, stopping the carriage.

Another soldier, not seen by either Gopal or Vyasa, approached from the side. "Who are you?" he asked. "What is your business?"

"I am Yatudhana," answered Vyasa, "and we are here for the sacrifice. This is my apprentice."

"A worker of magic?" questioned the soldier. "Let us see your skill!"

Vyasa held out his right hand, making a fist. He passed his left hand over his right, chanting "Hiranya!" When he turned his hand over and opened it, there appeared a palm-size, golden coin. "Here! This is for you!" He threw it up in the air.

The soldier stretched out a nearly skeletal hand and caught the coin. He looked at it, tossed it up once and caught it. "Ha!" He laughed with a pointy-tooth grin. "Don't you know what kind of magic amuses us?"

Vyasa turned to Gopal. "Get the barrel from the back."

Gopal jumped from his seat and climbed in through the back of the coach.

Getting suspicious, the soldier at the side walked to the rear of the cart, pushing the curtain aside with the tip of his spear.

On the inside, Gopal saw the tip of the spear coming past the curtain. A tiny skull, dangling from the tip of the weapon, looked at him. "Here it is," Gopal said, pushing a small barrel out the back and into the arms of the curious soldier.

The soldier fumbled, trying to catch the barrel and keep hold of his weapon at the same time.

"I think I might even have some extra cups," Gopal added. "Let me see." He searched through the bundles of clothing, all the time trying to remain calm. "Here they are!" Wiping the goblets clean on his sleeve, he handed one to the soldier.

"Well, what do we have here?" he asked, leaning his spear on the coach and propping the barrel on the step of the door. Removing the cork stopper from the barrel, the soldier poured some thick red liquid into the cup and sniffed. His amber eyes opened wide and glowed even brighter. A fiendish grin stretched across his face. He sipped . . . then gulped the contents of the cup. "Soma!"

"Soma?" yelled his companion, rushing to join him. "Let me see what you have there!" Pushing his friend to the side, he grabbed the other cup from Gopal's hand. Filling it with the nectar, he took a drink. After licking his white lips, he shouted to Vyasa. "You are good, magician!" Taking the barrel from the step, they set it down on the road and again sipped from their cups. "You may pass!" one yelled, as the warmth of the drink filled his cold body. The other lifted the barricade with one hand, while holding a cup in his other.

Gopal stepped backward, into the rear of the carriage. Vyasa took hold of the reins and ordered the bulls forward, while the two guards fought over who would get the next drink.

The sound the animals' hooves made on the road suddenly changed. The wagon must have moved onto more solid ground, for it sounded like cobblestone underfoot. The hooves clopped on and the rusty springs of the coach echoed louder.

Gopal climbed through a window at the front of the coach and again sat with the mystic. "What were they?"

"Yaksas!" Vyasa replied.

"They were small for soldiers."

"They are not ordinary soldiers," Vyasa explained. "Yaksas live on mlecchah, the herb of frenzy. They fight at twice the speed of Middle Whorl soldiers. When their weapons are exhausted they use their teeth. Some have been known to fight after their heads were cut off, their bodies swinging weapons and their heads biting and hanging on to their opponents. There are thousands upon thousands of them at Bhutanatha's command."

"And the others?" Gopal needed to ask. "The ones we first met . . . the ones we killed?"

"Those vile creatures were Krodhavasa, a Rakshasa race from the lowest planets of Bila-svarga. Bhutanatha must be recruiting from all over Bila-svarga."

Gopal only looked ahead, his eyes never straying from the reach of the mystic's beacon.

Without warning, the forest thinned, opening to a flat, lifeless plain. There were no trees, no rocks of significant height, nothing but flat land and pale blue mist as far as they could see . . . except in the distance, where a glowing, walled city waited.

TEN

IT WAS THE CITY OF ALAKAPURI. The extent of the fortification disappeared to either side, into a shroud of more haze, making it impossible to know how far the walls extended. Vyasa kept the trishnas moving slowly forward, toward a massive iron gate.

Gopal remembered the mystic's words on Bhu. "How many gates are in this city?" he asked.

Vyasa looked at him. "Why would that be of interest to you?"

"You said that everything I needed to defeat Kali would be found within the City of Nine Gates."

The mystic smiled. "There are some things you must do alone."

"Can't you help?" Gopal pleaded.

"I just did," said Vyasa.

The mist, almost consciously, gave way from the walls like a curtain drawn to the sides of a stage, revealing the victims of Bhutanatha's wrath. Hanging from chains were the tattered, torn, and decaying corpses of headless soldiers.

Gopal shuddered. He would never get used to the sight of death. He moved the wagon to the end of a long line. Others, here for the Mahayagna, also waited to pass into the city.

There were many carts, some oddly shaped and harnessed to more trishnas, to people, and even to children. There were beings from races throughout the Third Whorl. Some stood as high as the axle of the wagon, while others towered above the roof of the coach. There were Rakshasas. There were beings in garments of gold, of cloth, and of skin. On some of these, human heads were still attached. There were beings covered in their own natural fur.

There were faces without eyes, faces with three eyes, faces without mouths, and faces with more mouths than could be counted on one hand. There were beings from the subterranean planets, with two, three, four and more, heads and arms. There were beings that were part animal, for some, the lower part, and for others, the upper part. There were even visitors from the obscure planets of the bird and serpent races.

It was a menagerie that surpassed even Gopal's wildest imaginings. This wasn't the way he thought it would be. It wasn't supposed to be like this.

Two Yaksa guards, just as small as the soldiers on the road, stood under the gated archway, eyeing all who passed. Their reputation as warriors must have been well known. No visitor, small or giant, challenged any requests they made. Peering into wagons, they eyed the would-be entrants and allowed visitors to pass.

Vyasa was next and moved the wagon under the archway. Afraid of arousing suspicion, Gopal stared blankly ahead. Beside him, he heard the words, "The road is yours. Heed the power of Bhutanatha."

"What was that about?" he asked the mystic.

"Before the wars," Vyasa said, "the manus had created twenty hells as a punishment for those who committed the greatest offenses. During the wars, before Bila-svarga was sealed,Bhutanatha captured some of these hells to use as tools for his revenge. Here he keeps the captured souls of those who fought the Asuras. It is a warning to all who oppose the Pisaca," Vyasa warned. "Before we can reach the temple, we must pass through the Gates of the Preta."

Gopal knew the word. It meant "the newly dead." He knew that his being here, and his failure to perform this vidhi, would find him a place on the walls of Alakapuri. He was afraid.

Vyasa kept the wagon moving behind the long line of visitors, who were also forced to witness Bhutanatha's displays. The wagon moved closer to the first gate, above which hung the word: Tamisra—a hell so dark that it was impossible for Gopal to see his hand pressed against his face.

Within the darkness, cries like those of weeping children echoed above and below him. The voices sounded too tired to continue, but did. They were forced to. The dark hid everything. Only Gopal's ears still worked. The weeping swelled with each breath of the tormented as if each gasp would be their last. It never was. Their weeping echoed madness.

Gopal was about to whisper to Vyasa, but a hand closed briefly over his mouth, silencing him. He hoped the hand belonged to the mystic. Gopal chanted silently to himself and held the naga's claw tight. The claw brought comfort, even if the thought of its capture didn't. "Be strong," Gopal heard from beside him. "Think of saving your sister."

The next gate read: Kalasutra.

Here suffered the captive souls imprisoned within walls of copper that burned blue-hot. Prisoners were threshed like grain by invisible hands, only to become whole again. They would be threshed again for eternity or the end of Bila-svarga, whichever came first.

Next came the hell of Samghataka—the pressing.

Within the confines of this existence Gopal beheld an uncountable mass of bodies—more than could be counted by a manu. Here, beings from throughout the Three Whorls, beings that had opposed the power of Bhutanatha, pressed together into one unimaginable volume of flesh. It was impossible to tell where one body ended and another began. The contortion of limbs and faces ran the color from Gopal's complexion. He was forced to turn away from the multitude of crying eyes.

Seeming without end, next came the hells of Asipattravana, the sword-leaved forest; the hell of Tapana, the burning; the screeches of Kakola, the ravens; the stench of Putimrittika, the stinking clay; Lohasanku, the iron-spikes; and Rikisha, the frying.

Every scream became Citty's. Every eye, every face was his sister's. Gopal had discovered his hell. . . . Now, he had to find a way out. Turning from the tortures, he cried silently, trying not to reveal his fear to Vyasa.

The mystic moved the wagon under the sign: Dipanadi. Gopal prayed to the gods that it would be the final gate, hoping that his request would be heeded without spite. A narrow bridge spanned a river the color of blood. Moving swiftly, its torrents of boiling fluid carried within it bones, flesh, and clumps of hair. From many caves, imprisoned souls were cast into this raging hell. To Gopal, each tortured soul was Citty.

At last, they entered Alakapuri. It was too dark to see sky, as was the nature of Bila-svarga. Gopal gratefully breathed the stale Narakatala air. For a moment, he sensed some relief.

Twelve-foot-high poles lined the streets of Alakapuri. Atop each, like lanterns decorating the way to a festival, hung heads, their eyes bulging their fate. Other poles that lined the streets, shorter in height, held lanterns. Inverted skulls, filled with serpents' gems, hung from chains like baskets. Each glowed like red-hot coals, producing dim hues and casting an eerie light. Poles lined both sides of the road and ran off into the distant maze of walls and strange, dark buildings.

The air was thick with the scent of the freshly dead, while life filled the streets—least as life was known on Narakatala. It was like the market at Goloka gone mad, a nightmare to be dreamed and awakened from. In booths were merchants selling Pisaca potions, charms, and amulets, though the busiest vendors were those selling Soma. Groups of hooded figures stood in the streets. Some sat near the edges, gambling. One shook the skull he held, rattling the contents which he then poured into the street, bringing screams of delight from some of the participants and cries of dismay from others.

Streets ran in all directions, without plan. Like Goloka's marketplace, the streets were crowded. Gopal thought of that day on the roof, when his sister had come looking for him. She had told him to get to the field for the sacrifice. Now he was here to find his sister, who was to *be* the sacrifice.

Between the darkness and the always present mist, it was impossible to see very far in any direction, and everywhere they looked were dead ends. The dim lights did little good, always leaving a gap of darkness that moved along as they did, never showing more, before or behind.

The sound of the wagons' wheels on the hardened road echoed through the crowded streets. More Rakshasas laughed at the sizzling coming from another of the coveted fires. trishnas, with various faces, stood tied to posts, while others, for sale or trade, and in a variety of animal forms, carried bundles, pulled wagons, and took abuse without response in this dark market.

Food, if that's what it was, burned over gems. The smell from the stoves turned Gopal's stomach.

A hooded figure held a small cage, within which clung creatures no bigger than fingers. Human in form, they sang a siren song when their seller struck the bars with his taloned fingers.

"Not today," Vyasa replied to the silent offer. The mystic stopped the coach. "Listen," he whispered. The creaking of the wheels faded. They heard the muted sounds of a crowd in the distance . . . and music. Vyasa directed the trishnas to go on. Their wagon continued under the ghostly lamps, between the grisly decorations, among the crowds thick with the smell of the living and the dead, until reaching a walled street.

Their wagon came to a place where they could see into a plaza filled with a multitude of representatives of the Asura races. There were Rakshasas; Yaksas; Sarabhas; Bhurundas, the animal races of Patala and Sutala; the Kapota, a bird race from the planet Atala; and the serpent races, for which there were no names, from the planet Rasatala. There were also the feared Pisacas, the race of priests and mystics of Narakatala. All the worshipers of the black arts had assembled in a moving mass of shapes, colors, and sizes, waving weapons, beating drums, and blowing conchshell horns.

"A celebration," said Vyasa.

"Not for us," Gopal replied.

"What you see before you," the mystic warned, "could signal the end of our whorl."

Before a magnificent golden temple, the multitude chanted the name of Bhutanatha. The spires surrounding the temple's base hummed a strange tune to the chanting. The vibration had a narcotic affect on the crowds. Pisaca priests, carrying jewel-studded staffs that emanated beacons of blue light, walked among their devotees. Hooded robes covered the priests' heads, hiding their faces, but still they had no trouble moving among the crowds. The mist didn't part for their passage but flowed up their robes and out through their sleeves, hugging the priests like children grabbing the legs of loving parents. Drifting among the assemblage, as if carried by the mist, the priests offered lotus petals—powerful Pisaca magic—for their devotees to feed on.

An altar, rich with golden trays, jeweled goblets, and silver knives, rose out of the center of the assemblage. Other priests were already there, preparing for the sacrifice.

"Where is Citty?" Gopal cried, seeing the unholy display and fearing the worst. "Where could they have taken her? We have to find her!" The scent of the lotus flowers began to make Gopal dizzy. The spell of the Pisaca magic went beyond the confines of the temple grounds.

Vyasa touched Gopal's forehead with two fingers. "We need to keep moving. This is no place for us." Gopal's head cleared at the mystic's touch. "We need to find a place where we can rest and plan." He looked about, searching. "There!" Vyasa pointed to a small side street. "That looks quiet."

The streets around the arena were strangely vacant. The buildings in this part of the city looked more like the kind built on Bhu. Vyasa drove the coach to an alley and stepped down to the street, at the other end of which a pier jutted into a mist-covered lake. "The pier on the water and the mist floating above it makes me think of my hermitage at the bathing ghat." Again, they heard the Pisaca music. "If I'm to continue my quest," Vyasa said, looking at Gopal who stood, motionless, in the road, "you must complete yours."

The ever present mist made it impossible to tell the size of the lake. A large vessel, moored at the dock, gave some hint that the body of water was anything but small.

The sound of marching soldiers, coming down the street toward them, made all questions about the lake fade.

"Get to the front of the wagon," Vyasa ordered Gopal. "Act as if you are tending to the trishnas." The mystic flipped the hood over Gopal's head. "I will stay at the back."

A formation of fifty Yaksa soldiers marched past. The soldiers, as white and ghostly as the others they had encountered, were dressed in full battle armor. When the garrison passed, the armor, hanging loosely over their skeletal frames, clanged in unison, bouncing with each step.

Each miniature warrior on the perimeter of the formation held a spear that rested on his right shoulder and pointed straight up. Each pair of red eyes stared lifelessly ahead, casting a hundred narrow beacons on the road.

Within the center of the garrison was a break in the formation. Two prisoners, in chains, their heads high above those of their guards, were being forced forward by the tips of the spears held by their captors. The captives were obviously not Yaksas. . . . They were Sudama and Nimai!

Both were bleeding from their faces. Sudama's arms were held out, extended, strapped to his own dunda, now lashed across his shoulders like the top of a cross. Nimai was bound in a similar fashion to a spear shaft.

Peering from the back of the wagon, Vyasa saw their hands were covered with blood. The mystic knew that the Pisaca used fingernails for their rituals. Since nails continue to grow, even after death, they were believed to be filled with life energy, an important ingredient in Pisaca magic and mantras.

Gopal stood on his toes, straining for a better look. He ran to Vyasa's side. "What will we do?"

"Follow them," answered the mystic.

Leaving the coach, Gopal walked behind the mystic, always keeping to the shadows, which was easy enough in Alakapuri. The Yaksas were of one mind and never noticed they were being followed.

Gopal was angry with the student mystic and Nimai for getting themselves caught. He was here to save his sister, but now he had to worry about Nimai as well. "Where are they taking them? What will they do to them?"

"Even I do not know everything," the mystic whispered. "Just stay close to me. We will follow them as long as we can, and when we know more, then we can decide what to do."

The Yaksas marched their captives along the walled street until it wound its way to the rear of the temple. The few travelers on the otherwise desolate road showed more

interest in getting out of the soldiers' way than in paying
attention to two figures ducking in and out of the shadows
behind the formation. Two guards, standing in front of a
large wooden door, came to attention when the soldiers
drew near.

Gopal and the mystic ducked into a darkened doorway.
For a moment, the mist at their feet parted, revealing the
road and the cause of the odd, hollow sound the wagon
wheels had been making. What Gopal had taken to be
cobblestone was not stone at all. Imbedded into the
ground were skulls of every size and shape, of men, wom-
en, and children, and some that he couldn't recognize.
How many were his neighbors? How much of the road
had been paved with the army of Drona? Was one his
sister?

For the first time, Gopal became angry at Kali. It was the
Asura's fault . . . all that had happened, all that was hap-
pening now. "What can you see?" he asked impatiently.
"What's going on?"

"A Yaksa is talking to the guards. They are pointing to
Sudama and Nimai."

"Can you see Nimai?"

"Nimai is injured. He is down on his knees and resting
against Sudama's legs."

A Yaksa soldier turned his spear to the blunt end and
beat Nimai about the shoulders and head, yelling for him
to get to his feet. Sudama, enduring the blows from another soldier's weapon, tried to help the boy stand. Vyasa's
silence frustrated Gopal. It was his own fault that Nimai
was here, Gopal thought. Why hadn't he listened to his
friend and stopped complaining? It would have been better to have died with his father; at least his pain would have
been short. "What's going on now?" he demanded, still
unable to see from behind the mystic.

"Nothing," Vyasa whispered, knowing there was little
they could do at the moment. "They are letting them pass
through the door." The door slammed shut as though on a

vault, making a loud, empty sound between them and their friends.

The darkness made Gopal feel closed in and helpless. He needed to take action. "I say we go in after them."

"We will," Vyasa assured the boy, sensing his impatience. The mystic knew he and Gopal needed rest before they attempted a rescue. They would need all their strength. "We will do it my way," the mystic instructed, "when the time is right."

Some of the soldiers marched off, leaving ten Yaksas and the two original guards. Vyasa looked at the door he and Gopal were leaning on. "Does this building look abandoned to you?"

Gopal needed to release his frustration somehow. "Let's find out," he replied, thrusting his shoulder against the door and crashing in. "Looks like it!"

The lantern from the street barely lit the room, empty except for some broken clay pots scattered around the dirt floor. They found no signs of any recent inhabitants. The windows on each side of the front door were boarded over from the inside and another door, leading out the back, was held closed by a small wooden crossbar.

Vyasa closed the front door behind them.

"I'm going to see where these stairs lead," said Gopal. Too nervous to stay still, he disappeared up the stairwell, dagger in hand, before Vyasa could stop him.

Vyasa pointed his staff at the door and chanted: "Kastha-ghata-yati." A dim white spark appeared on the end of his tridunda, spreading outward, engulfing the door. After a moment, the light disappeared. "That should hold it shut," Vyasa mumbled to himself.

There was a crash from above and the sound of something breaking. Gopal tumbled down the stairs, his dagger still in his hand, followed by two Rakshasas.

Vyasa had his back to the door and made no attempt to intervene . . . at least not yet.

One of the Rakshasas leaped onto the boy, and Gopal

thrust his dagger forward, impaling his attacker. The creature's cries split the room. The Asura's trident slipped from his dead hand, coming to rest at Gopal's feet. Gopal tried to remove his dagger from the Rakshasa's chest, but it was stuck in the breast armor of the Asura.

The second Rakshasa jumped from the stairs, waving a club above its head. Gopal ducked, wondering why the mystic wasn't helping. He avoided the first blow and frantically tried to free his own weapon. His eyes flashed to the trident at his feet . . . to Vyasa, who was standing strangely at ease by the door . . . and back to the trident.

Gopal thrust his boot against the dead soldier's chest, which was stuck tight to the hilt of the dagger. With one more tug, the dagger came loose, and Gopal raised it, prepared to strike. The Asura was gone.

The Rakshasa lay at Gopal's feet, a trident jutting from the upper portion of the warrior's chest. A final gurgle of life bubbled from his dark lips. Vyasa stood against the door, the last syllable of a mantra fading from his lips.

Gopal didn't stop. He plunged his dagger down, striking the neck of the dead Rakshasa. Turning to the other creature, he again raised his blade and, after two more fierce stabs, separated the warrior's head from its torso.

Vyasa rushed to the boy, catching his arm as he prepared to drive the dagger into the Asura again. The mystic's eyes said everything. "I thought you said it was empty," Vyasa said, trying to calm the boy.

Gopal was trying to control his panting. "I thought it was."

"What did you find?" The question jarred Gopal from his thoughts.

"What?"

"On the upper level. I mean . . . besides these two."

Gopal looked at the dead soldiers and came to his senses.

"What did you find?" Vyasa repeated.

"There's another window with a good view. I can see down the street in either direction. Is it secure down here?"

"Now it is," said Vyasa. "Let us start with those soldiers across the way. Show me the window."

Gopal led the way up the stairs.

* * * * *

Within the dark, twisting passages under the temple, the point of a spear pressed firmly into Sudama's back, piercing his skin and drawing blood, forcing him forward down the damp, stone corridor. Lanterns, filled with serpent jewels, were positioned so he could see only a short distance.

Sudama knew he was descending deeper into an underground passage, but his greater concern was for Nimai. Only the fact that they were going downward kept the boy from collapsing. Nimai needed rest, and Sudama needed Vyasa.

The air thinned. Sudama took deeper breaths. The change in atmosphere had no affect on the guards, whose pale, blood-drained expressions remained unchanged. The soldiers brought the forced march to a halt, and an iron cell door opened on their right. Sudama's broken dunda fell from his shoulders when a guard cut the bonds, freeing the student's stiff arms, which fell lifelessly and painfully to his sides. Cold, skeletal hands pushed him into a darkened cell.

The two prisoners tumbled down some steps and into a stone-walled room. The floor was damp and soft under the mist. A single lantern hung from the high ceiling. The glow of more fiery jewels gleamed from the eye sockets of the inverted skull, casting red beams around the room. The lantern swayed above their heads, disturbed by the intrusion.

Sudama, on his hands and knees, groped about on the ground. A figure moved in the shadows. Someone . . . or something, was trying to stay out of the light.

A young woman emerged from the shadows. She had a golden complexion and long, red hair that curled to her shoulders like flames from a golden hearth. Sudama couldn't remember ever seeing a creature more enchanting. He was helpless from exhaustion . . . and from her glance. She walked, half-floating, toward him. Sudama fell, half conscious.

The woman kneeled, taking Sudama in her arms, which, along with her hands, were elaborately tattooed. She looked at him and said, "I am Usha, wife of Visvavasu—the King of the Ghandharvas . . . " Her voice was like music, and Sudama, relaxing, passed out.

Seeing the wounds to be more grave on the boy, Usha moved over to Nimai, stroked his bloodied forehead, and chanted in a soft siren voice:

> "I bind your life here firmly.
> Do not go away.
> With song I sing for your release.
> Be not afraid.
> You will not die.
> Vayu, return his breath,
> Eyesight and strength.
> Surya, hold off Death by your rays."

Raising Nimai's head she softly chanted:

> "Vaca-vadami-te."

Nimai opened his eyes and with Usha's help, sat up, revived.

Sudama woke to find himself lying on a mound of soil, with Nimai sitting beside him. "Thank the manus," Sudama whispered, feeling responsible for their capture and Nimai's suffering.

"Thank her," said Nimai, pointing to his rescuer across the room.

Usha was a strange, yet enchanting creature, whose eyes pierced Sudama's heart, intruded on his mind, tested his will . . . tested his vows. She sat against the wall, appearing innocent and childlike, though in truth she was neither. Her hair was red like blood, her skin was molten gold, hot to look at, yet appearing soft to touch. Her eyes were emeralds. Her glowing glance could pierce armor. Soft, white down covered her body—at least what was not covered by her gown, which she pulled up over her shoulders as she stood, tall, sleek, and entrancing.

"Who are you? Where are we?" Sudama tried to break the spell.

"As I said, I am Usha, wife of Visvavasu, the King of the Ghandharvas. We are in the dungeons of Bhutanatha."

From the look in Sudama's eyes, Usha knew she would have to repeat herself. He didn't hear a word; he was too busy listening to how she said it, for her words rang like a song. He couldn't avoid listening to the entrancing melody she made when she spoke. It took all his strength to overcome the bewitching powers of this divine creature.

"I will spare you," she said and waved her hand in a half-circle motion before the brahmacari's staring eyes. She uttered, softly, "Visrj," releasing him from her spell. At the end of her final breath, as the last syllable of her utterance reached and caressed his ear, his head cleared. He was able to think again.

"Ghandharvas, the winged race from Svarga." Standing, as if awakened from a dream, Sudama again realized his captivity.

"But you have no wings," said Nimai, who knew about her race from all the time he'd spent with Gopal.

"No," she sang, for every sound she made was still like music.

"If you are not a Ghandharva," Nimai continued, "what are you?"

"I am Apsarasa," Usha replied, walking toward Sudama. "Our touch has a healing effect." She smiled, touching the brahmacari on the check.

It wasn't healing that Sudama felt. Apsarasas were a race

of female sirens whose fathers came from other races. Although once considered witches, they were actually very limited in power. They could seduce men with a word or touch, and even kill should they desire to do so, but little else. Usha's power, however limited, took its toll, for once touched by an Apsarasa, a bit of the mind always remained enslaved. For how long depended on the will of the victim.

Sudama was losing consciousness again. He could no longer think of his captivity, or Nimai, or the search for Citty, or even of Vyasa. His only thoughts were of Usha, only of this wondrous creature, who was just a touch away. That was her power. With it, she filled his consciousness, his being. He jerked away from her hand, stepped back, and fell to his knees, weak. "*Jai Om*," he chanted, as if the mantra would shield him from this sorceress.

The neophyte mystic amused Usha. "You are stronger willed than your friend." She smiled, glancing at Nimai. "Don't worry; I know my powers. I have learned how much the men of your race are able to take. If I wished, I would do more than heal your wounds."

Sudama and Nimai's fingertips were no longer red with blood. Although their nails had not grown back, the skin had healed.

"Our touch has been known to make the men of Bhu lose their minds. Of course, their last thoughts could not be rivaled by the women of Soma." She smiled again. "Don't worry, I need you to help me. After all, if you are here, you also must be Bhutanatha's enemies."

Nimai stood; his strength had returned. "Maybe we can help each other," he offered. "We came in search of a friend, a girl, but the Yaksas captured us."

"There have been many otherwhorl women brought down to the cells." Usha was not interested in talking about women. She was more interested in Sudama. "In fact, you are the first—" she glanced at Nimai "—men I have seen." She stepped closer to Sudama.

The brahmacari didn't trust her. She might be part of

their punishment. He circled to the other side of the cell.

Usha enjoyed toying with him. A brahmacari, especially one studying to be a mystic, was a challenge to her.

"Where were they taken?" asked Sudama. He needed to get his mind off this siren.

"Who?" Usha asked, confused, having been distracted by the game they were playing.

"The captured women."

Usha gave up the chase. Like a disgruntled child, she sat in the center of the floor, resting her elbows on her bare knees and her chin in her hands. "They are probably being prepared for the Mahayagna. Bhutanatha is readying his entire army to join with Kali in a joint conquest of Bhu."

"Even Bhutanatha's magic isn't powerful enough to transport so many from Bila-svarga," Sudama said, looking up the stairs at the cell door.

"It is now!" Usha answered. "They have the Chakra."

Sudama's eyes widened. He moved closer, sitting opposite Usha. The news she offered broke the spell, giving his mind something to focus on. He knew of the weapon of Paramatma. "The Sudarsana Disc?"

Even Nimai knew of the weapon. "Its powers are said to be endless."

"They are also very strong. The least of them can transfer Bhutanatha's armies to any planet in the mandala," said Usha.

"How could Bhutanatha come to possess such a weapon?"

Usha explained how the Apsarasas and Ghandharvas had been made keepers of the disc after the Whorl Wars. Her husband had been tricked into a meeting with Bhutanatha, whose Yaksas slaughtered the king's delegation. They took Usha hostage, demanding that the disc be turned over to Bhutanatha. After Bhutanatha had a chance to try the disc to see if it truly worked, Usha was to have been released, but remained instead in Bhutanatha's dungeon.

Usha rose to her feet, turning in anger. The heat of her

fury warmed the room, as well as Sudama and Nimai.

"What about your husband's own forces?" asked Sudama.

"He cannot risk an attack with the power of the Chakra in Bhutanatha's hands," she said. "If you can help me get the discus—" she moved toward the two males, her siren scent bewitching them, "—then he will be free to attack and deliver us!"

Sudama laughed. "All we need to do now is get out of this room." He walked to the bottom of the stairs, looking at the cell door again.

"There are others who came with us," said Nimai. "Perhaps Gopal and the mystic will come to our rescue."

* * * * *

Gopal and Vyasa crouched at the window. The streets were deserted, except for the soldiers and the two guards across the way. The assembly in the temple arena still chanted. The sacrifice was still being readied.

"Can't we do something?" said Gopal.

Vyasa counted the soldiers again. "There are too many for us to avoid attracting the attention of the entire army. We must wait a while longer."

That was the last thing Gopal wanted to hear. His thunderous expression would have offended the devas, the manus, and Vyasa.

The mystic knew Gopal was still a boy. He needed to calm the youth. "I must tell you now why Kali is seeking the destruction of the Chayya. You already know of the Whorl Wars." Vyasa hoped to divert Gopal's attention, at least until he could figure a way into the temple underground.

Gopal looked from the floor to the mystic. The child in him, that spark he thought had been stilled forever, was awakened. He wanted to hear. Something inside wanted to forget everything that had happened and return to a time of wonder and stories.

Vyasa told Gopal the history of the mandala: how during the reign of the Chaksusa manus, the greatest of the mystics, Mantradrumna, had used ancient mantras, since lost to time, to churn the Ocean of Milk and produce the Nectar of Immortality. He invited all the devas to come and partake of the nectar, but did not invite the Asuras.

When the Asuras heard of the nectar, they marched toward the ocean with raised weapons. Before anyone could drink, a fierce battle ensued on the beaches.

Mounted on animals of the water, land, and sky, including animals with deformed bodies, both armies faced each other and went forward. The ranks of soldiers were like two oceans converging.

For the battle, the most celebrated Asura commander, Virocana, ancestor of Kali, sat on a magic flying vehicle. It was at times invisible and was equipped with weapons for all types of combat. Seated in this vehicle, Virocana, surrounded by his commanders and generals, looked like the moon rising in the evening, illuminating all the directions.

Sitting on Airavata, the elephant who can go anywhere in the Three Whorls, was the commander of the devas, Lord Indra, looking like the sun rising. Surrounding Indra, the commanders of the deva forces sat on various types of vehicles, decorated with flags and weapons.

The various races of devas and Asuras clashed violently, the Maruts with the Nivatakavaca, the Vasus against the Kalakeya Asuras, the Visvedeva with the Pauloma, and the Rudras fought the Krodhavasa. All wanted victory. All wanted to possess the nectar. In their desire, they severed one another's heads.

The elephants, horses, chariots, charioteers, infantry, and various kinds of animal handlers, along with animal riders, were slashed to pieces. The arms, thighs, necks and legs of the soldiers from both sides were severed, and their flags, bows, armor and ornaments were torn apart.

Because of the impact on the sand from the feet of the

armies and animals, and the wheels of the chariots, particles of dust flew violently into the sky, making a cloud that covered the Three Whorls. Drops of blood followed the particles of dust. When the dust cloud could no longer float in the sky it fell over all the planets and all the kingdoms.

Severed heads of heroes, their eyes staring and their teeth still pressed against their lips in anger, were scattered. Headless trunks, with weapons still in their arms, could see with the eyes of their fallen heads and attacked the enemy soldiers.

Virocana attacked Airavata and the four horsemen guarding the giant elephant's legs. Before Virocana's arrows could reach Indra, the king of the devas countered them with arrows of his own. These bhalla arrows intercepted and destroyed all of Virocana's shafts.

Virocana could not restrain his anger. He took up another weapon, known as kanti, which blazed like a great firebrand. Indra cut that weapon to pieces while it was still in Virocana's hand. Virocana used a lance, a prasa, tomasa, rstis, and other weapons, all of which Indra immediately cut down.

Then Virocana resorted to Pisaca illusions. A giant mountain, generated by mantra, appeared above the heads of the deva armies. From the mountain fell blazing trees. Chips of stone, with sharp edges like picks, smashed the heads of the deva soldiers.

Scorpions, large snakes, and many other poisonous animals, as well as lions, tigers, boars, and elephants, rained upon the deva soldiers, crushing everything. Hundreds of male and female carnivorous demons, completely naked and carrying tridents, also appeared, crying, "Cut them to pieces! Pierce them!"

Fierce clouds, harassed by strong winds, appeared in the sky. Rumbling gravely with the sound of thunder, they showered live coals, and a devastating fire burned the soldiers of the devas.

When the devas could find no way to counteract the magical atmosphere created by the Asura, they meditated upon the mercy of the manus, who sent the deva Paramatma.

When Paramatma, holding various weapons in his eight hands, became visible to the devas, the illusions of the Pisaca were vanquished by the effulgence of the weapon known as the Sudarsana Chakra.

Virocana took his trident and whirled it at Paramatma, who caught the weapon and severed his enemy's head with it. Paramatma flew over the battlefield sprinkling the Nectar of Immortality over all the dead deva soldiers, returning them to life. The devas then beat back the very same Asuras who had defeated them before.

Seeing their defeat, the Asuras cried.

Paramatma, standing before the Asura army, said: "For your offenses, I cause you to be sent to the lowest regions of the mandala for eternity. To ensure such, by the Law of Karma, I will cause the brink of Bila-svarga to be sealed until time does not exist."

Vyasa's plan had worked. At least for a few minutes, Gopal had returned to the position of the wide-eyed child, listening to fantastic stories about fantastic creatures. Gopal felt refreshed, as if he had slept. It brought satisfaction to Vyasa to see Gopal at peace, if only for a moment. The mystic's plan also reaped a second reward. The streets echoed footsteps as the soldiers left. Only the two guards remained.

"Have anything in your bag of tricks?" Gopal half-laughed, knowing the difficulty of the task ahead.

"Not in my bag, but in my mind," Vyasa replied. "Whatever minds those two have are weak at best. I might be able to get them to do my bidding."

Holding the middle of his staff, Vyasa got to his feet. Pointing the crescent at the two Yaksas, he chanted:

"Your minds,
Your purposes,

> Your plans,
> I cause to bend.
> You that are devoted to other purposes,
> I cause to comply!"

Something appeared to be happening. One guard held his head, appearing faint. The other leaned on the wall as if to rest. It was working.

Vyasa continued:

> "With my mind do I seize your minds.
> Your thoughts follow my thoughts.
> I place your hearts in my control.
> Direct your way after my course."

The guards shook their heads, trying to break free from the commands of a new master.

> "I call upon the three planetary systems.
> I call upon the deva Sarasvati.
> I call upon both Indra and Agni."

Vyasa then took a deep breath. "May we succeed in this, O Sarasvati!" He turned and walked toward the stairs. "Let us go!"

I've trusted you this far, thought Gopal, and I trust you now! Gopal caught up with Vyasa as the mystic held the front door open.

"Now, follow behind. Don't say a word. I have never tried this on a Yaksa. We will get them to let us inside. Are you ready?"

Gopal grasped the claw of the naga and swallowed, his throat dry. He tightened his grip on the handle of his dagger.

Quietly, they moved from the shadows of their hiding place, across the skull-cap road, to the guards who were standing at attention.

Vyasa didn't need to say a word, just think what he wanted them to do. The Yaksas turned. One guard removed a key from his belt and opened the door. His hollow eyes stared straight ahead, lighting the keyhole with their beams. The guards stepped into the lantern-lit passageway, followed by Vyasa and Gopal. The second guard waited and slammed the door shut. The noise echoed through the dim and misty corridors.

"It's even in here," said Gopal, looking down at the blue mist.

"Gopal, get the key."

The boy looked at the little, white-skinned guard.

"Don't be afraid."

Gopal cautiously bent over the tiny soldier and removed the key the guard had rehung on his belt. Quickly, he returned to his place behind the mystic.

"No, you hold it," the mystic said as Gopal tried to hand him the key. "You'd better arm yourself," Vyasa advised as he mentally ordered the two guards forward, keeping enough distance between him and the Yaksas so the guards could act as an alarm.

The guards' loose armor echoed through the passageways that felt and looked like the belly of some giant serpent. Footsteps coming from the opposite direction echoed down the corridor.

"What are you two doing down here?" Gopal heard from ahead of them. It was another Yaksa, and, from the tone of his voice, an officer. This Yaksa was a little bigger than the two guards, but not much.

The Yaksa officer growled. "Who told you to leave your post?"

Vyasa sent the two guards forward. The animated shells of the spellbound soldiers stared straight ahead, paying no mind to their superior.

The Yaksa realized something was wrong and displayed his spear. Noticing movement in the shadows up the passageway, he stepped between the two bewitched guards.

"Who's there? Come out, now!" he ordered.

Vyasa stepped from the darkness.

The officer stepped back at the sight of the tall mystic. The Yaksa hurled his spear, catching Vyasa by surprise, hitting him in the right leg.

Falling to one knee, Vyasa raised his right hand. His left arm held Gopal back when the boy sprang forward to defend the mystic. Vyasa twirled his finger in the air as if he were drawing a circle in space. Unnoticed by the officer, who was distracted by Vyasa's strange behavior, the two puppetlike Yaksas turned, lowered their spears, and impaled the officer, pushing his jerking, howling body face-first against the wall.

At Vyasa's command, the guards each placed a foot on the officer's back for leverage, and yanked their weapons from his body, causing him to slump to the ground, blood oozing from the two wounds.

Vyasa tilted his head as a command to Gopal, who rushed forward with his dagger and kneeled by the lifeless form. After looking down the corridor to see that there were no others, he sliced hard, separating the officer's head from his body. He rolled the two pieces farther into the shadows.

"It looks clear," he said.

Vyasa pulled the spear from his thigh and quickly sprinkled a sandalwood and tagara leaf mixture on the wound to counter the poison.

It was only then that Gopal realized the seriousness of the wound. He remembered the dead villager at Radha-kunde. Gopal ran back to Vyasa, afraid to ask.

Vyasa smiled to cover the pain. "Don't worry, I will still be able to help you find your sister. The poison did not have enough time to do much damage." Using his tridunda as a crutch, Vyasa motioned for Gopal to follow. Even if the poison wouldn't kill him, a spear was still a damaging weapon, and Vyasa felt the bite of its point. He limped down the passageway, keeping the Yaksas a safe distance ahead. They came to a row of cell doors, where Vyasa commanded the guards to halt.

There, jutting from the mist, leaning against the wall, were pieces of Sudama's dunda.

"Can you have them find the right one?" Gopal asked, looking at the Yaksas.

The mystic mentally ordered the guards to enter the cell with Sudama and Nimai in it. Obeying their master's will, they approached the door. One undid the latch.

No sooner had the guards entered than two figures leaped from the shadows. Grabbing the spears from the unresisting soldiers, they plunged the weapons into the already lifeless Yaksas.

"That was easy," remarked Sudama.

"A little too easy," added Usha.

Sudama moved to the bottom of the cell stairs. "I think there are more coming," he said as he readied the spear. A figure appeared at the door.

"Well done," Vyasa congratulated him from the doorway. The mystic was leaning on his staff. "You didn't look capable of such a feat when I saw you before."

Sudama lowered his spear. "Thanks to her," he said, pointing to Usha, who was standing at his side. The student noticed the blood staining his master's leg and rushed to the stairs.

Vyasa held Sudama back with the raising of his hand. "Pay it no mind," the mystic whispered, in obvious pain. Vyasa was more concerned with what he found in the cell. "An Apsarasa," he said, taking note of the tattoos that covered her hands and arms, "and one who is a queen."

"May I introduce you to Usha," said Nimai, "wife of Visvavasu." The boy was obviously both impressed and bewitched. "She saved our lives."

"I am sure she did," remarked Vyasa. "I am familiar with their powers." Vyasa descended into the cell. Sudama tried to help him when he reached the bottom of the steps, but the mystic again waved his student away. "If Sudama has come to trust you, then I will also. Just stay away from the boys. They are foolish enough to be lulled by your beauty. Do not entertain the thought of practicing your witchcraft on them. Is that clear?"

"You have nothing to fear from me, old man." Usha smiled, stroking her long, fiery hair. "We are all in need of a similar prize right now. I suggest we work together to accomplish it."

Vyasa nodded, still not quite able to trust an Apsarasa. "Remember, I have the magic to deal with your kind."

Gopal, curious at the delay, entered the cell. "Is everything all right? I heard some noise. Sudama! Nimai! You're alive!" He quickly searched the shadows of the cell for some sign of his sister. "Citty?" Noticing the figure of a female, he ran down the stairs and approached her. Getting closer, he knew it wasn't Citty. His eyes looked into Usha's. His legs grew numb. The tingling sensation moved the entire length of his body. The dagger slipped from his hand. Losing his balance, he grabbed the dungeon wall. "Who . . . is . . . this?" His eyes scanned every inch of the beautiful creature.

Usha reached out, her finger a breath away from Gopal's cheek.

Vyasa lifted his tridunda, a task made difficult by his wound, and pointed it at her, making her back off.

"She is called Usha, and she is an Apsarasa!" the mystic warned, his eyes turning from the creature. "You stay clear of her. Her powers are too much for you to handle."

Usha gave a bewitching grin, accepting the unintended compliment.

"I warned you," he sternly remarked, glancing in her direction.

Usha looked away from Gopal, finally releasing him from her spell, but Vyasa still had to shake the boy to get his attention. "Do you hear me?"

"Oh," mumbled the youth, as if awakening from a dream. "Yes . . . I hear you. I don't know what came over me."

"Well I do! Keep your distance from her." Again, Vyasa found Gopal's dagger. "Hold on to this. I am sure you will still need it."

They exited the cell, leaving the bodies of the guards where they lay. Sudama still felt the Apsarasa's spell and fought to control his mind. His concern for his teacher helped him. He approached Gopal, asking about the wound, and Gopal explained how it had happened. Then Sudama approached Vyasa. "Bhutanatha has the Sudarsana Chakra. He plans to use its power to transport his armies to Bhu."

"What about my sister?" pleaded Gopal, not realizing the significance of the information. "We came to find my sister!"

Nimai, sharing his friend's concerns, answered. "From what Usha told us, she is one of many they are preparing to sacrifice—as a benediction to use the discus."

"I think I know where she is being held," Usha interrupted. Vyasa looked distrustingly at the Apsarasa as she spoke. "There is a passageway that leads under the temple courtyard, to the sacrificial arena. If she is not there now, she will be brought that way. We should be able to find her."

"And what is in it for you?" asked the mystic.

"My freedom," replied the Apsarasa, " . . . and the Chakra, to be returned to the keeping of my race."

"Is there any chance she can help?" Gopal asked the mystic.

Vyasa nodded, wincing from the pain of his wound. He had no choice and turned to Usha. "Show us the way."

ELEVEN

WITHIN THE TUNNELS, below the temple courtyard, they followed the Apsarasa deep into the underground of the temple, through more winding passageways, deep below the surface of Narakatala. Each turn took them farther into the labyrinth, down through even darker passages where the air thinned even more, causing them to slow their pace. Usha grew impatient at their weakness. Vyasa's wound caused him discomfort; only his will kept him going. Sudama worried about Vyasa; only his concern kept the Apsarasa's spell at bay. Gopal worried about finding his sister, and whether they would ever return to Bhu. Only Nimai's attentions were totally on the Apsarasa; he had no defense. Soon, the path they followed came to another, which crossed theirs. "I don't know where the right leads," said Usha in her hypnotic tone, "but I do know that the passage to the left will take us under the altar."

As they continued to follow the siren, Vyasa whispered to Sudama, "I can't help wondering if you made the right decision in trusting her. If only my own charms could invade the Apsarasa's mind and read her real thoughts."

Usha suddenly stopped, holding up her hand. Sudama stopped next, fearing an accidental touch.

"What is it?" asked Gopal, hearing the sound of clay drums.

"It is the raga of tablas," said Vyasa. The mystic knew the special beat of Pisaca drums.

"Come," Usha whispered, "this way." They ducked under a low arch and saw a light farther down the passage. It was too bright to be from a lantern. They also heard voices. "It's not coming from the arena overhead," whispered the enchantress.

"We know that," responded Sudama, "but what is it?"

"Gopal, take Sudama and go on ahead," ordered the mystic. "See what it is. We will wait here." Vyasa trusted Usha up to a point, but didn't want to test his good fortune. The siren remained unusually calm.

Gopal was even more anxious, now that they were close to finding Citty—or at least learning if she was alive. He took his dagger from under his robe as he and Sudama crept along the passage, ever so slowly, measuring their distance to the voices by the clarity of conversation they were able to overhear. The others warily crouched in the shadows . . . and waited.

The voices came from lower in the dungeon complex. There was an opening, like a balcony, where their passage overlooked a lower room. Stairs led down into a small chamber. They cautiously approached, taking positions overlooking the bright chamber where, at the far end of the room, four steps led to an elevated platform and a seat. Along the walls more of the same ghastly lamps, brighter than any others encountered so far, were suspended from metal hangers, shedding their light on twelve Yaksa guards in full battle armor. With spears and shields at the ready, they were stationed between each lamp, their thoughtless eyes always staring straight ahead.

Seven hooded Pisaca priests, their long robes draping the length of their slim, long-limbed bodies, stirred the mist.

A tall man, dressed in royal robes . . . a *human* man, stood with the priests. They were all milling about in the center of the room, apparently waiting for someone. "When will he be arriving?" asked the human. "Kali wants to know if the discus is safe and when your master will be joining him on Bhu."

A voice echoed from under one of the robes. "Bhutanatha has made all the preparations for invoking the power of the Chakra. Will Kali be able to complete his share of the bargain?"

The emissary from Bhu reached for a scabbard. "How dare you! If Maya even thought you spoke like that she would—"

A figure entered from a doorway that was hidden from view by the stone stairs. Four more soldiers—Rakshasas this time—followed. Two of them were holding the four-eyed hounds of Sarama at the end of chain leashes. The priests fell to the floor, prostrating themselves. The guards stationed along the walls snapped to attention. Kali's agent removed his hand from his weapon and bowed his head with respect, and maybe fear.

"The dogs," whispered Gopal.

"Stay still!" Sudama said. "Maybe we are too high for them to notice." With not so much as a blink, Gopal became like stone. The animals raised their heads. Eight narrow red beams scanned the walls and the stairs leading to the two spies. Suddenly cheers echoed in the room, and the hounds turned their attention back to the priests.

"Do you think it's this robe?" whispered Gopal, the skin on his face nearly cracking. "Is it covering the scent of our whorl?"

"I can believe it. Thank the manus anyway."

"Jai Bhutanatha!" echoed from the hall below. "Glories to Bhutanatha," chanted the priests, still stretched out on the floor and sliding themselves, like serpents, to the sides of the room, allowing their lord to pass. Kali's emissary bowed at the waist when Bhutanatha walked past.

The Lord of Narakatala took his seat on the platform as his four bodyguards took positions behind him. The dogs were placed to each side of him, and again they raised their heads, sniffing the air. Their snorts were strong enough to agitate the clouds of incense that hovered above the floor, parting the fragrant white smoke. Bhutanatha laid his hand on the head of the dog to his left, calming the beast. The lord's eyes, gleaming a strange yellow hue, scanned the places the animals had abandoned searching at his command. Gopal and Sudama ducked from view, hidden behind the stone wall of the balcony.

The priest closest to the platform got to his knees, still keeping his head down, avoiding the master's stare. He addressed his lord. "All glories to you, Bhutanatha, Master of the Pisaca, greatest of sorcerers, controller of ghosts, second to none. We have followed your commands and have completed all preparations for the Mahayagna."

There was a pause.

"Where is the Chakra?" asked Kali's emissary, shocking the priests, who dared not speak without permission.

A soft, raspy voice that chilled the air replied. "Bring it forward." Bhutanatha held his hand out, waiting.

A guard held his left hand out to another, who moved closer at hearing the question. "It is right here, my lord," he replied, taking the relic from the other guard's hand. No longer standing erect, he cowered to within reach of Bhutanatha, who took the disc. One dog snapped at the soldier's wrist. "Move away," Bhutanatha ordered, brushing the Rakshasa away with an angry motion. Bhutanatha's eyes glowed when he beheld the Chakra. Holding it in two hands, he rubbed it front and back. Its touch gave him strength. He placed it by his left side.

The beast closest to the discus moved to sniff the prize. The creature also renewed its strength as its snout pressed the sacred symbol, making its beacon eyes glow brighter, before fading back to their former dismal glow.

"Is Kali prepared to complete our bargain?" Bhutanatha challenged, slamming the disc on the arm of his throne.

"My lord is prepared to consummate the alliance," said the messenger, "as soon as you turn over the disc."

"That will be very soon. . . . We are ready for the first sacrifice," Bhutanatha answered, eyeing the emissary and making the man very nervous. The dark lord petted one of his dogs, and the animal's eyes glowed, striking Kali's messenger. Bhutanatha grinned. "We will go to the arena."

The messenger from Bhu relaxed, and Bhutanatha turned to the guards behind him. "Bring one of the Middle Whorl women," he said. Rising to his feet, he stepped from the platform. "Come, let us go." The priests scrambled for places behind their lord, followed by the guards and the emissary. With the disc in hand, Bhutanatha led the group of priests, Rakshasa bodyguards, and Yaksa soldiers through the door to the plaza above and the multitude of Asuras waiting for the blood offering.

Beyond the range of Gopal's hearing, Bhutanatha asked a priest, "Are they close yet?"

"Like the crown on your head," the priest replied. "We are ready. The trap is set. A krtya has been placed in the cell and will feast on the intruders when they come to rescue the girl."

Bhutanatha smiled at the thought of the sight. "Imagine those fools from Bhu, thinking they could come here without being noticed and take what is now mine." The entourage passed through the door into another chamber.

"Go back and tell them what we've found," Gopal said. "I'll follow the two guards going for the girl. They may lead me to Citty. You bring the others here. This is where I'll meet you. Hurry!" Sudama, excited by their discovery but fearful of the danger, ran cautiously along the shadows to take the others the news.

Two soldiers climbed the stairs to where Gopal was hiding. He made a sanctuary of the darkness, relieved when they turned to go in the other direction, avoiding a confrontation. Gopal followed until they came to where the tunnel widened. There was a cell at the far end with thick vertical bars, running floor to ceiling, about ten feet in height. The width of the cell measured some twenty feet. It was impossible to tell how deep it was, since the only light came from more lamps hanging from the low ceiling of the tunnel, and the lanterns' glow fell short of the back of the cage. In the shadows of the prison were figures, huddled together. Two Rakshasa soldiers stood guard at the cell door.

"They are ready," announced the guard sent by Bhutanatha. "I need one." The weeping that had begun upon seeing the soldiers turned to screams at his words. One guard removed a large key from his belt and, with his sword held out, entered the cell.

"Get a good one," laughed the other. "The first sacrifice is usually the bloodiest. We don't want to disappoint Bhutanatha."

The guard in the cell pried the captives apart with his arm. He looked them over like a butcher choosing a fat lamb. "Here! This one looks good." He laughed and grabbed one of the terrified victims by the wrist, throwing her out to the waiting Rakshasas. The girl's cries turned to terror as the fur-covered hands of the two soldiers dragged her, screaming, through a door and up a darkened staircase to the altar above.

It happened too fast, thought Gopal. He was unable to see if the girl had been his sister.

The guard emerged from within the cell, slamming the door behind him. "Go ahead," he said to the other Rakshasa still with him. "There is no need for both of us to watch this lot. Go up to the top. I will stay!" The guard made no reply. They had done this sort of thing often and it was his turn. So, taking advantage of their arrangement, he rushed up the stairs to the arena. The captives' weeping had not ceased. "Quiet!" The remaining guard called back over his shoulder, repulsed by the sight and sound of these creatures from the upper whorl. "Because of you, I have to miss the sacrifice!" He held his sword up. "I should slit your throats myself."

The girl he had chosen had been taken into the arena. Drums and shenai played faster at her entrance, reaching a feverish pitch when she was pulled, screaming, up the marble steps of the altar and turned over to the priests. As if on cue, the sound of conch-shell horns blared from the crowd, and the priests on the platform drew back their hoods. Their heads had never grown hair, and the skin was as white and wrinkled as skin could be that had never seen light in a thousand years. These were the priests of birthright—the Pisaca, the special beings that had incarnated in Bila-svarga to serve as the hands and eyes of Bhutanatha. Their special place in this dark whorl was sanctified by their being born without the senses of the other creatures of the Bhu-mandala: their heads were without ears; their faces without eyes, without a nose. All that took shape on their blank masks of wrinkled white skin was a toothless slit that served as a vocal point, their connection to the dark whorl, their link to the vibrations of Bila-svarga.

From this one crevice flowed the blue mist that pervaded Narakatala, the mist that was their essence, their link with Bhutanatha, their source of sight, sound, and touch, their connection to all the creatures that moved within the blue cloud that hugged the ground. It was Bhutanatha's warning system. It was how they knew of the visitors from Bhu, and how they knew to set a trap for their lord's amusement, if not for their own dark entertainment, the trap that Gopal was about to spring. These small matters had been put in place, and the priests had confidence in their skill, for failure would mean a fate much worse than mere death. For now, though, they turned gladly to their immediate, and what they thought to be the greater, task.

The first priest tossed the captive onto the sacrificial table. In a terrified daze, she lay there, bound hand and foot to the cold marble where another priest tore at her garments, leaving nothing more than shreds of silk hanging from her sides. Her skin shrank from the dark cold that embraced her when her bare skin touched the smooth marble surface. She struggled to keep her mouth closed when another priest pried her teeth apart with a silver knife. The blade sliced her mouth, tore her lips, setting her mouth aflame. She gagged, trying not to swallow when they poured a sweet, warm liquid into her mouth and throat. . . . She *prayed* not to swallow. Her tears mixed with the Pisaca drug slithering down her throat, and all too soon her kicking and struggling stopped, and a warm sensation ran down her arms and legs making her glow. The drug had paralyzed her limbs and tongue, silencing her cries to Asura ears and to Gopal, who had heard it all.

The thought that it might be Citty made him sick. He wanted to rush up to the arena. Even death seemed welcome, if it would end his torment. He waited and chanted to himself, listening instead to the words Vyasa had spoken about using his intelligence.

Now Bhutanatha appeared to the screaming crowds, holding the Chakra above his head for all to see. Even without light the disc glowed brightly, spilling its luster over this evil lord's hands and head, sending its rays deep into the darkness of the skies above. "With this disc, there is nowhere in the three planetary systems we cannot travel!" Bhutanatha proclaimed.

The roar of men and animal races swelled. "To Bhutanatha, let this blood be offered," they chanted. Conch-shell horns raised their hollow sea notes above the arena as drums beat and shenais shrieked.

"By his power we will conquer," Bhutanatha promised. Swords were beaten against shields; spears were raised to toast this Evil whose time had come. Bhutanatha turned to the priests. "Begin the offering!" Once again he took his seat, handing the disc to a bodyguard. "Return this to my quarters and stay with it until I return!" With his hand he motioned for Kali's representative to sit beside him, where a seat had already been prepared.

Placing the Chakra under his vest, the guard left the altar and stepped through the door that would have led down to the cells . . . and Gopal. The soldier, more interested in what was going on than in carrying out his duty, stayed on the other side of the door to watch through a small barred window. He would take care of the disc as ordered, after the sacrifice.

The priest designated to lead the offering began the prayers of the Pisaca.

> "Take your seat, O Bhutanatha,
> With the priests, with your devotees
> And with the eyes and ears of the Asura.
> To all assembled in this arena,
> I praise this offering as worthy."

The priest sprinkled a mixture of ash and ground bone on the head of the girl. Taking a dish filled with Soma, he sipped, ceremoniously offering it to the other priests. The brass dish caught the girl's reflection, freezing her soul as the priest poured a fine line of the remaining drink down the length of her body, continuing his prayer.

> "Put this sacrifice
> Under the protection of your two dogs,
> Each with four eyes,
> The guardians and keepers of the way."

Next, he removed a knife and cut a handful of hair from the girl's head, which he tossed into the sacrificial fire. The two dogs raised their heads, aroused by the scent of burning human hair. The priest lifted the blade, slowly followed his design on the girl's flesh, and chanted:

> "May the brood-nosed, dark-hued pair,
> The life stealers, messengers of death

Who run in men's wake,
Restore to us at this hour
The power that we may again see
The sun of the Middle Whorl."

As the knife pressed deep, releasing the girl's life airs, the maddened cries of all who witnessed the dark deed rang forth. The drummers, seated along the foundation of the altar, renewed their rhythmic beating to restore order to the unholy mass. Musicians played haunting melodies on their shenais. Priests chanted "Bhutanatha. Bhutanatha," the eight syllables resuming the narcotic affect, quieting the assemblage.

Gopal heard the cries of the assembly. He had to know if Citty was still in the cell, or if his journey had been in vain. Creeping next to the dark wall, he made his way to the jailer. The guard had moved to the bottom of the stairs to listen to the ceremony above, enabling Gopal to get within arm's reach. Leveling his dagger, he plunged the blade into the sentry's back, under the guard's armor, pushing harder than usual, holding tight until all struggling ceased. Then he let the body fall to the floor and searched the dead guard's uniform, finding the key. Opening the door, he called softly, "Citty!"

From among the sobbing of the huddled captives, within the shadows of the prison, came a frightened voice. "Yes . . . I am here."

As karma would have it, the bodyguard at the top of the stairs had become worried about not having followed Bhutanatha's orders and descended into the dungeon where he found the body of the guard. Curious, he removed his own sword from its scabbard and stepped into the light.

Gopal, still opening the cell door, heard something and looked over his shoulder. The Rakshasa was coming across the corridor with sword raised and teeth gritted. With his own dagger still in hand, Gopal turned in time to dodge the first blow. His only advantage was the fact that the Rakshasa moved so slowly. Gopal moved away from the cell door so as not to place his sister in any more danger and jumped from under another blow. Raising his foot, he pushed the guard to the opposite wall and followed the stumbling soldier.

Hitting the wall, the Rakshasa shook himself to consciousness just in time to meet a thrust from Gopal's dagger. The sound of steel hitting steel echoed up the corridors. Seeing that Citty was about to exit the cell, Gopal cried, "Get back!"

The bodyguard took the opportunity to lay a blood-drawing gash to Gopal's left shoulder. The boy fell back, grabbing the wound with his dagger hand. Bhutanatha's guard grabbed the sword of his dead comrade. With a weapon in each hand, the Rakshasa lunged.

Remembering his confrontation with the Rakshasa at Radhakunde, Gopal held his ground until the last second and stepped to his right, avoiding the two swords of his enemy. Swiftly, he plunged his dagger into the guard's belly, but instead of entering flesh, his dagger clanged against the metal Chakra tucked under the guard's vest. The discus dropped to the mist-shrouded floor, and the soldier bellowed at his good fortune, turning to attack Gopal's wounded side. First he struck with the sword in his right hand, then thrust with the sword in his left, alternating hands.

Gopal managed to dodge each blade but was forced to back down the passage toward the cell and the rest of the captive women. Keeping his wits, he noticed the serpent-gem lamps hanging from the ceiling. He waited until the Rakshasa positioned himself below a lantern, then, seizing the moment, he swiped at the chain holding the flames.

The container poured its burning gems over the head of the guard. Like dry brush, the Rakshasa's head and shoulders burst into flames. The creature thrashed its arms in a futile attempt to extinguish the fire. Bouncing from wall to wall down the tunnel, he groped his way past the wounded boy, toward the cell, and plunged through the open door into the midst of the huddled and terrified prisoners.

Gopal ran to catch up to the inflamed Rakshasa, who pulled the door closed in his frenzy, relocking it. The straw-covered floor ignited as Gopal tried desperately to enter the cell, but the heat forced him back. Frustrated, he slammed his dagger against the bars. The fire consumed everyone.

Again there was nothing he could do. The manus had played with him, letting him come to this place. For what? They let him think the mystic could help him, but it was all in vain. He couldn't save his father or mother; he failed to save his sister. "I hate you all," he shouted, not caring if the manus, or the Asuras, heard his complaint. "You aren't fair! You cheated me!"

Suddenly, weeping came from the shadows to Gopal's left. The sight of a figure, huddled in the dark, ignited his heart. "Citty?" He ran to his sister, but his opinion of the manus didn't change. "It's almost over. I'm here with Nimai and the mystic. We will all get out of this." He extended his hand to her reaching fingers, noticing the unusual whiteness of his sister's skin. She must have been enchanted by Pisaca magic. Her hand felt cold to his touch—more than cold—like death. He pulled her from the shadows. Look what she has been through, he thought. This was the result of the black arts.

Gopal returned his dagger to his belt. Even with the sting the Rakshasa's weapon had left in his shoulder, he lifted Citty and, grabbing a robe that lay on the ground, covered her. With his sister in his arms, he ran down the passageway, the flames from the cell lighting the way when he kicked something. A metal object slid before his foot. Crouching down, trying to balance his sister in his arms, he found it—the Sudarsana Chakra. He tucked it under his robe, next to the naga's claw, and continued in haste.

"Someone is coming," Vyasa warned. The mystic, Sudama, Nimai, and Usha scurried to the cover of the shadows but came out again when Gopal appeared.

"You found her!" yelled Nimai, the spell of the Apsarasa temporarily overcome by his bond with Gopal and Citty.

Everyone congratulated Gopal, gathering around Citty, who was still held closely in Gopal's arms. Sudama noticed Gopal's wound, and tried to get a closer look at the gash, as did Usha.

"I'm all right," said Gopal, who was more concerned with his sister. "We can take care of it later."

"I can help him," Usha sang.

A look from Vyasa changed her mind. Gopal's wound did concern the mystic, as did the poor condition of the boy's sister, but there were other, more pressing matters to attend to first.

"I think she's fainted," said Gopal.

*   *   *   *   *

Bhutanatha, sitting on his exalted platform, noticed first the glow and then the smoke coming from behind the door. His eyes cast their own heated rays on the back of the head of a priest. The blank-faced priest turned to his master's words. "You said you arranged everything. They were supposed to be dealt with . . . as amusement."

The priest made no reply but breathed in the mist. The pale haze crept up the front of his robes and into the hole that was his face. "They were to have the krtya with them. Something is wrong!"

Bhutanatha rose. "The only thing wrong is that I trusted you." With a twitch of his right hand, Bhutanatha set the two hounds to tearing the priest apart. After witnessing the execution, the Lord of Narakatala called his remaining bodyguards to attention. With the two dogs, they descended into the smoke-filled tunnel while the other priests continued the ceremony, each having moved up one step in rank.

"What about your agreement?" called the emissary, chasing after Bhutanatha.

* * * * *

The celebration was short-lived, for the sound of conch-shell horns meant their presence had been discovered. "Quickly, we must find our way out," said the mystic, glancing again at Citty's complexion. "There will be soldiers flooding these corridors."

"What about the Chakra?" Usha asked, her limited powers unable to detect the relic just feet from where she stood. "I found the girl for you. You were supposed to help me find the Chakra." No one answered, not even Gopal. Maybe he could get back at the manus for all they had done to him. He had the weapon and wasn't going to give it up.

Now Sudama got a better look at Citty. "Something is wrong with the girl," he said.

Vyasa knew they couldn't stay where they were any longer. "We must take care of Citty on the outside."

"The Chakra!" Usha insisted.

"We will take care of it," Vyasa assured her, "but not now."

"I know the way back!" announced Sudama. Gopal felt his belt for the dungeon keys, relieved that he hadn't lost them.

Vyasa looked at Usha. "What about you? Are you coming with us?"

"I don't have the disc!" Gopal remained silent. The growls and barks were coming down the tunnel.

"We will worry about that later," Vyasa advised. "Come with us." They ran, following closely behind Sudama. The pain in Gopal's arm grew under the burden of his sister's weight. In his relief at finding her, he refused to let anyone help carry her.

Vyasa was having trouble keeping up. "Go!" the mystic ordered.

Sudama slowed the pace and still found his way easily. Ahead stood the entrance to the dungeons. On their left was the crumpled corpse of the Yaksa officer. "Just a short way now," he assured them. The sound of the dogs was closer. "Quickly!" the brahmacari yelled. Gopal took out the keys, tossing them to Sudama. The student pressed the door open.

"We should head for the coach," said Gopal. "I hope it is still there" Nimai helped get Citty through the opening, and Gopal got his first good look at her. "Citty!" Her eyes glowed red and her skin . . . "Vyasa, come here! Something is wrong." Vyasa, now dragging his leg, approached the frightened boy. "Her skin, it looks almost gray now," Gopal cried, "and her eyes . . . What have they done to her?" Vyasa didn't answer; even he wasn't sure. "I won't leave her," Gopal shouted. "You know everything. Do something!"

"I am afraid that even I am still a student when it comes to matters of the Pisaca." The mystic thought a moment. "There is a class of healers—the Pandu—expert in the Art of Ayur. Sudama knows of them. They live near the city of Niyana Bhiram." He looked to his student. "You will need to get her there."

Sudama nodded. "What do you mean? Aren't you—?"

"Nobody is going to get back if we don't move, and I mean now," interrupted Usha. "I want the Chakra and I need you alive to help me." The dogs' barking echoed through the doorway. "They have our scent and will be on us soon."

Vyasa looked at the opened door and the mist pouring from within the dungeon. "Of course," he mumbled, "Why didn't I see it before?"

"See what?" Gopal became even more anxious. "See what?"

Sudama stepped closer. "We'd better hurry . . . "

"The mist. They can follow us in the mist. It is their eyes and ears. That is why things have been so easy for us."

"Easy?" shouted Gopal.

Vyasa explained. "Bhutanatha has known of our presence from the start." The sound of the dogs was closer now.

"Now is the time to use whatever you know," advised Usha. "You'd better do something fast."

Vyasa stood with his back to the door of the dungeon. Sudama stood next to his teacher so Vyasa could lean against him. The mystic held out his tridunda, directing the staff at the mist in the center of the road. The crescent on the tridunda burned red.

"Agni shall fly against our opponents,
Burning against their schemes and hostile plans.
Thy thunderbolt, O Indra,
Shall advance to deceive the enemies."

With those words a bolt flashed from the staff and flew round at speeds no one could fathom. In a circle, it moved above the mist as Vyasa continued.

"Confuse the enemy with the impact of fire,
Let Vayu scatter them to either side."

The circling light lowered and now moved within the haze, clearing a space. "Quickly," Vyasa directed. With Sudama's help, he led them into the mystic circle. The barking stopped, replaced by the sound of confused yelping. "They will regain their senses shortly. We need to go before they alarm the garrison. Get Citty to the wagon. Sudama, do you remember the charm to endow a beast with swiftness?"

"Yes, Master."

"Good! I will ride in back with the girl until we get to the city's main gate. Then let me out. I think I can hold off our pursuers." Before Sudama could ask the meaning of the statement, Vyasa ordered. "Go!"

They moved down the street as quickly as possible, the ring of mystic fire hiding them from the senses of Bhutanatha. As Fortune would have it, the wagon, with the trishnas still harnessed, was waiting. Nimai climbed up front with Sudama, while the others helped get Citty inside. Sudama

picked up the reins, then recognized the type of beasts he
was to drive. "Trishnas?" He looked over at Nimai. "I
don't know if it will work on trishnas," said Sudama.

"Just do it!" Nimai said. "Vyasa knows better than
you."

Sudama chanted:

> "Swift as the wind, be thou O beasts,
> Fleet as the mind!"

With the final command, "Acva-palay," he whipped the
reins. At the completion of the last word, as the last sound
fell from his lips, Sudama's hands, clasping the reins,
glowed white. Nimai's gaze fixed on the light. The beam
emanating from Sudama's hands moved the length of the
reins to the horns on the trishnas' heads. Then the glow
filled the bodies of the beasts, who gave a snort, bowed
their massive heads, dug their front hooves into the
ground, and, like lightning bolts, darted down the street
with the mystic's ring staying in its place around the coach.
The trishnas' sudden movement almost pulled the reins
from Sudama's fingers. "I have no control!" he cried as
Nimai gasped.

Before them lay a body of water. They were going the
wrong way! "Turn around! This is not the way," said Vyasa,
looking through the front window of the coach. Sudama
found he could not slow the trishnas, so he tried to turn
them in the right direction. He managed to turn down a
street on his right, away from the lake.

There, up ahead," Vyasa said. "I recognize the wall. The
gateways should be to the left." Just as they made the left
turn, a garrison of Yaksas appeared behind them. "Remember," yelled Vyasa, unaware of Sudama's predicament
with the trishnas. "When you reach the gateway . . . "

"What?" Gopal looked down at his sister and then at
the mystic. "You can't leave us!"

"I must stop the soldiers, or no one gets back. Don't

worry, I will catch up with you. You have everything you need. Sudama will show you the way and help with the girl. Get to Niyana Bhiram." When the wagon passed under the entrance, Vyasa leaped from the back onto the skullcap road. The pain in his leg radiated when he hit the ground. Another figure landed beside him. It was Usha. "What are you doing?" With the staff as a crutch, Vyasa forced himself to his feet. The Yaksa guards at the gateway charged.

"I am not leaving without the Chakra." Usha dodged the first spear and grabbed the Yaksa who wielded it. She released her touch, and the Yaksa squirmed and died.

Vyasa was in no position to argue. He met the attack of the second guard with his tridunda, knocking the soldier off his feet. The garrison was coming down the street with spears held out and shields in place. Hanging from the walls of the city were the remains of the soldiers who had fallen to Bhutanatha. There was only one way out. Taking his staff firmly in his right hand, and putting his weight on his good leg, Vyasa pointed at the skeletons and recited the chant reserved for a treta-mystic—the mantra to animate the dead.

> "Come forth, I adjure you,
> Into the world of the living.
> I draw you toward the life of a hundred autumns.
> Releasing you from the bonds of death,
> I stretch forth your life thread."

The wind grew at Vyasa's feet. The dirt and mist swirled like a funnel around the mystic. The end of his robes twisted around his legs.

> "From Vayu I give you breath."

The wind moved to the wall, shaking the lifeless bodies like bamboo wind chimes.

"From Vivaswan, I give you sight."

A flash from his tridunda jumped from soldier to soldier, illuminating their frames.

"I strengthen your hearts.
The life airs blow upon you
As one blows on a fire just kindled."

Against the walls, the sound of bones clanged against metal as the skeleton soldiers stirred within their rusting armor and the mystic fell into a deep trance.

The dogs could again be heard. "Quickly," Usha warned, taking out her own dagger.

Without opening his eyes, Vyasa lifted his staff with both hands, his legs straining to keep him upright.

"I command you to emerge
From the Realm of the Dead.
I have saved you
For the powers that must be combatted.
Be free from your bonds. Live again!"

The headless soldiers stirred. Hands scraped the chains that bound them. The skeletons pushed against the stone wall with their bone feet, visible through their decaying boots and sandals. The chains that bound them snapped. First one, then another, then many of the animated soldiers fell to the ground like hail.

The Yaksa garrison had reached the gateway. Surprised by the mystic's powers, the soldiers came to an abrupt halt. Even the dogs were held back on chains by their handlers. Then a howl emanated from within the ranks, and the dogs were released, followed by the screaming soldiers. Like waves, the two forces met. The dogs singled out an animated soldier and attacked in a frenzy, tearing at the pieces of decaying flesh that hung from his arm.

The clanging of metal on metal, and the sounds of metal on bare bone, echoed as the battle raged. Yaksa spears lodged in the exposed ribs of Vyasa's animated dead as Vyasa's soldiers were lifted above the heads of Bhutanatha's soldiers, to be dropped to the ground where their brittle frames were crushed into powder. Swords were raised and blade met marrow as the Yaksas hacked and stabbed their way through the mystic's diversion.

The first Yaksa to get through the barrier attacked Usha with his spear. Vyasa, using his tridunda, knocked the weapon to the ground in time for Usha to sink her dagger into the Yaksa's stomach. The enemy fell dead.

"My army cannot hold them for long," Vyasa warned. Without heads and eyes to guide them, the mystic's army spun around blindly, swinging their weapons without guidance, hacking in a frenzy at anything within reach. Some blows met Yaksas, but most met each other. Swords and axes severed comrades' arms. Animated limbs swung their weapons on the ground, some finding Yaksa flesh, most spinning uselessly. The animated army was slowing the Yaksa advance, but not stopping it. The skeleton army was nearly defeated.

"Back into the city," yelled Vyasa when, from out of the dust, a four-eyed hound lunged at the mystic. Vyasa turned to Usha's warning just in time to repel the teeth of the beast with his staff. The dark creature caught the tridunda in its fangs, wrestling it from the already wounded mystic. Vyasa lost the contest for the staff. The hound bit and clawed, finally breaking it.

Usha offered to help, but Vyasa feared the siren's touch. Instead, he took a spear from the ground for a new crutch. Together, in the confusion, they found the way back through the gate and into Alakapuri as more soldiers ran past, rallying to their comrades' aid. Vyasa and Usha hid in a darkened alley as a garrison of soldiers marched past, led by Bhutanatha himself.

"They have someone with them," whispered Usha. "It

looks like another Middle Whorl girl."

"It's Citty," said the mystic.

"Then who is in the wagon?"

* * * * *

With the runaway wagon racing along the roads of Nara-katala, Sudama remembered the way back to the Rudra temple and did all he could to keep the wagon going in the right direction. That was all the control he had when, ahead of them in the road, he saw the two Yaksa guards holding shields and spears. Nimai was frightened, but Sudama had no choice . . . he couldn't stop the coach. He would have to go through.

As the wagon approached, the guards took their stance and prepared to throw their spears. The Yaksas held their ground as Sudama headed straight at them. The soldiers launched their spears. One went over the coach, and the other hit the seat between Sudama and Nimai. The trishnas broke through the wooden barrier. "Don't touch it," yelled Sudama. "Poison!" The out-of-control coach ran over the soldiers, who had been trampled under the hooves of the trishnas. A Yaksa head fastened itself with its teeth to the hitch of the wagon. Nimai froze at the sight, but Sudama couldn't let go of the reins.

Gopal saw it and called to Nimai. "Use the spear! Break it loose." Nimai didn't move. The head of the Yaksa was gnawing through the wooden hitch, and the wagon would crash if Nimai didn't act. "Please!" yelled Gopal. Then, after thinking for a moment, he took another approach, knowing Nimai's commitment to the law. "Nimai, as your simha, I command you to do it." Nimai turned. The thought frightened and sickened him, but he loosened the spear from the wood. "Don't touch the tip." Gopal warned. In disgust, hating what Gopal was making him do, Nimai pried the head loose. The head, screaming words that were foreign to Bhu, bounced under the coach and away from them. Nimai tossed the spear to the side of the road.

Gopal grew more anxious and looked out the window. "We should be there. I remember this terrain. Take your spell off." Sudama didn't acknowledge Gopal's request, but instead cast his eyes downward. Gopal thought the brahmacari couldn't hear him. "Slow this thing down! Citty is looking worse."

Nimai grew nervous. "I told you not to trust magic. I told you not to leave Goloka."

"I can't," mumbled Sudama under his breath, finally replying. The student tried to keep the racing bulls under control, afraid to turn his head or take his eyes from the winding road.

"What? What are you mumbling?" yelled Gopal from the window. "I can't hear you. Stop the coach!"

Sudama turned to the window. "I can't. I don't know how." Gopal wasn't sure he had heard correctly. He was afraid to believe what he thought Sudama had said. "It was the first time I used that charm, and I don't know how to end it."

Nimai's eyes raged. "I can't believe this! Damn you mystics and your mantras! The manus are punishing us!"

Gopal reached through the window, grabbing Sudama's shoulder. "Sudama! Try to remember," he begged, shaking the brahmacari. "Concentrate."

"It's coming up! There on the left, beyond those trees," yelled Nimai, turning his attention back to the road. "We are going to go past it!"

"Please, Sudama," Gopal pleaded. "Think quickly!"

"I can't remember what I don't know!"

"That does it," Nimai yelled. "We are going to die here." He prepared to leap from the coach.

Sudama, seeing Nimai stand, reached to catch the boy and yelled, "Stha!" the treta-mystic word for "stop." Immediately, the trishnas came to an abrupt halt, throwing Sudama and Nimai from the coach and onto the road. Inside, Gopal smashed headlong into the window frame.

Nimai got to his feet. "Stop? . . . Of all the ridiculous spells in the Three Whorls! Mystics will be the death of me."

Sudama, holding his head, came to the wagon from the other side of the road. Remembering the passengers, he ran and opened the back curtain. "We're fine," said Gopal, lifting Citty. With her in his arms, he climbed out.

"How is she?" Nimai asked.

"At least the ride didn't hurt her," Gopal answered, looking at Sudama. The brahmacari made no remark. Gopal, wanting to move on, urged, "Let's get back through the portal. Citty needs our attention now." Leaving the wagon where it stood, he took them through the thicket into a small clearing, with the protective ring still around them. "There, on the other side. See it?" He pointed to a marble structure rising from the mist. "Quickly, let's get there before we find we've been followed."

Reaching the mirror image of the Rudra temple, Sudama stepped forward. "This, I remember," he announced, and chanted the mantra of travel. "Yanti deva-vrata-devan."

With some skepticism, they repeated, "Yanti deva-vrata-devan."

The familiar quiver rose from Gopal's feet and traveled up through his legs. He and Nimai took a firm hold on Citty, and, walking up the steps, disappeared through the doorway. Sudama, keenly feeling the absence of his master, followed. Stepping through to the other side, Gopal placed Citty on the altar and, finding the body he had left behind, was soon sitting back down into himself. Moving the stiff limbs, he hesitated, and then stood to his feet. Sudama and Nimai were doing the same.

"Ah! This feels good. Nothing like warm flesh covering these bones," said Nimai, standing and stretching. "Vyasa was right."

Sudama was wiping Citty's forehead. "She is in some

kind of trance. Exposure to the air and food of Narakatala must have poisoned her. If we don't get help, she will be transformed into jiva-mrtyu—the living dead."

Gopal was confused. "Citty's body?"

"Since she was taken whole by the Pisaca," said Sudama, "her body is still one." Sudama sounded knowledgeable, and Gopal believed in the brahmacari.

Vyasa's body still slumbered against the wall of the altar. "Vyasa!" said Nimai. "I hope he has better luck with the mystic arts than we did."

Sudama came to the defense of his master and their art. "I have seen the things Vyasa can do. There is no greater mystic in the Three Whorls."

"Let's get my sister into what little sunlight is left," interrupted Gopal, more concerned about Citty. "The sun's rays are purifying. Maybe it will help slow the process and give us more time to get help." He started to lift Citty off the altar. "Nimai, give me a hand."

"I will care for the body of my master," said Sudama, who knew a mantra that would protect his teacher. Except for a few differently placed syllables, it was similar to the charm Vyasa had used to make the door appear in Radha-kunde and the path that took them up the cliff to the ashram. To all who would enter the crematorium, it would seem empty.

Outside in the late afternoon light, Nimai helped Gopal make Citty as comfortable as possible, then joined Sudama at a small fire he had created. "Why are you just sitting there?" asked Gopal, worried about Citty's condition and their safety. "Didn't you hear what Vyasa said for you to do? You are to take us to the city of Niyana Bhiram."

"We are safe for now," Sudama answered. "I sprinkled one of Vyasa's charms around the clearing. It will protect us until sunrise. The dark will be upon us soon, and we can not risk traveling at night if we are to carry your sister. Besides, who knows what has happened on Bhu since we left?"

"What about the dvar portal?" asked Gopal. "Shouldn't it be sealed?"

"Not until Vyasa has come through," warned Sudama, prepared to defend his master. "I have used a charm to repel the Pisaca . . . for a while at least."

Gopal was still concerned. He knew that Sudama was right about the dvar, and that they couldn't get very far before nightfall anyway. Maybe they would be safe for now. "I've never heard of Niyana Bhiram," said Gopal, thinking he had heard of all the cities. "Is it on Bhu?"

"Yes," Sudama explained. "The city is famous among mystics for magic and healing."

"Maybe you should go and live there," Nimai teased. "I'm sure you could learn a thing or two."

Sudama prepared to lash out at the boy's insinuation, but after catching Gopal's grin, he relaxed. "Maybe I could learn something." Then he remembered Gopal's wound. "Let me look at that."

Now that they were relatively safe, Gopal realized that his left arm and hand were sore. "My fingers are stiff. It's hard to move them."

Sudama examined the wound and ran his fingers down Gopal's arm to the hand. Gopal was curious. "What did happen on Narakatala?" Sudama's look questioned Gopal's meaning. "I mean," Gopal explained, "why did you lose control of the charm?"

"It's not having Vyasa's help," Sudama admitted. "Vyasa was always with me before. It was the first mantra I tried on my own." Sudama wanted to forget the experience. "The bleeding has slowed. Fortunately, the blade that hit you had no poison." Gopal nodded. "Rakshasas prefer to kill with their own power. They don't usually use magic." Sudama stood. "There should be some herbs around that I can use for a poultice. Healing charms, now that's something I have no trouble with." He left and collected the necessary ingredients. Gopal was made more comfortable, although Sudama told him that he might never regain the full use of his left hand.

When the night came, Gopal, knowing he wouldn't be able to sleep, volunteered to take the first watch. "I'll wake one of you to relieve me," he said as he took up position on the edge of the camp.

"Fine," came Nimai's sleepy reply from where he lay near the warm glow of the fire. Night closed around them like a blanket, and all but one welcomed the dark of Bhu.

TWELVE

AT THE SIGHT OF THE SUN rising over the sleepy encampment, surrounded by lush green forests and clear streams, it was difficult at first to remember the horrors they had seen, or the chaos that Bhu had undergone in such a short time. With the dew beginning to dry, and the dark giving way to dawn, Gopal thought about Narakatala and the condition of his sister.

Sudama finally rose from his place by the now cooled embers. Leaving Nimai sleeping, the brahmacari found his way to the stream for morning oblations and a much needed bath. He found Gopal sitting by the water and realized then that the boy hadn't asked anyone to take the watch. "Have you been up all night?" he asked, startling Gopal.

"I'm not tired. I have other things on my mind." Gopal sat on a rock overlooking the stream. The water cascaded into a clear, shallow pool near his feet. It was a relief to again smell the wild tulsi that grew in abundance in the shade of the palasa, pipal, and sami trees. The monkeys were a welcome sight, and even the lizards that scampered through the underbrush brought comfort in their familiarity.

Gopal was holding a shiny metal object. "I found it in the dungeons," he confessed.

Sudama couldn't believe his eyes. He held out his hand. "The Sudarsana Chakra!"

"This is the disc Usha was looking for, right?"

"The very one."

"I thought so."

The Chakra looked like it would be hot to touch, the way it gleamed in the rising sun, but it was, in fact, cool. It had sent a strange sensation through Gopal's arm when he held it, and had brought a feeling of comfort and security, but he couldn't help feel guilty at the same time.

Now Sudama held it. "Look here, this is the mandala," Sudama pointed. "Carved here . . . in the shape of a lotus."

Gopal wondered why Sudama hadn't questioned his having the object. Was it all right that he had kept it hidden from Usha? Gopal looked at the disc as if seeing it for the first time. Lost in his contemplation and guilt, he hadn't noticed any carvings.

"This shows the wheel of the cosmos. In the center . . . here." Sudama pointed with his raw fingertips. "This is the sacrifice, and this circle contains the five beings for sacrifice."

Gopal looked closely. "Yes, I see them: a lamb, a cow, a horse, a goat, and . . . a man?"

"There are sacrifices for all modes of consciousness," Sudama continued. "There are five sacrifices and five elements, the senses and so on." He handed the Chakra back to the boy and pointed. "These are the three whorls surrounding the portal to Vaikuntha."

Gopal knew of Vaikuntha—more than knew, he dreamed of it! "The nonmaterial universe of all-sentient beings, inaccessible to even the devas. The home of the manus," he recited. How often had he read of it?

"This whorl," Sudama continued, outlining a circle that ran round the center of the discus, "is Sveta-dvipa, the Whorl of the Devas."

Gopal didn't want to appear ignorant. After all, he was educated as a simha. "I know of the devas," he assured Sudama. "Their lifetimes calculate in thousands of thousands of years, but they aren't eternal." This fact made Gopal feel somewhat equal to the divas, though that thought was an offense. "Even they have to petition the manus to serve for another lifetime." He thought of his offenses against the manus and added, "Even devas commit offenses against the manus."

"For such offenses," Sudama continued, unaware of Gopal's meaning, "they can be forced to transmigrate to the lower whorls." Sudama returned his attention to the Chakra. "This is where we are," Sudama pointed.

"Bhu," said Gopal. "Our planet is named for the Second Whorl."

"Yes, and from here we can achieve perfection in the various arts and be reborn on other planets . . . even as devas."

Gopal felt guilty again. "Unless our offenses cause us to take a birth in the Lower Whorl." He recalled the hells of Alakapuri. "I've seen all I care to see of that place."

"Narakatala is in the Third Whorl," Sudama continued, "farthest from the center. It is all there on the Chakra." He pointed for Gopal to see. "It is all set in motion by the wheel of time, divided by the twelve moons."

Gopal followed most of what the brahmacari said. Padma had explained it all before, but Sudama's knowledge impressed him. "You're very familiar with these things."

"It surprises you?" Sudama asked.

"Well," Gopal hesitated. "You are only a student yourself."

"My father was a great simha," Sudama replied. "Before I entered brahmacari life, I was educated by the finest teachers . . . in preparation to rule in my father's place."

Gopal was surprised. For some reason, it never had occurred to him that Sudama had a past. He had met him
with Vyasa and . . .

"I left my family and renounced my inheritance to learn
the mystic arts. I traveled to lands where I was unknown,
without the benefit of name, to search for a teacher. I offered my services to Vyasa in return for training in the Art
of Ayur. I had wanted to be a healer." Sudama stopped for
a moment. Gopal's questions had obviously probed deeper
then he had intended. Sudama looked down now, away
from the boy. "I later learned that my father had been
killed, and my family sold into slavery in Bila-svarga." He
kicked a stone into the water, disturbing the placid stream.
"The Family of Rsii had been destroyed by the Asura Kali
. . . with the help of Maya's magic." He stood and stepped
toward the stream, kicking more soil and rocks into the water, sending more ripples through the disturbed surface.
"If it hadn't been for Maya's magic . . ."

Gopal was uncomfortable with the brahmacari's display
of emotion, and was not sure how to act. Should he try to
console Sudama? What could he say? His own father had
met a similar fate. His feelings about being a simha were
mixed. After having met Vyasa, he wondered if the life of
an ascetic would be the answer to his problems.

Gopal walked to Sudama's side. Glowing in the water's
surface were both their reflections and the image of the
Chakra, highlighted by the newly risen sun.

"After what happened to my family," Sudama continued, "I stayed with Vyasa to learn the battle mantras of the
treta-mystic, offering my services for life. Now I am here
with you . . . destined to meet the Asura King." Turning to
Gopal, he handed him the Chakra. "Guard the disc. It
must not fall into the hands of the Asuras, and keep it hidden from the Apsarasa as well. I don't trust her. When we
meet Kali, use it to slay the demon. Its powers are beyond
my knowledge," he confessed.

Sudama's words made some of Gopal's guilt leave him.

Maybe he had made the right decision to keep the Chakra a secret. Gopal held the discus up, studying it carefully. "What's this?" He held it out for Sudama to look at again.

Sudama took Gopal's hand, turning the hand and the discus to catch the light. He read the inscription. "Man verily is sacrifice and with desire for the heavens, may be sacrifice."

Unseen, Nimai hid nearby in the brush. He had been looking for his godbrother and had overheard the whole conversation. He was less than happy with the idea of being kept in the dark. "After all I've done for him," Nimai thought, angry with Gopal, "why didn't he confide in me? I've been closer to him than anyone."

"I need to bathe now," Sudama said. The brahmacari looked more serious than Gopal had ever seen him. "Keep the disc secret. The fewer who know, the better."

Nimai ran back to camp to pretend he was still asleep. Maybe Gopal would still tell him about the discus. Maybe he had been hasty in his attack on his best friend.

Gopal, who had already bathed, placed the Chakra under his belt, next to the claw. Why me? he wondered, walking back to the clearing. Now he had two sacred objects to which he felt he had no claim. He wondered what reasons the manus could have for placing these in his hands . . . if it was the manus who were responsible. None of this was his own doing. He was still the tool of others, and the whorl, with its manus and its laws, was the puppet master.

Vyasa was using him to appease the Spirit of Foreboding. Sudama was using him to avenge his family. His sister needed him to break the spell that held her captive. Nimai needed to be cared for. Gopal remembered his vow in the mountain ashram. "I said I would do your bidding," he whispered, knowing that if the manus were truly as powerful as they were supposed to be, they would hear. "I know you like to toy with us," he remarked, not very happy with the idea, "but when my sister is out of danger, then I am on my own." He stopped, knowing that sometimes the manus took the form of animals, or entered, as spirits, into trees, plenty of which were about. "On my own! Do you hear?" Gopal entered the clearing where Nimai lay sleeping. "Wake up, wake up, you servant of nescience!" he shouted. "The sun has risen, and Brahma-murta has passed."

Nimai stirred. "A servant," he mumbled under his breath, "that's all I am to him." Gopal checked on Citty, but didn't mention the Chakra to Nimai.

Sudama stepped from the woods, straightening his clothing. "The water is cool and refreshing. It feels good to get the stench of Bila-svarga out of my nose."

"You must have been reading my mind," said Nimai. He ran off into the woods, less than pleased with Gopal or Sudama.

Gopal laughed at the sight of his friend leaping over bushes, trying to disrobe. Sudama joined him next to his sister. "Your friend is spirited," he said, joining the laugh at Nimai's expense. "He doesn't appear very learned."

"There are more things to be learned than can be found in books," Gopal responded in his friend's defense. There were more serious issues at hand, however, and Nimai's antics were soon forgotten. "I'm afraid she's still changing." Gopal turned his attention back to his sister. "Her whitened hair reminds me of the Yaksas."

"There is a mantra," interrupted Sudama, "that I could use to put her into sushupti."

Gopal, remembering the trouble Sudama had had with the charm on Narakatala, hesitated.

"It's a deep sleep. It might slow her sickness. And it will keep her from suffering from lack of food and water."

"At least until we can get her to Niyana Bhiram," said Gopal, having more faith in the directions of Vyasa than the inexperience of Sudama. He sighed. Citty was looking less like his sister as time passed. He had to have faith in

Sudama. "I'll make a litter to carry her," he decided.
When Nimai returned from the stream, Gopal was already
busily cutting bamboo. "Give me a hand," he told his
friend. "We can use this to carry Citty."

"Yes, master," said Nimai.

The apprentice mystic recited the spell.

> "I call upon you who are neither alive nor dead.
> Sushupti!
> Varunani is your mother, Yama your father,
> Sushupti!
> We know your birth,
> You are the child of the divine,
> An instrument of your father.
> Thus do we know you!
> Sushupti!
> Now do we call you!"

The forest stilled. A soft breeze swelled around the clearing.

> "Protect this girl from evil dreams."

Cittahari stirred, as if about to wake from the coma,
then, as suddenly, she appeared to be sleeping peacefully.

"She is ready to travel," said Sudama. "Bring the litter."
Sudama smiled, looking at the now peaceful expression
that covered the girl's face. "We have a long way to go."

"Sudama," said Gopal, "you and Nimai carry Citty. I
need you by her side in case of any change." Gopal looked
at the robe he had brought back from Narakatala. "What
should I do with this?" He lifted it on the tip of his sandal.

"The stench saved us once already," said Sudama. "I
have a feeling . . . "

"We'll take it, but only if you carry it," Gopal replied,
feeling close enough to the brahmacari to challenge him.
Sudama smiled. Gopal was right. There was a bond devel-

oping between them, a bond which Nimai noticed and silently resented.

Sudama rolled the rank-smelling garment up and had Gopal tie it to his back. He and Nimai lifted the girl's stretcher, and followed Gopal.

Gopal walked in front, next to Sudama. "How long will it take to reach Niyana Bhiram?" he asked.

"According to Vyasa, it should lie to the north. I figure a day to get through Talavana forest. That should bring us within another day's journey of the city of Toshana. From there I believe we will have another two days. We will know for sure at Toshana. I know some people there who can help us."

"If there is anyone left," said Gopal. "We don't know what's happened while we were gone. Maybe we should take it slow . . . for Citty's sake."

The dry warmth of the morning sun was welcome, compared to the damp darkness of Narakatala. Reacting to the pleasant surroundings, Gopal grabbed a handful of wildflowers, and sniffed their fragrance. Peacocks shrieked to their hens in the branches overhead. A monkey, startled by something unseen, scampered up the trunk of a nearby tamala tree. Gopal stopped in his tracks, holding out one arm to stop Sudama. His other hand reached for the handle of his dagger. Everyone laughed when a wild dog darted out from some undergrowth, chasing and barking at the monkey hiding in the high branches.

Seeing the animals, Gopal thought of the hunt . . . and of battle. "I don't know if I could be a soldier," he said. "I always wanted to travel and learn from great teachers."

"Our journey is far from over," answered Sudama. "Who knows where the manus, and your karma, will lead?"

Gopal smiled. "We will see what the manus have planned for all of us." They had reached a crossroad.

"Slow down," yelled Nimai, annoyed at not being a part of the conversation. "I need to stop and rest."

"I agree," said Sudama. "Let me see to your sister."

Gopal nodded and walked back to where Nimai had stopped. "How is she?"

"She has warmed up," answered Sudama, removing his hand from her cheek. "The mantra is working."

Gopal looked helplessly at the white-haired form of his sister.

"Here," offered Nimai, breaking Gopal's suddenly solemn mood, "I saved some nutmeats." He opened his cupped hands. They each took a few wild nuts and sat quietly, waiting, resting, listening to the sound of their chewing.

"What's that?" asked Sudama. Something was coming through the brush.

Gopal placed his hand over Nimai's mouth. "Sssh! What? What do you hear?"

Sudama sat up straighter. "There, off to the left." He pointed. "Something rustling in the underbrush."

"I hear it," said Gopal, turning to the snap of a branch.

Nimai pushed Gopal's hand away. "Maybe it's just another monkey," he hoped, looking in the direction the others were pointing.

From out of the woods, unaware of their presence, came a small, bent, old man who wore the dark green, homespun clothes of a begger. He hobbled out of the forest, using a short staff for balance, carrying an animal over his shoulders. He was too far away for Gopal to recognize the beast. Reaching the very center of the crossroad, the old man dumped the animal, its legs tied together, onto the dirt road, then he scurried back into the forest and was gone.

"What was that all about?" asked Gopal.

Nimai stood first. "I'll go see." He wanted to get back the respect he thought he had lost and ran to the road before anyone could do anything to stop him. Nimai reached the spot and touched the animal, which jumped. Nimai jumped too. "It's just a black goat," he yelled back, relieved.

"Did he say a black goat?" asked Sudama, sitting up straighter, suddenly alert.

"That's what it sounded like," said Gopal. "Why?"

Now Sudama was standing. "A crossroad! It was forbidden by the Laws of the Manus since before the Age of Dvarpa."

"What? What is it?" Gopal didn't like having to ask questions.

"Why didn't I realize it?"

"Realize what?" Gopal asked, getting upset.

"If this is going on, Kali's power knows no limit. Nimai! Come away from there," yelled Sudama, looking up. "Quickly!" he called, looking to the treetops.

Now Gopal was looking up . . . and back to Nimai, who was still standing at the crossroad, then crouching over the black goat.

There was a flutter above them. The branches of the trees became disturbed, dropping their leaves. A shadow passed Gopal's feet, skimming the ground. Is it another naga? he wondered, grabbing the claw at his waist.

"City will be safe," Sudama said. "Come with me."

Gopal followed the brahmacari to the crossroad. Again a shadow passed overhead that touched Gopal's bare skin and chilled him.

They reached Nimai. "What is it?" he asked. The goat kicked its bound legs and breathed quick short breaths.

"The crossroads," Sudama said again as if talking to himself. "I didn't think—"

Gopal couldn't stand it anymore. "What's wrong?" he demanded.

"That man has made a pact with a puttanah—the ghost of an evil mystic that feeds on flesh, and not only the flesh of animals. Their offerings are always left at a crossroad." There was a pause. "This worship was always forbidden by the Laws of the Manus." Again, the ground shadow skimmed the road at their feet. It slid across the road, and they looked up.

Something big soared high above the trees, darting against a backdrop of black thunderclouds and sun. It hovered, looking like a giant mosquito. Six long legs, or limbs, or arms—they couldn't tell which—extended from its body, hanging lifeless, like a sleeping marionette. The sun behind it made it difficult to see with any accuracy. The creature hung motionless in the air, except for its everbeating translucent wings that moved so quickly it was impossible to tell just how many wings the thing had. They were big, though, . . . and loud.

With a blur of wings, the sand in the road swirled into a whirlwind, and the beast landed. The puttanah stood about ten feet in front of them and was at least that much in height. A male or female, they could not tell. It had pointed ears that extended twelve inches beyond the top of its egg-shaped head, on top of which sat a golden crown. Long earlobes, stretched and fleshy, hung low to the creature's shoulders, weighted down by the many golden earrings that decorated the coarse, red skin. Two solid red eyes and a thick, black nose were embedded into its drawn and sunken, copper-colored face. From its mouth slithered a red tongue, four fangs, and a smile that stretched literally from ear to ear. The creature wore brass armor over a belly that was sunken from something Gopal fervently hoped was not hunger. From the back of its shoulders grew two pairs of wings that were not unlike a bat's, except for their color, which was white crystal. Leaflike veins pulsed, branching from where the wings joined the creature's back, pumping blood through each twisted vessel with such vigor that Gopal guessed the creature must have needed more than one heart to meet the task. But extra hearts did not give it compassion . . . quite the opposite.

What had been hanging limp from its body in the air turned out to be two scaled legs, thin as bamboo stalks and tipped with clawed feet, and four scaled arms that grew from the front of its shoulders. On their ends, sixteen elongated, bony-white fingers stretched to twice the size of its near-human hands. Black talons touched the ground when the creature dropped its arms to its sides. It said nothing, making Gopal wonder if it could speak at all. It looked past them and eyed the offering while scratching its black fingernails in the road.

"It's too late to back away," Sudama whispered.

"I am Jara," it shrilled, in a voice that was human, bird, and serpent all at the same time. "I was once a mystic of great and terrible powers, and now I am condemned by the manus to the life of a puttanah . . . also with great and terrible powers." It grinned a horrible grin.

"What is it you want from us?" Gopal asked, as calmly as he could.

"Why, the offering my devotee has left. That's all."

"Oh," answered Nimai. "It's fresh and ready. A feast for your greatness."

"How do you come to know of its freshness?"

Sudama wanted to stop Nimai from answering, but couldn't. "I inspected it for you."

"Did you place your fingers upon it?"

"Just one," answered Nimai, curious at the strange turn in the questions.

"You defiled the offering!" screeched Jara. The puttanah opened its wings and raised its four hands to the sky as if climbing invisible rungs in the air, lifting itself about eight feet from the ground.

"He didn't know," pleaded Sudama as Gopal reached for his dagger. Jara's eyes glowed at the sight of the boy's hand touching the handle. Three of the creature's four arms sprang out from its body, stretching to reach Sudama and the two boys, grabbing hold of them by the waists. With one in each hand, it raised them from the ground and hovered in the air with its wings beating furiously. Its hot, red eyes stared at Nimai, the spoiler, who froze at the hypnotic gaze. Gopal freed his dagger, prepared to strike as the puttanah spewed poison toward Nimai.

Sudama, holding his arms out before him, his palms aimed at the creature, chanted: "Astras!" The sound vibration released its magic—a mystic arrow—that hit the creature above its opened mouth, jarring the crown from its head and causing the poison to veer to the side while Gopal slashed at the arm that held him.

Surprised at Sudama's power, Jara dropped the three hostages, recoiled its limbs, and sank to the road. Nimai tumbled into the brush, still dazed, while the puttanah reared back, shaking violently from the sting of the mystic's charm.

Freed, Sudama moved between the trees on the right, again releasing a magic arrow. "Astras," he said, and another bolt streaked from his palms, this time striking Jara in the mouth, splashing blood from the creature's face. Screeching with pain, the creature whirled around to face Sudama, but noticed Gopal trying to sneak around to its other side. A limb sprang forth and coiled its long, thin fingers around the boy, again lifting him into the air. Turning to the mystic, it spit another dose of poison.

"Pratikina-pratikih!" chanted the apprentice. The poison spray deflected off a sound shield, and Sudama leaped for the cover of a large rock just as the shield faded.

Gopal, once again in the puttanah's grasp, stabbed repeatedly at the creature's flesh with his dagger. The monster, having lost track of Sudama, hissed and turned. Gopal looked up as the creature prepared to hypnotize him with its stare.

Undetected, Sudama had climbed to the top of a rock while the puttanah lifted Gopal above its head, opening its mouth like a huge sack, ready to devour the boy like a snake that swallows prey twice its size around. Sudama aimed his palms at the back of the puttanah's head, and chanted.

"O Agni, bring hither the mystic's fire.
Endow this missile with your power."

With the chant, "Astras!" a flash launched another arrow into the back of the serpent's neck. The creature dropped Gopal, but Sudama had been unable to control the power of the magic and the bolt went completely through the monster, splashing blood on Gopal and the ground below. Although not a death blow, the wound was grave. Jara turned to see Sudama on his knees on top of the rock, exhausted from his newly tried feats. The puttanah moved in for the kill.

Suddenly, Nimai, from out of the cover of the forest, threw himself in front of Sudama, and the puttanah grabbed Nimai by the neck instead. Snipping with its long scissorlike claws, Jara snapped Nimai's head from his shoulders. A flash of blue light—Nimai's atma!—sparked from the body and began drifting upward.

Seeing his best friend killed, Gopal cried a warrior's scream and raced to the rock, leaping onto the head of the demon, plunging the tip of his blade with all his might through the top of its skull, into the brain of the whirling beast. Jara reared for a final attempt at flight, trying feverishly to shake Gopal loose, only to fall dead to the ground. Gopal pulled the blood-soaked dagger from the puttanah's head and wiped the wet blade on the scaled beast, looking for the brahmacari. Sudama was on his knees near the rock, raising a dagger and bringing it down on something. "Nimai!" Gopal raced to Sudama's side.

Sudama knelt over Nimai's body. "He saved my life!" cried the student mystic. Nimai's head lay six feet away, cracked like an egg. Next to Sudama lay the body of the black goat. Sudama had cut the head from the goat and placed it on Nimai's body. Frantic, half mad, Sudama chanted a forbidden mantra.

"May Nimai's in-breathing,
And out-breathing remain here.
United here with spirit, this beast and this boy
Shall share in the sun, shall share the whorl

By means of this divine utterance.
Rise hence!"

Gopal saw the blue glimmer that was Nimai's life force
hesitate in its upward motion. He grabbed Sudama's
shoulder, trying to stop his madness. Sudama wouldn't
stop, and brushed the hand off, still chanting:

"Cast off the shackles of death
Do not sink from the sight of the sun.
Let this boy remain here, let him not depart.
I rescue him with this mantra
I snatch him from Death
Sound of limb, of mind, of sight,
Of ear, of touch, of smell, of tongue.
Life have I obtained . . . "

Without rest, without thought, Sudama kept chanting
into the night, within the darkness. He chanted until the
sun brought light again to Bhu, and the blue glow of life
had returned to settle within Nimai once again. Finally,
Sudama held his own forehead and cried, "I am weak."
Before Gopal could say anything, or understand Sudama's
true meaning, Sudama collapsed into a deep sleep.

For two days he slept. On the third day, Sudama opened
his eyes, jumping up as if his life depended on it. "What
have I done? I have offended Vyasa. I have offended the
manus. . . . I have offended Nimai. I have brought the
curses of a thousand births on my life."

Gopal had no idea what to say, but words formed. "You
saved my godbrother. You saved us."

"You don't understand," Sudama said, repelling the
words of comfort. "That mantra is forbidden to a neophyte. Only a treta-mystic can challenge Death." He
sobbed into his hands. "I have had only one life to learn.
What have I done?" Sudama's eyes showed madness. "We
can't defy the Law of Karma as set into motion by the

manus. Nimai was already the property of the servants of
Yama. He belonged to the Lord of the Dead. I stole him
back. I am a thief!"

Gopal grabbed the brahmacari at the shoulders, shaking
him, getting his attention. "Your mantras saved all of us."

But Nimai, who now wore the head of a black goat, also
woke, and saw his old head. Feeling the animal head now
resting on his shoulders, he tried to speak, but only the
cracked bleat of a goat sprang from his throat. His animal
eyes rolled in his head as he tried to control his half-animal
senses. Concentrating on his tongue, he finally cried out,
in a voice that was still only half-human, "Whhaaaat
hhhaaaaave you done to meeeeee?" Upon hearing his own
voice, he screamed through the mouth of the beast. His
voice cracked. "I aaaam neither aaaa man nor beast." Frantic, Nimai kept feeling his face and head, and wept with
animal tears.

For another whole day, Gopal tried to find the good in
Sudama's action, but was not really sure he ever would.
With time, however, Sudama began to calm down, and
Nimai began to get better control of his new tongue. Even
after Gopal convinced them to forget their bitterness for
City's sake, and to help him get the stricken girl to
Toshana, Nimai's thoughts were not equal to the deed.

With another day wasted, they gathered at the body of
the puttanah. Sudama noticed the markings on its chest.
"The sign of the Pisaca."

Gopal recognized it. "I thought you said it was a puttanah."

"Yes," said Sudama. "The worship of puttanahs has always been forbidden on Bhu. Now, without the simhas to
enforce the laws, and with the return of the Pisaca, it appears the former outcasts of this whorl have returned."

"I suggest we travel off the paths and roads from now
on," said Gopal. "Let's get City and be on our way."

Nimai and Sudama grabbed hold of the pallet, and they
group traveled through the night, carrying City.

"It isn't far now," Sudama assured Gopal. "It will take us a little longer, staying off the highway."

"Fine," said Gopal. "Are you all right?" he called back to Nimai.

Nimai twisted his head like a poor fitting garment. "Yes, I'm fiiine," he answered.

After walking for some time, Sudama looked back at Nimai, worried. "I need to rest again," he said. Placing Citty on the ground, he sat with Gopal. "I am afraid for Nimai, and for us." Nimai sat with Citty, running his fingers through the girl's snow-white hair.

"You're just feeling guilty again." Gopal knew the feeling.

"No! You forget. The goat was to be used in a sacrifice of the black arts. I don't know how much Pisaca magic remained in the beast." Sudama put his hand to his face. "What have I done? Nimai may be in danger . . . or he may endanger us."

"Nimai is my friend. We are closer than brothers. We have nothing to fear."

But Sudama wasn't satisfied.

* * * * *

Still on Narakatala, Vyasa had created another ring for protection from the mist, and, with Usha, followed Bhutanatha and his captive to the ship that lay anchored in the mist.

"We have to get on board," Vyasa whispered. His leg was hurting, and he tried vainly to keep his weight off it and on the Yaksa spear. "I have to rest. I don't think I can—"

She smiled. "I can take care of the guard."

Before he could say anything, Usha was on her way, appearing from out of the mist, unseen and unheard by the Yaksa. "Can you help me?" she sang, approaching the guard.

"What? An Apsarasa?" The sight of the siren enchanted even the Yaksa. "We don't get many of your kind on Nara-katala." The guard questioned Usha further but the trance of her presence overshadowed his words. "I have to sound . . . the . . . alarm," he stuttered, reaching for the conch-shell horn hanging from his shoulder.

"That won't be necessary," she chimed, grabbing his hand and the seashell. With her other hand, she took the short guard by the back of the neck, pulling his head forward until it rested on her stomach. "There, that's better," she hummed, embracing him with both arms. "Aren't you glad you didn't sound the alarm?"

The Yaksa, feeling the erotic hold of the Apsarasa, hummed his reply, then, releasing a short shrilled scream muffled by Usha's golden flesh, he slumped, lifeless. She dropped him to the ground and, using her foot, rolled him off the pier into the water, where his body made a strange sound when it hit the surface.

Vyasa hobbled from within the shadows to join the siren. "We need to see inside." Voices came from within the ship, and a light shone from a porthole. Checking again for more guards, they moved to the window, where they could hear Bhutanatha.

"We will get it back!" the dark lord screamed.

"Kali will not like what has happened here," said the emissary. "A few soldiers through a portal will not satisfy the Asura . . . or your agreement. I must return to Bhu with the news." The emissary left the room and the ship.

Bhutanatha stared, and his eyes glowed red. His anger shifted to his captive. Citty, her hands bound behind her, was forced to kneel before the sorcerer. She wore the vest of a warrior that hung down to her knees, and a tunic that reached as low. Under that, she still wore the same tight, white punja pants she had worn under her dress. Now, covering her head and encasing the waist-length black hair of a simha's daughter, was a warrior's leather skull cap that reached just above her eyes, and strapped to her back was an empty sword case.

"The girl for the Chakra?" asked Usha.

Vyasa nodded.

THIRTEEN

WHILE GOPAL AND HIS COMPANIONS MARCHED on, trying desperately to reach the city of Toshana, events were taking place that, unchecked, would change the face of the whorl—Kali was being crowned Simha of Bhu.

Far from their forest path, within the city of Hiranya, the new capital of Klesa, Maya had constructed a palace with her mystic powers, a palace that was peerless throughout the Three Whorls. Supported by columns of gold, it rose like a mass of new clouds lighted by the sun, with golden walls and archways so brilliant that it seemed to be on fire. Within this palace she built pools bordered with marble and set with pearls. A flight of crystal steps led from the marble edge into the water, where lotuses blossomed and fish and golden-hued tortoises played in their clear depths. Around the outside of the palace were planted tall, ever-blossoming trees of all descriptions that provided cool shade and whose fragrances were carried inside on cool breezes. Into this palace, now filled with representatives of the Rakshasa and Pisaca races, as well as the humans that had joined with the Asura, Kali himself came, dressed in royal purple. The Asura ascended the crystal stairs to his throne, where Maya waited to install her brother as Simha of Klesa.

Maya addressed the assembly, all the time working her mystic illusions. "Glories to our mighty guardian, slayer of enemies, who prospers his friends and allies." The crowd cheered their lord. "Clothed in grace, shining by his own lustre, this great Asura has entered upon immortal deeds." Casting her web of illusion, Maya soon had the assembly seeing what she told them to see. "To Kali, whose kingdom has come, arise, endowed with lustre." With these words Maya placed a crown, decorated with a single peacock feather—the symbol of the godhead—upon her brother's head. "Come forth as Lord of Bhu and conquerer of the Three Whorls." The assembly hall shook with cheers as Kali accepted the crown from Maya.

* * * * *

Still within the cover of the forest, tired, hungry, and fearing for the lives of both his sister and his best fried, Gopal pushed on. The journey took as long as Sudama had guessed it would, and, finally, the weary travelers reached the city of Toshana.

Things had changed while they had been in Bilasvarga. To enter Toshana, they had to force aside the main gate, which was now burned and battered, and hung lopsided from its giant rusted hinges. With the three of them sharing the weight, they forced one of the wood and metal gates to the side. On the backside of the opposite gate, scratched into the surface, was the symbol of the Pisaca, and, once inside, they found the buildings ransacked, with large gaping holes dotting the roofs. The once busy streets, now strewn with weeds, were vacant but for a few straggled villagers who hugged the shadows, trying to remain hidden from the strangers.

A hot wind swept the street, lifting the dry dust and

forming large clouds of sand that moved about the empty village like phantoms, pushing open doors and banging loose window shutters. When the dust clouds moved on, they revealed poles that lined the streets in all directions; atop each hung the headless remains of men and boys.

Sudama became alarmed and ran to confront a stranger huddled in a doorway. The brahmacari grabbed the man by the wrist and pulled him from the dark, only then noticing the bareboned frame and sunken cheeks behind which stared cold, dead eyes. Sudama forced the villager to face him. "What's wrong with you?" Sudama, frustrated, shook the man. "Is this how the people of Toshana welcome visitors?" Gopal and Nimai, alarmed at the loud cruelty in Sudama's voice, joined the brahmacari while still carrying the sleeping Citty. Seeing Nimai's goat head, the villager cowered against the door, shivering with fright. Sudama let loose his grasp.

"What's going on?" asked Gopal, seeing the pitiful figure and directing Nimai to rest his sister's litter on the ground.

"I don't know," Sudama answered. "It's as if we were the Yamaduttas."

"You are the messengers of Death!" snapped the figure from his corner. "You are Yama's henchmen," he cried, his head in his hands. Gopal crouched, placing his hand on the man's arm. The stranger pushed it away, and Gopal, startled by the sudden movement, reached for his dagger. "Kill me," the man screamed, extending his arms, revealing his fleshy ribs. "You have taken our farms, our wives and children. There is nothing left but my soul. Take it and leave me in peace." He slumped in the darkened corner, weeping.

Gopal stood, backing away. It was all too much like Goloka. The nightmare wasn't over. Things weren't getting better.

"Come," said Sudama. "Let's leave him. He can't help

us. We must find Dhanus, the healer we have come for."

"What about him?" asked Gopal, pointing to the broken stranger. "We can't just leave him."

"The wise lament for neither the living nor the dead," retorted the brahmacari.

Gopal, looking down at the sorry figure of the villager, then at his sister, again became fearful of the student's lack of experience. He lashed out. "How can you know?"

Sudama stepped forward. "There is nothing we can do for him!" He lifted his hand, pointing at Gopal, Nimai, and Citty. "It is the rest of you that concern me now, so get your sister while we can still do something for her!"

With the girl in tow, they walked the deserted streets, while frightened eyes peered at them through boarded windows. As they made their way through weeds that grew high on roads that were once busy with traffic, it was obvious that Death had cast his shadow over Toshana.

Sudama suddenly stopped in front of a seemingly abandoned building, its sole window also boarded over from the inside. Weeds grew as tall as a man's waist in front of the door. It was evident that no one had entered or left for a long time. A cracked, handcrafted sign, bearing the word "Dhanvantari," swung in the hot breeze. The nails that precariously held it were long since rusted.

"Physician?" asked Gopal.

"He likes to think so," said Sudama. Nimai scratched his fur-covered cheek, not understanding the meaning of Sudama's comment. "He was my teacher," Sudama said, looking at Gopal, ". . . before Vyasa." The brahmacari stepped through the weeds, crushing the long, wild grasses with his foot. Nimai was eyeing the grasses, then, fighting unfamiliar feelings, tried to look through the cracks of the boarded window. Gopal, worried, looked at his sister and the dark structures that surrounded them. He felt vulnerable standing in the open. "Is he still here?" Sudama wondered, knocking on the door. There was no answer.

"Whether he's there or not, we need to get off the street." Gopal didn't like feeling that eyes were staring at them from the buildings. Sudama agreed and knocked again. Slowly, the door creaked open about an inch. An eye stared from the cracked darkness.

"Who's there?" From within, came a hesitant, worn, and equally cracked voice. "How may I serve you?"

"Dhanus! It's me . . . Sudama!"

"Sudama?" The door opened another inch and then swung open with a long creak. An old man stepped through the opening. He was small in the door frame, only five feet or so. His face, wrinkled like a prune, but not with time, was framed by long black hair. It was not the hair of an old man. His arms were no thicker than stalks. His hands were dark, with fingers that twisted. He embraced Sudama.

How could this man have been a healer? Nimai thought.

The old man's face glowed with excitement, but his eyes stared blankly. "Sudama, my old friend." Realizing some unseen danger, Dhanus stepped back into the shadows. "Quickly! Come in. The streets of Toshana are safe for neither man—" Dhanus lifted his nose and sniffed. "—nor beast."

Sudama motioned behind him, and they all scurried into the dark shop. The front door slammed, a beam of wood falling across the threshold. Dhanus leaned his back to the door to rest. Inside was as quiet and desolate as the street outside. The dull, cracked walls were lined with empty shelves where bottles of herbs and potions of various shapes and sizes had once stood. Only the dark silhouettes of Dhanus's craft, that had long ago left their imprint, remained. A fireplace, with barely a flame, stood on their left, and the right side of the room, once a workplace, stood silent and cobwebbed. A stone trough, sunk into the wooden floor, was filled with gray, cold coals. Only spiders and mice worked the room now, making it seem all the more vast and barren. To the right, toward the back, was a door. From where he was standing, Gopal could see a sleeping mat and more shelves along the wall.

Dhanus broke the silence. "I am sorry to have to greet you in such a manner." He reached to his side, finding a stick to help support him. "Since the coming of the Age of Kali, there are few alive who can be trusted." As Gopal and Nimai placed the girl by the small fire, Dhanus sniffed the air again. "But enough. It isn't often I get visitors, at least friendly ones." Dhanus pushed himself from the door to the fireplace, taking a lantern from the mantle. With a piece of splintered wood he moved a small bit of flame from the fire to the lantern, igniting the oil and lighting the room. "Where are my manners? Please . . ." He motioned to the mats that lay before the fire. "Take seats, rest. I have water and some rice." He moved to a table, the only furniture left, on which stood a pitcher, some dented metal cups, and a tray.

Everyone sat quietly, and, although it was warm outdoors, they huddled by the fire. Dhanus threw another log on the small flame. It brought comfort, as did their host. Dhanus handed out the cups, pouring water for his visitors and handing the tray of rice to Sudama. The brahmacari looked at the meager offering and realizing it was all the food the old man had, he passed it to Nimai who lapped the rice with his black tongue. "What has happened here?" Sudama asked.

"Since Kali was crowned Simha of Bhu—"

Their voices rang out in surprise. "Crowned king?"

"Many lands have been laid waste, even worse than what you see here."

"He's taken over everything?" Gopal asked. "All of Bhu?"

"What about you?" asked Sudama. "How have you survived?"

"They have no use for a blind man."

Sudama moved closer to his friend, waving his hand in

front of the old man's face. "Dhanus, but how?"

"It is all right," the old man reassured Sudama, grabbing the brahmacari's wrist when it waved past. "When I tried to keep them from taking the things in my shop, they took my sight. But enough about me! What are you doing here? How can I be of service?"

Gopal answered. "My sister is sick. We need your help. Can you cure her?"

"I sensed something vile when you entered . . . an animal." Dhanus sniffed the air again. "But knowing you, Sudama, I trusted your sense."

Sudama explained. "The girl has been stricken by the Pisaca."

"And I was spared an early death by this mystic here," said Nimai sarcastically. Nimai explained how Sudama had panicked, giving him the head of a wild goat. Gopal grew anxious, moving to his knees and sliding himself across the floor to their blind host.

"Can you help my sister?"

Dhanus, using his stick and his hand, felt his way to Citty. Kneeling, he touched her head, mouth, and ears. Then, after removing her sandals, he felt the bottoms of her feet.

Gopal couldn't wait any longer. "Can you help her?"

"The soldiers didn't take everything. There are some drugs in my possession that are not for everyone, and there is one that I might be able to use on her." Carved into the mantle of the fireplace were two elephant heads. Feeling his way, Dhanus pulled on the tusks of the one on the right and from the elephant's mouth fell a packet, which Dhanus caught. "Get water." Sudama, the former student, jumped to the command. "It is called Tamopa— a stimulant." Dhanus said to his former student. "I could have shown you things!" Sudama didn't answer and handed Dhanus the cup. "If this doesn't wake the girl from her dark sleep," said the physician, "nothing will." Gopal watched anxiously as Dhanus poured drops of the drug into Citty's mouth. "Now, we must wait."

Sudama wasn't convinced that Dhanus would be able to help. "Do you know the way to Niyana Bhiram?"

"You still don't trust my way, do you, Sudama?" Sudama didn't answer. "You still prefer the ways of Ayur!" Yes, I know the way." Dhanus held his hand out for Gopal to take. "Help me up, and I will show you." He grinned. "Sudama, get some parchment from my workroom . . . in back. You," he tugged at Gopal, "get some charred wood from the fire for me to use as a marker. I will draw you a map." He smiled again, feeling triumphant over those who had maimed him.

They gathered at the table, and Sudama placed the parchment before his friend while Gopal guided the old man's hands to the edges of the paper. "I can still see in my mind's eye," he laughed, dragging the blackened stub across the surface of the sheet, sketching a mountain, a river, a forest, and the place where the city of Niyana Bhiram would be found.

"Thank you my friend," said Sudama, rolling up the map and tucking it in his belt. "You will come with us."

"No!" Dhanus answered. "I must stay. My life has been spent here, and this is where I wish to die. Besides, others may come . . . like you, in need of assistance, and I will be here to help."

Sudama, along with the others, looked into the flames dancing in the fireplace. The fire cast its warm glow on their faces, and their shadows stretched across the low ceiling behind them, dancing a strange dance to the crackling sounds of wood.

"You are safe here. Tonight, we will wait for the drug to take effect," said Dhanus. "You will leave tomorrow, before word spreads of your presence. If my boat hasn't been destroyed, you can take it. Sudama, you remember, we used to fish together." Sudama nodded. Then Dhanus returned to the mantle and took another packet from the open mouth of the wooden elephant head. He also took a pipe from the shelf above the fireplace. "I also have some svapna. It is the one pleasure I have left." He smiled. After removing some of the herb, he broke off a small piece of the resin and dropped it in the pipe.

"Svapna is smoked by the worshippers of Rudra. It induces a state of dreaming and is very relaxing." Dhanus smiled a sly smile. Gopal's eyes never left the bowl and hands of Dhanus. He watched intently as the man's fingers crush the herb into powder. Dhanus took a stick from near the fire and touched it to the flames within the fireplace. Then, touching the ignited twig to the pipe's bowl, he set the resin aflame. "Um," he sighed, inhaling the smoke and passing the pipe to Sudama.

"I cannot," said the student mystic, taking and handing the pipe to Nimai. "I am a brahmacari now. I took a vow."

"Thaat maay be for thhhe better," snorted Nimai.

"Still following that mystic?" Dhanus puffed. "Ayur is an ancient, dying art," he insisted. "Few learned men follow its ways anymore. The Art of Shastram, that is the way!" Sudama said nothing. "You still won't listen, will you?" Dhanus released another breath and the cloud of smoke passed under Nimai's black nose. Nimai took the pipe without hesitation, while Dhanus released a smoky cough and smiled a wide grin.

"I'm next," said Nimai, grasping the bowl. "I've heard about this. Some people say it can give visions of the heavenly planets." He laughed and puffed on the pipe.

"Not so hard," instructed Dhanus. "Don't blow out, just inhale . . . softly."

"I don't know if we—" Gopal worried.

Nimai breathed in, calming himself. Tears swelled in his reddened eyes. He exhaled the smoke, coughed uncontrollably, and handed the pipe to Gopal.

Gopal hesitated. First he sniffed the burning herb, surprised at the sweet scent. "This smells different from what I imagined." Sudama remained silent, shaking his head at the boy's curiosity.

"Don't listen to the mystic . . . take some," coaxed Dhanus, "and pass it around again."

Gopal looked at the anxious face of his friend, but took a puff, quickly passing the pipe to Dhanus, who again inhaled the fumes. Gopal leaned back, trying to feel if any changes were taking place. Nothing. The pipe made its way round the circle, still refused by Sudama, and reached him again. This time he didn't hesitate and inhaled a large amount of the smoke, coughing loudly. For some reason, which he couldn't yet understand, the others found his coughing hysterical, especially Nimai, whose laugh was more animal than human. Starting to feel frivolous, Gopal took another quick puff and passed it on.

Sudama was still concerned about Kali. "Is he really Simha of Bhu?"

"He likes to think so." Dhanus laughed. "I call him the Blue Jackal." Dhanus pointed at Sudama with the pipe stem. "Before he wanted to be a mystic, we shared many a pipe over such tales."

"Why the blue jackal?" asked Gopal, trying to keep his wits. The drug was beginning to take its toll. Something was happening to him. His body seemed to fade from consciousness, leaving him with the sensation that he was only a mind, peering out through eyes that were his windows.

"Tell him," Sudama urged. "You tell the story of the Blue Jackal better than anyone."

Gopal was having a hard time concentrating. The fire was especially interesting, as it seemed to possess its own consciousness—the way the flames danced on the wood, as if by design. He couldn't remember ever seeing such beautiful colors before. The sound of voices faded from his ears, and the noise of the crackling wood, like the beats on a kole drum, grew louder as Gopal stared into the multicolored flames. Soon, his eyelids became heavy, like the thick cotton pandals that had covered the market at Goloka. It felt comforting to close them, but in closing his eyes he had entered a new darkness.

Meanwhile, Dhanus started his story about a jackal named Fierce-Howl, who lived in a cave. One day the animal was hunting for food and wandered into the city after nightfall. There, the city dogs snapped at his limbs with their sharp teeth, and terrified his ears with their dreadful barking. The jackal, in his efforts to escape, happened into the house of a dyer where he tumbled into a tremendous indigo vat. Unable to find him, all the dogs went home.

Finally, the jackal managed to crawl out of the vat and escaped into the forest. There, all the animals caught a glimpse of his body dyed with the juice and cried out: "What is this creature enriched with that royal color? An exotic creature has dropped from the heavens."

Gopal wasn't hearing Dhanus's story. For him, images of shadows and light were taking abstract forms, then fading back into nothingness. Then the forms appearing before Gopal took familiar shapes, making him feel uncomfortable. An owl took form from within the darkness and flew off. He stared, somehow knowing there was more to come. Suddenly, a white cow took shape, and then a white bull. The two animals approached and tears ran from the eyes of the two beasts. They were unlike any animals he had ever encountered in all his years at Goloka.

The cow cried out, in a voice that was human . . . and in pain. "Please don't kill me!" she screamed, her voice quivering with terror. "Please don't kill me!" she begged, the words tearing at Gopal's heart. "I am Bhumi."

The Mother of Bhu? Gopal was unable to speak.

"Please spare me, I beg you!" the cow-mother cried.

Why didn't anyone else see this? Gopal looked around the darkness. He heard the voices of his friends, and laughter. Where were they? He couldn't find them. Why weren't they helping him?

Nimai and Sudama were right next to Gopal, listening to Dhanus telling how Fierce-Howl perceived the other animals' dismay and called to them: "Come, come, you wild things! Why do you flee in terror at the sight of me?" The jackal thought for a second how he could make use of their terror. "The manus anointed me as your simha." Hearing this, the lions, tigers, bakasuras, monkeys, rabbits, lizards, rats, and other wildlife bowed—

Still unable to move or speak, paralyzed by the vision, Gopal listened when the bull spoke. "I am Dharma, the personification of Bhakti. Without me, the mystic art will cease. Men of piety will perish! Please don't kill me!" the bull screamed. "Please, don't kill me!" the animal begged, in a voice of human sorrow and misery. Then, before Gopal's tear-filled eyes, the head of the bull tore at the neck, peeled and separated from its body, falling into the eternal darkness, while Bhumi continued to cry her plea. Gopal tried to break from the trance by covering his ears, hoping to block out the cries. At last the screams ended. He opened his eyes, and the vision faded.

The shadows that had been the cow and bull became the forms of Sudama, Nimai, and Dhanus, who was telling how Fierce-Howl was sitting in his court when he heard a pack of jackals howling. Fierce-Howl's eyes filled with tears of joy as he leaped to his feet and howled a piercing tone. When the lions and others heard this, they saw that he was merely a jackal and stood for a moment, shamefaced and downcast. "We have been deceived by a lowly jackal. Let the fellow be killed." Fierce-Howl tried to flee, but was torn to bits by a tiger.

"Are you all right?" asked Nimai, seeing the sweat rolling from Gopal's face. "You're trembling."

Gopal didn't answer. Frantic, he searched the room, trying to get a grip on reality. Sudama and Dhanus were laughing at the story. His sister was sleeping. He wiped the sweat from his face. "I'm fine. I must have been dreaming."

"Some dream," said Nimai, staring at his friend's contorted face. "You look as if you've seen a ghost!"

"Two of them."

Sudama wasn't paying attention to Gopal, but responded to the jackal story. "So Kali is the Blue Jackal, and we must find the tiger among us to tear this false king to pieces." He looked at Gopal, sitting squarely before him. "Are there others who know of Kali's true nature?"

"There are some kingdoms far to the east and north that remain free. Kali's armies have defeated most of the kings that didn't join him. Those that opposed him, and lived, have taken refuge in the mountains with small bands of followers. We who can see through the illusion of Maya know the truth." Dhanus lowered his voice. "I fear, though, that Kali's plan for genocide will continue."

Gopal finally became aware of the conversation taking place. "We met a villager when we first entered," he said, trying to shake the impression the dream had made on him. "He was mad with fright."

"There are a few people left in Toshana, and most are like the one you met. Kali took everything of value after Toshana fell. His generals claimed we were being punished. At night, soldiers came and took all the women and children, killing anyone who resisted." Dhanus was tired from all the talking, and, rising, placed another log on the fire. "We have been desolated by the Asura. The lands lie in waste. We have even heard of man-eating among the soldiers of Kali's armies. I sicken when I think of the horrible fate of Bhu." The svapna had made them all very tired. "I must rest now," said Dhanus. "You are safe here."

Nimai yawned, lying down next to Citty. Sudama found a place near the fire and made himself comfortable. Gopal looked around the room again. The flames in the fireplace had returned to normal, so he also lay down and folded his arms across his chest, staring at the fire until sleep overcame him.

Later, within the dark stillness of the room, broken only by a stubborn spark flaring up with a gust of air, Nimai stirred. Something had touched him. He opened his eyes to meet Citty's gaze.

Her eyes were vivid red and, although Citty's lips were still, a voice filled Nimai's head. *Why do you let them use you so? You are nothing but a slave to your simha and the mystic. Look how they have mocked you.* More than her words, the spell of her eyes worked their magic on the weak-willed boy. *A goat! That is your reward. They made you into a goat.* Between the effects of the drug, the spell of the krtya, and the black magic cast on the animal head, Nimai was easy prey.

"Gopaaal did keep the Chaakraa a secret from me," Nimai blurted, always fighting to control his tongue. He looked at Sudama, who was sleeping soundly. "I hate this aaawful head I aaam forced to wear."

The glowing eyes spoke again. *Why should Gopal have the discus? You deserve it. You have been his loyal friend. You deserve more than that mere boy and the brahmacari have given you. I can help you gain power beyond your dreams. I can get you the riches of a thousand simhas. Just serve me . . . and my master.* Nimai listened. What he heard, he believed. His own weaknesses made him an easy mark for the krtya's enticement. *You must help me, if I am to help you,* she bargained. *I am still too weak. Get me the old man.*

Nimai wasn't sure what Citty meant. In his bewitched state, he woke Dhanus. "Dhaanus," he whispered, shaking the old man's arm. "Dhaanus, I thhink your drug is worrking. Come look aat thhe girl"

Dhanus woke, the svapna still heavy in his mind. Half sleeping, trusting Sudama's choice of friends, he crawled to where Citty lay. Running his hands along the form before him, he felt the shape of a young girl, but something told him it wasn't so. He sensed movement in the body, a life force separate from the body he touched. A vibration reached within his mind. A paralyzing sensation froze his limbs and tongue. Fear seized him.

With the girl directing, Nimai lifted a log and hit the

old man over the head. Dhanus slumped to the ground
where a cold hand grabbed his neck, and the foreign voice
gloated. "You are worn and my strength can match yours,
even now. Soon I will be strong enough to meet the others." The form that was Citty's rose from its resting place.
Hold him still, Nimai heard within his own mind. Under
the power of the krtya, Nimai obeyed. The creature's skin
turned black. Its teeth no longer fit in its mouth. With
hair turned red and wild, the krtya revealed its true form
to Dhanus and killed him. "This first sacrifice seals the
pact." Nimai was put back to sleep.

*   *   *   *   *

On Narakatala, Bhutanatha was glaring at his captive.
"Your friends must have fortune looking out for them,
for my creation wasn't quite ready to do my bidding.
When my krtya comes to full strength—" A priest entered the room, getting Bhutanatha's attention. The
priest began whispering to another. "What is it?" said
the dark lord.

The priest came forward to address his master, bowing
as he spoke. "Kali has captured the devas, Bhumi and
Dharma, my lord. He plans to sacrifice them to invoke
the Brahmastra weapon. He may no longer need the
Chakra."

Another priest, standing next to Bhutanatha, kneeled at
his lord's side. "When the energy of the weapon is conjured and set into motion, it can penetrate any barrier, be
directed at any target. With the Brahmastra, Kali's conquest of the Three Whorls is guaranteed, even without the
Chakra."

"I want that Chakra!" Bhutanatha screamed, stamping
his boot on the wooden floor. "We must join Kali before
we end up with nothing."

"The Chakra?" Usha whispered from their hiding place.
"Bhutanatha doesn't have it? Then who controls it?"

"It sounds like my companions have stumbled on to more than they anticipated," Vyasa answered, quieting the Apsarasa. "It is the news of the Brahmastra that bothers me most. We must get the girl and get back to Bhu quickly."

Citty, still kneeling before Bhutanatha, was exhausted from her captivity, but was, as always, defiant. With pride she wore the warrior's vest taken from a Rakshasa at Goloka, and, even in her weakened condition, two Yaksas had to keep hold of her.

"We may still have a prize for Kali," Bhutanatha calculated. "My priests tell me you are of the Race of Chayya." Citty looked defiantly at the Dark Lord. "I hear Kali has given the Chayya a special place in his black heart."

"A curse on you . . . and the Pisaca," she yelled, only to be silenced by the smack of a Yaksa hand across her face. The blow drew blood from her cheek.

The priest near Bhutanatha whispered. "She is spirited. Her life force is strong. I could use her—"

"Not just yet," his lord advised. "She will serve us, one way or another." Bhutanatha looked at the two guards holding the girl. "Take her to her cell." Lifted by the arms, Citty was dragged from the room. "Get me a report from our search parties," Bhutanatha bellowed, banging his drinking cup against the arm of his seat, splashing himself and the floor. The lower-status priests ran to mop up the spilled nectar with their robes. "Get away from me," he screamed, slapping a priest who was unfortunately within reach. "I want the heads of those thieves! I want the Chakra! Offer a simha's treasure to anyone who returns my prize! Contact Kali. Make him use his soldiers to help search. Now! Do you hear?" The priests cowered, backing from their lord. "I'll have all your heads. Now go and make ready to sail. I want to be within the safety of my castle until the Chakra is returned."

"What do we do now?" asked Usha.

"We must get on board," Vyasa replied, holding his

wound and looking for a means to that end.

"But the Chakra!"

"You help me get the girl—" the Yaksa wound stung again, making the mystic wince. "—and I will help you get the discus. That was our deal."

FOURTEEN

WITH DAWN, THE SILENCE of the room and Gopal's less than restful sleep were invaded by Sudama's frantic shouts. "Everyone, get up, get up, come quickly. Dhanus! Dhanus!" Opening his eyes and stretching his legs, which had gone stiff from sleeping on the hard floor, Gopal rose and rushed to the brahmacari's side. "Gopal, something has happened to Dhanus."

Nimai also stirred. "I had the strangest dream," he mumbled, rubbing his temples. Sudama was standing over the body of Dhanus. "His throat's been torn open," Nimai heard Sudama exclaim. The brahmacari knelt in a pool of blood.

Gopal ran to Citty's side. She was still sleeping. There were no signs that she had been touched. "Is it the work of Maya?" Gopal asked.

"Or the black arts?" responded Sudama, looking at Nimai. "Didn't anyone hear anything?"

"Only my head baaanging," mourned Nimai, still sitting on the floor, rubbing the space between his bushy eyebrows. "I feel teeerrible."

Sudama placed his hand under Dhanus's blood drained face. "Why Dhanus? Why him?"

"Maybe for helping us," said Gopal. "Maybe someone knows we are here." He looked around the room, expecting to see something unusual, but nothing was changed. "How did it happen?" wondered Gopal, standing over their dead host and looking around the room, at the boarded door, the boarded windows, the ceiling, the still-hot embers in the fireplace. "Why not kill one of us?"

"Pisaca or Maya," said Sudama. "Either way, we must leave. Our time is up here—" Loud banging at the front door and the voices of soldiers left little room to discuss their options.

"Dhanus! Dhanus! Open up!"

"Soldiers," whispered Gopal, removing his dagger.

"Come on, Dhanus," yelled the voice. "You may be blind, but you're not deaf."

"Not yet," laughed another.

"They don't know we're here," said Gopal, taking control. "Sudama, get a fire started. Nimai, help me get Dhanus's body over there." Gopal pointed to the foundation of the fireplace and started to drag the body toward it without waiting. "Let's prop him up here." He leaned Dhanus against the wall next to the fire. "Hurry with that fire, mystic."

Sudama hesitated, at first doubting his ability, then called on Agni as he had heard Vyasa do so often, and the wood ignited. "Now take some thin pieces and light them like torches," Gopal commanded Sudama, who paused, unsure of Gopal's motives. The boy snapped his order. "Quickly!"

"Open this door, or we'll break it in," yelled the soldiers, banging harder. The old wood on the door cracked.

"I am coming," responded Gopal in a crackling voice, trying to imitate the dead healer. The soldiers were suspicious of the disguised reply and beat the door harder, this time with the handles of their swords. "All right," whispered Gopal, ready to divulge his plan. "When I open the front door, Sudama, you throw those torches at the soldiers. Nimai, give me your dagger." Nimai, confused, hesitated. "Hurry!" Nimai turned his dagger over to Gopal. "I'll stand behind Dhanus and throw this at the first soldier to enter. Nimai, get Citty into the back." Nimai still looked puzzled, as did Sudama. Gopal started to remove the crossbeam. "I don't want them to know we are here." The soldiers splintered the wooden door. Gopal released the hold, and suddenly the soldiers were inside.

Sudama quickly hurled both torches, blinding them with the light. Gopal's dagger throw found its mark in the first soldier, who, grabbing for the piercing metal in his chest, fell to the floor. Two more soldiers, equally surprised by the sudden opening of the door, tumbled on top of their dying comrade as Gopal ran to the fireplace. Taking a burning log with the end of his dagger, he rolled it along the floor while motioning for Sudama to get to the back room. Gopal quickly grabbed the oil lamp and tossed it onto the log, which exploded in flames. The soldiers clambered to their feet, and the oil splashed one, setting the man aflame. Screaming, the soldier swayed wildly about the room, getting the other soldier's full attention. More soldiers entered, releasing a score of arrows at the figure of Dhanus while Gopal and Sudama sneaked into the back.

"Whaat's going on in thhhere?" asked Nimai, holding one end of the girl's stretcher.

"Dhanus is holding them off," Gopal laughed. "Come, the soldiers weren't expecting our reception, and I doubt they knew we were here. Let's try the back way." He led them through the door and out. "We will go to the river, and from there, find our way to Niyana Bhiram."

Flames gutted the old shop. Conch-shell horns sounded their alarms just as Gopal, with Sudama and Nimai carrying Citty, reached the shoreline of the Sarpa River. "It's there," Gopal said, pointing at the rushing current and a small wooden boat tied to the shore.

"Just like he said," said Sudama. The conch-shell alarms grew in number.

"They will be coming," Gopal reminded the others. "Let's get to the boat." Carrying Citty, they placed the stricken girl in the center. Nimai got to the front, while Sudama helped Gopal push the boat into the current. The distance between them and Toshana grew safer with each passing second. Together they sat in back, with Gopal holding the small rudder.

"Now," said Sudama, "let's take another look at that map." From his belt he removed the map Dhanus had sketched.

"Do you mystics haaave aaanything for a hhheadache?" Nimai called, unable to control the animal part of his mouth. Sudama looked up at the boy, but soon turned his attention back to the map.

Gopal had a question. "You claim to know the village of Toshana."

"Yes," mumbled the brahmacari, turning from the sketch. "I thought I did. Why do you ask?"

"Vyasa told me to seek the City of Nine Gates. Did Toshana have nine gates?"

Sudama, amused by the strange question, answered, "No, I can only count two real gates. There are some roads and paths leading in from different directions, but I can't say there are nine gates. Maybe he meant Niyana Bhiram. I don't recall such a place . . . at least not in this whorl." Sudama turned back to the map. "I recognize this mountain," he said, pointing to the center of the map. "It must be Mount Kuru."

"This river Dhanus drew, winding its way past the mountain," Gopal said, moving his finger up the bending line, "looks like a snake. That must be the river we are on," he realized, pointing to the water around them.

"Sarpa—like a serpent," said Sudama. "This is the Sarpa River."

"Here it is!" Gopal happily announced, pointing to the

north-western portion of the map. "This must be the city of Niyana Bhiram, in the midst of this forest." For the rest of the day they sailed with the current, with Gopal watching both the river and his sister, waiting for Dhanus's cure to take effect. Sudama watched the shoreline and the mountains in the distance. Nimai stared at the others, mumbling to himself and Citty.

As the sun got low, Gopal remembered the weaver they had met going to Radhakunde, and how he had said not to travel the waters at night. He felt lucky to have come this far on the river without incident. "I don't want to tempt the manus," he said, turning the rudder. The boat started for the shore. "We'd better camp for the night. There are some high grasses there." He pointed with a jerk of his head. "Let's wait until morning to continue."

"I agree," Sudama replied. Nimai just looked ahead at the shore.

*   *   *   *   *

Still in Bila-svarga, Vyasa and the Apsarasa had little difficulty climbing aboard Bhutanatha's ship. "We will need to find where they have taken the girl," Vyasa whispered.

Usha's senses were sharp. "Soldiers," she warned, running to hide behind a level in the ship's deck. Vyasa, trusting her instincts, followed.

Six Yaksas came on deck. "Prepare to leave," yelled one, ringing a small brass bell to bring more soldiers up from below. "Detach the lines, and be quick, or Bhutanatha will have all our heads."

The Pisaca ship left the dock without rocking or swaying as ships ordinarily do. It sailed, parting the mist, floating on the waves. There were no sails . . . no oars. . . . Only the power of the black arts moved the vessel. While the crew performed what few duties they had, all Vyasa and Usha could do was to stay hidden.

"What is a krtya?"

"What?" Vyasa couldn't believe Usha didn't know. "A witch like you . . . not familiar with the krtya?"

"Just because I practice the art, that doesn't mean I understand the Pisaca."

"True," the mystic agreed. "When it comes to the Pisaca, there is much for all to learn." He explained what he knew. "Conjured by mantra, the krtya usually takes female form, in this case, that of the girl, Cittahari. They live simply to execute the task of the maker."

"What did Bhutanatha mean when he said 'when it reaches full strength'?"

"The krtya lives on blood. It feeds on the living like a nursing child. It must have been placed in the cell with the captives so it could feed and grow. When the mist let Bhutanatha know we were coming, I think he tried to use the krtya against us." Vyasa paused. A Yaksa had come too close, but soon the danger passed. "Something must have gone wrong," he whispered. "The krtya wasn't ready. Gopal mistook it . . . we all did . . . for his sister."

"You aren't concerned that this creature is with your friends?"

Vyasa smiled. "My student will be able to take care of the krtya," he said confidently. "I have taught him well."

"Then what is your concern?" Usha was curious about the motives of the mystic.

"After we get the girl, we must stop Kali from using the Brahmastra."

"First, you must help me regain the Chakra," Usha reminded the mystic as the shore disappeared from view and fog closed around the ship, erasing all trace of land. "Can you swim?" asked Usha.

"No," Vyasa whispered. "I never needed to know how."

* * * * *

Before dawn, Gopal was up. The shore was peaceful, undisturbed except for a few birds fishing along the water's edge. Tall grasses and brush covered the land, reaching all the way to the foothills of a mountain, the one Sudama had called Kuru. If he hadn't experienced the events of the past few days, Gopal would never have guessed that the whorl was in chaos.

He woke Sudama. "We have about an hour before the first light," he whispered. "I am going to see if I can find some herbs or fruit growing nearby." Sudama turned and stirred, hearing, but half asleep. "Watch my sister. I'll be back soon, and we will continue on the river."

Gopal was feeling confident, maybe too confident, having led their escape from Toshana. He thought that his father would have appreciated his courage and welcomed the chance to prove his worth. He couldn't do mystic tricks like Sudama. So what could he do? He challenged the manus to answer him.

"What is my karma," he called out, walking along a path normally trodden by animals on their way to drink from the river. "After I remove the curse from my sister," he asked, "am I supposed to fulfill the wishes of Vyasa and confront Kali? When will I be free to make my own destiny?" Today, the manus didn't answer. Gopal didn't know the answers either, but this was the first chance he had had, in a long time, to be alone. As much as he loved his sister, he still needed time by himself to "air out his mind," as he called it.

Feeling safe, he removed his sandals, and, slinging them over his shoulder, walked closer to the water's edge, allowing the cool mud to seep between his toes. The wetness under his feet, the sound of the water rushing by his side, the dark, clear sky of Bhu dotted with black thunderclouds hanging overhead, and a cool breeze coming off the river felt great to see, to smell, to touch. He even imagined bathing in the river.

He was almost at peace when something grabbed him from behind. A hand covered his mouth; two more grabbed and held his arms behind him. He tried to pull away, squirming like a fish in a net, but his captors held him even tighter. A sharp pain ran up his wrenched arms, across his shoulders, and into his neck, stiffening his joints. A hair-covered hand grasped his mouth. So foul was the stench that he nearly gagged.

"Hold him tight!" he heard. A figure moved from his side to face him.

They were dvid-dvids—mountain demons, part-ape, part-dog, and barely human. Is this how the manus were to answer him? Another came from behind to join the first. The dvid-dvids' bodies were totally hairy, except for a sash worn around each of their waists. The fingers wrapped around Gopal's arms must have been six or seven inches long. The creatures' feet, also covered with hair, were bootless, with long, clawed toes that left prints in the sand as they hobbled along.

"Is it one of them, Trnavarta?" it growled, saliva drooling from its mouth.

"It must be."

"We'll be rich!" the creature cried, wringing its hands and jumping up and down in place.

"Calm down, Dhenuka!" howled Trnavarta. "It's only one. We were told there would be at least five. Vatsasura! Vyoma! Hold him tight." The leader moved closer to sniff the prize. Taking Gopal by the hair on his head, the dvid-dvid moved the boy from side to side, examining him. "He looks like he would make a good meal," he snarled, revealing his yellowed, canine teeth. "This hair would make a nice decoration." He grinned, running a claw through Gopal's hair.

Dhenuka, the smallest of the pack, became excited and again jumped up and down, throwing his arms wildly into the air. "Can we eat him? Can we eat him?"

Trnavarta, without turning from his captive, swung his arm back, catching Dhenuka across the face, sending him to the ground on his back. "Stop all the chattering! How can we collect the reward if we eat him?"

"Well? If we aren't going to eat him," complained Vatsasura, still holding Gopal's arms, "then what are we going to do?"

Trnavarta let go of Gopal's head, sniffing at his own hand for remnants of the boy's sweat. He licked his hairy fingers as if Gopal's scent might substitute for eating their captive. "Let's take him back to the cave. We can decide what to do with him there." Again the creature rubbed its finger over Gopal's sweated brow and licked the salted digit clean.

The one called Vyoma tore a piece of cloth from Gopal's shirt, using it to gag him. Another piece was ripped off and used to bind his hands, enabling Gopal to see the two hair-covered creatures that had been holding him so tightly when they took positions at his side, grabbing him by the arms.

They were taller than Gopal, but because they walked bent over, he stood about even. As they dragged him, he found it difficult to keep pace since they stepped forward first with one leg and then hopped on the other. As if the smell of these vile creatures wasn't bad enough, the two scampering ahead defecated as they walked. Shocked by the offensive display, Gopal tried desperately to avoid stepping in their droppings, but wasn't successful.

After about thirty minutes, Gopal saw cliffs ahead, and a cave opening showed above. They forced him up the rocky path to where bones scattered the ground at the entrance to the cave. There were skulls of horses, cattle, and buffalo, and smaller animals, rodents, he thought. The others were without a doubt . . . human, the gnawed remains of adults . . . and children, so many that he had to step over and between them as he was forced into the mouth of the cave. Was this his karma? A meal for dvid-dvids?

The stench was even worse when he entered the darkness. One creature scurried ahead, and Gopal was told to wait. In a minute or so, a light shone from within. Dhenuka lit a torch and walked about the cave, igniting more torches that stuck out from holes in the walls. It would have been better to remain in the dark, for the light revealed the source of the foul smell. Around the ground were more bones and half-eaten carcasses. Piles of stool were everywhere. Ammonia permeated the dark, dank air. Along the damp, moss-covered walls, bundles of various sizes—booty from caravans—had been torn open. Their stores—cloths of cotton and silk, cooking utensils, tarnished pots, broken clay bowls, and vases—were scattered about the ground. There was nothing of real value, just the discarded remnants of the dvid-dvid's pillaging.

Forced to enter, Gopal was finally pushed into a corner and tied by the neck to a short length of leather, a leash, secured to a spike protruding from the cave wall.

"Someone will need to go back and see if there are others," snarled Trnavarta, scratching his genitals. "Dhenuka! You go!"

"Why me? Why me?" the smallest jabbered. "Always me. Always me. Dhenuka . . . do this. Dhenuka . . . Always Denu—"

Trnavarta slapped the back of his hand across the babbling face of the little dvid-dvid, making a wet, smacking sound. "Get moving and stop complaining, or next time we run short of food. . . . Now get going!"

Dhenuka, his stub of a tail between his legs, cowered, and reluctantly slunk from the cavern. The three remaining dvid-dvids paced nervously, finally settling into a corner where they shared the remains of some carrion. Gopal wished they had covered his eyes with a blindfold. At least then he wouldn't have to see these disgusting creatures. . . . It was bad enough he had to smell them.

* * * * *

Still at the river, Sudama became worried and woke Nimai. "Gopal must have gone too far ahead. Wait here with the girl. I want to go and see if I can find him."

Nimai wiped the sweat and flies from his cheeks. "Hurry, it's getting hhhot agaaain." Rising, he crouched at the shore, lapping water.

After journeying for some time, Sudama became suspicious when he noticed the footprints of a boy in the mud. "He must have taken his sandals off," he whispered to the morning. "Foolish boy, where does he think he is?" The brahmacari, his guard up now, followed the heedless steps, reaching the site of the abduction. Placing his own foot into a large print in the wet sand, he recognized the long toes as the imprints of dvid-dvid claws. He silenced himself, not knowing if the creatures were still close, and turned his back to the river, knowing dvid-dvids' dislike of water. He crouched, motionless, searching the brush and tall reeds. Feeling secure, he again turned his attention to the prints. They went in that direction, he reasoned. I'd better go back and get Nimai. We shouldn't be separated. Continually watching the brush behind and around him, not trusting even the sound of birds, he made his way back.

Nimai saw Sudama coming. "Whhhere's Gopaaal?"

"I'm afraid we have more trouble. I found dvid-dvid tracks. They must have Gopal."

Nimai understood the seriousness of the news, for Gopal had read him tales of the creatures, but, like so many other stories, he hadn't believed. "Waas there—" he stumbled over his words, trying not to bleat, "—aaany blood?" Citty twitched.

"No, he may still be alive."

"Whaat aabout . . . Citty?" Nimai reminded, still enchanted.

"We will take her with us. Help me hide the boat first." Grabbing the small craft, they pulled it up onto the shore, turning it over and covering it with grass. Then, Sudama led Nimai to where he had found the tracks.

*　*　*　*　*

In the cave, Gopal tried desperately to undo his bonds, but all attempts proved fruitless. The dvid-dvids continued to fight over the rotting meat, drooling and passing wind throughout their meal. Trnavarta, the biggest and most foul, whose whitened fur covered his head like a crown, kicked at the others, snapping if they came too close. Vyoma, the second largest, and more brown than the others, got up and walked over to Gopal, checking his restraints. Satisfied that they were secure, he squatted in front of his captive, this time just to sit, much to Gopal's relief. "The bounty on your head is said to be a treasure," Vyoma growled. "Kali and Bhutanatha will reward us—"

"Shut up!" barked Trnavarta from across the cave. "Let's get him to do the talking." The leader, still gnawing on a bone, stood to his feet, suddenly dropping the chewed marrow. It was immediately pounced on by Vatsasura. Trnavarta joined Vyoma and Gopal. The dvid-dvid leaned over Gopal, who crouched in the driest place he could find. The dvid-dvid ran his long black fingers through the boy's hair, making Gopal worry that their hunger would overpower their greed. Then, Trnavarta extended a claw from his longest finger and dragged the talon across Gopal's forehead, scratching down the side of his face, over the gag crossing his cheek, and across the width of his neck. Gopal swallowed his own breath, anticipating the worst. But Trnavarta continued his teasing by moving his claw to the back of Gopal's neck, where, with one quick flick, the dvid-dvid snapped the gag. Folding his claw into his hairy palm, Trnavarta placed his knuckle under Gopal's chin, lifting the boy's pale face. "Now . . . my tender morsel . . . tell us where your friends are . . . and maybe we will decide not to eat you first."

"Friends?" Gopal questioned, realizing the dvid-dvids weren't very smart. They hadn't even thought to search the area where they first found him. "I'm traveling alone."

With long strands of saliva dripping from both sides of his mouth, and spitting mad, Trnavarta let out an ear-piercing howl and smashed Gopal across the face, drawing blood. Recomposing himself as quickly as he had lost his temper, the creature leaned forward, catching the droplets of blood with one extended claw. After licking the rich fluid, he reached for more, this time offering it to Vyoma, who still sat by Gopal's side.

Vyoma licked his lips and purred, pleased with Trnavarta's gift. "It tastes so sweet. Sweeter than even my mother's milk."

"Before or after you ate her?" yelled the red-furred Vatsasura, rolling on his back, his legs pulled up with his knees against his chest, and howling with laughter.

Vyoma's appetite had been awakened. "Let's eat him now!" he begged, standing to his feet.

Vatsasura, hearing the word "eat," held in his banter and dropped the scraps he was licking, scurrying over on all fours. "Eat?" he growled. "Give! Give me!"

"What will it be?" asked Trnavarta, standing and grabbing Gopal by the neck. He lifted the boy against the damp wall. "Friends or food?"

Gopal imagined himself torn to shreds. He knew he couldn't give up his friends. Something slipped from his belt, clanging when it hit the hard cave floor. Trnavarta's eyes gravitated to the round, shiny object at his feet. He tossed Gopal to the side, farther than the leash would allow. Gopal's neck wrenched when it reached the length of the cord, but the force served him well, for it loosened the spike.

Vatsasura dove for the shiny object first, followed by Vyoma. Reaching the unusual relic, they got to their knees, each snarling at the other. Tugging and growling, they spit and hissed, the hair on their backs standing stiff. Trnavarta stood over the two, and, grabbing each by the back of the head, banged them together. They fell to the ground, both dazed, dropping the object of their fancy. Trnavarta retrieved the disc from the dirt. "What do we have here?" he pondered, not realizing he held the real purpose for Kali and Bhutanatha's reward. "A golden disc?" He tossed it up and down, trying to guess its weight.

Vyoma and Vatsasura came to their senses. "What is it?" Vyoma asked, standing to join his leader.

Vatsasura, holding himself, paced in place. "Let me see! Let me see! I can't see!" he whined, pushing Vyoma to the side. "Is it worth anything?"

"Shut your mouth!" Trnavarta snarled, hitting Vatsasura, forcing him back against the wall, and dropping the discus.

Vyoma, seizing the chance to hold the shiny object, pounced on the disc. Trying to hide it against his body, he hobbled into a corner. "Give it back!" demanded Trnavarta and motioned for Vyoma to heel.

"No!" Vyoma barked, still huddled in the corner and cradling the disc. "It's mine now!"

Gopal leaned against the cave wall, temporarily forgotten. He squirmed on the ground, thinking of the vile surface. The spike! It was hanging from the wall. Had the dvid-dvids noticed? He thought not. Carefully, hoping they were diverted, he tugged with his neck, and the spike came loose with a puff of dirt and fell to the ground. He feared the noise would attract attention, but the dvid-dvids were busy tugging on the discus. He squirmed some more, hoping to get closer to the wall and farther from their sight. He slid himself in the dirt, and the cloth binding on his hands loosened.

*   *   *   *   *

On the path, Sudama had found the dvid-dvid tracks. "Here, over here."

Nimai came running from the opposite direction. "Whhhich waay?"

Sudama pointed to the ground. The tracks led away from the river. "They go off . . . toward those cliffs," he answered, unaware that they were being watched. "There are dvid-dvid droppings all over," he warned. "Watch your step."

They again lifted Citty's stretcher, and Nimai looked down at the trail, disgusted. He couldn't let go of his burden to pinch his black nose closed.

"Wait until you smell a dvid-dvid," said Sudama. "They have to be the most foul—" He stopped. "Quiet, I heard something." The sound of a heavy foot broke the silence. "Over there. Down!" He motioned for Nimai to rest the litter.

"Whaat do you think it is?" whispered Nimai.

"I don't know. I wish I had my staff," said Sudama. "I don't know if I can depend on mantras."

"Here," offered Nimai, handing the apprentice a stone, as the brush on their left crushed under the weight of something large, rushing and then leaping into the air. It released a blood-curdling howl. The sun was blotted out above Nimai, and the weight of the creature pressed him to the ground, making him unable to move his arm. With his free hand he grabbed the creature around the neck. He could see only its fangs, yet even in the terror of the moment, he couldn't help noticing the horrible stench. Yellow saliva dripped from the creature's opened mouth. Its hot, foul-smelling breath blew into his face. Nimai screamed the cry of a goat, startling the dvid-dvid and making the creature hesitate to bite the boy's throat.

By now, Sudama had risen to his feet, and, raising the stone, brought it down on the back of the creature's head. Howling and chattering at the same time, the dvid-dvid rolled off Nimai. Screaming, it brandished its fangs and claws, trying to cope with the pain. Sudama prepared to strike a second blow. "Kill it!" screamed Nimai. Sudama hesitated. Again Nimai screamed. "Kill it!" Sudama brought the stone down on the dvid-dvid's face, crushing its nose. The creature gasped for breath. Unable to find any, it collapsed.

"That vile thing deserved death," Sudama reasoned, trying unsuccessfully to convince himself that he had done right. "Again I have fallen to my emotions."

Nimai, recovered from the shock of tangling with the dvid-dvid, was trying, without luck, to brush off the horrible stench that filled his clothing and nose. "I caan't breathe. Every time I take aaa breath, I smell that horrible odor. It dripped saaaliva on me."

Sudama looked at what he had done to the dvid-dvid. "At least you still have a nose to smell with, Nimai. You're lucky it didn't rip your face off."

Nimai was touching his animal face. "Maaybe, I would raaather be dead!"

Sudama needed to get away from the dvid-dvid, and from Nimai. "Stay here and watch Citty. I'll be right back. I am going to check ahead."

When Sudama was out of sight, Citty's eyes flashed open. Her red glare cast beams on Nimai, who was trying to clean himself with wild herbs. "Get me closer to the dvid-dvid," the krtya called. Nimai had no choice. While Sudama searched ahead, the krtya fed, growing stronger. When it finished feeding, Nimai, like a faithful servant, cleaned the krtya's face, and hid the dvid-dvid's body.

* * * * *

In the cave, Gopal had finally freed his hands when Trnavarta lunged at Vyoma. With claws extended, the two creatures came together in a clash of fur, teeth, spit, and blood. Trnavarta had no difficulty subduing Vyoma, and once on top of the smaller dvid-dvid, plunged his fangs into the back of Vyoma's neck. Vyoma, held under the weight of his leader, tried in vain to free himself from Trnavarta's clutches, but Trnavarta tore at Vyoma's flesh until Vyoma stopped struggling. His head slumped forward, held to his body by a few strands of fur and muscle. Trnavarta reared his head. His long hair thrashed. Again he plunged his fangs into Vyoma's head, digging his teeth through the skull. The smaller dvid-dvid kicked wildly, then shuddered, ceasing all movement. Gopal feared he would be next.

Vatsasura, recovering in the corner, was drawn by the scent of Vyoma's blood. Leaping from the shadows, he landed on Trnavarta's back, knocking them both to the ground. Trnavarta, invigorated by the battle, bucked like a horse, throwing the other dvid-dvid over the top of his head. Hunched on all fours, fangs exposed, his hair standing on end—making him appear twice his size—and still dripping the blood of his first kill, Trnavarta leaped some ten feet into the air, landing on Vatsasura.

Since the fight had moved a safe distance away, Gopal found his chance and grabbed the discus from the dead Vyoma's hand, crawling on his own hands and knees through the scattered cloth, bowls, and bones to the far side of the cave, hoping to reach the opening.

Vatsasura had tossed Trnavarta to the side, temporarily gaining the upper hand. Vatsasura's eye-shine suddenly beamed from the darkness to meet Gopal's stare. Opening his mouth and baring his canine teeth, Vatsasura raised his arms above his head and, waving them wildly, ran from the shadows toward the boy. More with reflex than with thought, Gopal threw the only thing he had—the discus! Flying from his hand, the Chakra grew in size, reaching eighteen inches in diameter in time to sever Vatsasura's head. So quick and clean was the spinning motion of the disc that the dvid-dvid's body continued running across the chamber, unaware of its loss. Headless, it reached Gopal; confused, it collapsed, spewing blood from its neck.

Trnavarta witnessed the magic of the disc but, controlled more by animal instinct than intelligence, realized only that Gopal was now unarmed. The last dvid-dvid, down on all fours, sneaked along the dark wall to the side of the unsuspecting boy. Hurling himself from the darkness, he knocked Gopal to the ground. Gopal, dazed by the surprise attack and by the wonder of the Chakra, lay motionless as Trnavarta stood to his full eight foot height, circling and taunting the human. The creature, about to pounce, became distracted by a glow which grew, brighter and larger, from the area where the disc had landed. An effulgence, too bright to look at, gave off a warmth that filled the cave. Reaching about six feet in height, the glow floated along the ground, moving toward both of them.

Again, the dvid-dvid's animal instincts took over. Turning to face it, Trnavarta snarled and spat. The incandescent apparition moved closer. Backed into a corner, the dvid-dvid leaped into the air, onto the glowing form, and instantly burned, like an insect hitting a flame.

The smell of a dead, burning dvid-dvid was worse even than the smell of a living dvid-dvid, Gopal thought as he sat up. Would he be next? The crackling of the dvid-dvid's body reminded him of the game the Rakshasas had played on Narakatala. As strange as it seemed, a smile crossed his face when he thought how the Rakshasas would have loved the loud crackling that Trnavarta made, but soon the crackling ended, and the glowing form moved again.

Slowly, moving backward on his hands and feet, Gopal found himself against the wall, with the blazing form slowly approaching. He used his right arm to shade his eyes from the light. Gopal stood tall, prepared to meet his fate. "*Jai Om,*" he chanted, feeling the being's heat.

"I do not intend harm, Prabhu," the radiance spoke.

Gopal tried to look from behind his arm, but the light was so bright, he had to close his eyes. "What are you?" he demanded, opening one eye and looking at the floor. "What do you want from me?" He looked for a means of escape, but knew he could never make it to the cave entrance.

"I am the Chakra," it replied, "and I serve whoever possesses me."

Gopal looked to the spot where the Chakra had originally fallen. The discus was gone. Sudama had said its powers were great. Maybe this was true. Maybe the manus were

going to work for him now. "Your light is blinding me."
The glow subdued until tolerable. Anything but relaxed,
Gopal removed his arm from in front of his face to find a
glowing human form standing before him. "You take the
form of a man?"

"I am the Sudarsana Chakra, weapon of Lord
Paramatma—the guardian of the manus."

"This is an illusion, a spell of some kind," Gopal protested, for there were no distinguishable features on the
glow.

"Bhutanatha realized my power of interplanetary flight.
For you, I served as a weapon—that being your desire. Did
I not perform well in ridding you of the dvid-dvids?"

It had helped him by killing the dvid-dvids. "Yes,
but—"

"I am the servant of whoever possesses me," repeated the
Chakra, "and you are now my master."

Gopal was too frightened to think of the true meaning of
those words. He wanted the thing to leave him, or at least
to return to its previous form. "Then return to the form of
the disc," he hesitantly commanded. The glow shrunk back
to its six-inch golden form, and Gopal quickly picked up
the disc. Almost afraid it would change again, he placed it
back under his belt. *For the moment*, he mentally ordered
the Chakra, *stay that way*, then he walked toward the light
outside.

*   *   *   *   *

When Sudama returned, Nimai convinced the brahmacari that the dvid-dvid smelled so bad that he had had to
roll it into the brush or he would have thrown up. Happy
to be rid of the thing, Sudama didn't question the boy's
words, and together they lifted Citty's stretcher to resume
their search.

After following the path for a short distance, Nimai
cried out, "There! There's a caaave." He pointed to the

cliffs ahead.

Sudama looked up in the direction Nimai had indicated. "Someone is coming out. Down," said the brahmacari, lowering his end of the litter.

"It looks like Gopaal," whispered Nimai. "Gopaal! Gopaal! Down hhhere!" he yelled, waving his arms, to the consternation of the brahmacari. Gopal looked down and waved back.

* * * * *

On the Pisaca ship, the Yaksas had fallen into their routine. The deck quieted and the stowaways felt safe enough to continue their search. They had just made their way to the decks below when Vyasa whispered, "Soldiers . . . talking in that room." He pointed to a closed door across the hall. The laughter of too much drinking came from the other side. Quietly, the mystic and the Apsarasa crept down the ship's narrow hall, with Vyasa using the walls to support him. As in the dungeons before, it was Usha who decided the direction when they reached a bisecting passage. Vyasa peeked around a corner. "Your instincts were correct again," the mystic whispered. "There are two guards in front of a locked room." He stepped back, resting against the wall, trying to catch his breath.

The Apsarasa also looked. "I don't think I will have time to bewitch both of them," she admitted.

"Allow me," Vyasa offered. The color had drained from his face.

"You are too weak," said Usha. "Let me help you." She put out her hand, with one finger extended.

Vyasa pushed it aside with the spear. "I am fine," he insisted. Practicing his art would give him the concentration he needed, the diversion he needed to overcome the pain of his wound. "I can do it," he urged. Vyasa moved past Usha to a place where he could see. He held out his left palm, fingers extended at the Yaksas.

"Gatavedas shall confuse them.
Maghavan, deprive them of their senses.
Indra, confuse the hostiles who contend against us.
Agni, turn them against each other."

Usha was unable to see and could only hear the mystic's words. "What are they doing?"

Vyasa turned away from the guards. "They will eliminate each other," he explained, but turned back to be sure. The guards were restless, unable to stand still. They paced around the hall, looking at each other. "Like the wind," Vyasa continued, "scatter their thoughts to opposite sides." The guards backed away from each other and leveled their spears. "Cause them to slay their enemy!" The soldiers lunged at one another. Both slumped forward, impaled on the other's weapon. Slowly, they crumpled to the floor, and the ship jerked, tossing Vyasa and Usha to the wall.

Getting to his feet, Vyasa rounded the corner with Usha. Stepping over the bodies, Usha said, "There are things we can teach each other."

"Maybe at another time." Vyasa removed the wooden beam from the door and opened it as Citty turned to the entrance, ready to fight for her life. The door slowly pushed inward. The dim light from the hall fell into the cell, but the girl couldn't see the face of the figure who entered.

"Citty?" Vyasa called into the dark.

Citty knew it wasn't the voice of a Yaksa or Rakshasa. The voice was that of a human. Vyasa entered the cell, and Citty recognized the mystic she had seen at the istagosti.

"I have been sent by Gopal," Vyasa assured her as Usha also stepped into the cell. Citty quickly forgot her captivity, overwhelmed by the creature that stood behind the mystic. "This is Usha. She is here to help us."

"Soldiers," the Apsarasa suddenly warned and pushed Vyasa farther into the cell, her touch catching the mystic off guard.

The door was pulled shut from the outside, and the wooden beam replaced. "Now we have three to trade for the Chakra, should my krtya fail," laughed Bhutanatha from the other side. He pointed to the dead guards. "Remove these two fools and assign someone who will not be so easily swayed by an old mystic's game."

FIFTEEN

OUTSIDE THE CAVE, the friends were reunited. "It's good to see you," admitted Sudama. He took Gopal by the shoulders and shook him vigorously. This exhibition of emotion by the brahmacari surprised Gopal. After a brief pause, Sudama actually embraced him.

Nimai didn't like the display. . . . Gopal had always been *his* friend. "Wee killed aaa dvid-dvid," screeched Nimai, standing proudly with the dvid-dvid's clawed finger in his hand, as if he had singlehandedly killed the creature. He also walked over to Gopal for an embrace, but was overwhelmed by the stench of the lair. The dank silence permeated the earthy dark, making Nimai forget his intended embrace and wander to the place where Vyoma lay dead. Nimai pressed his hand over his mouth for fear of being sick.

Gopal ran to check on his sister. Sudama followed, giving him the bad news. "I'm sorry, there hasn't been any change. Dhanus's drug had no effect." Gopal's expression paled. "Let's move her closer to the entrance. The sun might do her some good." Leaving Gopal with Citty, Sudama went looking for Nimai. Upon entering the cave, he found a dead dvid-dvid. Gopal went to Sudama's side and was looking down at the gutted Vyoma when Sudama began quoting from the Song of Kartikeya—the Book of the Warrior. " 'Happy are the warriors to whom such fighting opportunities come unsought, opening for them the doors of the heavenly planets.' Maybe you were meant to be a warrior," he proclaimed at the sight of the carnage, " . . . although you may have gone a bit far," he added, focusing on the hollowed skull of the creature.

"Oh—" Gopal tried to explain, "—I didn't do that. They were fighting among themselves. . . . The big one did that!" He pointed to the bloodied corpse of Vatsasura. "I was forced to kill that one," he admitted, pointing to the headless body lying in a pool of half-dried blood.

"Aaand this must be the rest of hhhim," said Nimai, holding Vatsasura's severed head by its hair, peering closer, examining the black, glass-eyed stare of the dead creature. "Haaave you ever seen aaanything so ugly?"

"Now smell your fingers," said Gopal, laughing, thankful for the humorous interruption.

Nimai dropped the head, which made a hollow clunk when it hit the floor. Hysterical, he wiped his hands on himself, on the ground, on the cave walls. "I'll neeever get this smell offf me." He dropped his hands in frustration, holding them as far away as he could, repelled by his own smelly fingers.

"I did find some weapons," said Gopal, walking to the collection he had gathered from around the lair. "They're old, but useful." Sudama and Nimai gathered around. Gopal showed them the arsenal: an old bow and a handful of arrows, a frayed rope, a splintered club, and a stained and yellow conch shell that smelled more of the sea than of battle. "At least now, we're armed." Neither Sudama nor Nimai reacted.

*   *   *   *   *

Within the belly of the Pisaca ship, trapped in the cell, Vyasa fought the power of the Apsarasa's spell. The wound no longer stung his leg, but now, Usha's touch stung his heart and mind as he fought to keep control of his senses, refusing to surrender to the siren. He turned to face the Apsarasa and chanted the mantra to break her spell over him.

> "As the wind stirs up the dust and the clouds,
> Thus may all misfortune, placed by your charm,
> Go away from me!"

Citty was frightened and confused. She didn't know if she had been rescued or not.

Vyasa couldn't think of their captivity. He had to deal with the Apsarasa, or everything would be lost. He continued:

> "Go away, O spell of sirens.
> Do not stand and track me like some wounded animal.

"You will not put me under," he challenged.

Usha tried to explain. "You fool, I was try—"

Vyasa kept chanting.

> "As the sun releases darkness,
> Abandons the night and the streaks of dawn,
> Every misery prepared by your spell,
> Do I leave behind."

With those words he passed his hand through the air between him and the Apsarasa. For the moment, he had won.

Citty couldn't hold back. "What do we do now?" she asked.

Vyasa turned to the girl. "We are not lost yet!"

"We must deal with Bhutanatha," warned Usha. "and his soldiers."

Vyasa, having regained strength of mind and body, paced the length of the cell, rubbing his chin. It was not the pace of anxiety, but of deep thought. After a few minutes, he spoke. "First, we have to change the course of this ship."

The two females looked up from their seats on the floor.

"But—" Usha started to say.

"If I can direct it to the shore . . ." Vyasa didn't hear her. He was talking aloud, to himself. He found this to be the best way for him to solve problems. "That's it! Even if we crash on the rocks, we would still have a chance to escape."

"What?" Usha stood and blocked Vyasa's path, forcing him to pay her some mind.

Citty also stood and confronted the mystic, as an ally. "What exactly is your idea?"

"There is a mantra to change the course of currents." He turned and paced again in the smaller space left him.

"You are taking the chance of sinking this ship," Usha realized, "with us trapped in here."

Vyasa smiled thinly. "That is right, and I don't even swim."

"Anything is better than being in the hands of Bhutanatha," Citty admitted. "I say, do it."

Usha knew they were out of choices. "Try your spell, mystic. The girl is right."

Vyasa sat in a lotus position in the center of the cell floor. Reaching down, he placed his palms on the deck. "We are in the lowest deck. I can feel the current vibrating through the wood." Closing his eyes, he uttered the mantra.

"From the time when the cloud-serpent was slain.
Var became your name."

He paused. With the creaking of a thousand boards, and the twisting of a thousand coils of rope, the Pisaca ship screamed. The rafters fought to keep control against the mystic's charm. "I can feel the current changing course. The ship is fighting it."

"The *ship* is fighting it?" Citty gasped. "What do you mean, the ship?" She looked to Usha for an answer. There was none.

"This ship is alive!" Vyasa answered, quickly continuing his battle of wills with the vessel.

"These waters, as do all waters, support Varuna.
When the manus stood within you,
You flowed according to their will.
In his name, I call you to me.
Surrender your life's breath and luster."

At that, the three captives were hurled across the cell. The walls of the prison buckled as the ship turned to Vyasa's mantra.

"The walls are leaking," said Citty.

Usha grew worried. "We Apsarasas aren't fond of water."

Vyasa stayed in control and sat in place. His calm hands again pressed to the floor, feeling the wet wood.

The guards, realizing the disruption was the work of the mystic, tried to enter the cell. "The door is bent," said one. "It won't open."

"Move aside, you fool," yelled the other, beating his sword against the warped wood. The first guard joined him. Their banging added to the tormented cries of the ship, and the transcendental sound vibrations of the mystic. The ship's screams grew louder. Waves crashed against the living hull. With each furious splash, water found its way through the parting seams, forming puddles on the cell floor. Usha chose her steps carefully.

Vyasa continued chanting.

"I see them. I hear them.
The waves cry out; their voices come to me."

The ship rocked and tossed itself into a frenzy. Citty
strained to hear Vyasa's voice, now drowned out by the
crashing waves and the soldiers' frantic banging. The
Yaksas' fear of their lord's anger gave them added strength.

"Here, you waters, is your heart," Vyasa chanted louder.
"Come ye mighty ones by my path. I am conducting you!"
Again, the ship threw them across the cell, but this time,
guided by Vyasa, the vessel crashed into the rock-covered
shore. The outer wall gave way to the stone, showering the
captives with shredded wood and water. The banging at
the door ceased. The soldiers had been thrown down the
hall.

"Quickly," Vyasa called, keeping his senses. "Through
the opening, before the ship recovers." He ran toward the
twisted beams and siding. Usha guided Citty ahead of her.
Vyasa stepped with one foot to a rocky ledge. The ship rose
and sank, fighting to break free. Grabbing the ledge,
Vyasa extended his hand. "Now, before the ship breaks
free." He pulled Citty onto the rock. Staying in place, the
mystic looked at Usha. The only way she would make it was
if he pulled her across. He would have to touch her. Vyasa
held out his hand. Usha grabbed it, pulling herself across
the space that widened between the shore and the broken
hull. Vyasa started chanting to protect himself.

Just then, the guards broke down the door and entered
the flooding cell. "There!" screamed one, pointing with a
now blunt sword. The other released his spear through the
gap in the hull, hitting Usha squarely in the back.

* * * * *

At the cave, after moving the new-found weapons outside, Gopal stood over his sister. "We still need to get Citty
to Niyana Bhiram."

"Wee will never get her thhhere in time," said Nimai. The concern he still felt for the girl overcame the animal half of him for a moment.

Gopal touched the Chakra in his belt. "It may still be possible." He took out the discus. Nimai made no comment, but his goat eyes glowed red at the sight of the discus. "The Chakra is supposed to have the power of flight," Gopal exclaimed, placing it on the ground. "It must be true, for Bhutanatha has offered a handsome price for its return. The dvid-dvids were after some reward but didn't even realize they had the object of Bhutanatha's quest." He stared at the Chakra, lying in the dirt at his feet. "I've seen it change form."

"It is true," said Sudama. "The Chakra is said to have many powers." They stood, looking at the golden disc.

"Chakra," said Gopal sternly, not knowing how to do it, or how else to say it. "We wish to fly to the city of Niyana Bhiram." Nothing happened.

"There is a word for the vehicles the devas use to travel," said Sudama. "I think Vyasa called them . . . vimanas. Yes, vimanas, that's it. Try chanting that."

Gopal looked down at the disc. "Vimanas!" The disc began to glow, first a little, then brighter. "It did that in the cave . . . and then it killed the dvid-dvids." Nimai and Sudama stepped back, but not Gopal. He stood his ground as the glow again grew larger, but this time remained in the shape of the disc. Finally, when it was large enough to hold all of them, it stopped. "Do we get on it?" Gopal wondered.

"Yes," answered Sudama. No one moved.

Then Gopal took the first step and placed his sandaled foot into and on the glow. Nothing happened. He placed his second foot on the discus. "I can feel it humming," he said. "It's sending a tingle through my body." Sudama and Nimai, carrying Citty, joined them. The disc jerked, jarring them from their feet.

Suddenly, the Chakra rose from the ground and hovered

above the cave entrance . . . and then it flew. The wind felt refreshing against their faces, especially for Nimai and Gopal. It was cleansing as the Chakra skimmed the air. Like a sled on ice it pierced the sky, unwavering in its mystic flight. Everyone felt excited and bewildered at the same time. Sudama wondered if anyone knew how to make it stop.

Gopal could see the path they had followed to the cave. "There," he pointed, "the Sarpa." Thinking his words to be a command, the Chakra descended, flying low, skimming the water. A cool mist rose from the waves, spraying them. Conch-shell horns echoed through the valley. A dust cloud, moving toward them, rose along the sandy bank downriver. "Soldiers?" asked Gopal.

"Chariots!" replied Sudama. His experiences before he became a student of Vyasa enabled him to tell the difference between the dust of foot soldiers, of horses, and of chariots. "We've little time." Quickly sitting again, they lifted from the surface and were about ten feet from the ground when the first charioteer came into view.

The sight that greeted the soldiers was quite unexpected, and the lead chariot came to a screeching halt. Being warriors, the surprise wore off quickly. The archer behind the first driver had already released his arrow and was loading and aiming a second. The other chariots gathered in a V formation. The archers on board released their volleys.

Gopal thought quickly. "The shield!" he yelled at Sudama. "Make the shield."

Quickly, with Gopal's confidence driving him, Sudama moved himself between the shower of arrows and the riders of the Chakra and chanted, "Pratikina-pratikih." The shield of sound opened like an umbrella, as the arrows, like hail, pounded on, then bounced from, the transcendental barrier, breaking the tips and splintering the shafts. The soldiers threw their spears and followed those with even more arrows, but the discus was out of range and flew downriver.

After some time, a forest, looking much as Dhanus had sketched it, appeared in the distance. "I can see the city," said Gopal.

"Set us down in the woods," Sudama urged. "I can imagine what would happen if we landed in the market." The Chakra hovered above the woods. "There." Sudama pointed below.

Gopal directed the Chakra to rest in the clearing, scattering and frightening deer and nesting birds beneath. Once on solid ground, they stepped off the disc, which then returned to the small golden form.

"Gopal and I will go into the city," Sudama said, looking at the goat-headed Nimai. "I think it will draw less attention."

Nimai looked rebellious at the thought of being left behind again. "I know you want to come," consoled Gopal, wrapping his arm around his friend's shoulders, "but I need you to protect Citty." He smiled and wrinkled his nose in disgust. "What we don't need is this smell." He pulled at his own shirt.

Sudama remembered the robes from Narakatala. Before anyone knew, he had them unbundled and waving in the breeze.

"These aren't much better, but compared to stale dvid-dvid, Narakatala might smell good." There was no argument from Gopal.

"It might provide a better cover," said Gopal, covering his clothing with the robe he had worn before. There was still a hint of the oil he had sprinkled on it.

Sudama was looking through the forest behind them. "The soldiers from Toshana know which way we went. They are sure to come here. We must hurry."

"Shall we take the weapons?" asked Gopal. "What do you think?"

"We just want to get information," said Sudama. "Maybe they would be better left with Nimai."

"I have had some luck with bows," said Gopal. Sudama

didn't argue, but left the rope, the conch shell, and the club behind. Gopal carried the bow and the Sudarsana Chakra, hidden as always next to the naga claw. Excited and relieved at what he thought to be the end of his journey, Gopal walked toward the lights and sounds of Niyana Bhiram . . . a city that was strangely loud for a such a mystical place.

SIXTEEN

FAR FROM HER BROTHER, on the shore of the Black Sea, and still within the dark kingdom of Narakatala, Citty cried. "Usha is dead." Her brief exposure to the Apsarasa was enough to nurture attachment to the siren.

The Pisaca ship had finally pulled itself free from the rocks and drifted into the misty water before the guards could release anymore weapons. Unaware of its damage, the ship faltered, rocking and moaning, trying to maintain balance. The cold waters rushed into the cavity in its side, catching the guards in the swell where they were quickly grabbed by the waves. The cries of other Yaksa soldiers rang from the ship's belly. Having sustained so much injury and taking on water rapidly, the ship cried out one last time and sank like a stone, vanishing into the mist of the cold Narakatala waters.

Vyasa, having overcome the spell of the Apsarasa once again, touched Usha's face. "She is in turiya-samadhi," he said. "I have seen great mystics put themselves into this trance to heal their wounds, but—," Vyasa grunted, and, with a quick jerk, removed the spear, "—I don't know if the trance works against weapons of the black arts." He tossed the spear into the waves that crashed below them. "We will need to get her to her husband's people, the Ghandharvas. Only they will be able to help her." He paused. "That task will take a far greater mantra than I possess."

Citty was confused by the hopelessness Vyasa displayed. "There must be a way."

"You don't understand. No one knows where their kingdom is. . . . I know it's on an upper planet, but they are innumerable. It would take forever to find the right one."

"You are a mystic!" said Citty, sounding very much like her brother. Like him, she refused to admit defeat. "I've seen your powers. Think of something!"

Vyasa looked out over the now quiet sea, his mind transcending the lightless confines of Bila-svarga. Suddenly, he remembered the conversation he and Usha had overheard between Bhutanatha and his priests. "The Chakra. Gopal has the Chakra. The discus can take us to the Ghandharvas."

Citty delighted in the news, but was still in the dark. "Where is Gopal?" she asked.

"I sent them to Niyana Bhiram to get help for you—"

Citty's brow furrowed. Vyasa knew her question. "I will explain on the way. We must leave here. I can't believe the sinking of that ship was enough to finish Bhutanatha." Taking hold of Usha, whose touch was rendered harmless in her current state, they set out for the portal through which Vyasa had originally come. Vyasa followed the shoreline, finally reaching the outskirts of Alakapuri. Once again, by using mantras, spells, charms, and plain wit, he and Citty sneaked past the city's fortification, and, following the road he and Gopal had used earlier, finally reached the Rudra temple and the dvar back to Bhu.

* * * * *

Meanwhile, Gopal had reached the gate of Niyana Bhiram, ready to end his unwanted journey. The entrance to the city was crowded, and from the sound that was coming from within, it was even more crowded on the inside. Seeing the gate, he wondered. "How many gates are there in Niyana Bhiram?"

Sudama shook his head; he didn't know. "Let's walk behind this cart," he suggested. "We may draw less attention." He tugged at Gopal's robe.

"Our smell alone will keep people from getting too close," Gopal replied.

Although once a mystic retreat, with the coming of Kali Yuga, Niyana Bhiram was now busy with vendors, a haven for charlatans and soldiers. It was evident the moment Gopal passed through the gates. "Astrology!" he heard. "Let me read your stars and find your fortune!" barked a man from within his shop. "A mere coin I ask you to invest."

"Come here, your palm can tell me your future," screeched another. "I can find you a beautiful wife, for only a small price."

"I have one for you now," called a woman from a balcony. Leaning over a flower-garlanded rail stood six women. Long hair, dyed the colors of wheat, teakwood, and sandalwood paste, brushed their colored cheeks. "Come up here!" their procurer called again. "These women are better than wives. These you can use for your pleasure and throw back when you're done." She laughed, a hacking mulish laugh, and was joined by the women with her. Crowds jammed the street, pushing to get a closer look at the goods for sale. Gopal stopped in his steps, taking a long look at the pleasures offered from above. Sudama had to pull him on.

"Slaves! Young, strong, take your pick. These children will eat little and serve well," yelled a man. "I'll even throw in the mother, at no extra cost!" This brought cackled laughter from the crowd. "Come, take a look!"

"What has happened to this place?" Gopal whispered, pushing through the mass of people. "What has happened to Bhu?"

"It's the influence of Maya," answered Sudama. "It's—"

"Make way there!" came an order from behind. A strong arm pushed Sudama to the side, separating him from Gopal.

"Make way!" a voice commanded. A formation of fifteen human foot-soldiers plowed a path through the crowd, like elephants through bamboo. Behind followed a Rakshasa garrison on horseback.

I've lost Sudama, thought Gopal, trying frantically to see to the other side of the street. When he finally caught sight of the brahmacari again, he didn't take his eyes off him. He wasn't ready to be alone. Standing within the always pushing crowd, listening to the shouts of the vendors, he wanted it to end. The market, a thing that had been his cherished treasure, no longer attracted him. This scene actually repulsed him. Waiting for the garrison to pass, he couldn't help listening to a man reading bumps on another man's head.

"Want me to read your bumps?" cried the man, spotting the wide-eyed youth.

"Let's be on our way!" Gopal heard from behind. Sudama grabbed his arm, dragging him away.

"Maybe this place can no longer give us the information we seek," Gopal worried.

"Let's try anyway," said Sudama, stopping suddenly. Two soldiers, left to patrol the market, were giving them odd looks. Gopal and Sudama turned away from the soldiers. A sign hung over a nearby door. It read: Nila Udumbara, in fresh blue paint on a bright yellow background.

"The Blue Lotus?" Gopal asked. "What is it?"

"It doesn't matter," replied Sudama. The two soldiers were asking questions of the bump reader. "I would trust anything in there, faster then what's happening on this street." Pushing Gopal by the shoulders, they dodged through the crowd and entered.

* * * * *

Back at the clearing, Nimai had been summoned by the krtya. He had to obey. "Your friend has the Chakra, and I am still too weak to challenge its powers," she said, "and now you have allowed them to take more weapons." Nimai stared into the hypnotic glare of the creature's eyes, able only to listen. "Hide the weapons you have here. Tell them they were stolen by thieves. Until I can get the discus and gain my strength, I will need your help."

* * * * *

The Nila Udumbara, although bleak on the outside, opened to a well-lit courtyard, crowded with low tables and sitting mats, each occupied. Singing, drinking, and gambling filled the incense-scented air. Musicians took seats on a platform, and, lifting a flute, ektar, tablas, and kole, they played a tune that seemed to quiet the crowd. Very much like in Alakapuri, thought Gopal. The scent of something familiar mixed with the incense. "Do you smell it?" Gopal asked, searching for the source.

"Smells like svapna," Sudama replied.

"We don't have time to waste," Gopal quickly reminded the brahmacari, remembering his dream. "We came for information."

"Maybe we should find a place to sit," Sudama suggested. "It would make us less suspicious." He paused, looking around the room. There were no soldiers. He saw a table become empty. "There, those men are leaving."

Gopal pushed his way through the crowd, reaching the table just as another man was about to sit. "We saw it first," Gopal challenged, shoving the drunken stranger away and quickly sitting on the mat.

"I am called Mokra," came a voice as soon as they had taken seats. "How can I serve you?" Gopal looked over his shoulder at a large, dark skinned man, his clothing and turban as faded and dirty as his face.

"One who robs wealth?" questioned Sudama.

"A suitable name for the proprietor of this establishment, don't you think?" Mokra looked down at Gopal and grinned through the spaces in his teeth. "Don't you think?"

Gopal stared up at him. "I suppose," he replied. Their table was wet with spilled drinks and food. A pipe with three stems sat in the center. Cold, black ash filled the bowl.

"I can't take your wealth until you drink. Or would you prefer something else? What will it be?"

Gopal looked at the pipe. "A drink!" He turned to Mokra. "What's good here?"

"For you? . . . How about Ananda-panam? The drink of bliss! Guaranteed to fill you with delight."

"Yes, yes, bring . . . " He looked at Sudama, who shook his head in disagreement. " . . . one drink!" Gopal just wanted the man to leave, which he finally did. "Look, we came for information," he whispered, resting his elbows on the table's grimy surface. "I doubt this is where we will get it. Maybe we should leave?"

Sudama, like Vyasa, was conscious of the boy's impatience. "Move around the crowd. Maybe you can find some loose tongues." He remembered the drink. "I need money. We can't arouse suspicion."

Gopal handed the brahmacari the last two coins given him by Stoka. "I can't believe I still have these." He rose and stepped from the table. "I'll be back."

"Here you go," Mokra announced, "your drink." Noticing the empty seat, he asked, "Where is your friend?" He looked among the faces of the crowd for the boy, making Sudama suspicious. "You still want it, don't you?" For some reason, Mokra seemed more interested in Gopal's whereabouts than was warranted.

"Yes." Sudama handed the coins to Mokra, who turned his attention from the crowd.

"Yes, I think this will do fine." Mokra walked away from the table, mumbling. "It will do just fine. Yes." There was a strange look on the proprietor's face.

Across the courtyard, Gopal was looking for someone who could help him. This is useless, he thought, seeing only drunkards and gamblers.

"I see you carry a weapon," said a stranger. Part of Gopal's bow jutted from a tear in his robe. Quickly, he covered it. "I am called Bharuji," said the man. Gopal met the stranger's dark stare. It was like the stare of the naga. "I find it curious that one who dresses and smells like a mendicant would have a weapon." He moved to grab Gopal's garment.

Gopal quickly moved his hand up, grabbing the stranger by the wrist. "Perhaps there are things in this whorl that are better kept secret," the boy said.

"You seem protective. Maybe the bow carries some value? Will you wager it?"

"I have no desire to gamble; that's not why I'm here!"

"Maybe it is," came a voice from behind. Sudama whispered, "Behind him. See the one with the ashes marking his forehead?" Behind the one called Bharuji, a tall willowy man stood, prepared to serve his master. "Is that your slave?" Sudama asked.

"The Pandu?" Bharuji laughed, as did four to five others that stood close, listening. "In the Age of Kali, this fool is every man's slave!"

"Then we will take him." Sudama's words surprised Gopal, who wasn't prepared for this.

The offer heightened Bharuji's interest. "Kamala," Bharuji called. The man hobbled forward. As if arranged beforehand, a serving girl came past on her way to the kitchen, a raw fish held above her head in a dented, brass tray. Bharuji snatched the fish. "I will place this, and you will snatch it with an arrow," he offered. "If you hit it, you get the man. If you miss, I get the bow and whatever else you might be hiding under that robe."

"You said you were good with a bow . . . right?" whispered Sudama. Gopal only nodded, wary of the stranger's interest. "We—*he* accepts," Sudama answered.

"You must hit the eye of the fish," Bharuji challenged.

Gopal thought, The naga was harder than this! "I can do that."

Bharuji suddenly added, "I get to choose the place for the fish."

At the far end of the courtyard stood three chariots. Bharuji whispered to his slave, who took the fish and ran to the closest vehicle. The Pandu, at his master's direction, hitched up the horses and tied the fish to the axle, between the wheels. Then the slave took a place on board, reins in hand. An audience gathered, sounding like a variety of jungle animals laughing at the challenge.

Gopal was not about to back down. He had come this far to save his sister. The Pandu was his last hope. "I'm ready," he said, removing the bow. Taking the weapon in both hands, he took a stance, spreading his feet wide, and flexed his left arm which was still stiff from his wound. He looked at the fish. "I see the axle," he mumbled. "I see the fish. I see only its eye."

Bharuji raised a dagger. "When I drop my arm, my slave will drive through the courtyard to the gate. You have to hit the eye of the fish . . . through the spokes of the wheel."

When the stranger reached up, Gopal became momentarily distracted by a symbol on the man's arm—the symbol of a Pisaca! He couldn't think of that now. "I see only the eye," he chanted, "only the eye. . . . "

Bharuji winked at the snickering audience and dropped his hand. The horses reared. The target moved.

Gopal steadied his stance, looking only at the eye of the fish spinning round. The wagon moved rapidly across the yard. "Only the eye," whispered the boy. "Only the eye!"

In another moment he would have what he needed to save his sister. He would be free! He pulled back on the string. His left hand was numb. Would this old bow perform? Would the arrow fly straight? Whispers and wages passed between the onlookers. Gopal released the shaft across the courtyard . . . through the whirling spokes of the chariot wheel . . . into the eye of the fish!

When the Pandu returned with the fish, the arrow still in place, Bharuji became furious. "I have been tricked by a child," he said, kicking a table aside. Catching the boy unaware, he knocked the bow from Gopal's hands and threw him to the ground. "Maybe I should remove that tongue from your mouth." The crowd laughed and snorted at the prospect. "It is too sharp for a boy like you and will probably get you hurt. Yes?" Bharuji turned to the crowd for approval. "I think I will take it and keep it for myself . . . to use as a weapon. I will also see what else is under that robe." The crowd laughed even more. Bharuji, with his dagger displayed, lunged for Gopal.

From the floor, Gopal reached under his belt. Before anyone was aware of its presence, the Chakra flew into Bharuji's neck. The surprise alone made Bharuji drop the dagger. The crowd fell silent. Bharuji grasped his throat as blood dripped down his chest. His hands vainly tried to close what he thought to be a flesh wound. Before the now silent audience, Bharuji's head tumbled from his shoulders to his feet, coming to rest against Gopal where the boy still sat on the wine- and soup-stained floor. Then, Bharuji's body crumpled.

Even before it hit the floor, news of the incident rumbled through the crowd. The onlookers whispered excitedly and spilled out the door and into the streets, spreading the news.

Gopal stood to his feet, rushed to the headless corpse, and removed the disc from the back of Bharuji's neck. Sudama emerged from the panicked audience with Gopal's bow drawn and the Pandu beside him, never taking his eyes off the faces that surrounded them. Motioning for Gopal to join him, he parted the crowd and quickly led them outside. Conch-shell horns sounded. Alarms ran through the village. Word spread quickly of the strangers in Niyana Bhiram. Gopal led them through the flow of the street, where they blended like drops of water in a stream. He finally hid the discus from view. "Let's get away before they realize what this weapon is and who we are," he said. "That information would bring a fair price in this market."

"The entire city will be after our heads," said Sudama. The Pandu ran along behind them as they quickly made their way out of the village and into the woods. Torches, the sounds of seahorns, and the thunder of horses' hooves pounding down the streets meant Niyana Bhiram was not sleeping tonight.

*　*　*　*　*

Far from Niyana Bhiram, at the palace at Hiranya, Kali was alone with his sister in their private chamber, and he was frightened. "What can we do?" Kali was pacing, his hands nervously clasped behind his back. His black, wrinkled skin hung loosely over his small, crooked frame. Dark, scraggly hairs hung from his chin and head, upon which lay the crown. "I don't like it. I don't like the idea that a few rebels can evade our soldiers . . . and that Bhutanatha. Why did you agree to ally with him? Why do we need him? Why aren't you able to find them with your own powers?"

Maya was quick to anger, especially at the ignorance of her twin. "You fool! They have the Chakra! It shields them from my eyes."

Kali cowered, afraid his sister would unleash her frustration on him. "What about Bhutanatha? Why do we still need him?"

"He controls the Third Whorl and that we need! Once we have the allegiance of that fool, and his army, I will dispose of him. Our armies are ready to invade Sveta-dvipa, but we need more forces. My powers are not enough against the combined forces of the devas . . . and the Chakra, should they regain it," Maya fumed. "Right now we have to deal with finding the Chakra. It is the only weapon I fear." A knock came at the door of their chamber. "Enter!" Maya called.

"Maya!" Kali panicked, looking at his true appearance. "I can't let anyone see me like this!"

His sister turned to him and chanted.

"I cover all eyes. All eyes I do shut to truth.
All eyes that shine on you will gleam with wonder.
I place illusion in their hearts.
Their thoughts are mine."

The door opened. A soldier entered, followed by the emissary that had been sent to Bila-svarga. They both bowed before the magnificence and beauty of their king and queen. "What news have you?" Maya asked, standing next to a throne.

Kali sat next to his sister, holding his royal shield and sword. "You heard your queen," Kali bellowed. "Answer!"

The emissary bowed again. "We traced the Chakra to the city of Niyana Bhiram. Your soldiers are right now tearing the city apart and searching the hills."

"Enough about the Chakra." Maya waved her delicate fingers, momentarily entrancing the messenger. "What about Bhumi and Dharma?"

"The captured devas are being brought here. They will arrive soon. I have already made preparations for the ceremony to invoke the Brahmastra."

* * * * *

Still within the temporary cover of the darkened woods, with the sound of conch-shell horns growing in the distance, Kamala thanked his rescuers. "How can I repay you for saving me?"

Gopal wasted no time. "My sister has been stricken by the Pisaca." He was relieved that his ordeal was coming to a close. "We were told that your people have knowledge of such things."

"Yes . . . and no," the Pandu replied.

Gopal stopped walking. "This is impossible! Vyasa said—"

"Yes, I have knowledge of such things," Kamala assured the boy, "but I am not able to help you myself."

That did it. In his mind, Gopal cursed Vyasa and the manus. He cursed his birth. He cursed his life.

"But you can still help us?" Sudama knew there was more.

"There is no cure on Bhu, but, for my freedom," the Pandu offered, "I can give you the location of the Kalpavriksha—the Tree of Wants."

Gopal was still too angry to answer, so Sudama answered for him. "Agreed."

"It stands in the garden of Ushana-shukra," the Pandu revealed.

Sudama wasn't pleased. "Only the greatest of mystics can attain entrance to the gardens!" The brahmacari knew it was beyond his experience. "We need Vyasa."

"You have the Chakra," said the Pandu, aware of its powers.

Gopal had had it. He was not giving up. He was not going to be defeated. He would save his sister and beat the manus at their own game. He thanked the Pandu, and with new hope they hurried back to Nimai and Citty.

"Well," Sudama greeted Nimai, seeing the boy up to strange activities. "What are you doing?"

Nimai was still burying the weapons. The voice of the brahmacari startled him from his trance. The krtya turned slightly, forced to release her slave. Nimai stood, open-mouthed, bewildered by his own actions.

"You startled him," said Gopal, thinking he knew Nimai better than anyone. "I can see what he's doing. He's burying the weapons to hide them from the soldiers."

Nimai nodded and mumbled, "Thaaat's whaat—" he stopped to get control, "—I was doing." The sight of his friend temporarily overcoming the krtya's spell, he began removing the weapons from the hole he had dug.

Gopal rushed to Citty's form. Looking down at the face of his sister, he removed the Chakra from its hiding place. "We go to Ushana-shukra!" He placed the Chakra on the ground and, with Nimai helping, placed his sister on board. Sudama took a seat next to the girl, helping the others hold her. Nimai hoisted the rope, conch-shell, and club onto the disc. Then Gopal uttered the word for flight, just as an army of torches scoured the hillside. The disc glowed brightly in the night sky and, like a comet, carried them across the heavens, through the sea of stars.

SEVENTEEN

THROUGH THE OUTER COVERINGS OF BHU, into the space between the planets of their whorl, the Chakra flew. The sensation of flying through space was like being under water. There was a constant pressure surrounding every inch of Gopal's being. He didn't have to hold his breath, but he wasn't sure that he was breathing. He couldn't tell. Whenever one of them moved, even the slightest, they could see some form of barrier that encased them, as if their moving had ignited a force field. It was as if his body was suspended in a solution of space and time, floating in a sea that was the Bhu-mandala.

Obeying Gopal's will, the disc landed in the garden called Ushana-shukra, on the planet at the edge of the whorl—the planet Soma. The garden was filled with mandara and parijata trees. Colorful and fragrant manjari, kusuma, kundini and mritsna flowers—flowers he had till now only read about—were before him to see and smell. Celestial birds—maruta, jivana, and pavana—of magnificent beauty, sang hypnotic songs and flew from the trees, frightened by the intruders in their glowing vehicle. Familiar peacocks, always with their hens, ran from their path displaying their plumage. Giant arka butterflies, masterpieces of artistic design, flew from flower to flower, sipping the abundant nectar. Even the bees that buzzed overhead made music with their wings, more soothing than anything heard on Bhu. Enchanted by the magical surroundings, Gopal left the Chakra in its flying form, carrying with him only the bow. Sudama had the conch-shell horn and the rope. Nimai didn't want to carry both the club and Citty, so he left the weapon behind.

Fine vrnda grass that felt like silk against their bare ankles covered the ground. Across the clearing, a waterfall cascaded from a cliff, carrying its liquid beauty into a sparkling pool that formed at its feet. Still enchanted, they carried Citty to its waters and listened as the splashing of the falls made music like the strings of a vina—the lute of the devas. "This is truly aaa heavenly plaaanet," said Nimai, intoxicated by the colors, fragrance, and sounds. Seeing his head reflected in the pool, he dipped his hands in the pond to erase the image. The small waves lifted the lotus flowers floating on its smooth surface, but the waves changed the sweet melody the waterfall had played with its splashing. Nimai sniffed the air with his goat nose. Something wasn't right.

Gopal realized what it was. "It's an alarm!" He took his bow from his shoulder, turning to look behind them.

"Whaaat are you taaalking about," Nimai questioned, annoyed at the prospect. "We are—" In the clearing, through which they had just passed, a small thatch hut appeared where nothing had been only moments ago, between them and the Chakra.

"Someone was expecting us," said Sudama.

"I hope it is aaas guests," grinned Nimai, half-joking.

Gopal wasn't amused. He was tired of it all. "Let's accept the invitation." He moved forward as the others followed, still carrying the sleeping krtya, when something became visible, squatting on the roof of the hut. Something female, with arms extending an abnormal length down between her legs, rested on hands with long claws that dug into the dried grass roof. Her matted hair hung down over her bare shoulders, reaching her feet. She sat, felinelike, watching the uninvited guests. "Namas te!" called Gopal, tucking the bow under his arm and folding his hands, palms together, head bowed.

"Greetings!" purred their host, and, lifting her hand, licked the extended claws.

"We have traveled a great distance, from the Whorl of Bhu, in search of the Kalpavriksha. It is our last hope. Has our journey ended? Are you the caretaker of the tree?"

"I am called Mangudi." She took her hand from her mouth as something behind Gopal caught her curiosity. "What is that they are carrying?"

"It is—" Gopal was answering as Mangudi vanished, reappearing in the doorway below.

"I don't like this," whispered Sudama, looking to all sides.

Gopal continued. "It is my sister they carry. She has been stricken by the Pisaca. We were told that a tree with the power to heal her exists in these gardens."

"That may be true," came another voice, this time from the left. Gopal leveled his weapon and turned in different directions to see if more would appear. "Such a tree, if it did exist, would surely be able to cure such an ailment," the second sorceress continued, "and such a deed would bring a heavy price."

"What will we get if we point out such a tree?" asked a third voice, this time from behind Sudama and Nimai. "The power of such a tree is special, and we, as its new guardians, have special needs that must be met before we can divulge its secret."

"Maybe that's all of them," Gopal guessed. "Be ready."

The last two arrivals vanished and reappeared next to Mangudi. "These are my sisters," she mewed, standing erect and running her hands over the heads of the other yatudhanis. The two sisters rubbed lovingly against her legs. "This is Canda," she said, petting the sister on her right, "and this," she said, licking her other hand and rubbing it on the cheek of the sister crouched by her left side, "is Sadanvas."

"Please!" Gopal begged, stepping forward, again holding his palms together.

"Be careful," Sudama warned.

"We can see that your powers are truly wondrous," Gopal said, "but I need to help my sister. Surely you can have pity on a young girl."

The two crouching stood at Mangudi's side. "We can do almost anything," Sandavas answered. "Are you willing to give us almost anything for what you seek?"

"Enough with the riddles!" blurted Gopal, ever impatient. "What is your demand?"

Canda and Sadanvas again vanished, leaving Mangudi alone. "Why . . . blood." Mangudi grinned, exposing a glistening fang from the right side of her salmon lips. "We will help save one . . . if you give up one!"

Gopal raised his bow. "Enough is enough! You want blood?" He stepped forward and launched an arrow. The yatudhani vanished, and the arrow hit the wall of the hut.

"Up there!" said Sudama, pointing to the rooftop.

"His blood is hot!" Mangudi purred from the safety of her perch. Her eyes filled with the vision of the boy. "Maybe we can have him." She pointed her long claws at Gopal. "In return for showing them the tree . . . of course."

"Of course," came the echoes of two invisible voices moving from here to there. The sisters appeared, one on each side of Gopal.

Gopal stepped forward again, standing tall, unafraid. This must be his karma—to die so his sister might live. Wasn't that the duty of a simha? Of a brother? Yes! "I am willing to give my life. It is my fault that we are here. It is my duty!" Sudama thought hard for a mantra to use. If only Vyasa were here. Nimai wondered if they would be satisfied with just one victim.

"No!" Sudama, raising his hand like his teacher, screamed, "Maha shakti!" Canda reared her head at the transcendental sound. The vibration pierced the air before the yatudhani, and she vanished. Mangudi leaped from the roof onto Gopal's back when he turned at the sound of Sudama's cries. "Pratikina-pratikih," chanted Sudama, creating the mystic shield over Gopal. Unaware of the meaning of the chant, Mangudi revealed her fangs, attempting to drive their needle points into the boy's shoulder. A howl pierced Gopal's ear. Mangudi fell, her fangs broken. She squirmed on the ground, her hands at her face, blood coming from her mouth.

Without hesitation, Gopal raised his bow and released another arrow through the wrists and neck of the sorceress. The yatudhani danced in a pool of blood, her screaming ending only with the cessation of life. Gopal turned from Mangudi, ready to help his friends. But Nimai, who was again at the will of the krtya, had moved Citty's body next to the dead yatudhani. Gopal thought he was moving his sister to safety.

Sudama, frustrated by Canda's tricks, hesitated again, not sure if he could conjure more battle charms. Sadanvas prepared to take advantage of his moment of doubt and leaped through the air at the mystic. Seeing Sudama falter, Gopal prepared another arrow. As Sadanvas flew toward her prey, Gopal's arrow flew to meet her in the air. Wounded, she merely knocked Sudama off his feet and landed, bleeding, on the ground nearby. Still not defeated, Sadanvas rose to her feet. Gopal readied another shaft. Finding the source of her pain, the yatudhani vanished.

Sudama, however, had not been forgotten. Canda had reappeared behind the brahmacari as he lay watching Gopal and the other sister. Gopal pointed the bow at the open air and chanted, "Jai Om," letting loose the shaft. The arrow hit its invisible mark, bringing the dying creature back into view. She struggled, and, with two arrows dangling from her body, she leaped and grabbed Gopal by the legs, dropping him to the ground.

Sudama was too enthralled by Gopal's display to see the creature circling to his left. Suddenly feeling her presence, he turned to face her. She leaped for his throat, and, frantic, he searched his mind for the right mantra. "Astras," he chanted, and the mystic arrow the command released impaled the sorceress. The yatudhani slumped to the ground, and the source of her existence seeped from the wound.

Gopal was struggling to reach the arrow knocked from his hand as the last yatudhani tugged at his legs. Sudama, knowing he could not reach Gopal in time, removed the conch shell from his shirt. Gopal pulled the weight of the sorceress with him, crawling back, stretching for the arrow that lay within inches of his hand.

As Sudama blew on the crusted seahorn, the cracked note resounded through the gardens. Sadanvas released her grip to cover her ears. Without her weight on his legs, Gopal reached the arrow, and, instead of using the bow, leaned forward, sinking the arrow into the yatudhani. The sorceress's gargled scream mixed with her blood as she fell forward. Gopal backed away, letting her struggle and die.

All this time, Nimai was with the krtya. With the smell of blood to guide her, she reached for the source of her strength and nourished herself on the dead sorceress. In seconds, the krtya was fully developed. Finishing her transformation into the likeness of Citty, the krtya stood.

And Nimai, still bewitched, stood for his master. The krtya closed on its hypnotized victim, her arms extended for an embrace . . . of death. Gopal and Sudama looked in wonder at what they believed to be Citty. Nimai was helpless.

Suddenly, a bolt of light struck the krtya in the back, pushing her into Nimai's arms. Another bolt, appearing from nothingness, hit her again. The force of the blow was too much for Nimai's strength to hold. He fell to the ground with the still-disguised krtya.

Gopal and Sudama, the spell broken, expected more yatudhanis. The air behind the krtya had wrinkled. The space in the air widened, and the source of the bolts appeared. It was Vyasa. Running to the creature, the mystic pulled Nimai to the side and chanted, "Maha shakti!" as Bhutanatha's creation screamed and rolled in the grass.

"Has Vyasa gone mad?" Gopal screamed, running to the mystic.

"Maybe it's not Vyasa," Sudama replied.

Reaching the mystic, Gopal saw his sister, healthy and beautiful at last, lying in pain on the ground. "Have you gone mad?" he screamed again, believing the manus had once again pulled victory from his grasp. "The gardens have cured her!"

Vyasa didn't have time to explain. The mystic grabbed Gopal's dagger and hacked off the arm of what the boy still thought to be his sister. "Stop!" Gopal grabbed at the mystic, but Vyasa pushed the boy back. The mystic's face was more serious than Gopal had ever seen it, more serious even than at the yagna.

"Watch," Vyasa instructed. "Reveal all form. Do not hide yourself." The krtya howled an inhuman howl. "Reveal to the mystics!" As if shot, the krtya twitched and squirmed. "Reveal the krtya! Reveal the hand of the Pisaca." Taking the krtya by the hand, and holding it up, Vyasa struck another arm from the creature with Gopal's dagger. Citty's features changed. Her skin turned black. "Reveal the eye of the kasyapa, the four-eyed bitch. Make the krtya evident."

Vyasa moved to the figure's side and severed her blackened leg. Her two eyes became four, then reddened and glowed. Her teeth grew, no longer fitting neatly in her mouth. Her hair turned red and grew wildly in all directions. Vyasa appeared to calm now. He had the krtya under control. With less urgency in his eyes, he hacked off her other leg. The dismembered, blackened limbs shriveled like prunes. "This thing that regards this form as her resort, that do I kill!" With one last blow, Vyasa severed the head, and it too shriveled, along with the trunk. Everyone stood shocked by the spectacle. The pieces dried and turned to dust.

"What is happening?" demanded Gopal. "What happened to Citty?"

"Not Citty." Vyasa smiled his mystic smile again and handed the blood-stained dagger back to Gopal. "A krtya!"

"A krt-whaat?" asked Nimai, remembering he had been embracing it, but little else.

"We learned that Bhutanatha had substituted this creature for Citty," Vyasa said, turning to Gopal. "You ruined his plans when you took it too soon. It was supposed to kill all of you and get the Chakra back."

"What about my sister?"

Vyasa turned to the space where the portal had appeared and chanted: "Om mani padme, om." The air wrinkled again, opening the portal from which the real Citty stepped. "The jewel in the lotus!" Vyasa announced, proud of his feat. "Your Citty!"

Gopal met his sister's embrace, but noticed something about her was different. "Your clothes! What are you wearing?" He looked closer. "It's the vest of a warrior," he shouted, stepping back. There was his sister, finally dressed the way she had always wanted—like a soldier. Then a thought occurred to Gopal. "How did you know where to find us?" he asked the mystic.

Vyasa smiled. "I knew the Pandu in Niyana Bhiram would send you to the tree."

This was not the first time Vyasa had impressed Gopal with his foresight. The young simha's relief at seeing his sister turned to concern as he saw the body of Usha. "Is she dead?" he asked.

"She was wounded by a Yaksa spear. She is in a trance." Vyasa walked to where they had gathered around the Apsarasa. "I need the Chakra to get her to her planet. It is the only way we can save her."

Gopal didn't want to give up the discus. Having the power it gave him made him feel good and special. It was his power over the manus. "For the return of my sister?" he asked.

"That was the arrangement," Vyasa reminded him. "I must return Usha to her people, and quickly."

"What about us?" asked Gopal, hoping it was all over.

"You must continue your vidhi to subdue Kali."

"Since we have Citty back," Gopal argued, "maybe we can use the disc to find a place to live in peace."

"As long as Kali rules, there is no peace. He is right now preparing to sacrifice Bhumi and Dharma to invoke the Brahmastra, a weapon that will mean the destruction of the whorl."

"Will this never end?" Gopal demanded.

Vyasa placed his hand on the boy's shoulder. "It will," he answered, "when you stop Kali."

"The tree," said Gopal. "Can we use it?"

"Your only chance to stop the Asura is in the City of Nine Gates," the mystic reminded the boy. "The tree can only be used once . . . to return you to Bhu!" Gopal put his chin to his chest. "I will show Sudama the secret of the tree." Vyasa was looking curiously at Nimai. "Then he will explain the strange appearance of your friend." Citty, also, had to be told how Nimai had gained the head of a goat, all of which further agitated Nimai. When the tale was done, they helped get Usha to the discus.

"May I have that weapon?" asked Gopal, seeing the club still on the Chakra. The mystic didn't answer, so Gopal took it anyway.

Vyasa chanted the mantra to give the disc flight. "Stay together!" The disc lifted above the gardens and disappeared into the cloudless sky. After watching the glowing shape vanish, Sudama guided them to a lone tree. Its branches held plump, golden figs.

"It's only aaa fig tree," said Nimai.

Sudama didn't reply. "Take a fruit, bite into it, and repeat after me. Stand together . . . close." Everyone moved within arm's length. Sudama stood in the center. "Parashakti!" he chanted.

"Parashakti!" Gopal and Citty repeated. Nimai finally joined them, realizing he had lost his chance to change back. The tree was his last hope, and it had to be used to return them to Bhu, to finish a vidhi of which he wanted no part.

"Srotapanna," Sudama chanted. The air quivered. "We will now enter the stream that flows unseen between the planets of the whorl. Srotapanna . . . repeat it!"

"Srotapanna," they chanted, and the gardens faded.

EIGHTEEN

WHEN THE BLUR CLEARED, they were dizzy from the journey. Without a word, all looks turned on Sudama.

"Where are we?" Nimai asked. The place was unfamiliar.

"Where Vyasa wanted us to be . . . I suppose," said Gopal.

Before them loomed the face of a temple. Citty ran to the top of the leaf-strewn steps for a better view of the surrounding area. "I can't see anything from here, just more trees."

"The carvings look familiar," said Sudama, noticing the reliefs above the entrance. Citty moved down a step, turning back to look at the stonework above their heads. Sudama and Gopal joined her. Nimai sat on the bottom step, drawing circles in the dirt with a twig and mumbling to himself.

"What can you make out?" asked Gopal. The reliefs were worn thin.

Sudama hesitated, wanting to be sure. "I know it's a Nrisimhadeva temple. There!" He pointed to the left side of the relief. "It looks like the story of the lion-headed avatar."

Gopal recognized the deity in the relief as the spirit that had appeared at the istagosti—the one that Vyasa had said told of the vidhi. Maybe Vyasa was right. Maybe this was his karma. "Where's Citty?" Gopal asked, looking around the steps and not seeing her.

"Here, come here!" Citty stood in the darkened doorway of the temple. "At least it's cool in here." Turning, she went inside. Gopal ran after her. He wasn't going to let Citty out of his sight again.

Sudama followed. "Nimai," he called. "Come up here!" Nimai didn't move. "At least get out of the sun."

Nimai looked over his shoulder, keeping the same distorted face. He dropped the twig, stood, and turned to accept the brahmacari's invitation. The only light entering the temple was the sun coming through three skylights in the multicolor, tiled ceiling. The floor and walls were inlaid with marble, which caused the cool temperature. Along the walls stood rows of marble columns. Their footsteps on the dusty floor echoed in the emptiness of the room, disturbing the cobwebbed stillness.

"I don't think anyone's been here in a while," said Citty, standing in front of a raised altar that reached to her waist. She wiped her fingers along the altar's edge, moving a small mound of dust.

Sudama, Nimai, and Gopal had wandered off in different directions, looking behind the rows of pillars. Sudama walked up stairs that led to the altar platform. Exploring the back, he found a smaller altar, ornately framed in teak and sandalwood. "Here," he called.

Gopal and Citty met him there. Nimai stood leaning against the main altar's equally ornate ledge. "What did you find?" asked Gopal.

"A room . . . and food." Sudama emerged with his arms full. "Fruit and water."

"I'm hhhungry," Nimai admitted, a black tongue

sweeping his upper lip.

Citty smiled. "You're always hungry." Gopal walked away from the altar. "Where are you going?" called his sister.

"To keep watch."

Sudama handed out meager meals on banana-leaf plates. "I'll take one to Gopal," he offered and found the boy sitting on the top stair, in front of the temple.

"The sun is setting," said Gopal, seeing Sudama with the food. "The last rays look like a veil, the way the light glistens, as if the sun's rays were made of a fine cloth and someone draped it." Gopal broke a blackened banana with his fingers and ate. He swallowed. "Are we all going to die?" he finally asked.

"Is my brother pondering the unanswered questions of the universe?" teased a voice from behind.

Gopal turned. "To think we risked our lives to save you!" He reached to grab Citty as she came near. Avoiding her brother's hand, she turned, running back into the temple. Gopal stood and chased after her. Sudama smiled, happy at not having to answer. He chose to stay outside on the step.

"Uhhh?" mumbled Nimai, spilling his food to the ground. Citty had jumped onto the altar, grabbing him to use as a shield from her brother. Things were almost normal again.

"Come here, you nit," Gopal demanded, running across the slippery marble.

"Nit? That's it!" she threatened, throwing Nimai to the altar floor. "That's the last time you call me that and live." Laughing, she leaped from the altar onto her brother, and they fell, wrestling and rolling in the dust as life and laughter filled the abandoned temple. Even Nimai smiled.

Abruptly, Sudama came running through the door, hiding behind the wall. "Soldiers! Coming down the road!" Gopal and Citty stopped their horseplay. Remaining flat on the floor, they crawled through the dust to the doorway, opposite Sudama. Nimai hid himself behind the little wooden altar.

The thunder of horses drew near, shaking the temple floor. Mounted Rakshasas rode past the temple on horses as richly decorated as they were, in full battle armor, helmets glistening in the last rays of sunlight. The armor on the horses clamored under their weight as the ground moved beneath their hooves.

There was a moment of relief. The dust on the floor of the temple settled, but before Gopal could relieve the tingling sensation in his arms, the ground rumbled again. A phalanx of charioteers, soldiers from Bhu who had betrayed their own kind, with armed bowmen standing tall, paraded past. The large, golden-painted wheels stirred the dirt and dust that blew up the temple steps into the doorway and the hidden faces. These men were followed by a regiment of Rakshasa foot soldiers, each armed with a shield and spear. A short sword swayed at each man's side as they marched in unison to the beat of a hundred drums.

The regiment passed, but was followed by three horse-drawn wagons—cages—that carried the cramped and crushed forms of women and children, packed so tightly together that their only movement came from the jostling of the wagon on the rut-covered road. The captives bumped up and down as one solid mass. Arms hanging through the bars dangled lifelessly like cloth dolls. . . . They could not all be alive.

Finally, after what seemed a lifetime, the last formation came round the bend. These were not like the professional soldiers who had already passed. This last group, mostly Rakshasas, marched in broken ranks, their spears displaying decapitated heads. Even armor and weapons varied from soldier to soldier. Before them, they drove two animals—a white cow and a white bull. They must have been taunting the captives with their spears, as was evident by the blood on the animals' hides.

Gopal remained hidden until the last begrimed soldier passed from view. He motioned for his sister to stay still, and leaned out through the open doorway of the temple. Without saying a word, he got to his feet, and stepped out.

After waiting a moment, Sudama and Citty followed. Sudama spoke. "The cow was Bhumi, and the bull was Dharma. They are the devas Vyasa told us about."

Gopal knew who they were. For the first time, he understood. He looked back at the lion-headed relief. "Vyasa is right," said Gopal. "It is my karma. I see that now! I saw this on the day when we smoked the svapna. I have been chosen to stop Kali." Gopal was undaunted. "We know which way our road leads."

"They aren't very far ahead of us," said Citty, looking after the soldiers. "We should wait for night and continue under the cover of dark."

Gopal nodded. He turned in the direction the soldiers had traveled. A road wound its way around the wooded hill and into a wide valley where, on the flat plains, a city stood.

NINETEEN

WITH NIGHT AS THEIR CLOAK and the moon as their torch, Gopal, Citty, Sudama, and an unwilling Nimai made their way down the valley road. The wind was blowing from the city and swirled dust into their faces as they traveled.

"It smells like a slaughterhouse," said Gopal. He remembered the wagons they had seen. "Only I don't think it's animals."

The terrain of green hills that spilled out from the forest ended abruptly, as if an artist had deliberately ended his painting mid-way. The canvas continued with a scene of dry, barren, blackened soil. Stumps jutted from the hard, parched earth. Dried trenches, where streams had once run, now sustained only weeds and low, wild brush. The air was still, devoid of life. The land had been touched by the Asura. This desolate road led to a walled city, but there were no guards or soldiers, nothing to stop them from entering. "This must be a trap," said Citty.

"Maybe not," answered Sudama. "Maybe guards are not needed here. Vyasa described this to me. It is Hiranya—the

capital of Klesa." Still, they entered the city cautiously.
Streets were quiet, but for small groups of gaunt men and
women huddled around open fires. Lining the streets in all
directions were wooden buildings, cramped together,
while rats, larger than any seen in Goloka, or even on Narakatala, scurried across rafters. There were no trees, no bushes, no living things, but for the hollow-faced, pale-skinned
shadows of men and women. The stench became thick
now, carried on black smoke that rose above roofs in the
background. It lay heavy above them, like a giant lid
pulled over the entire city. The black sky rumbled and
sparked. Sudama recited:

> "There will be cloudless thunder.
> And bolts from a darkened sky.
> The rays of sun have declined,
> And the stars fight among themselves.
> A dark wind blows through the streets,
> Blasting dust everywhere,
> Adding dark to nighttime.
> And the clouds will rain blood."

Gopal was curious. "What was that?"

"Something Vyasa taught me," said the brahmacari.
"There is no need to guard this place. This is a place of
death! Only the jiva-mrtyu live here."

"The living dead?" Gopal looked at Citty. That would
have been her fate!

"This is the caaapital of the mighty Kaaali?" Nimai
bleated, more goat in his voice than human now. He was
losing the battle with the animal half. He spun around to
look behind him. A horse-drawn wagon approached, driv-
en by two priests.

Gopal called, "Get into the shadows."

"Pisaca," said Sudama and Gopal simultaneously.

The blank-faced priests broke the heavy silence of the
streets. "Nectar!" sang one from his slit. "Come taste the

nectar. Share the celestial realm." The wagon stopped, and the priest who was driving exchanged the reins for a small metal gong. The unholy sound echoed through the nearly vacant streets. "All knowledge and bliss is yours through the mercy of Kali!" they called. Doors opened. More inhabitants, in worn and torn clothing, their bodies frail and dirty, scurried like rodents from their nests. As weak as some appeared, they dragged themselves to stand around the wagon. The priests tossed the lotus petals to the wretched creatures, who fought each other for a taste of the enchanted flower.

A bewitched petal landed at Citty's feet. She bent to pick it up. "No!" Sudama pulled her back. "It is the charm they used in Alakapuri. Just touching it will be enough. You will become as they are." He pointed to the jiva-mrtyu, reaching for their fiendish addiction. Citty kicked the leaf behind her . . . in front of Nimai.

The priests signaled. As quickly and silently as they had appeared, the throngs scurried back to their holes, their arms and mouths filled with petals. The streets returned to their eerie quiet as if nothing had taken place, as if the entire scene had been imagined. "Nectar!" they heard the priests cry, and the wagon moved on.

Nimai looked down at the petal. What could it hurt to take it? Sudama wasn't even a mystic yet. What could he know about such things? Watching to see that no one saw him, he quickly scooped the leaf into his hand.

"Let's go on," said Gopal, leading them through more slums. "How many gates do you think are in Hiranya?" he asked to all and none. No one could answer. At the center of the city they found a wide, deep moat spanned by a narrow bridge. "The other Hiranya!" Gopal declared. On the far side of the moat stood the glistening, domed palace created by Maya's magic, rising high above the sights and smells of the slums. Tall and plump men and women, from Bhu and other planets, were dressed in silk and gold and wore headdresses of pearls and feathers. They walked, dressed in long, flowing gowns, arm-in-arm along the brightly lit streets. Crowds paraded up a jewel-paved walkway leading into the golden temple. The music of shenai and drums spilled from within the multilevel building as wandering musicians entertained guests on the many balconies that wound around the outside of the temple-palace. A variety of birds, harvested from many lands and planets, flew and walked on the walkways. Jewel-studded fountains, which surrounded the structure in the centers of the many-gardened plazas, flowed with wine.

Surrounding the palace, as far as Gopal could see, were glowing, white, bi-level homes, each with its own private balcony. More gardens, crowded with fragrant flowers and colorful vines, decorated the fronts of each home. Lanterns hung outside each door, shining their light on the splendor within each abode.

From his position within the dark shadows of the slum, Gopal noticed the many guards on the opposite side of the bridge and pointed them out to the others, who still gazed with wonder at the island.

Sudama noticed that something was wrong with Nimai. "Are you all right?" he asked.

Nimai removed his fingers from his mouth. "Nothing's wrong," he said. "I had something sticky on my fingers. It's all right now, I got it off."

"This needs to be done carefully," said Citty.

"I don't think a mind trick would work," Sudama admitted.

Gopal took command. "We must find another way." He looked both ways down the street. "Let's see if the moat runs all the way around." Following the canal, they came to yet another bridge and more guards. "Maybe we should go back to . . . between the two bridges," he suggested. "I have an idea."

"How caan we cross over the moaaat?" Nimai challenged, as they reached a location out of the light of the palace, and without any visible entrance to it.

"Sudama, hand me your rope." Gopal uncovered the bow he carried under his robe. "Can you create another shield?"

"I can try," Sudama answered, unsure of Gopal's intentions.

Gopal took out his old dagger while Sudama uttered the mystic vibration for the shield. Gopal cut the rope in half, and, taking an arrow, he tied an end of the rope to the shaft. "Mystic," he ordered. "when I shoot the arrow across, I want you to use your knowledge to make the rope stretch."

"But—" protested Sudama.

"Do it," Gopal ordered. "It is my vidhi!"

"There . . . that tree straight across!" Pulling back, he said, "I see the tree. I see that knothole. . . ." He let loose the arrow.

"Upavita," chanted Sudama, watching to see what would happen. The rope streamed over the moat, magically stretching, and, whether by the hand of a mystic or the skill of a boy, the arrow came to rest in the targeted trunk.

Taking his knife again, Gopal cut three more pieces from what was left of the rope. Citty tied the end of the line that was attached to the arrow to a post.

"Now, hold your shield," Gopal directed Sudama. "We'll suspend it from the line like a tray and slide across." Citty proudly helped tie loops in two of the smaller pieces of rope and fastened them securely. Gopal asked, "Who wants to go first?"

"Sudaaama's chaaants!" cried Nimai. "We caaan't trust—"

"I'll go," said Citty, and with her brother's help she climbed on the shield. Nimai was not pleased, but said nothing more.

"Turn on your back and pull yourself across. Take the end of this last piece of rope and pull it across. Ready?"

"Will she be able to do it?" Sudama questioned.

"Just stretch the other piece," Gopal answered. Citty pulled herself across the moat to the arrow anchored on the other side, and the second piece of rope, with Sudama's help, stretched like the first had. Sliding off the shield, she tied the end of the newly stretched line to the shield. Gopal tugged to get it back. Nimai went over next, followed by Sudama, and finally Gopal.

"Maaaybe we shhhould split up," suggested Nimai. "We might be aaable to cover more aaarea."

"I agree," said Citty.

Gopal wasn't sure. "Vyasa said to stay together."

"How could hhhhe know whhhaaat we would find?" Nimai stuttered, his human half giving in to the beast.

Gopal was pleased that Nimai was trying to help. "All right. Citty, come with me. I'll keep the bow."

"I haaave thhe club," said Nimai.

"You go with Sudama." He handed his dagger to his sister and the two parties circled the palace in opposite directions. Gopal and Citty found the bridge they had come upon earlier. Its jeweled entrance shone like a star. "What do we do?" Gopal saw the ornate garments of the guests. "We can't just walk up there looking like this." He lifted his stained and torn robe.

"I see our wardrobe coming now." Citty smiled, pointing to three men strolling along the street. They were dressed in the finest blue and green silk robes. "Get back in the shadows," she ordered. "I'll get them in here." She looked back as Gopal hid. "Remember, don't mess up the clothes!"

From the dark, he watched his sister as she removed her warrior's vest and cap. Her hair fell over her shoulders as the men approached the alley. A soft voice called from the shadows. "Soma and pleasure? Help a poor devotee of Kali collect a proper offering for her master."

"Who's in there?" one man asked.

Citty took a step forward, barely into the light.

"She's young," said another. "We do have time before

the ceremony."

Citty quickly stepped back into the shadows, and the seekers of pleasure ventured in after her. "Where are you, girl?" called one. "Come now. We want to get another look at you."

"Here," offered another, jingling coins in his palm. "Let us see more of what you have to offer."

"How about this?" yelled Citty, swinging the dagger across the head of one stranger, knocking the man to the ground. The others looked on in horror at their friend, lying in his own blood. One felt the point of an arrow tip. The other faced Citty, who still brandished the dagger.

"Get against the wall," Gopal ordered, "and get out of those clothes." The prisoners hesitated. "Now!" he yelled, jabbing with his arrow. Frightened and trembling, the men hurried to the wall and undressed. Citty took the clothes from the one on the ground. Grabbing her vest and putting it back on, she covered it with the rich garments. Gopal turned the prisoners around, securing their hands. "Rip some strips of cloth and put some across their mouths," he told his sister as he donned the other captive's garments. Leaving the men bound and gagged, Gopal and Citty left the alley and joined more of Kali's guests on their way to the palace.

Mixing with the growing multitude of guests, Gopal and Citty walked up the walkway, under the large arch, and into the palace. The domed ceiling of the large hall was gilded with pure gold and decorated with jewels from a hundred conquered lands. The stars, glowing through the opening at the very top, sparkled along with the precious stones until it was impossible to tell which were the real celestial lights.

A maze of walkways led to five levels of balconies that jutted over their heads. Each overflowed with guests, drinking, talking, and listening to the musicians that strolled among them. Across the room, on a large, golden platform, stood the altar. Large pillows, embroidered with

gold thread, lay around the sacrificial firepit. Priests came
and left, bringing the various articles needed for the ceremony. Knives and incense were set on a jewel-studded,
marble table. Above the altar, a door opened onto a small
isolated balcony, on which stood two golden thrones.

"*Jai Om*," Citty mumbled just in time, for Gopal was
becoming absorbed in the goings-on.

"*Jai Om*," he repeated.

"Is that Nimai?" Citty suddenly asked.

Gopal looked, spotting the back of Nimai's animal
head. "Nimai?" He grabbed Nimai by the shoulder, turning him around, and saw the glass-eyed, animal rage of his
godbrother. "What's wrong? Where's Sudama?"

"Leave me alone!" Nimai yelled, in a deep-toned rasp,
no longer the voice of Gopal's friend. Nimai's battle with
the bewitched goat had been lost, and he knocked Gopal's
hand away. Then, turning, the goathead boy ran into the
crowd that was still swelling around them. The music and
noise grew louder.

"Nimai!" Gopal cried. Nimai disappeared into a sea of
color, sound, and bodies.

Citty felt the influence of the room closing in around
them. "We will have to find him later." She tugged on
Gopal's arm, worried for her brother and herself, realizing
their friend had already succumbed. "There! Over there
. . . a door. Come on! We must get out of here! Before it
happens to us."

Gopal struggled to keep a grip on his sister's wrist as she
towed him along, trying to get him away from the mesmer-
izing affect of the temple room. The whole time, he was
looking behind him . . . for Nimai. Drawn by his attachment to his childhood friend, and the narcotic effect of the
temple hall, Gopal broke from his sister's grasp, to be swallowed by the crowd.

On the opposite end of the assembly hall, the altar platform was crowded with priests and dignitaries from the
lands that had allied with Kali. The balconies around the

domed hall overflowed with guests, as did the main floor of
the palace room. Soldiers, unseen before, were everywhere
now, but mostly on the main level, close to the altar.
Swords, tridents, axes, and spears waved above the heads of
the assembled military might.

"Arise!" cried a priest, stepping to the front of the platform. "You, as nebulous specter, together with fiery por-
tents, Yaksas, Rakshasas, Asuras, Pisacas, to all our allies
from Bhu. Rise and behold our lord!" The screams and
cheers were deafening. "The brood that is below and in the
heavens, and the human powers upon the Middle Whorl,
shall be obedient to the plans of Kali!" Another frenzied
outbreak of screams arose from the assemblage as the priest
turned, pointing to the balcony above the altar. Two figures, Kali and his queen, came through red curtains.

Gopal, alone now, and barely able to keep his wits, followed the priest's pointing finger, looking for the object of
his vidhi. There, stepping to the edge of the railing,
dressed in the robes of a simha, was a man of magnificent
stature. He was tall and handsome, dressed in royal robes
of silk and gold. In his hand, he held a shield embedded
with gems. A mighty, jeweled sword hung from his waist.
Atop his head was the peacock-feathered crown, decorated
with more gems. Between his clothing and the jewels, Kali
glowed more radiantly than Surya—the deva of Light.
Then Maya stepped forward, taking her place next to Kali.

Gopal stopped chanting when his gaze fell upon the enchantress. Her illusions were working their tricks. To
Gopal, she was the woman—the dancer—he had seen in
the market of Goloka. Long black hair flowed down the
front of her body. His eyes caressed each inch of this creature, whose sight intoxicated his mind. The thin, transpar-
ent material that draped over her tall, slender frame
hugged her body, revealing every curve through the flimsy
garment. The wet, perfumed oil that covered her smooth,
soft skin, seeped seductively through the clinging fabric,
taunting all who stared. Hypnotic blue eyes glistened when

she removed the veil from her face, uncovering her lotus-shaped lips. Turning from their devotees, the king and queen took seats on their thrones. Gopal was left famished. His eyes and mind hungered for more.

The priest began the hymn.

> "The devouring flesh shall fasten itself
> Upon our enemies,
> Together with the power of the Brahmastra.
> Arise thou divine spirit. Do thou, O magic,
> Create and operate the Brahmastra.
> This tribute is offered to you."

The priest turned to the twins. A tumultuous roar filled the dome. No longer chanting, Gopal wandered closer to the altar, trying to see more of Maya. Unseen by her brother, the ever resourceful Citty had managed to get on the altar, among the human priests, trying to see the sacrifice. Undaunted, Citty continued her own chanting under her breath while her brother stood in a trance.

Before the crowds, before the dark twins, a priest led Dharma to the center of the platform and tied the bull's neck to a marble table. Another priest, with a silver axe, stood next to the bull. The animal turned within his shackles and screamed, "Please don't kill me!"

The priest continued his prayers.

> "By virtue of a compact
> Broken by the denizens of the lower planets.
> By virtue of the agreement, broken by Bhutanatha,
> Do I call the forces of the Brahmastra,
> Who on this side will conquer."

The glistening axe was raised. The light from the unholy tool struck Gopal's eyes. The blade fell. Dharma's head lay on the marble slab. The pitiful pleas ended. The bull's body, still tied to the table, jerked, then slumped to its knees, his life air released.

Now, another priest brought forth a golden bowl and placed it below the bull's neck, filling it with the blood that flowed from the murdered deva. Dharma's life fluid was then poured into the sacrificial fire.

"All the Three Whorls we will conquer through this oblation," cried the priest. "Glories to Kali! Glories to Maya!" The soldiers in front of the platform raised their weapons and danced in place to the chants of the priests and the sounds of the drums. "By the bolt of the Brahmastra, this blood of Dharma do we mold into the weapon of destruction." More blood was poured as the bare hands of the priests mixed the blood with the hot ashes. The priest's scorched flesh gave birth to a black cloud of smoke that rose from the fire.

> "Counting its dead by thousands, this weapon,
> Born from the smallest particles of matter,
> Will pierce and scatter all who oppose us.
> For with this weapon we usher in Kali Yuga,
> The Age of Kali!"

The multitude danced and chanted while the altar was cleared of the carcass. Then, another priest brought the celestial cow forward. Gopal, still bewitched, stared helplessly. The black cloud now swirled above the sacrificial fire, taking on an unnatural shape. Bhumi was dragged forward, crying. Her head was tied to the same slab. Gopal stood across from the cow-mother—the mother of Bhu. She strained to look at him, the chains digging into her skin when she twisted her head. "Please don't kill me! Please don't kill me!"

But another sound entered Gopal's clouded mind; from another balcony, close to the altar, it rang out. It was the cracked sound of an old seahorn. Then a voice chanted something different from the rest of the crowd. Slowly, the words pierced the spell.

"Whenever yonder person in his thought,
And with his speech, offers sacrifice
Accompanied by oblations and benedictions,
May the manus,
Smite this offering before it takes effect!"

Gopal woke. That voice! It was Sudama's. The priests on
the altar faltered in their hymns. The brahmacari was trying to stop the sacrifice.

"May the manus mar this work.
Scatter this sacrificial blood.
May that which yonder person offers
Not succeed!"

Sudama grabbed the railing in front of him for support,
the crusted conch shell in one hand. The utterance of the
charm and his inexperience drained him. The powers he
tried to invoke were too great.

"You can do it," encouraged Gopal. "It's working.
Don't give up!" The priests on the altar, understanding
the meaning of Sudama's mantra, ran from the platform.
Gopal stood bewildered by the sudden change of events.

Citty suddenly appeared at his side. "Come on!" She
ran to the bound cow, her dagger out. Reaching the animal, she undid the chain and cut at the straps. The deva
was free. "You must protect Bhumi." She tossed her brother his dagger. Gopal pulled his robe over his head, and,
placing the dagger into his belt, readied his bow as the
whirlwind of fire and smoke, created by the priests, broke
free and soared.

"There! There, you fools!" Maya rose from her seat,
leaning over the gold railing. "The mystic!" Kali huddled
behind his consort. Two more guards joined her on the royal balcony. Soldiers rushed to the altar platform. The soldiers in the crowd who didn't scatter organized to assail the
mystic's balcony.

Citty? Gopal couldn't find his sister. He searched the altar . . . the crowd. There, above him, using the shield of mystic vibration to protect Sudama, was Citty, repelling the spears and tridents of Kali's soldiers.

Sudama pointed to the priest, who remained on the altar below. "Back do I tie both your arms." The priest was unable to move; his arms had suddenly twisted behind him. "Your mouth I shut." The priest gagged on his own tongue. In the confusion, Gopal led Bhumi from the altar to the main floor. He had one arrow left. "And with the fury of Agni, I destroy this oblation." The flames on the altar exploded in a thousand directions, setting fire to tapestries, sitting mats, soldiers and priests. Then, invoking the mystic missile, maha-shakti, Sudama hurled it at the priest, impaling and forcing him back into the sacrificial pit, igniting another explosion and snuffing the unholy flames.

Another voice entered the battle of charms as the soldiers tried to fight past Citty to get to the mystic. Maya prepared to duel with Sudama.

"Like a god-begotten plant, hated by the wicked,
Meant to wipe away this sacrifice,
The curse of this rival shall be vanquished by me!"

Sudama's body numbed. His lips froze. Citty was too busy fighting to help the mystic.

"From the hellish planets,
I call this curse to be suspended."

Sudama fell from sight to the back of the balcony. More soldiers stormed their position, keeping Citty at her task. Gopal turned to Kali's balcony. Kali was unguarded, and Gopal readied his bow, his last arrow aimed at the Asura. Then the words of Vyasa entered him. "To kill the snake you must cut off the head. To stop Kali, it is Maya who must be killed."

He turned his aim on the new target and focused the last arrow on the heart of Illusion. His own heart beat loudly. His hands began to sweat. He pulled back on the bowstring. His left arm and hand were numb and stiff. He had a clear shot. He pulled back . . . another inch. The bowstring was taut and cut into his fingers.

This was what he had waited for . . . for all the pains he had suffered, for all the lives that had been lost, for crushing the whorl as he knew it. This was his vidhi! This was his karma! No manu can take this moment from me! he cried within his mind.

Then someone knocked the bow from Gopal's hands and it lay on the floor at his feet, crushed and broken. There, holding the club, was Nimai. Without a word, Nimai gave a triumphant grin and swung the club again, hitting Gopal on the left shoulder.

"Nimai!" Gopal raised his arm to repel another blow. Nimai!" he pleaded. "It's me! It's me!" Nimai raised the club again, prepared to kill. Gopal's last arrow was on the ground before him. With his eyes blazing red, and laughing the laugh of an Asura, Nimai brought the club down. Quickly, Gopal grabbed the arrow, plunging it into the belly of his friend. Nimai's face turned to horror at his fate. Behind the eyes of the goat, Gopal saw his friend for the last time. Nimai dropped the club and doubled over, falling to the ground, dead.

"I curse you all!" Gopal screamed at having committed this unspeakable act. "I curse all the manus!"

Maya completed her spell. "From the fire it rises with a thousand suns to protect us on all sides." She wasn't directing the mantra at Sudama; she was calling upon the form of smoke circling above the altar. "Protect me," she commanded. The black cloud assumed the form of a winged man. "Let not ill will overcome us. Let no hostile schemes spoil our intentions." Maya's blue eyes turned to red. Her hair electrified, standing on end. "I call upon Brahmastra,

Destroyer of Whorls! Fly to the curser!" She hurled her creation at the helpless Sudama.

Citty was doing all she could with the shield and a Rakshasa dagger to hold back the overwhelming swarm of attacking soldiers. The Brahmastra hovered, then, after taking a momentary position at the side of its mother, it shot across the width of the temple, launched at its target. The entire side of the palace: balconies, soldiers, onlookers, stone, wood, glass, and marble, vanished in the explosion that followed. The force threw Gopal and everyone else to the ground. A burst of light filled what was left of the temple room, then faded.

Stunned, but alive, Gopal brushed the debris from his body and rubbed the flash from his eyes. Sitting up, he found Bhumi next to him. She had also been stunned by the power of the blast. His next thoughts were for his sister . . . and Sudama. He turned to where the balcony had been. The side of the temple was gone, collapsed into a pile of stones and rubble. Dead soldiers were strewn about the debris, where arms, legs, and heads mixed with the stone and twisted beams. Some stones on top of the pile rolled down. Dust kicked up from near the bottom of the mound. A few more stones rolled aside, and a hand pushed up from within the pile. Citty, dragging the limp body of Sudama, rose from the dust. Dropping a now visible, broken and dented shield, she held the Rakshasa dagger above her head.

On the balcony, Maya, in all her arrogance, remained, with Kali still hiding behind her. When she raised her hands, the Brahmastra appeared above her head. Hate emanated from all her pores as she pointed at Gopal's sister. At her command, the Brahmastra shot toward Citty, this time revealing claws on the end of its cloud fingers.

Citty swung at the beast bravely. It brushed the girl to the side, knocking her, bleeding, to the ground. Maya laughed at the sight. More soldiers entered the temple room, but Maya held them back. Then, waving her hand like a puppeteer, she caused the Brahmastra to fly to the uppermost part of the partially collapsed ceiling, and, sporting the grin of conquest, dropped her hand, pointing her finger at the wounded girl. Maya's weapon descended.

Gopal was helpless without the bow. "It is in the City of Nine Gates that you will find the strength and knowledge you will need," he mumbled. His frustration reached a new height. "There is no City of Nine Gates! It was nowhere in the Three Whorls!" Suddenly it dawned on him. How foolish he had been! The answer had been with him all the time, something so simple, something he had learned as a child from his father. The body has nine openings—nine gates. Gopal *was* the City of Nine Gates. It wasn't up to special weapons or the manus. He had to make his own destiny! Now he understood.

While Maya was distracted, he removed his dagger, the blade that had been lost so many times and so many times had been returned to him. He ran to the collapsed altar. Any spell the Asuras had over him vanished. "I see a thin, frail, skeleton of a man, with black skin hanging over a puny frame. Dark, scraggly hairs hang from his chin and head. He wears a false crown of gold and jewels."

Gopal stared into the glowing, yellow eyes of this creature that had caused his whorl to disintegrate. How could this miscreant have managed to deceive so many? He remembered the words of Dhanus. "The jackal! He is only a jackal!"

"What do you see?" He smiled. "I see jackals.

"What do you see?" he whispered. "I see Illusion.

"What do you see? . . . I see Maya."

He pulled his right arm back, the dagger held tight.

"What do you see? . . . I see her face.

"What do you see? . . . I see her forehead.

"What do you see? . . . the spot between her red eyes."

Taking a deep breath, he chanted, "*Jai Om*." Then, with complete control of his mind, with all his senses focused, he hurled his dagger . . . striking the Asura queen in the forehead, releasing her life airs.

The dagger stung Maya's head and being. Petrified at her defeat, Maya shriveled, dropping, lifeless, to the cold floor of the balcony. More terrifying than the death cry of the naga, more piercing than the cries of the Rakshasas, more chilling than the chants of the Pisaca, more horrible than the screams of the dvid-dvids, more startling than the shouts of the Yaksas, more soul-shattering than the moans of the krtya . . . Maya's last howl shook the palace walls, which lost their brilliance, appearing dull and ordinary to all who could still see.

Hearing her cries, the Brahmastra turned to the call of its mother, distracted. Quickly, seeing her chance, Citty raised her wounded body to one knee and lifted her dagger. Chanting, "*Jai Om,*" she severed the creature's head.

Before he could rejoice, Gopal turned to the hot bite of a soldier's arrow and tumbled from the platform with the reed embedded in his back. Looking at the balcony, he caught one last glimpse of the demoness whose beauty, now crumpled and shriveled like the dead krtya, faded with her life. Kali, seeing the fate of his consort and power and knowing his true identity would be revealed, abandoned the balcony for safer ground. Feeling faint, Gopal heard the flutter of birds. In the night sky, an army of winged beings blotted out the stars, and Gopal passed out.

TWENTY

AMONG THE SMOLDERING RUINS, within the shattered walls and dome of the now dull palace, Gopal woke, head spinning, dazed, his vision no more than swirling shadows. His eyes slowly focused. Citty sat beside him. "Sudama?" he moaned, trying to sit up. The pain in his shoulder and back was more than he could bear. Citty placed her hand under his head, pillowing it, trying her best to make him comfortable. Tears were all she could offer.

"Sudama is dead," answered a familiar voice.

"Vyasa?" Gopal whispered, almost too weak to speak. A trickle of blood seeped from the corner of his mouth when he turned his head.

"I'm afraid I came too late. When I returned Usha to her people," answered the treta-mystic, "Visvavasu wouldn't believe my story until he could speak to his wife."

"Something came through the opening in the dome," rasped Gopal, catching a breath.

Another familiar voice answered. "It was the Ghandharvas."

"Usha?"

"Yes, Gopal." Her face was as enchanting as the first time he had seen her, her skin as golden and pure, her eyes like hypnotic jewels. "I wanted to thank you for returning the Chakra . . . and for saving my life." Holding out her finger, she looked at Vyasa, who nodded his approval. Then, she touched her hand to Gopal's wound. "I have learned much from this mystic." Gopal sensed the healing effect of her touch. "You've no need to worry," she assured. "My touch will only heal you. When the Ghandharvas brought me out of my trance, I explained to my husband what you had done. Unfortunately, we were too late to save the young mystic."

Gopal sat up with the help of his sister and looked over his shoulder. "Nimai?" he cried.

"We found his body," said Vyasa. "He had fallen to the Pisaca. There was nothing I could do. His body had to be burned.

"We have killed what was left of Kali's soldiers," a voice interrupted, a voice that had the same affect on the ear as the Apsarasa, with words like music. "Some have managed to run off or are hiding within the city, but I'm afraid Kali has evaded us."

Gopal turned and saw the most beautiful creature he had ever seen. Standing before him was a tall, golden-skinned man, with long, curly red hair like Usha's. His body was bare, except where smooth down covered his shoulders and back. From his back, two pearl-white wings extended, as perfect in shape and dimension as the rest of him.

"Allow me to introduce the King of the Ghandharvas," said Vyasa, gesturing to the splendid creature.

Visvavasu turned to the boy that up to now he had only heard about. "I am told you saved my queen's life." Gopal only stared, offering no reply. "I want to thank you and apologize for not believing the mystic. We don't usually trust humans. I hope you will be well, in any case."

"Thank you," Gopal stuttered, his mind taken with the creature.

"As I was saying," Visvavasu said to the mystic, "my soldiers are tracking down and killing all of Kali's soldiers in the palace and in the streets. Do you wish me to do anything else here?"

"No, that is more than I can thank you for."

"I will leave a small party to escort you from the city. So, if there is nothing else . . . Usha?" Visvavasu extended his golden hand to his wife, who climbed into his arms.

Usha looked once more at Gopal. "Again . . . thank you. I am sure we will meet again." With her farewell, Visvavasu let out a high-pitched trill and took to the air, followed by hundreds of his winged soldiers. The Ghandharvas filled the giant dome, flying up through the top like giant white swans. Visvavasu's generals, from outside in the streets, echoed his call to the rest of his army. The sky outside also became dotted with flying Ghandharvas.

"We should see to Sudama's body," Vyasa reminded Gopal and Citty, turning to where it still lay.

Gopal reached out for Citty to help him up. "Will you be all right?" she asked. He nodded, and she let go, keeping her hands within inches should he fall.

He balanced shakily for a moment, still dizzy. "I'm fine. See to Sudama."

The palace had all but been destroyed. Fires had spread to most of Hiranya and in most places burned out of control. The dead littered the floor with the rubble. Sudama's body was being carried out on the shoulders of Ghandharvas as Gopal walked with Vyasa. "Was Bhumi saved?"

"You are Gopal. It was your destiny." Vyasa gave his all-knowing smile. "She has been safely returned to Svetadvipa."

"And the War for the Mandala?"

"With the Chakra returned, the devas may, in time, be able to reclose Bila-svarga and find the rest of the dvars."

"I wonder," said Gopal. "Will Bhu ever return to how it

was . . . before? Will there ever be peace again?"

"Nothing stays the same," replied the mystic. "It is the way of the whorl, but now, with the Ghandharvas as our allies, others will soon join the fight against the Asuras."

"What about Dharma?" asked Gopal. "What does it mean that Dharma is dead?" He stumbled over the rocks and wood at his feet.

Vyasa caught him. "With Dharma gone, it means the knowledge of the treta-mystic will probably end with me. Unless, of course, another can be found to take the deva's place in Sveta-dvipa."

With Gopal, Vyasa, and Citty walking behind, the Ghandharvas carried Sudama's body from the palace to a garden that had been prepared. Standing outside, Gopal looked over the gutted city. "What will happen to Hiranya?"

"It will probably fall prey to thieves, until it is finally abandoned . . . and forgotten with time. Come, they are ready for the cremation." Vyasa had chosen a place in the garden with an unobstructed view of the west. There he had directed that a shallow pit be dug. After Sudama's body was shaved and bathed, and Citty had gathered flowers to make a garland, Sudama's body was placed in the pit on a bed of kusha grass, flower petals, and cut wood. As more wood was placed on top of the body, Vyasa circled the pit three times and chanted the prayer of the dead.

> "You depart, we remain.
> Subside into the lap of Bhumi, our mother,
> The kind and gracious maiden,
> Who is soft as wool to the generous giver.
> From the womb of nothingness may she preserve
> you."

As three fires were set around the body, Vyasa chanted, "To Agni, Sva-ha," and put twigs into the first. "To Kama,

Sva-ha," he chanted, putting wood on the second fire. "To Anumati, Sva-ha." He placed wood on the final fire and chanted more of the prayer.

> "Make a vault, O Bhumi, do not press down upon him.
> Grant easy access. Afford him shelter.
> For he who is born, death is certain.
> For he who dies, birth is certain."

The mystic looked at Gopal and Citty, who sat on the ground, exhausted and drained. Gopal thought of markets and caravans, of rooftops and dancing girls. Citty fingered her warrior's vest, remembering her mother, Lila, and her father, Padma. Together they recalled the days when they had scared each other with tales of demons that never grew larger than their imaginations, of friends who had shared their dreams and fears.

Vyasa spoke. "The actions of Sudama's past life will determine his next birth," he explained, continuing the rite of passage into the next body. "Depending on which of the three fires reaches his body first, his atma will either enter the heavenly planets, the hellish planets, or return to another womb and be reborn on Bhu. If all the fires reach him at the same moment, it means Sudama will enjoy Sat Cit Ananda—eternal bliss and knowledge—in Vaikuntha, with the manus."

Gopal and Citty realized at the same time that Vyasa had not disclosed which fire meant which end. So together they sat, nervously watching. Slowly, the fires crept toward Sudama's body. Whether by the will of the manus, or the blink of a mystic's eye, neither could say, but a sudden gust surrounded them on all sides, carrying all three flames simultaneously to the body, igniting the bed of wood. . . . The smoke carried Sudama's atma to Vaikuntha.

With Sudama's atma freed, and his own vidhi complete, Vyasa chanted from the Song of the Godhead—the

Book of Bhakti:

> "Never was there a time that I did not exist.
> Nor you, nor all these kings. Nor in the future
> Shall any of us cease to be."

He turned his gaze to Gopal and Citty. "I have helped you complete your vidhi. Maya is dead and Bhumi has been saved. Now you are Simha and must join with the others to restore peace to the whorl. I have completed my task in this life." Prepared to gain the prize he had strived for over the length of three lifetimes, Vyasa at last took control of his senses and mind. Absorbed in samadhi, within his body, the mystic raised his life force on the airs of Vata, to his heart, to his throat, and to his head, where it burst forth through the sacred part of the skull, straight up, into the clear, crisp sky. Finally, before the reddened eyes of Gopal and his sister, the mystic's body burst into flames.

Gopal had known Vyasa would come to this when the boy had completed the vidhi. He wondered if it was one of the reasons he had resisted. Vyasa had filled the void left by the death of Padma. Now, what did he have? Nimai was gone. Sudama was gone. He was no better off than when he had started, or so he thought, but he knew Vyasa was right. It was the way of the whorl.

Vyasa had received the prize he sought, and maybe, when the time was right, and Gopal had lived other lives, perhaps he, too, would be worthy. He looked to his sister, who waited on his words. "His task was done for this life. He fulfilled his karma," said Gopal.

"But what about us?" asked Citty, also feeling alone.

Gopal picked up a Rakshasa dagger from the rubble, slipping it into the empty sheath that still hung from Citty's back. "We are Dvija—the twice born descendants of the First Root-Race of Chayya, of the First Order of the Varna." He touched the claw of the naga, still hanging from his side. "As Simha of Goloka, I must see to my people." Leaving the funeral pyre burning, and under the escort of the Ghandharvas, Gopal and Citty began their long journey back to Goloka.

Half-Light
Denise Vitola

Commander Ariann Centuri's betrothed is killed by the bat-faced Benar, and she is stricken with a terminal mind-bending disease. Suddenly she finds herself wedded to the Viceroy of the Galactic Consortium of Planets . . . and fighting for her life. **On sale December 1992.**

Thorn and Needle   Paul B. Thompson

Miyesti is a perfect city where lamps blaze without wicks and voices speak from the air. When two intriguing travelers journey there to destroy its mysterious new techno-god, powerful forces collide. **On sale now.**

Kingslayer   L. Dean James

In this sequel to *Sorcerer's Stone*, young Gaylon Reysson, the new king of Wynnamyr, must learn to use the magical sword Kingslayer. Will he capture a glorious victory for his people—or destroy himself and the world he hopes to save? **On sale now.**

PRISM PENTAD
Troy Denning

The Amber Enchantress:
Book Three
Sadira, the beautiful sorceress loved by both Rikus and Agis, is torn between the dark power of sorcery and the need to use magic to protect the planet's fragile ecology. *On sale October 1992.*

The Obsidian Oracle: Book Four
When Tithian, the power-hungry king of Tyr, sets off on a perilous journey into the Athasian desert, Agis follows. Tithian searches for an ancient oracle that will allow him to become an immortal sorcerer-king, but what the two men find may lead to the salvation of Athas--or its destruction. *On sale Spring 1993.*

The Cerulean Storm: Book Five
Armed with the Obsidian Oracle, King Tithian I leads his former slaves--Rikus, Neeva, and Sadira--on a desperate mission to save the world. But when the journey into the mysterious Sea of Silt begins, old hatreds and passions prove as dangerous to the party as the enchanted fleets and terrible dust storms that batter their tiny caravan. *On sale Fall 1993.*

On Sale Now--*The Verdant Passage & The Crimson Legion*

BOOKS

The Cloakmaster Cycle

Beyond the Moons   David Cook
When a spelljamming ship crashes into Teldin Moore's home
on Krynn, a dying alien gives him a mysterious cloak that
makes him the target of killers and cutthroats.

Into the Void   Nigel Findley
Teldin is plunged into a sea of alien faces when his ship
is attacked by space pirates. The mind flayer who rescues
him offers to help him learn how to use the powers of the
cloak--but for whose gain?

The Maelstrom's Eye   Roger E. Moore
Teldin allies with a gypsy kender and is reunited with an
old friend, but they must fight to find a genius slug to learn
more about the cloak. Both scro forces and the elven
Imperial Fleet are in hot pursuit.

The Radiant Dragon   Elaine Cunningham
A radiant dragon who also possesses a key to control of
the *Spelljammer* joins Teldin in his search for the legendary
ship, but the quest is interrupted by the coming of the
second Unhuman War. On sale November 1992.